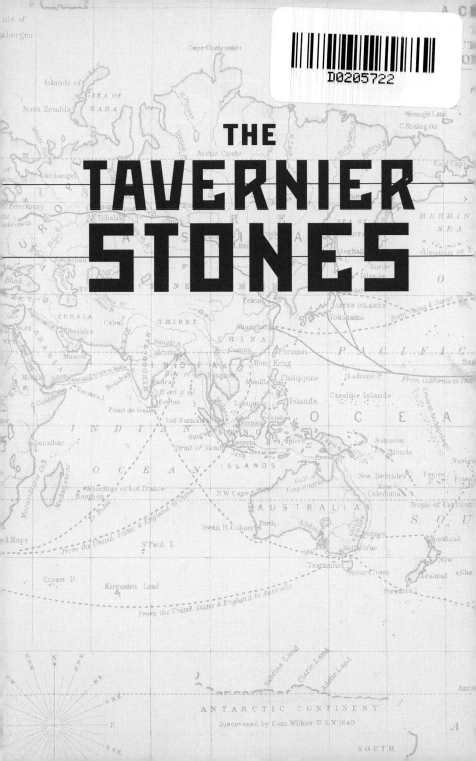

THE
TAVERNIER
STONES

Praise for Stephen Parrish's
Tavernier Stones

"From the opening pages to the closing scene, Stephen Parrish has created a literary mystery, one with adventure, history, cartography, jewels, and unforgettable characters. I was swept away. But even more, I can't recall the last time that I finished a mystery that also moved me so much. The characters will stay with readers long after they stay up all night finishing this story."

—Erica Orloff, author of *Freudian Slip* and *The Roofer*

"An utterly compelling adventure that pulls you along on a rollicking ride and doesn't let go until you turn the last page. The writing just sparkles."

—Patricia Wood, author of *Lottery*

"Relentlessly fascinating, Stephen Parrish's *Tavernier Stones* is reminiscent of Dan Brown's *Lost Symbol*, but this treasure hunt based on real historical figures involves ancient maps, complex codes, and a cache of mysterious lost gems. It's one hell of a good time."

—Mark Terry, author of *The Fallen*

"*The Tavernier Stones* has something for every reader: adventure, intrigue, information, and no small amount of wit. An exciting debut from a talented new author, this novel delivers the goods."

—Debra Ginsberg, author of *Blind Submission* and *The Grift*

"*The Tavernier Stones* is a sparkling, multi-faceted gem of a fast-paced thriller."

—Eric Stone, author of the Ray Sharp series of detective thrillers

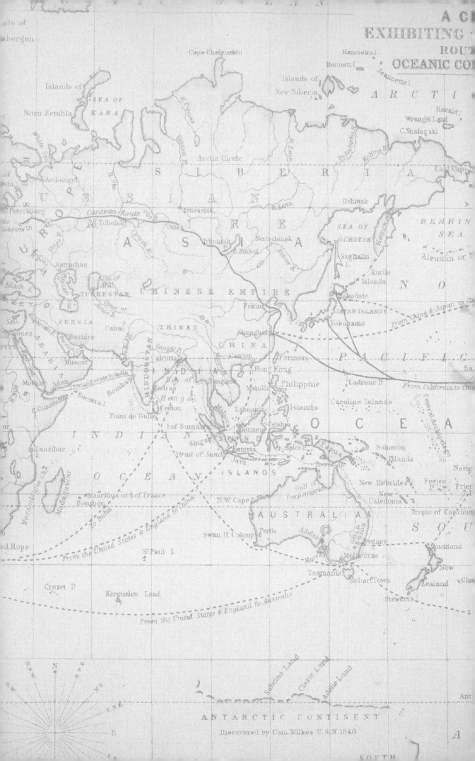

THE
TAVERNIER
STONES

A NOVEL

STEPHEN PARRISH

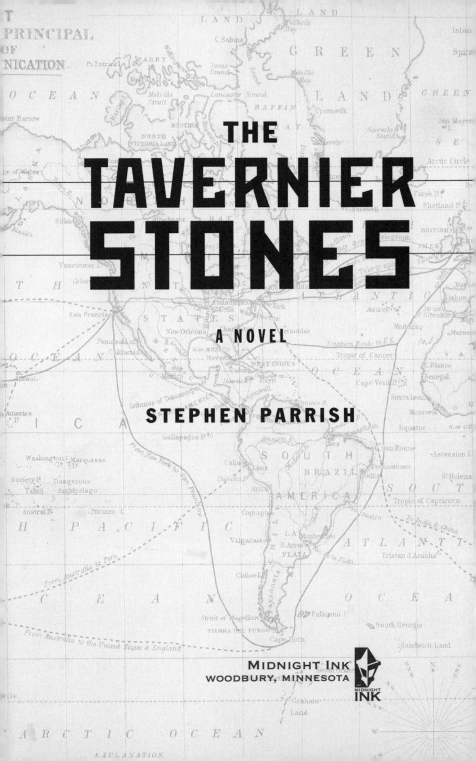

MIDNIGHT INK
WOODBURY, MINNESOTA

FIRST EDITION
First Printing, 2010

Cover design by Kevin R. Brown

Cover credits: Paris stamp: © iStockphoto.com/Marisa Allegra Williams; ruby: © iStockphoto.com/Bryan Reese; India stamp: © iStockphoto.com/Ray Roper; East German stamp: © iStockphoto.com/Linda Steward; ancient world map: © iStockphoto.com/Graffizone

Excerpt from "The Grauballe Man" by Seamus Heaney, first published in *North* (Faber & Faber, 1975), is reprinted by permission of the publisher.

Excerpt from "The Education of a Geographer" by Carl O. Sauer, first published in the Annals of the Association of American Geographers, Volume 46, January 1956, is reprinted by permission of the publisher, Taylor & Francis Group (www.informaworld.com).

Midnight Ink, an imprint of Llewellyn Publications

Library of Congress Cataloging-in-Publication Data
Parrish, Stephen, 1958-
 The Tavernier stones : a novel / by Stephen Parrish.—1st ed.
    p.   cm.
 Includes bibliographical references.
 ISBN 978-0-7387-2056-2
 1. Tavernier, Jean-Baptiste, 1605–1689—Travel—Fiction.
 2. Cartographers—Fiction. 3. Gems—Fiction. 4. Gemologists—
 Fiction. 5. Treasure troves—Fiction. 6. Theft—Fiction. I. Title.
 PS3616.A7685T38 2010
 813'.6—dc22
                                                    2009050083

Midnight Ink
2143 Wooddale Drive
Woodbury, MN 55125-2989

www.midnightinkbooks.com

Printed in the United States of America

For Sarah,
who believed unconditionally in her father

ACKNOWLEDGMENTS

Kevin Aicher. Paul Baumann. Valerie Beguin. Every cartographer who has ever lived. Terra Clarke. Dave, Doug, and Dan. Betsy Dornbusch. Brian Farrey. The Gemological Institute of America. William Greenleaf. The former Gross Diamond Centers of Louisville, Kentucky. Sarah Hina. The University of Illinois Department of Geography. Mel Johnson. Kay Jewelers of Champaign, Illinois. Librarians everywhere, thank God for you. The University of Louisville Department of Geography. Dave Mull. Erica Orloff. Pat, John, Dave, and Joe. Patsy Parrish. Sarah Parrish. The former R. R. Donnelley Cartographic Services in Lancaster, Pennsylvania. Ann Schein. Herwig Schutzler. Miss Snark. Heike Specht. Susie Stivers. Dave Stong. Alicia Tártalo. Teachers should be paid like doctors. Mark Terry. Becky Zins.

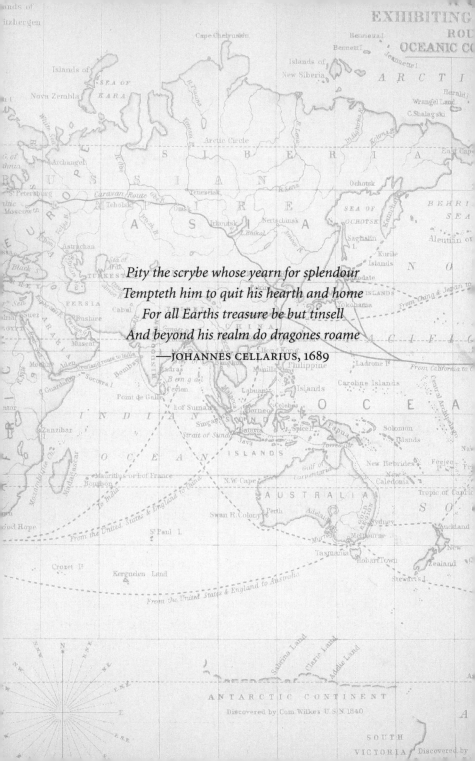

Pity the scrybe whose yearn for splendour
Tempteth him to quit his hearth and home
For all Earths treasure be but tinsell
And beyond his realm do dragones roame
—JOHANNES CELLARIUS, 1689

ONE

"THERE'S A DEAD GUY out there."

Kommissar Gerd Pfeffer first heard it from the dispatcher, who was quoting the boys who had found the body. He repeated the phrase in his mind as he drove to the scene: *There's a dead guy out there.* It would make an appropriate epitaph, he thought. There had been lots of dead guys out there. There would be lots more.

A narrow, overgrown road led Pfeffer into the Holmmoor, a bog north of Hamburg. Thickets on either side of the road strummed his car in irritating chords. Not far ahead, a gallery of rubberneckers, some with binoculars, peered into the woods. The focus of their attention was half a dozen police officers huddled like marooned buccaneers under a tarpaulin they had erected on an island of stable ground.

Pfeffer parked his car on the road, because the rains had turned the berm into a purgatory of mud-choked grass. The rest of the trip would be on foot, and cautiously: he was crossing from the real world into the bog.

It was one of the oddest calls he had received during his career as a homicide detective. Two boys had spent the weekend camping in the bog, on a patch of ground that had not yet thawed. Their campfire thawed it, and combined with the heavy downpours of late, as well as the strange temperature fluctuations of a typical Hamburg spring, up the body came.

First, the boys said, the peat began to crack. A fissure radiated slowly outward from the center of the fire, rending the mossy soil along a zigzag path as though etched by a lightning bolt.

Fingers emerged from the crack. The boys saw only their black tips and thought they were knobby roots, or maybe pieces of glacial till.

The tips grew into appendages. The appendages joined in a palm. When a thumb finally appeared, the boys extrapolated what lay beneath.

They laughed; it couldn't be happening. They rolled on the ground laughing. Their sides ached and their eyes filled with tears, it was so funny. Then the realization sank in that here indeed was a human hand, and following it now was an arm. And soon to come, no doubt, was the rest, some of which—the head in particular—might be too gruesome to behold.

They ran, stumbling on rubbery legs, their young minds filled with images of a root-hairy dead man loping after them. By the time the police arrived, the arm had finished sprouting. It jutted straight into the air, flecked with peat, its fingers splayed widely like the comic image of a drowning man counting to five. The police immediately concluded the body was one of the so-called bog people, dozens of whom—some more than two thousand years old—had sprung out of the ground throughout that part of Germany.

Pfeffer stepped from one clump of grass to another, advancing toward the tarpaulin. Walking on the peat gave him the sensation of unsurefootedness, as though he might sink up to his neck on any step. He did sink—four inches here, eight inches there, nothing there—you never knew. The water, stained by the peat, was the color of strongly brewed tea.

The bogs around Hamburg had been disgorging Iron Age corpses for as long as Pfeffer could remember. Humic acids in the peat acted as embalming fluids that stained hair and beards red and tanned skin black. Bones decalcified, turning the corpses into leathery bags filled loosely with internal organs and a menu of last suppers, typically barley and linseed gruel. Most strikingly, features were so well preserved that except for the tanning, a modern-day public could see exactly what the victims looked like—could stare them in the face.

They died with quiet dignity or cringing in horror. And the resignation or anguish or shock their expressions communicated at the moment of death, when the executioner weighted them down in watery graves, was preserved for the millennia.

As Pfeffer reached the tarpaulin, the rain started up again. A young Polizist emerged from under the tarp, covering his head with a clipboard. He greeted Pfeffer with a firm handshake, then led him safely around shaking pools of stained water. The other officers remained under cover. They stared in fascination at a lump of soggy human remains.

The victim—for so they were calling the thing—lay on his right side with his right arm stretched out straight above his head and his left arm pressed close to his side. He resembled other bog people in that his skin had darkened to the value of burnt umber and his woolly hair and prickly beard were the color of rust. And it was clear he had been murdered or sacrificed: deep, angular stab wounds perforated his chest and abdomen.

But Pfeffer noticed that his garb was more modern than that of other bog people, who typically wore only sleeveless capes, probably because the linen used for the rest of their outfits couldn't survive the peat acids. He estimated the victim's clothing was from the Middle Ages or some other time long ago, but clearly not the twenty-first century: he wore breeches that stopped just below the knee, stockings over his calves, and broad metal buckles on his shoes.

So it wasn't an ancient pagan sacrifice after all. Nor was it a recent murder.

An oval signet ring encircled the victim's right middle finger, on the hand that had sprung up on the boys. Bezel-set in the oval mount was a dark stone slab. Pfeffer used his thumbnail to scrape the ring clean of peat. Carved in the slab were the initials "JC" and an image of one woman helping another place a basket of grapes on her head.

The young Polizist had been watching him closely while he examined the body, and as Pfeffer inspected the ring, the young man suggested, "Jesus Christ?"

Pfeffer shook his head. "He would put his own initials on a signet ring, don't you think?" Squatting in the spongy grass, he surveyed the scene for a moment, then asked, "Have you turned him over?"

"We dug him up and laid him there, otherwise he hasn't been touched. I was waiting for you to arrive before I moved him. You know how bent out of shape the anthropologists get when they find anything disturbed."

Pfeffer thought the way the dead man clenched his left fist was odd, as though he had been holding something dear to him when he died. Furthermore—and this had been fermenting in the detective's subconscious the entire time—there was just the hint of a smile on the man's face. But surely that was only Pfeffer's imagination, or one of those ironic effects of the retarded rate of decay in the peat. People did not, in fact, smile as they were being stabbed. They didn't. Really.

He looked into the man's eye sockets. They had obviously sunken since his death, but it was nevertheless obvious they had been deep-set to begin with and had done their share of glaring at lesser intellects. Pfeffer shivered as he experienced the sensation the cavities were looking back.

"Open it," he ordered.

"Excuse me?"

"The fist. Pry it open."

The Polizist motioned for another officer to step over and help him. As they gently lifted the arm, the young man said, "Sir, if I may, are we doing this out of curiosity?"

"Call it professional intuition. I want to see what he held onto for dear life."

"But the anthropologists—"

"Open it."

Getting the fingers to uncurl required the use of pocketknives. The glinting red object that rolled onto the ground before the fist clamped tightly closed again caused the remaining officers to collide with one another as they evacuated their tarp shelter and pressed in for a closer look. It also sent a buzz into the roadkill gallery, whose frustration over a dearth of news had only festered under the drizzling rain.

If Pfeffer hadn't known better, he'd have guessed the thing was genuine.

The drizzle increased to a steady downpour, and the young Polizist, studying the corpse, blurted out something spontaneously: "'As if he had been poured in tar, he lies on a pillow of turf and seems to weep the black river of himself.'"

"What the hell does that mean?"

"Nothing. Just an English poem I read once. Come to think of it, it was Irish."

Pfeffer took another look at the bog man's leathery face. His skull had long since decalcified, leaving the outer skin pinched and distorted. His features were already caving in from rough handling and sudden exposure to ruthless compounds in the air.

It *was* a smile, Pfeffer was sure of it. The man had known something profoundly amusing the moment he died, so amusing he was still smiling even after being stabbed in the chest, even after centuries of submersion under the quaking peat.

TWO

John Graf wasn't compiling or editing maps as he normally would be on a weekday morning. Instead, he was reading from the *Lancaster Intelligencer Journal* opened unabashedly on his light table. The newspaper's front-page headline was one the like of which he'd never expected to see.

His appearance, reflecting back at him from the glass surface of the light table, revealed his Amish upbringing: short but unruly auburn hair, a close-cropped beard, and hands made rough from spending the first twenty of his twenty-seven years on a farm.

He glanced up at the other cartographers occupying cubicles around him; all were reading newspapers. All were captivated by the same improbable headline, not that they would return his glance otherwise. The first impression people came away with when they met John was that he preferred they leave him alone. It was a correct impression. But he could only hope they didn't come away feeling insulted. His eyes stared frankly and uncritically, and if he made people feel transparent, he compensated by finding no flaws in their vitreous souls. He didn't analyze, he didn't judge. Most of the time, he didn't care.

His closest acquaintances—he had no real friends—considered him a deeply introspective man. The Amish, it pained him to acknowledge, considered him an outcast.

John's parents and siblings still lived on a farm east of town, but only his sister Rebecca would speak to him, reluctantly. The Amish community had expelled him for committing the offense of enrolling in high school. After graduating, he had compounded his predicament by attending nearby Franklin & Marshall College. His wanderlust attracted him to geography, his passion for maps to cartography.

The city of Lancaster had grown up alongside John and his Amish neighbors. As a result, its architecture, dominated by narrow row houses composed mainly of red brick and mortar, was almost as plain. And like the Amish, it had remained anachronistic well into maturity.

John noted many signs of maturity in the town: wrought-iron fences bent from sheer weariness. Warped wooden shutters shedding their louvers. Rusted mailboxes with ill-fitting lids. The sidewalks, undermined by pioneering tree roots and colonized by stubborn tufts of grass, undulated erratically, forming chains of concrete blocks in tectonic collision, making obstacle courses for small children and large bugs.

The P. Lorillard Building, a former warehouse of the long-defunct P. Lorillard Tobacco Company, stood at the corner of Prince and James. Built in 1899, it served as an elegant example of Beaux Arts classicism with its three-story-high pilasters and large blind arches. Now it was home to North Star Maps, the most prestigious custom mapping firm in the country. The cartographers who worked there were proud of their building; some even believed they could still smell the lingering aroma of drying tobacco leaves.

A newspaper headline normally would not have distracted John from his work, not even a coast-to-coast news flash printed in enormous bold type. Even those he saved for after work, to read while he ate his frozen dinner of Salisbury steak, mashed potatoes, and "dessert" (*peel back cellophane cover before microwaving; perforate foil with tines of fork*). But today all the staff was buzzing about the front-page news. The body found one week ago in a bog north of Hamburg, Germany, had been identified by University of Hamburg historians. They used the victim's distinctive signet ring as their primary clue and were aided by his clothing, a forensic analysis of his remains, and ultimately his portrait.

Yes, his portrait. It was here, reproduced on the front page of the newspaper, from an original in sanguine chalk.

The man had been—and still was, most of him—Johannes Cellarius, a noted seventeenth-century cartographer, son of a Polish wine merchant who broke with a long family tradition to join a prosperous guild of European mapmakers. In 1689, at the peak of his career, he disappeared without a trace. Historians respected Cellarius for upholding vigorous standards during an era when mapmakers still relied on the hearsay of excitable voyagers and decorated their maps with fantastic beasts that allegedly roamed the unexplored lands.

John turned the page and read on.

The signet ring found on Cellarius's right middle finger was solid gold—in fact, 22 karat. It was set with an oval slab of chalcedony. The image engraved in the chalcedony, one that would stand out in relief when pressed into wax, was of one woman helping another place a basket of grapes on her head. Copied from a detail on the ceiling of the Sistine Chapel, the image was known as the Michelangelo signet.

University of Hamburg historians were able to ascribe Cellarius's breeches, stockings, and shoe buckles to the seventeenth century; he had dressed himself on the morning of his death in the manner of a middle-class craftsman of the 1680s. Forensic scientists suggested a date of death that was in close agreement with the date of the craftsman's disappearance.

But as far as John was concerned, the picture nailed it. The newspaper had printed a photograph of the corpse's head side-by-side with a reproduction of the chalk drawing. The prominent forehead, protruding brow, and deep-set eyes that were so conspicuous in the drawing were unmistakably shadowed in the photograph. Despite three centuries of metamorphosis in the bog, the resemblance was striking.

It was Johannes Cellarius. There was no doubt about it.

Judging from the drawing, Cellarius had the gentle, pampered face of royalty; the long, wild hair of an eccentric intellect; and the passionate eyes of an artist. To John Graf, it was as though Don Quixote had quit his windmills and settled down to engrave roads and rivers.

Who would have thought a seventeenth-century cartographer would make the front page of a modern newspaper? Some of the other cartographers at North Star were now running upstairs to the library to dig up anything they could find about Cellarius. But John remained at his light table. Let them scramble for stuff. He was an avid map collector, buying facsimiles whenever he couldn't afford the originals, and he probably had all the master's work in one form or another at home. He continued reading the article.

By some accounts, Cellarius had been done in by the jealous husband of his lover, the Palatinate beauty Hildegard Weinbrenner. The eleven perforations of his chest and abdomen—from blows delivered by what the autopsy suggested was a pickax—attested to violent murder. The last map Cellarius completed, its ink barely dry when it was discovered in his studio after his disappearance, was one of Hildegard's homeland, the lower Palatinate—modern-day Rheinland-Pfalz.

But that wasn't the end of the story. Something was clenched tightly in Cellarius's left fist, and when the German police officers who were called in to investigate a possible homicide pried open the fingers, a large red gemstone rolled out.

It was a ruby. It weighed more than 57 carats. Some said it ranked among the best ever examined.

There was a brief controversy over the stone at first, started by a Hamburg jeweler who suggested it was only red spinel, like the so-called Black Prince's ruby garnishing the British Imperial State Crown. From biblical times to the Industrial Revolution, all red stones, including spinel, were popularly known as rubies.

To end the controversy, a team of mineralogists flew in from the University of Heidelberg. It took them only minutes, using a refractometer and a spectroscope, to declare the ruby genuine. The newspaper article included a close-up photograph of the stone; in the background, slightly out of focus, were three beaming technicians in lab coats.

John felt the presence of someone behind him. Annette, a woman who occupied the cubicle across the hall, was looking over his shoulder.

"Now that's what I would call gruesome," she said.

He glanced at her, then back at the newspaper. "When I've been dead for three hundred years, I hope I look every bit as good."

Annette was a frequent visitor; John's workspace served as her break room. He had disciplined himself not to peek across the hall while she leaned over her light table, because the profile of her breasts constituted his greatest professional distraction.

"We really ought to step out together sometime, Amish boy. When do you think that might happen?"

When God forgives the serpent for deceiving Eve, John thought. Normally he would banter with her, but he was in no mood today.

"I know you like girls," Annette continued. "I saw you with one once."

"No, you didn't. You couldn't have."

"Yes, I did. But don't worry, your secret's safe with me. She actually looked pretty good—from the eyebrows up, anyway. Cute bonnet."

"You must be talking about my sister."

"Ah. Back to work I go!" She hurried across the hall and returned to her seat.

John watched her lean forward to peer into her computer screen, then he forced himself to turn away and focus instead on a picture frame mounted on the wall of his cubicle. Displayed in the frame were two unembellished quotes in an antique gothic font: "I am told there are people who do not care for maps, and find it hard to believe." And: "Show me a geographer who does not need them constantly and want them about him, and I shall have my doubts as to whether he has made the right choice of life." The first was by Robert Louis Stevenson, the second by Carl Sauer.

He wasn't going to get any work done today. Of all historic figures, the one he admired most—the one whose creative style and work ethic he most emulated—had made a return appearance. In the flesh.

———

John's house on Nouveau Street was within walking distance of the P. Lorillard Building. The house was equipped with a window air conditioner, but John had tested it only once. It blew a gale of icy wind in his face, and he immediately shut it off. The only other gadget in his otherwise austere quarters was a microwave oven he used to heat up his frozen dinners. He didn't feel he had a choice; he couldn't so much as bake a potato.

He spent the evening in his living room, poring over the newspaper article and digging up references in books. He didn't know the first thing about gemstones. And like everyone else, he couldn't imagine what connection Johannes Cellarius might have had with them.

Johannes Cellarius! Face to face with the greatest mapmaker of all time—dead for over three hundred years!

He stared long into the evening at his facsimile of Cellarius's last map, the one whose ink was barely dry when the great cartographer disappeared from his studio. He had no idea what he was looking for. The map was of Germany's lower Palatinate: its roads, villages, and topography.

He remembered the warnings of mapmakers of old, who drew boundary lines at the limits of the known inhabited world and wrote, "Beyond this place, there be dragons." He remembered the warnings but didn't intend to heed them.

Water was set to boil for coffee. A frozen dinner went into the microwave. Maps and facsimiles came out of a cabinet. Within minutes, the professional life of Johannes Cellarius was comprehensively delineated on the living room floor.

They made up the core of John's personal collection: maps of the Americas, Europe, the Holy Land, even the moon. Maps so beautiful they continued to sell in facsimile for framing and hanging. Maps so accurate, navigators could still use them without danger of getting lost or hitting a reef.

Hamburg, where Cellarius kept his studio, was but one of eighteen major cartographic capitals of seventeenth-century Europe. And what a time to be a cartographer! Europe and Africa were familiar; continental outlines of the time looked much as they did on modern maps. But the Orient was still a mystery, and exploration of the New World was just getting underway.

John gladly would have traded centuries with Cellarius. The modern globe was too well explored for the spirited adventurer; there weren't any significant blank places left. Even the ocean floor was thoroughly charted. And they were mapping celestial bodies as fast as they found them—not that a spirited adventurer stood much chance of visiting any of those. All John could do was gaze at Cellarius's maps and dream.

And exquisite maps they were. Uniquely among cartographers of his time, or any time, Cellarius signed and dated each copy. He was one of the first to recognize that maps were not only tools of navigation and geography, they were also works of art. He did not publish atlases, but his maps were so often copied by his contemporaries that some atlases contained little more than thinly disguised Cellarius reproductions.

The creations eventually diffused into the general trade, losing more and more identity with each generation. Cellarius, perhaps the most obscure of the great cartographers, arguably had the most pronounced overall influence on the look of modern maps and on the high standard for accuracy that subsequently characterized the industry.

John was prone on his living room floor, his chin propped up in his hands, his elbows planted in the carpet like a bipod. The hour grew late, and he failed to notice the chimes of his grandfather clock.

Cellarius's studio occupied the north bank of the Norderelbe, location of the present-day St. Pauli fish market. He was a character at the docks, welcoming the mariners when they returned from their voyages so that he might profit from their knowledge: "I endeavor to be good to them, to provide for their many wants after their long journeys upon the sea; to bring them foodstuffs and drink and tobacco, and to have readie the fairest maidenes of the wharf, reserving these latter in advance with a modest deposit. In this manner I am the first and only to acquire such information as I may seeke concerning the new landfalls, though owing to certain priorities I am usuallie suffered to wait for the next morning to get it down on parchment."

Reports of travelers varied in reliability. Sea-going navigators were frequently off by profound longitudinal distances, owing to shifting winds and currents. Land-going navigation was not all that much easier, hampered as it was by the difficulty of estimating distance traveled over rough terrain.

Cellarius said of one reporter: "Where might take me three days to arrive, might take him three weeks, for he is either modest of his overland feats, perpetualie lost, or delayed by the brothels, and I suspect all of these. The only other possibilitie being that villages migrate upstream and down, and hills are but ripples in the land like folds in a rugg that go hither and thither when trod upon."

In a letter to another, Cellarius was more caustic: "You do not find east by pissing into the wind and watching to see which way it will flye. Nor do you learn navigation in a canoe, which is obviouslie where you have learned it, and napped through the lessones besides. My cat navigates a good sighte better, and he has been dead a month and more."

And to another: "Your sounding man was clearlie intoxicated."

Cellarius was unscrupulously honest; if he didn't know the source of a river, he didn't invent one. Instead, he truncated the river to show that it was still unexplored, or unreliably explored. This practice incited men to push upstream in search of sources. "For," in Cellarius's words, "there is no call to pack ones staff and bootes like a blank place on a map." Likewise, if he was unsure of a boundary, he suggested it with a dotted or dashed line. In the seventeenth century, trustworthy explorers removed at least as many features from maps as they contributed to them.

John packed his maps and facsimiles back into the cabinet and went to bed with the warning of the ages on his mind: *Beyond this place, there be dragons … there be dragons …*

Cellarius's last map of the lower Palatinate bothered him. It had always bothered him, but he had never been able to put his finger on the problem. For some reason, the map had lurked in his subconscious ever since he'd first laid eyes on it.

What was it about that sheet of parchment? What was he seeing but not recognizing?

Also crowding his thoughts, as his head sank into the pillow, were images of Johannes Cellarius before and after: the affluent craftsman sitting proudly for a portrait, his deep-set eyes gazing poignantly at the artist, and the gnarled corpse, limbs in disarray, cavernous eyes staring vacantly at the sky.

John knew his interest in Cellarius was more than professional, more than academic, more than a mere expression of respect. It was mystical, as though the two were related by blood, and the three centuries that separated them had been compressed to a single moment by layers of placid and biding peat.

THREE

DAVID FREEMAN WAS DAYDREAMING about rubies. He knew he ought to be preparing himself for the next half-hour or so, because the nuances of his speech and body language would be crucial to the success of his mission. But he couldn't help it. The stones in the window were exquisite.

It was a compliment to the owners of Nineveh & Shimoda, a jewelry store on Sansom Street in Philadelphia. It was the only compliment David would have for them today.

David, whose real surname was Feinstein, considered himself fortunate to have been born with a face few people could recall; it was the kind of blurry composition police artists always seemed to produce from witness descriptions. Every time he saw a "wanted" poster, he thought, *That could be me.* Sometimes it was.

He wished he were taller—at least as tall as other grown men approaching thirty. In an effort to compensate, he always stood as straight as he could, and the practice lent an aura of arrogance to his posture.

Accompanying David to Nineveh & Shimoda was his girlfriend, for lack of a better word. Sarah Sainte-James, whose real surname was Smith, had once been a model for the women's underwear advertisements that appeared as supplements to the *Philadelphia Inquirer*—until squabbling incidents with photographers, some leading to bites and scratches, resulted in their unanimous refusal to work with her again.

"Are you ready?" David asked.

"Yes."

"You remember everything I told you?"

"Yes, for Christ's sake."

He looked her over. Her skirt was short, too short for any purpose other than exhibitionism. But today's target, a man David had followed down crowded city streets, had voyeuristic eyes that aimed low.

"Hitch it up," he ordered.

"Come on, David, give me a break."

He grabbed the waistline of the skirt and pulled it up a couple of inches. "There," he said. "It's showtime."

David had chosen a day for the duo's first visit to Nineveh & Shimoda when both the manager and assistant manager would be present. It was important that the manager see them. But it was the assistant manager, one Mr. Bowling, who was centered in David's crosshairs. Bowling was in his early thirties, wore circular, wire-rim glasses, and combed his tenuous filaments from ear to ear. He leaned toward the heavy side but packed it well into rumpled suits. His ties never quite reached to his belt.

It was his eyes, though, that gave him away: he always feared that the person he was trying to sell something to was not going to buy something from him. David had followed him after work one day, noting his taste for legs and his insecure gait. They had parted at the bus stop. It was all the destination David needed to know.

Once inside the store, he assessed the security. The jewelry cases were made of unbreakable acrylic rather than glass, to deter smash-and-grab thieves. Motion detectors peered down from strategic corners of the ceiling. And although the store was large, it was well lit and there were no blind spots; the owners were able to watch every transaction from a glass-walled booth, one they presumably also used to close big sales and conduct appraisals.

The booth was dark at the moment. Either the lights were off or the wall consisted of one-way glass. If the latter, David had a problem; the diamond solitaire case faced the booth, so any sleight of hand employed on Mr. Bowling might go down in full view of someone charged with making sure Mr. Bowling didn't fall victim to sleight of hand.

High and low electronic beams spanned the store entrance. A surveillance camera with a wide-angle lens spied on the sales floor. And broad, flat mirrors covered the walls; these not only created the illusion the store was larger, they allowed staff members to observe customer behavior when their backs were turned. The owners might not have been any good at selling jewelry, but they apparently had experience getting ripped off.

David took Sarah's hand and led her through the store. The two peered timidly into showcases, whispering and pointing. The manager, a study in corpulent dignity, stood near the darkened booth with his hands clasped behind his back and his feet planted far enough apart to keep his balance. David could already read his mind: *Here comes one.*

The assistant manager, Mr. Bowling, had posted himself in the geographic center of the store, where inexperienced salespeople tended to think they enjoyed a statistical advantage. He kept glancing at the other salesperson on duty, a densely freckled redhead in a low-cut blouse.

David had to reach Bowling before the others took advantage of an open field. But as he maneuvered closer, the manager launched himself on an intercept course, and the redhead stepped out from behind her showcase, stretching her facial muscles into a rehearsed smile.

David took three quick strides toward his target. "I know you from somewhere," he said to Bowling.

The manager stopped.

The redhead, who had already been offering a handshake from several yards away, retracted her arm and used it to smooth back her hair.

Bowling scanned David's face in confusion; the recognition was not mutual. "I ... um ..."

"College Park," David said. "You were a student there, weren't you?"

"Why, yes. Yes, I was!"

"And we were in the same ..."

"... class together?"

"We sat next to each other! Don't you remember?" David was as much into Bowling's face as he could get. He wanted to crowd out the competition. From the corner of one eye, he watched the manager lean back against a case and put his hands in his pockets. From the other, he saw the redhead hurry toward the entrance to greet a customer entering the store.

"Right," Bowling said. His eyes still darted about David's head and figure, looking for some detail that would trigger recognition. "The class was ... what was the class?"

"Think! What was the biggest lecture you had?"

"Ah ... chemistry?"

"That's it! We sat next to each other in chemistry." David scratched his jaw. "Or maybe I sat directly behind you. Yeah, that was it. I saw a lot of you, but you probably saw little of me."

The manager had by this time shifted his attention to the customer the redhead was pestering. He could not, of course, intrude on old friends, or even old acquaintances. David and Sarah belonged to Bowling.

Bowling's confusion faded as quickly as his blush. "Good to see you again," he said. And then, his confidence returning as well, "So what brings you into the store?"

David looked at Sarah shyly. Sarah squeezed his hand. "Tell him, honey," she said.

"Well," David stammered, "we're sort of looking for engagement rings."

"Actually, we're not engaged yet," Sarah clarified. "We have to wait for our families to schedule a dinner party for the announcement. But we're ready to pick out the ring. Aren't we, Delbert?"

David smiled. "Indeed we are."

"Well." Bowling clasped his hands. "Did you have anything in particular in mind?"

The two bowed their heads slightly. David nudged Sarah. "Go ahead," he whispered.

"A diamond solitaire," Sarah declared.

Bowling nodded without expression, but David could hear his thoughts: *Sounds like a good plan.*

"Of very good quality."

Bowling nodded again, this time pursing his lips to show approval. *No shock there. That's what they all want.*

"VVS, or better, if you have it."

A smile wound up on the assistant manager's face. *I think I'm going to be glad I got out of bed this morning.*

"In, say, the 3-carat range."

Bowling stiffened visibly but quickly regained his composure. "Step this way," he said. "I have some pieces I think will interest you. And I'm sure I can come up with the right price for an old classmate—if you catch my drift."

David grinned at Sarah: "I *told* you I had a feeling about this store."

They moved over to the diamond solitaire case, where Bowling showed them an array of round brilliants between 2.5 and 3.5 carats. David knew it was unlikely Bowling would show him a stone weighing exactly 3 carats, or even very close to it, because the size was so great. The heavier the finished product, the less sympathy cutters had for integers and quarter increments; their mission became to maximize weight retention.

Bowling routinely inspected every stone under a loupe before handing it to David, clearly in adherence to store policy. And he inspected each one again before returning it to its velvet-lined display box. This was to make sure, by checking the internal characteristics of the stone, that the one making the trip out of the case was the same one making the trip back in.

After examining and reexamining five or six stones, David settled on one that weighed 3.17 carats and had a color Bowling described as "E, nearly the top of the scale. The clarity," he explained, "is VVS1—but you don't have to trouble yourselves about such technicalities. It's a beautiful piece."

Bowling demonstrated use of the jeweler's loupe to David, who first tried to view the diamond from too far away, then from too close, finally settling into focus about an inch from the magnifying glass. David studied the cut of the stone and made quick estimates of its significant proportions. "VVS" meant the stone's inclusions were very, very small, visible only under magnification. David couldn't see any through the loupe, but a microscope was needed to make the call. He detected a dab of pink nail polish near the culet and memorized its size and shape.

A tag was fastened to the shank, but it wasn't going to be a problem; it was standard industry issue. And as though to make David's job even easier, the price and inventory number on the tag were hand written.

As he louped the stone, he noticed that Bowling was also louping Sarah, trying but mostly failing to keep his eyes off her legs. She was openly flirting with him and probably overdoing it. The circumstances were good, as good as they got; he hoped she wasn't going to screw things up.

He handed the ring back to Bowling and said, "I assume you can do something about that price."

Bowling first louped the stone, and David saw that he was mostly just checking the dab of fingernail polish. Then he jotted a number down on a sales slip and pushed it humbly across the top of the case.

Still too pricey. Probably to compensate for all the other sales the man had failed to close. David wanted Bowling to anticipate a windfall, but failing to bargain would look suspicious.

"That's a nice gesture," David said. "Now, if you wouldn't mind making a real effort."

Sarah reached across the case and grabbed Bowling's hand, the one still holding the ring, and pulled it closer to her. "Oh, Delbert," she said. "This is the one. I'm absolutely sure of it."

"Sweet*heart*," David drawled in a low voice. "Let's not be hasty in making our de*cision*."

"But we've been shopping for so long, and we've looked at so many. This ring was meant for us, I can *feel* it. Don't you feel it too?"

Bowling obviously felt it: as Sarah's eyes gazed lovingly at the ring, her fingers subtly caressed his hand and wrist. She tried to clear a dust particle from the crown of the diamond by forming her lips into a tight circle and blowing on it. But the steady stream of warm, moist air went into the palm of Bowling's hand instead.

David rolled his eyes. "Mr. Bowling, sir, we will go home and think it over." He cast a critical look at Sarah, who seemed hypnotized by the sparkling stone. "And it looks like we'll be back."

"I'll hold her for you. I mean, *it*—I'll hold *it* for you." Blushing, he extracted himself from Sarah's grasp.

"I'd … appreciate that. And I'd also appreciate you chiseling down the price some more."

David wasn't concerned the ring would be gone when he returned. Stones of such size moved so slowly, they could spend years in a jewelry case. But salespeople liked to give the customer a sense of urgency by putting pieces on temporary hold, fully aware the urgency was theirs, not the customer's.

"It was a little loose when I tried it on," Sarah complained. "Does that mean I have to pick out a different one?"

"We'll make it fit," Bowling assured her. "It's a simple process that takes just a few minutes."

"And you promise me it's a good diamond..."

"It's a beautiful diamond. But maybe you're asking the wrong man. I've never met a diamond I didn't like."

David shook the assistant manager's hand and looked him straight in the eye. "Neither have I."

———

After the couple left the store, Bowling jubilantly announced to the manager, who had been hovering within earshot, that he had bagged the big one. The manager offered reserved compliments and reminded him to turn over the sale if it appeared he would lose it. Bowling agreed good-naturedly but swore to himself he wouldn't split the credit. Not for this one.

There was a joke going around the small company about Bowling. It seemed that few of his customers who said they'd be back ever came back. According to the joke, the "be-back bus" waited around the corner with its engine running. As soon as his customers left the store, the bus ran them over and killed them.

No, he thought, these two would be back, and he'd be damned if he was going to split the sale. The discount price was just enough to push him past all other salespeople at Nineveh & Shimoda to the top of the May performance chart. Past even Felicity, who with her lustrous red hair and low-cut blouses had been capitalizing on the need young men had lately for gold chains and earrings.

He inserted the ring into a small brown envelope, labeled it with the name the young man had given him—Delbert Farrington III—and locked it in the safe.

Meanwhile, in a phone booth on Chestnut, David placed an order for a chunk of raw cubic zirconia, enough to cut a 4-carat stone. The color had to be precisely E, and the stone had to face up VVS or better when cut.

Sarah, who was pacing outside the booth, occasionally rubbing her bare thighs, knocked on the glass to hurry him up.

"Yeah, yeah, yeah ..." He waved her off.

He also ordered a Tiffany four-prong setting with an 18-karat gold shank and an iridium-plated, white gold head. The hallmark was easy: Weatherfront Findings, Inc., a large manufacturer, employed a simple lightning bolt. It was a standard mount, a routine job. Afterwards the two walked down Chestnut to their car.

"God, I'm hungry," David said.

"When are you ever *not* hungry?"

"A hard day's work always gives me an appetite."

"David, you spent the morning watching reruns of *Gilligan's Island.*"

"It's the quality of work you do, not the quantity. By the way, how many different shades of pink fingernail polish do you have at home?"

"I have everything, you know that. And I might as well tell you now, I'm retiring after this one."

"You said that last time."

"I *mean* it this time."

"The hell you do."

"You know how embarrassing this skirt is? Everybody's looking."

"Then wear a longer coat. Now be quiet while I do some conceptualizing."

"I'd like to see *you* in a miniskirt on a cold day." She laughed. "Christ, what a picture that would make."

"Shut up, would you? Would you just shut up?"

FOUR

"LET'S GET SOMETHING STRAIGHT before we start this morning." Harry Tokuhisa, North Star Map's chief cartographer, had stopped next to John Graf's cubicle and was waving a tabloid in the air.

"And what would that be?" John asked.

"Elvis," he said gravely, "is *dead*."

Tokuhisa had a youthful face that belied his years of experience. When John had first met him, he had wondered what the boy could possibly know about maps. Then he had seen the man's work.

Annette peeked out from her cubicle across the hall. "I beg to differ, Toke," she said. "I have it on good authority that Elvis is, in fact, alive. I don't care to reveal my source, but let's just say *enquiring minds want to know*."

Tokuhisa turned to John. "I have a new quote for your wall, by some guy named Bentley. Are you ready? Listen to this: 'Geography is about maps, but biography is about chaps.' Pretty good, huh?"

John winced. "Is there anything new in that paper about Cellarius?"

"In *this* paper? You've got to be kidding." He continued down the hall and resumed his social rounds. John heard him speak to the cartographers in the next pair of cubicles: "Let's get something straight before we start..."

For John, it was also time to make his own rounds. He was the project coordinator of a series of maps, in various stages of production, for a Bible history textbook. He went from cubicle to cubicle, looking over the shoulders of cartographers absorbed in the point, line, and area symbols glowing on their computer monitors. This would have bothered them were he like most other coordinators; mapmakers tended to be private and defensive about their work. But there was an unobtrusive way about John's inspections that made these mapmakers feel they were sharing their work with a colleague rather than submitting it to a supervisor for judgment.

He asked an occasional question, offered some thoughtful opinions, and mostly just tried to assure the cartographers that someone cared about what they were doing and was confident of their talent.

The Bible maps were well designed: the colors were transparent, the terrain art was spectacular, and the overall look was clean and legible. John studied each proof and waited for gut responses to his one unconditional criterion: would he be willing to frame and hang this map on the wall of his living room?

A map was a portrait, and one cartographer's vision often differed greatly from another's. The technology of map production had improved dramatically since the days of quill pens and compasses, and especially since the arrival of computers. But the fundamentals of cartography—the compilation and generalization of geographical data—had not changed much at all.

In fact, maps were not so different, to John's way of thinking, from the crafts made and sold by many of the Amish. John considered mapmaking a craft. He worked with his hands, he was proud of the quality of his work, and he served a profession as old as any other graphic form of communication. The only Amish crime he was committing was not working in or near his Amish home.

His father should have been proud as well. He wasn't, but he should have been.

John had been a devout member of the Old Order Amish until he had first expressed an interest in going to public school, then had insisted on it. In response, his church district ostracized him. As did his own father, who left the house now whenever John came by to visit. His sister Rebecca was the only one of his five siblings who would speak to him, and with her back to him, at that.

Of John's four brothers, only one worked on the farm. The others were part of a mobile construction crew. The family was on the verge of breaking up; there wasn't enough farm to go around. Some of the neighboring heads of household had busted up their estates and dealt the odd parcels to their sons, so that all might make a living from the land, however meagerly. The Graf family had decided to keep its farm intact and bequeath it to the oldest son. John's father, Clarence, thus semi-retired, or "got out of the way," as the Amish put it.

John was Clarence's oldest son. If he failed to assume his role as heir to the estate, and soon, it would go to his next younger brother, who had already returned to the property and taken up reins.

It had long been John's dream to go to college, and he knew he didn't stand a chance without an English high-school diploma. The Amish didn't believe in higher education, which they defined as anything beyond grade school. When word got out, and it soon did, that John had enrolled in high school, the bishop ordered the ministers to call him to the carpet during the next preaching service, conducted every other Sunday.

John was interrogated in public about his behavior, and he answered that he had no regrets. That without high school he couldn't attend college. That without a higher education he couldn't pursue his goals. That higher education was neither a weapon against God nor against the community, *die Ordnung*, or *Gelassenheit*.

He waited outside while the congregation debated the issue. When they called him back in, they told him he was expelled from the church for six weeks.

Six weeks later, John was still in high school, so in his absence the congregation voted unanimously, as required, to excommunicate him.

Even his father had voted in favor of it.

It was something of a moot point, as John had already moved out of the house. He could still come back if he wanted to; all he had to do was kneel and confess his wrongdoing, a choice Rebecca reminded him of routinely.

The worst part of it all was what excommunication implied: *die Meidung*, or the shunning. Except for minimal, necessary socializing, Amish church members were forbidden to interact with shunned members. They could interact as they liked with nonmembers, that is, with those who had elected *not* to take baptismal vows. But those who had taken the vows and broken them were treated as outcasts, even by their own families.

John attended Franklin & Marshall to study geography and cartography, to feed an insatiable curiosity about the world. He worked his way through college, letting himself out as a farm hand, mechanic, carpenter—whatever he could get.

At F & M, he grew weary of fellow students staring at his austere dress, and he grew lonely because would-be acquaintances treated him as they would a priest: with distant respect. So he changed his wardrobe. The buttons on his pants gave way to zippers, the hook-and-eye fasteners on his coat to buttons, the suspenders to a belt, and the wide brimmed hat was put away.

He continued to dress simply, however, preferring dark gray pants and a white shirt. And he grew a beard. He kept his Amish clothes for when he visited Rebecca; he couldn't bring himself to enter his old house in English dress.

A zipper had been the hardest change to reconcile himself to. What if you got your you-know-what caught in one of those?

Maps were more to John than portraits of faraway lands. Although he always claimed it was a passion for graphic arts that attracted him to cartography, he'd known even from early childhood that maps constituted a metaphor for his ruling passion: to discover his proper place in the world.

————

At lunchtime, John waited until the hallway traffic cleared, then he unrolled Cellarius's Palatinate map on his light table, placing weights in the corners to prevent them from curling.

The map was hand-colored in yellow and blue, and where the two combined, in various intensities of green. A warm red, almost orange, contributed highlights and deepened the heavier shadows. The line work and type were black. Some laypeople considered the design gaudy. But such maps had to be judged according to the standards of the time in which they were made.

Cellarius had employed silver and gold foil in the compass rose. His calligraphy, simple yet ornamental, was timeless. He had filled the margins with a delightful sequence of medieval runes, composing a border:

...

It was a dramatic stylistic departure from the single black line used to delineate the borders of most other maps of the day.

For the first time in history a cartographer had accurately depicted the cultural features of the Palatinate. A twenty-first century traveler using the map could find his way around with ease. The towns of the region—Kirn, Idar, Oberstein, Kaiserslautern, Zweibrücken—were drawn in a graphic style, each cultural element exaggerated in scale. Many of the roads had not changed since Cellarius's time other than when they were paved. Buildings appeared in perspective, and the churches, castles, and stately homes still standing were immediately recognizable.

But there was nevertheless something about the map that bothered John, something that had lurked in his subconscious from the first moment he laid eyes on it. Until Cellarius's resurrection from the bog, the Palatinate map had merely been the last one he had completed. Now that it was clear Cellarius had been murdered, his final professional effort demanded greater scrutiny, and John could allow the subtle naggings to surface. He stared at the map for several more minutes, then impulsively picked up the phone and dialed a number.

"You say the Palatinate map was never commissioned? He just did it for the fun of it?"

"I wouldn't say it was for the fun of it," replied Dr. Carl Antonelli, one of John's former cartography professors at Franklin & Marshall College. "But it's true there's no record, none that has come to light anyway, that anyone ordered this map from Cellarius."

"You've seen the original pressing, haven't you?"

"Yes, at the University of Southern Maine. I assume they still have it. Cellarius only made one print from the copper plate, which was itself quite unusual. Part of the margin was torn off; the upper right corner is completely gone."

"Not according to my copy."

"That's because they don't print facsimiles in any form other than a square or a rectangle. Your copy probably has an extrapolated margin. By the way, this is the only regular square map Cellarius ever made; all the rest have one dimension longer than the other. Were you aware of that?"

"No."

"The interesting thing about the margin of the Palatinate map is that it contains those strange symbols, the so-called runes, almost like a message or a cipher. They don't appear on any of his other maps, and no one's been able to figure them out."

"If they might be significant, why haven't they been followed up with some kind of cryptological analysis?"

"Well, John, you have to admit, that map's a little obscure. You and I don't think so, but to the rest of the world it's just a dusty old piece of paper, one of thousands of its kind. How many cryptologists do you know who collect maps? For that matter, how many cryptologists do you know at all? Maybe somebody's done something with it, I don't know. But nothing's been published on the subject, I can tell you that."

"I just figured they were abstract graphic designs."

"And they may well be. You know what the funniest thing is about the Palatinate map to me? The latitude-longitude grid. It conforms to no standard geographic grid, past or present, nor does it correspond to any particular unit of measure. Historians of cartography have long concluded that Cellarius merely drew an arbitrary grid. But you know as well as I do, that wasn't his style."

"Maybe that's what's been bothering me."

"There's another thing: the biblical quote that appears— oddly—in English."

John read directly from his facsimile: "'All the rivers run into the sea, yet the sea is not full; unto the place from whence the rivers come, thither they return again.' Ecclesiastes, chapter one, verse seven."

"That's the one. There's no obvious reason why this particular quote would appear in this particular language on this particular map."

"It's hard to know where to begin."

"What are you after, John? You wouldn't be trying to solve a murder mystery; I know you better than that."

John hesitated. What to tell his former professor? That he had a mystical connection with a dead cartographer? That he felt compelled to learn what happened to him, and the compulsion was already becoming a distraction?

"It's just the historian in me demanding closure," John said.

"Well, take it from a professional historian: the only thing more elusive than truth is truth in the past. If I were you, I would attack this mystery from the opposite angle."

"Meaning?"

"From the angle of the ruby found in Cellarius's fist. You know, the sister cities of Idar and Oberstein, both of which appear on the Palatinate map, are centers of a substantial gem and jewelry industry."

"No … I didn't know."

"Have been. For centuries."

FIVE

"WATCH THIS," DAVID FREEMAN said. "It's called the French Drop." He held up a quarter, pressed between the thumb and fingers of his right hand, and began reaching for it with his left hand. "Just as the coin is about to be snatched by your left hand, allow it to drop into your right palm. Then keep your eyes on your left hand as it moves away, to reinforce the idea that it's the one holding the coin. Let your right hand go slack, to suggest it's empty."

He was sitting in a beanbag chair that hemorrhaged beans every time he shifted his weight. On the floor next to him were the typical paraphernalia of an amateur magician: cards, coins, ropes, handkerchiefs. The news was on TV, but the anchor's voice only served as background noise in the room.

Sarah Sainte-James occupied the only other chair in their South Philadelphia row house. She was staring into a hand mirror, brushing her hair. David secretly clocked her. She'd been at it for nearly twenty minutes already and had yet to begin the other side.

"Very nice," Sarah said.

"Here's another one. It's called Finger Palming. You pinch the coin gently between the middle knuckles and palm of your right hand to hold it in place, and you turn the hand over as though to transfer the coin to your left hand." He demonstrated. "Your left hand makes a grasping motion, as if it took the coin, and your eyes remain focused there to reinforce the idea, as before."

"I'm wetting my pants." Sarah transferred her brush from the right hand to the left without any effort at sleight of hand.

"This is the most important one, the so-called Classic Palm, the epitome of the palmer's art. You hide the coin in the *center* of your palm without any help from your fingers." He raised his right hand to show the quarter; Sarah didn't bother looking up. "The trick is to keep your hand as straight as possible, without any tension or unnatural angle that would give the secret away. You almost have to convince yourself the hand really is empty."

"I could just shit."

"I've been sleeping with a quarter in my palm. This morning, for the first time, it was still there when I woke up. But that's the right hand; I still have to work on the left."

"Why don't you practice palming while washing the dishes?"

"Somebody once told me that if you can type fifty words a minute with a coin palmed in each hand, you've mastered the art."

"Or you could do the dishes. Since the drain is clogged, you wouldn't risk losing the quarter."

"The neat thing is, there's no difference between a coin and any other circular object, like a diamond ring."

"You could paint. You could paint the apartment with a coin palmed in each hand. In fact, since the rooms are so narrow, you could do both walls at once, holding a brush in each hand and a coin in each palm."

David let his shoulders slump. "Am I to understand the dishes need washing? Is that what this is about?"

"No, the dishes are washed, thank you. You are to understand that if I weren't here, they wouldn't get washed. That's what this is about."

"Sure they would. I couldn't stand a dirty kitchen. But why do women always blame men for not doing what's already done? You complain about the laundry, for example, yet you do it. Why should I then concern myself with it? Do you really want me to take my clean clothes out of the closet and wash them again, so I can say I did the laundry?"

"Very well," Sarah said, putting her mirror down. "What about dusting? The apartment has not yet been dusted."

"And it needn't be. Dust is perfectly acceptable. Dust gives the place character. Besides, what if somebody looked in the window and saw me doing it?"

"And vacuuming? Does dried mud on the carpet give the place character?"

"No, but I have an answer to that. Vacuum cleaners are designed for women, not men. When they are made so men don't have to bend over constantly to use them, maybe men will use them more often."

"It was men who designed them, you know."

"The same goes for washing dishes and all that other kitchen work: the countertops are too low."

"And the cobwebs on the lamps in your workshop? Are they too low for you?"

"Cobwebs keep the place free from flies."

"It looks to me like you're trying to grow new lampshades. By the way, when do you think you'll get around to investing the ten seconds it will take to change the bulb on the bedroom ceiling?"

"If it's so easy, why don't you do it, and save yourself the trouble of nagging me about it?"

"You know, David, even in the Polak jokes the bulb gets changed. It may take three or four of them to do it, but at least the job gets done."

He raised his hand to silence her. There was a news report on the television about the seventeenth-century cartographer who had floated to the surface of a bog. As was true of many people, the story of Cellarius's disappearance and rediscovery had captured David's imagination. The media delighted in showing pictures of the corpse.

The news camera panned the bog where the body had been found, but of course it was gone. All there was to see was a phalanx of detail-hungry reporters, some craggy birch trees, and a few anonymous spectators waving to the camera.

The body was being stored in a low-temperature chamber at the University of Hamburg and was unavailable for view. A news team had nevertheless perched outside the room and focused its lens on the door. The sign merely read *Privat*. Viewers could only imagine what was on the other side.

Coverage shifted to the Smithsonian Institution in Washington, D. C. Dr. Cornelius Bancroft, curator in charge of the institution's mineral and gem collection, filled the screen. The news camera scanned the curator's figure, from his tennis shoes to his ponytail, as though to point out an incongruity.

"Hey," Sarah said, "isn't that—"

"Shh!"

41

Dr. Bancroft was explaining his theory: that the ruby found in Cellarius's fist was one of the lost Tavernier stones of popular European folklore.

David caught his breath, sank deeper into the beanbag chair, and stared at the screen. The lost Tavernier stones were almost as legendary as the Holy Grail. Prospectors, treasure hunters, and quacks had been searching for them for over three hundred years.

Bancroft based his theory on a comparison of the ruby's color and clarity with those of a similar stone described by Tavernier. But opponents of the theory, whom the TV news reporter also interviewed, were quick to point out that the *cut* did not match any of the drawings made during Tavernier's seventh voyage—the entire account of which, at any rate, was commonly understood to be a hoax.

Bancroft countered that the ruby must therefore be a *recut*. "Finally we have a direct link," he said, "to the largest cache of gemstones in history."

David was well acquainted with that cache. Jean-Baptiste Tavernier, a seventeenth-century Marco Polo, had made six journeys to India during his career as a trader and brought back hundreds of precious gems. He described his journeys in his memoirs, which contained painstakingly made drawings of enormous jewels in the Indian royal treasury—jewels like the 280-carat Great Mogul diamond, the 242-carat Great Table diamond, and a flawless 285-carat ruby—that were never documented again.

At the age of seventy-nine, he came out of retirement to become the Duke of Prussia's ambassador to India, and thus embarked on his mysterious seventh voyage to the Orient. According to history, he never arrived.

But according to legend, he did: he bought the Great Mogul, the Great Table, and dozens of other priceless stones, and was robbed and killed on the way home to his barony in Switzerland. Somewhere in Europe, perhaps buried like pirate treasure in an oaken chest, a hoard of incomprehensible value awaited the first person who could identify and piece together the relevant clues. The hoard had been studied, glorified, and intensely hunted since its disappearance in 1689.

The same year Johannes Cellarius vanished from his Hamburg studio.

Bancroft produced a glass model of the 285-carat ruby reproduced from Tavernier's drawing and compared it to a hastily made plaster model of the ruby found with Cellarius in the bog.

"One of the facets on the bog ruby could possibly be the same as this one on the Tavernier stone." He oriented the glass model so the camera could get a clear shot of a trapezoidal facet. "Enough of the stone was cut away, in fact, to make one or two *additional* rubies, at least one of which might retain some more of the original facets. Such a stone could also be extant. It's just a matter of finding it. Unfortunately, it might be in someone's private collection, unavailable for study, or even in another bog somewhere, for all we know."

"Bancroft, you asshole," David blurted out. "You don't know a ruby from rhubarb."

The news report continued with harsh criticism from the community of academic mineralogists, especially those at the Field Museum of Natural History in Chicago. Tavernier was neither robbed nor killed, they said; he died of pneumonia on his way to a diplomatic post, his travel bags empty of gemstones.

David turned off the TV and paced the room.

Sarah put her brush down and looked at him sympathetically. "You should call him," she said. "He was like a father to you."

"I don't want to talk about it." He ran his hands through his hair, then picked up a fistful of plastic beans from the carpet and studied them as though they were jewels. "The lost Tavernier stones. Christ, do you suppose?"

"The reporter didn't seem to think so."

"What the hell does he know? Bancroft knows. He's uncovered the first irrefutable proof the stones really exist." David let the beans spill through his fingers. They bounced and scattered on the carpet. "Where's the nearest public library?" he asked her. "Do you happen to know?"

"What do I look like, Shakespeare?"

He needed to learn as much as he could about Cellarius. The media kept referring to a particular map, one the cartographer completed just before disappearing. Given the likelihood that what Cellarius was working on when he died had something to do with his death—a likelihood supported by evidence he took to his grave—the last map was as good a place as any to start.

Start what?

Start nothing. You know goddamn well what.

You started it before but couldn't finish it.

That was then. This—this is altogether different.

What angle will you try this time?

Whichever one it takes.

SIX

THE BLANKET OF NIGHT covered all four time zones. Whereas the East Coast already slept, the western zones were just clearing away dinner plates or getting ready for bed. The blanket of night provided scant protection from mundane hardships of the day, and it failed utterly as a buffer against impossible daydreams.

In Guymon, Oklahoma, a widowed grandmother put her small granddaughter to bed and wondered, childlike, about the prospect of finding large gemstones, about the difference such a windfall would make in their arduous lives. She tucked the little girl—her legal ward and the principal drain on her social security check—under a thin white sheet, leaving only her frowsy face and delicate fingers exposed to the ogres of the night.

In Gallup, New Mexico, a grade-schooler complained bitterly about being sent to bed so early. After testing every excuse in his kit, he sighed gloomily and resigned himself to mere anticipation. Searching his gravel driveway for rubies would just have to wait until tomorrow.

A Bakersfield, California, jeweler locked up his store for the night and headed home, vowing to someday carry a line of wares that would attract the carriage trade. Despite his ambitions, the jeweler knew in his heart that his best customers would always be high-school seniors.

The blanket of night continued its smooth glide around the planet until Wednesday morning dawned in Western Europe, where fortune seekers woke to the news that had broken in America the day before. The lost Tavernier stones, the greatest treasure in history, a legend on par with the Ark and the Grail, had finally relinquished a clue.

The race to find them was underway.

———

Kommissar Gerd Pfeffer woke with a dry, sticky mouth, a ringing in his ears, and a dull pain in his sinuses, the result of the previous evening's debauchery. He stared into his bathroom mirror at the stubble on his chin and the razor poised to shave it off. The image had appeared in his mirror every morning since around the time he turned fourteen. But the fourteen-year-old would not have recognized the man with veins on his nose and bags under his eyes.

A gang of neo-Nazi skinheads had set fire to a Turkish boy during the night, after first dousing him with kerosene. Early that morning, a Herbertstrasse beat cop found a whore sprawled dead in her window showcase, blindfolded with a necktie but otherwise exhibiting no clue how she died. There was even one from the Rheinland about a new Satanic cult that sacrificed virgins by throwing them from the top of the Loreley.

Another typical day in the valiant battle against bad guys. The world wasn't any safer, Pfeffer realized grimly, than when he joined the Polizei a quarter of a century ago. The notion that the human species was prey to no predator on earth was a silly one, after all; every gun-toting hood was a predator, one who served a purpose not unlike that of a lion in the Serengeti.

Pfeffer looked at the man in the mirror looking back. He knew he fit the mold of an old cop: a barrel-shaped torso, the lower end spilling over a narrow belt. A gruff voice that got little exercise except when speaking tenderly to his cat. An insolent stare, aimed most accurately at stupid subordinates.

A cheating wife.

He had been subconsciously ducking signals for months, but it was his wine cellar, oddly enough, that had tipped him off. The two of them—his wife and "Mr. Dick"—sampled from the collection routinely while doing it in his home, without the least bit of consideration for the value and rarity of the wines. If not for the latter, Pfeffer might have forgiven them the "it."

No, that wasn't true. The affair hurt him deeply, more deeply than anything ever had before. He had Mr. Dick's license plate number, because he'd arrived home one day just in time to see the man drive off in a Saab. A simple phone call would get him a name and address. If he wished.

The question was, what would he do with them when he got them?

To his way of thinking, there was only one honorable way to treat a man who entered his home, drank his wine, and soiled his wife. But there was an obstacle to Pfeffer's way of thinking, and it wasn't ethics. It was the German judicial system, with which he was all too familiar.

Every time he thought of the two of them together and imagined what they did to each other, he got so upset he struggled to calm his breathing. But he couldn't stop thinking about it. His wife was the love of his life, and he had assumed the feelings were mutual. He could see the man's hands reaching under her skirt. He could imagine her unbuckling his pants . . .

He snatched up the phone and dialed a München-Pullach number from memory.

"*Bundesnachrichtendienst.*"

"Reinhard? Is that you?"

"Gerd? Long time. Haven't they given you a gold watch?"

"Not quite yet. Listen, I'll be needing some sensitive materials squirreled my way."

"Gerd, I'd do anything for you, even help you find the goddamn lost Tavernier stones. But I can't give you anything that's not on the register. What are you after?"

"The goddamn lost Tavernier stones."

After a few seconds of static, Pfeffer continued: "And if you help me, all the notes I have on what your son Lucien did last year while vacationing on the North Sea coast . . . will disappear."

The intelligence agent cleared his throat. "What is it exactly that you want?"

"Everything your people come up with."

"And what Lucien did . . ."

"The world will never know."

———

One of the houses on Rosenstockstrasse in Mainz, Germany, a Queen Anne with a hipped roof and asymmetrical cross gables, had delicately turned spindle work on its wrapped porch that was finally the shade of cornflower blue the owner wanted: the painters had gotten it right on the fourth try.

The owner, Frieda Blumenfeld, was just finishing her breakfast and beginning the long, impatient wait for her husband to leave. She shouldn't have held her breath, however, because he discovered the newspaper under the dishes where she had tucked it and poured himself another cup of coffee.

No matter. She would gaze out the window until he was gone, pretending to be lost in thought.

She had a clear view of the house across the street, a Victorian that hadn't seen a fresh coat of paint in five years. A VW sat shamelessly in the driveway. She smiled; at least one neighbor's finances were even more precarious than her own.

The houses on Rosenstockstrasse were old money mansions, vine-encroached trophies of an earlier generation, most of them ageing gracefully in the shade of large plane trees. Greek columns were common, as were full-width porches, balustraded balconies, and real working window shutters. The architectural styles were mixed but could be summarized as "eclectic stubborn dignity."

Frieda Blumenfeld, the most eclectic, stubborn, and dignified resident of Rosenstockstrasse, felt that her most distinctive physical feature was her hair. It had grayed to the value of soft graphite and was highlighted with needle-length streaks of frost. She had long refrained from either dyeing or cutting it, and now it fell to her lower back in a ponytail bound in three places. She knew she was supposed to shorten it or shape it into a bun or otherwise act like an old lady. But she couldn't bring herself to discard the one remaining vestige of girlhood.

The feature she didn't like, and considered shortening, was her nose.

She fought to keep her chin from doubling and her butt from expanding, but the unforgiving cycle of seasons was winning the contest. In fact, her hair, nose, and cheerlessly pale blue eyes were combining to make her look like a witch.

A banker by trade, she had inherited a respectable sum of old money from her mother, from whom she had also inherited exquisite tastes. The money wasn't enough to place her and her husband at the top of Mainz society, but it was enough to place them within its bosom.

Old money wore so much better than new money. People with old money grew up wearing it, whereas those who came upon it later in life never seemed to be able to make it fit. Nevertheless, some of the new-money people were flaunting the staggering size of their portfolios, pushing the blue bloods lower down on the guest lists.

In an effort to catch up to them, Blumenfeld had invested her inheritance, all of it, in a sure-bet commodities venture: chicken futures. Trouble was, the chickens had no futures. When the price of feed soared during a drought, farmers all over Europe massacred their chicks rather than raise them with feed that was more expensive than the price they, the chickens, would bring at maturity.

For nine agonizing days, Blumenfeld watched her commodity go limit down and her fortune erode. She suffered nightmares of hungry baby chicks chasing her around the bedroom, peeping incessantly, pecking at her with their nasty beaks. The consummate blow came when she was arrested for having embezzled her bank clients to meet a preposterous margin call and led out of her office in handcuffs.

The worst thing about prison was the food. She got used to the noise—to mentally ill inmates wailing all night long—but despite two years of training her palate, she never got used to the food.

The best thing about prison was the sex. She was a lesbian married for the sake of convenience, the greater part of which was appearance. She had long come to think of males as superfluous to the planet.

She was still able to support the façade of wealth, but only because she owed no money on either the house or the car. The furniture was getting a little hairy, though. When one of her society friends recently suggested she splurge on a new living room arrangement, even giving her the name of a favorite interior decorator, Blumenfeld slipped and answered that she didn't care to spend her money so frivolously. The society friend only stared back, her expression blank, her eyes blinking.

The car, a BMW that had cost as much as a small airplane, was three years old now, and everyone knew it. In another year or so, it would become a downright embarrassment.

Like her husband.

Finally... *finally*... he put the newspaper down, stretched and yawned, and stood up from the table. Moments later, he donned his hat and left the house.

Herr Blumenfeld had taken a job as a retail clerk in an art supply store downtown, and it was only a matter of time before one of their acquaintances discovered this tidbit and realized how bad off they were. "It's just a hobby of his" wasn't going to fly: Herr Blumenfeld was color blind and couldn't draw a decent stick figure. The job was necessary, though, to pay for certain can't-do-withouts such as maid service.

Frieda Blumenfeld required her husband to leave the house each morning through the back door and to instruct anyone who asked that he was out and about doing volunteer work—

something perfectly acceptable for a wealthy, middle-aged man to do. But it was just a matter of time.

As soon as he was gone, she picked up the phone and dialed a number.

"Gebhardt."

"Hallo, Mannfred. *Ich bin's.* I have just read a most fascinating article in the *Frankfurter Allgemeine.*"

"I know which one you mean. I read it too."

"Then you know why I'm calling."

There was a long pause at the other end. "If you mean to ask whether I'm willing to devote my spare time to an enterprise that will almost certainly result in more frustration than satisfaction, more pain than profit … one that will toe the line of the law, cross the line, leave the line far behind … one that might even get me shot at … then yes, I think I know why you're calling—again."

"My dear Mannfred, you exaggerate."

"Do I?"

"Perhaps you should have one of your morning drinks to relax you. It's past noon somewhere in the world."

"I've already had two."

"Then a walk, perhaps."

"To Switzerland?"

"*Touché.* You do pay attention, after all. There's a partial reproduction of Cellarius's last map on the back page of the features section. Did you notice anything odd about it? In particular, the runes decorating its margin?"

She heard the rustling of newspaper pages in the background.

"That one must have gotten past me," Gebhardt said.

"Well, the world will soon notice, and it won't be long before somebody figures out what they mean. By the way, it may not be obvious to you, but I *am* waiting for an answer."

"You've already predicted what my answer will be, otherwise you wouldn't have called."

"That's what I like about you, Mannfred. You know me almost as well as I know you."

"When do you want to start?"

"Today. We begin by collecting information. And I shouldn't have to say this, but I will anyway: don't speak to anyone."

"This will blow over in a week or so, you know. The press will tire of it, and everyone will forget."

"Not everyone. Drop by this afternoon. I'll have a list of tasks for you."

"I have a job now, remember?"

"Quit."

"*And* an opportunity to go straight. Today is Wednesday. I'll come by Saturday and we'll talk. If I like what I hear, we'll talk some more. Now, if you don't mind, I still have time for another beer before I go to work."

"You owe me."

Gebhardt remained silent.

"You owe me," Blumenfeld repeated, "and I want the debt repaid. I need a complete facsimile of the map that appears in the newspaper. A partial won't do. I'll give you until Saturday, if you insist, but I cannot wait longer."

After another lengthy silence, Gebhardt said, "I have a feeling I'm going to wish they'd burned him and scattered his ashes rather than stabbed him and buried him in a bog."

"Nonsense. Have another beer. See you on Saturday. *Auf Wiederhören.*"

"*Tschüs.*"

Gebhardt had once told Blumenfeld that everything men did to improve themselves, they did to improve their chances of acquiring women, and thus spread their genes as widely as possible. Blumenfeld had a different opinion. She had a different opinion about most things, as a matter of habit, but this time it was a direct result of experience: she had served as Gebhardt's alibi in defense of a brutal sexual assault.

That was the debt he owed her. And that was the danger he posed.

Following her release from prison, Blumenfeld had set out to restore her estate. Together with a partner, she involved herself in an elaborate sting, raising capital of her own by begging and borrowing from former business associates. The target was a wealthy Dutchman who would put up most of the money for the purchase of shipping containers in Bremerhaven. Containers she, Blumenfeld, and her new partner didn't intend to buy.

It wasn't until the Dutchman and Blumenfeld's partner absconded with the money that Blumenfeld realized she had been the real target of the sting. She bore them no malice. To be sure, she hunted down the partner, who soon afterwards died in a house fire. She lost all track of the Dutchman. But she appreciated the lesson she had learned. "We" in every subsequent job translated to "me."

She'd needed someone to start the fire. A prison acquaintance suggested a young, clean-cut associate named Mannfred Gebhardt. Problem was, Gebhardt was about to stand trial for sexual assault. Several people were prepared to testify they saw him with the victim, but nobody had yet offered to remember he was elsewhere when the victim was assaulted.

Blumenfeld sometimes wondered to what extent she could excuse Gebhardt's precipitate nature by attributing it to the abuse he had received as a child. An uncle had tied him to a bedpost and had his way with him, even going so far as to invite friends over to share the treat.

But the girl Gebhardt had assaulted was underage. And every deed had its penance, regardless of the circumstances that brought it about.

SEVEN

THE NEXT MORNING, JOHN took the day off and visited the campus of Franklin & Marshall College. It was the first time he had ever taken a day off from work, and the request surprised Harry Tokuhisa.

"You're not sick," Harry clarified.

"No, sir."

"And nobody died."

"No, sir."

"You just need to take care of … personal matters."

"Yes, sir."

"Very well." He signed John's leave slip grudgingly, as though it were an execution order. "As soon as you're able, tell me what's really the matter."

"Yes, sir."

Like most private universities, F & M relied heavily on endowments. And like most private university libraries, the Shadek-Fackenthal Library bore the burden of its donors' legacies. The pride of the library was one of its annexes, the Erwin Raisz Institute of Mapping Sciences.

Some 30,000 individual map sheets, most printed before 1900, constituted the heart of the collection. They filled long aluminum cabinets stacked to the ceiling of one of the building's underground floors. Nearly one hundred pre-nineteenth-century globes populated a single room. The globes looked so much like round-headed people waiting for medical appointments that students usually referred to the room as the "waiting room." Officially, it was the Amos Lithgow Room, in honor of the institute's chief benefactor, though even some of the officers of the university were unaware of the name.

The building had cost Mr. Lithgow fifteen million dollars and the college its open-air tennis and basketball courts. The glass-and-steel construction was a new look for F&M, one not welcomed by every alumnus.

John Graf, a visiting alumnus clutching a sheet of paper covered with symbols he did not understand, decided to try his luck at the main library building. He thought he would have the best chances with a history librarian on the third floor. But the only staffer present took one look at the symbols and suggested he try the math department instead.

The math department was on the second floor of Stager Hall.

"You say you're a writer?"

John smiled despite himself. It wasn't really a lie; wasn't everyone a writer?

"Yes," he said, "I'm researching an article about the Tavernier legend, and I was hoping you could give me some advice."

"Who do you write for?" Dr. William Moulton, a mathematics professor who happened to have his office door open, seemed genuinely intrigued. John allowed his hopes to rise.

"Well, I'm freelance, actually."

"Oh. Have you published any books?"

"Not as yet."

"Oh. I'm a sci-fi buff myself," Moulton explained, leaning back in his chair. "The trouble is, nobody wants to write mathematical science fiction. They just want to write about combating aliens and exceeding the speed of light. The best science fiction, I think, would be based on mathematical concepts, for example non-Euclidean geometry. I just don't understand why nobody's doing it."

John sighed. "I don't either. Certainly everyone would want to read stuff like that."

"Well! There's a niche for you, a wide open one."

"Too bad I wasn't very good in math."

"Yes. That's a necessary—but insufficient—condition." He slapped his thigh and started to laugh, but caught himself when he realized his visitor didn't share the humor. "Now then, what was it you wanted me to look at?"

John handed him the creased and wrinkled page. He had arranged the runes from the border of Cellarius's last map in rows of twenty-five characters each:

```
7>ᗡᖴᘓᖴᗅᗷᗴᗅᘉᗅᘉ>7ᗷᗷL>ᐱᑌᐱᑌᖴᑀᖴ
ᘓᐯ<ᑌᐱᐯᗴᘉᖴᘈ<ᑌ<ᖀᖈᗅᘈᑀᖴᘓᐯ>ᘉ7ᗴ
Lᖴᗩᗴ>ᖀᗅᗴ7>ᗡᖴᖴᗅᖴᗴᗴᗅᘉᗅᘉ>7ᗷᗷL
>ᐱᑌᐱᑌᖴᐱᐯᗴᗴ>ᖀ>ᗩᖀᗴᗴᖴᐱᐱᖀ7ᒃᐯᐱᐯ
77ᖀᘓᘉᗅᗩᗅ><ᐯᐯ>ᐱᐯᑌ>ᖴᖴᗷᒃᐱᘈᒃ>
ᑌᒃᗴ7ᘈᗴᑀᗅ᠇ᗷᗅᘉ>ᐱᘉᖀ<ᒃᘈᘉᘉᐱᗴᗅᒃᐱ
ᘈᘉ7ᑀᒃᗴ>ᗴᐯLᗷᒃᑌ>ᒃᗗᘉᖴᘈᘈᑌᖴᐱᑌᖴ
>ᗗᗴᗗ<ᗴᖀᖀᘈᘉᗴᖀᗴᑌᑌᗗ>ᗗᒃᗅᖴᗗᘈᒃᗴᒃ
ᖀᒃᘈᗴᗴᘈᐯᘈᖀᒃᗗᘈᖀᒃᖴᐯᖴᗘᗘ<ᐯᗗᒃᘈᘈ
ᒃᐱᖴᑀᖴᖴᗗᐱᘈᑌᘈᗴᒃᒃᗴᒃᒃ>ᘈᐯᗗᐱᘈᗘᗴᒃᗗᒃ
ᘈᖴᗩᑌᗗᘉ7ᘈᗘLᖴ7ᘈ7ᘈ᠇ᗴᘈᑌᑌᐱᖴᐱᗗᗗᘈᐱ
```

"The library sent me," John said. "They thought, being a mathematician, and mathematicians being interested in ciphers, you might be able to make something of this."

Moulton looked at the sheet and frowned. He turned it sideways, then upside down, and continued the quarter spins until it was right-side up again. It quickly became clear to John that the man had no idea what he was looking at. But the examination continued another full minute for John's benefit.

"I'm afraid not," Moulton finally confessed. "There are too few characters—I count only 275—to do a decent frequency analysis, a character association analysis, and so on. There's software available for that stuff, but you'll need a lot more ciphertext than you have. Is the solution in English—do you know?"

John shrugged.

"Oh, well. Have you tried the people at Fort Meade?"

"What do you mean?"

"They've got a secret underground cryptology operation going on there. Most mathematicians who are into this kind of thing end up working for the government and never publish anything. But they'll tell you the same thing I'm telling you: without a decryption code, you'll have to come up with a whole lot more ciphertext to conduct any worthwhile analyses."

Moulton slowly handed the paper back, then looked at his watch and yawned. "Was there anything else?"

Before leaving campus, John stopped by the cafeteria in the Steinman College Center. From his table near the window he was just able to see the blue-capped spire of Hensel Hall next door. Although Hensel Hall served mainly for musical performances, it reminded John of a chapel, and its presence had always comforted him. The spire, visible from off-campus, was an F&M landmark.

He had taken the crumpled sheet out of his pocket and was gazing absentmindedly at the runes when someone sat down across from him at the table. He looked up to find Dr. Joseph Quimby, one of his former history professors, smiling in greeting.

"Well, what do you know," Quimby said. "A ghost from Christmas past."

"It's been a long time," John admitted. Quimby hadn't changed: an oval face, bulbous nose, and bald pate made him look like a clown without makeup. Still, he was one of the best teachers John ever had.

"That's the way of it, you know. I teach my students all I can, then I kick them out of the nest, and the moment they learn to fly, they forget who taught them. Do you know that out of hundreds of students I have every year, year after year, the only ones who return to visit are the ones who got a D?"

"So now you know why I've never visited. You gave me a C."

"I didn't."

"Oh, yes, you did. In medieval history." John had worked harder in that class than any other in his life.

"That explains it. My killer course. You might have gotten the highest grade."

They shook hands warmly.

"Seriously," John said. "I've always meant to visit. It's just something I never seem to get around to doing."

"I understand completely, what with your job taking you so far away. Where is it, way over on James Street, right?"

John felt himself blushing. "Come on. Don't rub it in."

"So what brings you here today?"

He tapped his tray. "The food, of course. I got addicted to it during the four years I spent here, and I can't break the habit."

"Is the pigpen keeping you busy?"

"Now, listen. North Star may not be a palace, but I wouldn't exactly call it a pigpen, either."

"No, I mean the pigpen cipher."

"Excuse me?"

"That page you've been studying." He pointed to the sheet of paper in front of John. "It's written using the pigpen cipher. Didn't you know that was its name?"

"Ah, no, I didn't."

"No wonder you got a C in medieval history. The pigpen was popular in the Middle Ages, especially among Freemasons."

Quimby took the sheet from John's hands and smoothed it out on the table. "Let's see if we can improve your grade."

EIGHT

ELEANOR HALL, FEATURES EDITOR of the *Chicago Tribune*, slammed the door of the conference room as she entered. Her naturally red hair looked like it had caught fire. She threw a current edition of the *Trib* onto the conference table, where four of her junior editors sat wringing their hands, knowing that unscheduled staff meetings only meant bad news.

The paper spun several times on the polished table.

"What's wrong with this picture?" she asked when the paper came to rest.

The four remained silent. Finally one of them raised his hand.

"Justin?"

Justin cleared his throat. "Ma'am, ours is the only major newspaper in the country not to reveal the identity of the pigpen cipher?"

"Ah! I suspected something was amiss."

She sat down at the table, closed her eyes, and ran her fingers through her hair. "All right. This Tavernier affair is dominating the news. Actually, it's overwhelming the news. I want stories. Your assignment is to interview puzzlers, historians, cartographers, treasure hunters—everybody. The jewels aren't going to be found; the real treasure here is the opportunity to sell newspapers. My boss knows it, and he has made sure *I* know it, and now I'm making sure *you* know it. Any questions?"

"Yes, ma'am." Justin closed his eyes before speaking. "Is there any travel and expense money available?"

Eleanor Hall glared at him. "Tell you what, Justin. If you wear out your shoes walking between your PC and my desk because you're bringing me stories, I'll personally buy you a new pair."

———

David met Sarah at a diner on Market Street, where she was nibbling on a plate of fries. He joined her in the booth.

"Did you get it?" she asked.

He removed a folded envelope and a small plastic bag from his shirt pocket. He unzipped the bag first and showed her a four-prong Tiffany ring mount. Stamped inside the shank were "18K" and the image of a lightning bolt.

"How much was it?" Sarah asked.

"Three hundred dollars."

"You could have gotten it from a jobber for less."

"True, but the jobber would come with a disconcertingly wide gap in his face known as a mouth."

David unfolded the envelope next, after first pressing it between his thumb and fingers to find the lump, and removed a colorless, amorphous stone from the soft blue tissues inside. It looked like an ordinary piece of abraded glass.

"We have until Sunday," he said. "That's the last day of the month."

"Don't put it off until the night before, like you always do. You know how you tend to underestimate these jobs."

The waitress arrived to take David's order. Sarah listened, blinking in disbelief, as he itemized a quarter chicken, coleslaw, potato salad, French fries, fluffy butter biscuits, a half-dozen zesty chicken morsels, and a cardboard envelope containing Granny's apple pie—a pie that, when bit into, would release the thermal energy of an exploding star.

"That's enough food to make a starving fat man cry for mercy," Sarah complained, wrinkling her nose. She pushed her own half-eaten plate of French fries away. Then she watched as David's eyes followed the waitress back to the kitchen.

"Satisfying?" she asked.

"Oh, she could satisfy me, all right," he replied. "She could do it easily. In fact, I bet she could do it lying down."

"That's one of your traits I respect, David. You don't hide your crushes. If you did, I might have to get jealous. And suspicious."

"They don't call it a crush anymore, honey. Nowadays, it's known as a hard-on. By the way, did you get the job?"

She rolled her eyes. "No, one of the photographers recognized me."

"Well, give it a few years. When you're old and ugly they won't recognize you, and maybe they'll want to take your picture again."

"You're sweet."

When the food arrived, David ploughed into it as though the platter were an open-pit mine.

"How can you stand gnawing on bones like that?" Sarah asked.

"I'm higher up the food chain than they are. I don't lose any sleep over it."

"If you saw what they do to it in the kitchen, you might."

"The thing about food is, the more hands that touch it, the better it seems to taste."

"At a five-star restaurant, maybe. But not at the Poultry Palace."

"Move over a little bit so I can watch the waitress while I eat. Hurry, she's about to bend over."

"You're disgusting." She picked up a French fry and nibbled on it halfheartedly. "Any progress on the ruby?"

"Not yet, but give me a couple of days. If other portions of the recut exist, and if they're as big as Bancroft says they are, there'll be photographs of them somewhere, you can be sure of that."

"Can I help in any way?"

David almost choked on his food.

"I guess that means no," Sarah said in mock resignation. "At least I could help look for maps."

David shook his head. "Every idiot with a pipe dream has his name on a waiting list at the libraries. The poster shops are sold out. The distributors that *supply* the poster shops are sold out. Granted, people have been looking for this treasure for three hundred years, and the ruby is the first real clue to emerge. But even I don't get it. It's the Cabbage Patch craze happening all over again."

"You have contacts at College Park."

"I already tried."

"And?"

"No way. It seems one of the vice presidents has put a hold on all that material, apparently for the personal use of his sociopathic offspring."

"It sounds like a lot of people are already working on the mystery."

"Oh, not more than three or four thousand in Philadelphia alone. I have to find somebody, anybody, who has copies of Cellarius's maps. The natural kind of person to look for, of course, is a cartographer." He glanced at his watch and pushed his chair away from the table. "Before someone else beats me to it."

———

Mannfred Gebhardt watched Frieda Blumenfeld size him up as he settled uncomfortably into a chair. She had complimented his looks so many times in the past, she didn't need to repeat the words again: he was younger looking than his thirty years, a quality she clearly envied. Clean-cut, with hair appropriately short for a man, whatever that meant. And he always wore a tie, a habit that met with her approval. He tried to remember whether he always wore ties before the Blumenfeld Era, or whether he had started doing so merely to garner her favor. He was sure the precipitate intensity in his gray eyes was always there, because he'd heard it from others.

Blumenfeld's living room was a microcosm of her paradigm, a showcase for her tastes, accomplishments, and ambitions. She warmed visibly as she entered the room, much as an architect did when visiting a building he had designed. Gebhardt knew that some of the oil paintings were fakes, especially those whose signatures raised the eyebrows of visitors. But the inevitable question—Is this real?—had become simple for Blumenfeld to answer: Oh, *please*.

On the other hand, she seemed to relish explaining how she had discovered the Etruscan vase in a quaint little shop in Cerveteri during a stopover while visiting Rome. So many times had she told the story, she apparently had forgotten the little forger with bad teeth who had personally delivered it to her house, and that her visit to Italy had been on a bus tour, one that did not include Cerveteri.

Like Blumenfeld, Gebhardt lived in Mainz. But unlike his worldly and sophisticated partner, he occupied a room above one of the department stores downtown, rather than a highbrow mansion on Rosenstockstrasse. Blumenfeld had never visited the place, but that didn't stop her from superciliously predicting that his carpet was wearing through to the floorboards and paint was peeling from his walls.

The paintings, figurines, and other knick-knacks in Blumenfeld's living room were charming, Gebhardt conceded. But they may as well have had those little cards in front of them that said, Do Not Touch or If You Just Broke It, You Just Bought It. The living room was for show, not for living. At the same time, there was the slightest hint of fatigue about the floorings and furniture. Yes, he thought, Blumenfeld's home was descending toward his own, which—she was correct—did indeed have holes in the carpet and cracks in the paint.

Blumenfeld put on a pair of reading glasses that were clipped to opera-length eyeglass chains made of gold filigree. When the glasses rested on her nose, the chain fell in loops on either side of her face and resembled mechanical jowls.

"'Ruby and sapphire,'" she recited from a book, "'are the same mineral—corundum—differing only in their color. When chromium atoms replace some of the aluminum atoms in corundum, a red color results. Iron and titanium impurities account for blue.'" She looked up from the book, her eyes peering at Gebhardt over the rim of her glasses. "Were you aware of that?"

"I confess I was not." Gebhardt knew he was in for a tiresome afternoon; the old woman was already affecting her stage voice. "I suppose this exercise has a point."

"Saturation, my dear Gebhardt. That's how you solve a complicated problem. Mathematicians have practiced it since the days of Archimedes. Saturate your consciousness with the facts of the problem, and your subconscious mind will go to work on it as well. It sometimes happens that you awake in the morning with the solution reverberating inside your head. Now listen." She flipped to a page she had marked. "'The ancient Indians,'" she read, "'believed rubies vanquished enemies, and when ground up and consumed, served as a love potion.' You see, Mannfred? Hope for you yet if we find them."

"For us both."

"Here's something. 'From Burma, the oldest source of rubies, comes a legend about a mystical valley strewn liberally with the precious stones. The valley was so deep, the bottom couldn't be seen from the summits. To get at the stones, gem hunters cast pieces of freshly butchered sheep into the valley, knowing as they did that rubies adhere to raw meat.'"

"Do they?"

"Of course not. But the legend continues: 'Vultures would snatch up the meat and carry it to the summits, and the people only had to chase the birds away to recover the stones.'"

"At least those people had something to work with."

"'Red spinel was often confused with ruby; such stones were known as balas rubies. Perhaps the most famous balas ruby is the so-called Black Prince's Ruby, a 170-carat spinel in the center of the Maltese Cross on the British Imperial State Crown. Its history is murky; no one knows how it came to the Tower of London, where it shares the crown with Cullinan II, the Second Star of Africa … and 2,800 other diamonds.'"

"You're drooling, Frieda."

"Oh, if security weren't so tight …"

"Well, you studied stealing in college. Breaking and entering surely must have been part of the curriculum."

"Finance, Mannfred. I studied finance."

"A rose by any other name."

"Well, let's talk about *your* major: classics. On a ranking of most useful subjects to least useful subjects, yours would place just about … oh my, it falls off the list altogether!"

"If it weren't for historians—"

"But you didn't study history, you studied Greek and Roman mythology. You studied events that never happened, documented in languages no one ever speaks. If you had really studied history, you might be able to help me with this research. Speaking of which … where are the maps?"

"They—will—be—here."

"Now, don't get petulant. Your ways are impractical, just like your choice of major, and you know it. If you were a little less idealistic, you'd have a political party of your own by now, instead of a handful of unemployed friends who throw rocks at public speakers and can't even score a hit."

"*You're* one of my friends, Frieda."

After a moment of silence, Blumenfeld said, "I prefer to see myself as your mentor." She opened a notebook and signaled for Gebhardt to crouch on the floor next to the coffee table. Once he did, it was hard for him to concentrate on anything but the chains dangling from her glasses; they did a synchronized dance each time the old woman bobbed her head.

Blumenfeld drew a pair of tick-tack-toe grids and a pair of large *X*s, then filled each partitioned space with a letter, or a letter and a dot.

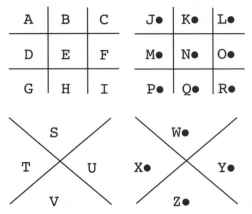

"It's as old as the hills but didn't get much use until the Freemasons adopted it to encipher their printed rituals. The modern form consists of four grids, the first two of the tick-tack-toe variety, containing nine letters each, the second two resembling large *X*s, containing four letters each. A dot occupies each space of the second tick-tack-toe and the second *X*. There are enough spaces for twenty-six letters of the alphabet, entered top to bottom, left to right.

"Thus the letter A resembles a reverse L, O resembles an E with a dot replacing its center stroke, S resembles a V, and Y resembles a less-than sign, filled with a dot. Using the pigpen is simple: you pull out the shape associated with the letter of choice and add a dot as appropriate. This is how Johannes Cellarius would have spelled his name in pigpen; your name is underneath."

⊐⌐⊓⌐⊔⊐⊡⊡⊡∨ ⌐⊡⌐⌐⌐⊔⌐⌐<∨
⊐⌐⊡⌐⌐⊐⊐ ⊓⊐⊔⊓⌐⌐⊐>

"Impressive," Gebhardt said. "So what does the text in the margin of the map say?"

"Regrettably, it comes up gibberish." She flipped to the front of the notebook and showed him her decipherment:

```
gxkqvqmnvhvhtgmmctvbzbrer
owubvsnhrfybuifqokqwsxhge
cqdnxiqngxkqvqmnvhvhtgmmc
tvbzbresmnxitjierivviglzs
pgiohagatysstewbtrrdgnkmx
bkegoefprjehtzhiypohhzepv
khgfkmxescjektmahrknbrzbq
tjejumiioheimbbjtjeeqafmn
imfdmfsniejfpnrsqlfywaenf
dvrkrrdvokdmnjvtewazgleia
kqabjhglcrpnplpokbzrzaalv
```

Gebhardt rose from the floor and returned to his chair. "*Now* are you finally convinced the shit is just border decoration?"

"Not at all. It's likely a deeper layer of decipherment is needed."

"Wait a minute. You said there was room for twenty-six letters. There are more than twenty-six letters in the German alphabet."

"I would be surprised if the language turned out to be German. In fact, I'm betting one of us is going to have to employ his Latin skills."

They stared at each other for a moment, then Gebhardt broke away and looked out the window. He wondered whether he could get his old job back.

"Don't start panicking yet," Blumenfeld said. "I know Latin was not your strongest subject. You have time to brush up. Meanwhile, I found it prudent to learn what other ciphers were popular in Cellarius's day. There were several, but the most common was one called the Vigenère. Unfortunately, we need a keyword to make the Vigenère work, or even to establish whether or not it was used."

Blumenfeld gestured for Gebhardt to view her notebook again. He rubbed his eyes, then got up and stood over the coffee table with his arms crossed. Blumenfeld was going to attack the puzzle relentlessly until she solved it. Until she could replace her Etruscan vase with a real one.

"The modern version," she said, "a derivation of the one originally devised by Blaise de Vigenère in his 1586 *Traicté des Chiffres*, employs a polyalphabetic sliding tableau." She turned the page in her notebook and showed him the 26 x 26 table she had drawn.

	A B C D E F G H I J K L M N O P Q R S T U V W X Y Z
A	a b c d e f g h i j k l m n o p q r s t u v w x y z
B	b c d e f g h i j k l m n o p q r s t u v w x y z a
C	c d e f g h i j k l m n o p q r s t u v w x y z a b
D	d e f g h i j k l m n o p q r s t u v w x y z a b c
E	e f g h i j k l m n o p q r s t u v w x y z a b c d
F	f g h i j k l m n o p q r s t u v w x y z a b c d e
G	g h i j k l m n o p q r s t u v w x y z a b c d e f
H	h i j k l m n o p q r s t u v w x y z a b c d e f g
I	i j k l m n o p q r s t u v w x y z a b c d e f g h
J	j k l m n o p q r s t u v w x y z a b c d e f g h i
K	k l m n o p q r s t u v w x y z a b c d e f g h i j
L	l m n o p q r s t u v w x y z a b c d e f g h i j k
M	m n o p q r s t u v w x y z a b c d e f g h i j k l
N	n o p q r s t u v w x y z a b c d e f g h i j k l m
O	o p q r s t u v w x y z a b c d e f g h i j k l m n
P	p q r s t u v w x y z a b c d e f g h i j k l m n o
Q	q r s t u v w x y z a b c d e f g h i j k l m n o p
R	r s t u v w x y z a b c d e f g h i j k l m n o p q
S	s t u v w x y z a b c d e f g h i j k l m n o p q r
T	t u v w x y z a b c d e f g h i j k l m n o p q r s
U	u v w x y z a b c d e f g h i j k l m n o p q r s t
V	v w x y z a b c d e f g h i j k l m n o p q r s t u
W	w x y z a b c d e f g h i j k l m n o p q r s t u v
X	x y z a b c d e f g h i j k l m n o p q r s t u v w
Y	y z a b c d e f g h i j k l m n o p q r s t u v w x
Z	z a b c d e f g h i j k l m n o p q r s t u v w x y

"Both sender and receiver must know the keyword. Repeating it above the cipher text in a one-to-one correspondence, the receiver finds each letter of the keyword in the vertical alphabet, then traces across into the tableau to the corresponding letter of the cipher text. Tracing up from that point, he identifies the plaintext letter in the horizontal alphabet. For example, the keyword 'ruby' would direct the receiver to interpret *klfyjosc* as follows:

R U B Y R U B Y

k l f y j o s c

T R E A S U R E

"The Vigenère was in common use during Cellarius's life, so it's as good a place as any to start. Breaking the code boils down to discovering his choice of keyword."

Gebhardt went back to his chair. "It looks like we have a hard road ahead of us on that one."

"We? Do you have a mouse in your pocket?"

He stiffened. "Come on, Frieda. This isn't my thing."

"Make it your thing. Weak as your Latin may be, it's stronger than mine. Who knows? Maybe you'll yet vindicate your impractical ways. But don't worry, I'll be working on it too. The only certain connection that exists between Cellarius and Tavernier—the only real lead we have—is the ruby that was found in Cellarius's fist. Indeed, it is this very object that leads people to suspect the runes constitute more than mere border decoration. Without it, there would be no treasure hunt. So I also need you to acquire every available photograph of large and famous rubies. The whole world knows what the bog ruby looks like. Sooner or later, somebody is going to match it up with its sisters."

"Acquire?"

"For free. We're on a budget."

"I see."

There was a knock at the door, and the maid entered the living room.

"Not now, Hannelore," Blumenfeld said. "We're extremely busy."

"But a gentleman is here with a package for you. He said he had to deliver it to you personally."

"A package?"

Gebhardt cleared his throat. "It's, ah, you know—the things."

"The things? Oh, the things! Well, by all means, show the gentleman in!"

Hannelore left to fetch the visitor, and Blumenfeld said to Gebhardt, "My dear Mannfred, you came through, after all."

"Yes. And you were saying? About my impractical ways?"

A bearded old man with spectacles entered the room, carrying a cardboard tube. Blumenfeld took the tube from his hands, unrolled its stack of maps onto the floor, and peeled through them until she found the one she was looking for.

"This is it," she said, beaming. "The Palatinate. And sure enough, Idar-Oberstein is depicted in exquisite detail."

"Planning a visit?" the dealer asked.

"Oh, one of these days, perhaps."

"I'll be going there shortly myself."

Blumenfeld and Gebhardt exchanged glances.

"To buy a piece of jewelry for my wife," the old man explained. "Next month is our anniversary."

Blumenfeld smiled. "Then may I suggest a ruby?"

The man shrugged. "Why not? After forty-five years of anniversary gifts, it makes little difference. She already has everything she wants."

"Take some raw meat with you," Gebhardt suggested.

"Excuse me?"

NINE

THE MONA LISA OF the Smithsonian gem collection was the Hope diamond, a rare blue and reputedly flawless stone weighing 45.52 carats. It held court in its own private vault built into the wall.

On Saturday morning, John shouldered his way through the rapidly assembling tourist crowd until he could peer through the bulletproof glass at the legendary diamond. The background of the display was light blue, no doubt to improve the stone's appearance, which was dull and inky under an intense monochromatic beam of light. John thought it had the color of the sky at dawn, just before the sun appeared.

Dr. Quimby had suggested the visit. "You know about Cellarius," he said. "Now you know about the pigpen cipher. What you don't know anything about is the stone found in Cellarius's fist."

Glass models of other famous diamonds, secured in museums and private collections elsewhere, rounded out the exhibit. Among them was the 68.09-carat Taylor-Burton diamond. It struck John as funny that a glass replica of a stone Richard Burton gave to Elizabeth Taylor would draw at least as many gawkers as the genuine version of the Hope. Whoever wrote the exhibit's placard had a wry wit: "We have seen individuals, governments, and even marriages fall victim to malevolent rocks. Apparently the only institution immune to them is the museum; none has yet suffered from owning a gemstone."

John moved on to the next exhibit, the one he had come to the Smithsonian to see: the lost Tavernier stones. It came as no surprise that tourists and day-trippers crowded the display cases. He had to wait for the currents and eddies to favor his drift toward the front, where he steadfastly held his position to study the replicas and interpretive text at his leisure.

The most famous stone in the group was the Great Mogul diamond, which Tavernier sketched in 1665 but whose whereabouts since were unknown. It weighed about 280 carats and looked like half a hen's egg covered with flat facets. Another missing behemoth, the Great Table diamond, was a slightly tapered, rectangular step cut with one truncated corner. Tavernier had sketched and weighed it in 1642, and had even made a model, which he sent to a prospective customer in Surat. He claimed it weighed 242 carats. No one ever laid eyes on it again.

The glass replicas sketched a chronology of old Indian styles: uncut stones, including perfect octahedra known as "glassies." Point cuts, octahedra with polished faces. Table cuts, the result of grinding down apexes. Rose cuts. Double roses. Mogul cuts, rose cuts with high domes.

The Tears of Venus, a pair of moguls weighing 40 carats each, were thought to be among the lost Tavernier stones. According to Tavernier, the cutter was fined rather than paid because he had cut them to match rather than retained as much weight as possible.

Likewise, the Ahmadabad, a 94.5-carat stone reportedly "of perfect water." It resembled an egg covered with facets of various polygonal shapes and was distinguished by a large natural—an unpolished area of the original surface—at its pointed end.

John stared long at one replica in particular, a rare table-cut ruby many believed to be the mother of the stone found in Cellarius's hand. The Smithsonian had dubbed it the Tavernier ruby. It had a legend, one first related by Tavernier himself.

So deadly was the stone, it was said to have dripped blood. A shah cast it into the Krishna River as a sacrifice to the gods. But obviously the gods rejected the offer, because when the shah cut into his fish dinner the next night, the stone rolled out onto his plate.

The shah's brother filched it. Attempting to flee the palace on his pet elephant, he was struck and fried by a bolt of lightning. The brother's wife led a successful coup and had the shah beheaded. She was prying at his fingers to recover the stone even as his head rolled away in the dirt.

Everyone who touched the Tavernier ruby, according to the exhibit, died a writhing death—including Tavernier himself.

But the feature attraction in the exhibit was a molded replica of the ruby that had been found in Johannes Cellarius's hand, now known simply as the Cellarius ruby.

Oval brilliant cut; 57 carats; pigeon blood red. Displayed side by side with the replica of its 285-carat table-cut mother, the exhibit slanted its presentation to make visitors believe the recut theory. Interest in the gems was so great, tourists were pressing their fingers against the glass window of the display to come as close as possible to touching the replicas.

After leaving the room that housed the National Gem Collection, John tested doorknobs in the hallway outside until he found one unlocked.

It was behavior he had never understood about himself, something he had picked up since entering the English world—where all doors had locks, and rarely was anything behind them worth securing. Once in a while he was cornered into explaining that he was only looking for a bathroom, "real nearby, if you know what I mean." He considered unlocked doors invitations to satisfy his curiosity about the English and locked ones challenges to his resolve.

The unlocked door, labeled "Staff Only," opened to what looked like a specimen preparation laboratory. Saws, grinders, and buffers rested on long tables strewn with mineral specimens, fragments, and dust. On the other side of the laboratory was another door, and John was about to cross the room and test *its* knob when he heard scratching noises coming from beneath one of the tables.

Then he saw tennis shoes and realized a man was down there, doing something on his knees. He took one quiet step backwards.

"Well, don't just stand there," the man said. "Come on in."

"Sir?"

"You're from the press, aren't you?" He raised his head above the table. "You're half an hour late."

The man stood up and dusted his hands with vigorous slapping actions, as though he had just completed repairing a machine (he had plugged one in), then stepped around the table to greet John. He was fortyish and sported a long ponytail despite a receding hairline. He wore a solid green tie loosely knotted, a wrinkled blue suit jacket, and a pair of faded jeans. The tie was marked with stains that might have once been ketchup. He kept glancing around the room although no one else was there, as if he were used to people surrounding him, watching him—or not watching him, it was hard to tell which.

"Dr. Cornelius Bancroft," he said. "Curator in charge. And what paper are you from?"

"Uh, the *Lancaster Intelligencer Journal*."

"That's funny. I could have sworn the appointment was with a Virginia paper."

Oh, crap. John was about to turn and run, but then figured he'd been telling lies all along, one more wouldn't hurt. He said, "I called you from Virginia when I made the appointment."

"That explains it. Well, shall we start? I'm afraid I'm just about the only research staff member here today, but at least you'll get to see everything."

Bancroft showed John an electron microprobe, an x-ray diffractometer, infrared and atomic absorption and emission spectrometers, and even an old wet lab equipped with streak plates, goniometers, and Bunsen burners.

"We keep the wet lab mostly for sentimental reasons," Bancroft said. "Nowadays, what we attend to are isotropic and crystal structure analyses, physical properties at low temperatures, elasticity, infrared absorption … you know, I could give you some technical literature if you're having trouble getting all of this down."

"I'm getting it," John said. His notebook was filling up with nonsensical scribbles.

At the end of the tour, the two men entered Bancroft's office, where John accepted the offer of a seat and a cup of coffee.

"Every summer I go to Tanzania," Bancroft said, "to study tanzanite deposits, what we know in academia as blue zoisite. It's sort of my specialty. What the hell, the National Science Foundation pays for the trips. Actually, my dream is to discover a new mineral and name it for myself: *Bancroftite.* What do you think?"

"Excuse me, Dr. Bancroft, but what I really came for was information about the lost Tavernier stones."

He nodded. "Of course you did. Everyone does." He rose from his chair and gazed at a map of Tanzania hanging on the wall behind his desk.

"So ..." John began.

"So, if you saw my first television interview, you know about as much as I do. If you want more, you can read the exhibits outside. There's also quite a bit of literature on the subject."

"Well then, sir, who *is* the expert?"

"No one here on the staff, really."

"Someone, somewhere else, on some other staff?"

He chuckled. "There was a kid, he used to be a mineralogy student of mine at College Park. He made a major study of the lost Tavernier stones. The guy was sharp, too sharp for his own good. I think he became obsessed with actually finding the things, and it went to his head. He was the one, by the way, who cut the replicas we have on display."

"Where is he now?"

"Probably in jail. He went bad right after his father, who was in the jewelry business, got taken by unscrupulous business partners and blew his brains out. It's tragic, too; the boy was a brilliant student, and he loved minerals and gems. He knows more about the lost Tavernier stones than anyone else alive. I'll give you the last address I have, but I doubt you'll find him there. When he dropped out of school, he dropped out of everything—life itself."

Bancroft shook his head and smiled. "I have to give the guy credit. When he's bad, he's good. He got caught palming off Chatham emeralds as the genuine article. Got hold of some Chatham rejects, some really flawed stuff, I don't know how, and cut it to look like natural crystals. Then he cemented the crystals in matrix and tried to sell them to museums. They passed the Chelsea test, of course, and their index of refraction was within limits, but some staff mineralogist on the ball at Los Angeles County routinely checked long wave fluorescence and got suspicious."

"What's his name?"

"Feinstein. David Feinstein. Last I heard, he lived in South Philadelphia, in a hole on Volta Street. But if you want to save yourself some time, check the state penitentiary first."

"You miss him … don't you?" John regretted the question immediately. Bancroft lowered his eyes and bit his lower lip. Then he rose, took the empty coffee cup out of John's hands, and opened his office door, indicating the interview was over.

"He was like a son."

TEN

David's first task Saturday evening was to grind and polish a small window on a relatively flat part of the cubic zirconia, so he could see inside the rough stone and study its internal characteristics. He had spent the better part of the last two days in his workshop—a spare bedroom outfitted with lapidary equipment—meticulously calipering the stone, punching a calculator, and drawing diagrams. He had skipped baths and meals, and was so absorbed in his work he didn't even hear Sarah's admonishments.

Although cubic zirconia contained none of the inclusions usually associated with diamonds, it did often contain spherical bubbles and small uncrystallized masses that would give it away.

David powered up the lap, inserted the rough into a tang, and rested it briefly on the rotating wheel. He smiled as he thought of the popular misconception of a diamond cutter at work: a round-shouldered man striking out facets with hammer and chisel, collecting the chips later to set in cheap jewelry.

After magnifying the window, he was confident the raw crystal would at least meet the VVS grade; at ten power it appeared flawless. He would need to put the finished product under his microscope to make sure, but he didn't think there was any danger of Mr. Bowling scoping the stone. The assistant manager could not be intimate with the internal characteristics of every diamond in his inventory.

An experienced gemologist could recognize cubic zirconia from its relative transparency: facet junctions were more visible through the table of a slightly tilted stone. But even the most experienced gemologists would exercise caution and test the stone with a thermal conductivity probe.

The first step in fashioning was preforming. David clamped the rough in a vise, orienting it so the vertically-mounted saw blade, a thin steel disk embedded with diamond powder, would remove about one-third of the rough. The large, flat surface on the remaining two-thirds would become the table of the finished stone. After the blade had cut through, he dopped the stone by gluing its new table to the end of a wooden dowel with wax. The dop would act as a handle during grinding, to protect David's fingers from heat and friction.

He imagined what it must have been like to cut and polish the lost Tavernier diamonds. In Tavernier's time, grinding wheels had to be powered by foot or running water. Stones were shaped by manually rubbing them against each other, often for weeks at a time. It was a wonder ancient cutters could make a facet at all.

Sarah appeared in the doorway, dressed in her nightgown, rubbing her eyes. "David," she said softly. "It's bedtime. You can finish this in the morning, can't you?"

As he got deeper into the job, David forgot he was working with cubic zirconia. The stone's sole purpose was to mimic a diamond, and not just any diamond, but a particular stone that had become, for the moment, his Holy Grail. As he fashioned the CZ, he kept a picture of the diamond in his mind and strived to metamorphose the hunk of artificial compound before him into that stone. It was no longer CZ, as far as David was concerned; rather, it was the diamond itself, trapped inside a formless hunk of transparent medium, and it needed liberation to do justice to light as only a diamond could do.

He remembered the allegory of the little girl watching a sculptor at work and asking, when he had finished, how he had known there was a lion inside the marble block.

"David, I'm worried the noise will wake the neighbors."

It was time to cut the bezel facets, the eight surfaces adjacent to the table that would take the shape of kites when the crown assumed its final form. David fitted his faceting machine with a copper lap and lubricated it with a large wad of water-soaked cotton. Then he inserted the dop arm into the 40-degree hole of the jamb peg. As soon as he finished one facet, he rotated the dop 180 degrees and ground another. He checked his work often with a ten-power loupe, each time returning the stone to a different place on the spinning lap, arcing gradually toward the center like a phonograph stylus to avoid uneven wear on its copper surface.

"If you're hungry, I could make you something. Then I really have to get some sleep."

The defining attributes of a gemstone were beauty, durability, and rarity, and diamond qualified exceptionally each time. Some people considered other gemstones to be more beautiful, but experts like David, who had acquired a taste for the idiosyncrasies of diamonds, were able to appreciate the difference; there just wasn't the same romance associated with topaz or lapis lazuli.

Jade was more durable, but nothing was as hard. Other gem species were rarer, but rarer also was demand for them.

Diamond was dull in the rough; there was no obvious promise of its potential when cut, no suggestion of the brilliance and dispersion flat facets would reveal. Indeed, raw quartz was more attractive. Why, then, did the ancients prize it so?

Until the eighteenth century, India had been the sole source. The rarity and extreme hardness of the diamond earned it a reputation for mystical qualities. It had the power to ward off illness, evil spirits, and bad luck of all sorts; thus it became a talisman, for if a diamond was indestructible, so was its wearer.

It guaranteed victory in battle. It brought wealth and virility. It even served as a fountain of youth.

During the Middle Ages, diamonds were reputed to have curative powers, especially when ground and consumed. The proof was obvious: poor people, who didn't own diamonds, suffered from more diseases than rich people, who did.

Diamonds made their wearers invisible.

Diamonds raised them from the dead.

David checked his stone once again under magnification, then returned it to the lap.

Sarah, still watching from the doorway, whispered a eulogy: "'Identify that activity, the success or failure of which is irrelevant to your pursuit of it, and you will find your one true passion.'"

"Did you say something?" David asked. He turned, surprised to find her standing there.

"No, David. I'm just now going to bed." She left, and the only sound in the room was the humming of the lap's electric motor.

"Good night," he whispered after her. "And sleep well. Tomorrow's a big day."

ELEVEN

THE RELIEF DAVID SAW on Mr. Bowling's face was unmistakable. The tension the poor man had endured the past week, wondering whether David and Sarah would return to Nineveh & Shimoda on Sunday morning, was enough to make any salesman nauseous.

It was the last day of the month, and David knew it was also the last opportunity for a struggling salesman to pull his numbers up and meet or exceed his monthly quota. That Bowling's expression went from tortured to peaceful the instant the two stepped into the store was proof enough that one or more of the other employees was ahead of him on the May chart.

David's suit was different from the one he had worn during their first visit to the store; it was the only other suit he owned. Sarah, likewise, was in her "Phase II" miniskirt, one so provocative she could hardly sit in a chair in public. A trench coat was draped over her arm. She held onto it as though it were a life preserver.

On the way into the store she had whispered to David, "I'm not going to kiss him. The last one tongued me."

"You'll do exactly as you're told," he had replied.

Now the two leaned over the showcase like children in an ice cream parlor. David asked Bowling if they could see the ring again. After retrieving it from the safe, Bowling louped it quickly before presenting it to David with a flourish. David, his hand shaking ever so slightly, gently eased it onto Sarah's finger.

"Nothing has ever looked, or felt, so right," Sarah said. "Oh, dear. I promised myself I wouldn't cry."

She returned the ring to David. As she did, she accidentally knocked her purse off the showcase, spilling its contents onto the floor. When she bent over to pick up the articles, she gave the assistant manager an ample view of ...

No underwear.

David handed the ring back to Bowling, who had the dazed look of a man who would never, ever recover from what he had just seen.

"Let's not wait any longer, Delbert," Sarah said. "Let's get it right now."

They quickly agreed on a price. Bowling would continue to hold the ring for the young couple until they returned with Delbert's "daddy" in tow. They had to pry him off the golf course and bring him to the store personally, so he could pay with his platinum credit card.

"You do accept those, don't you?"

Sarah kissed David on the cheek. Then she leaned over the showcase and kissed Bowling full on the mouth.

"Oh my," Bowling said. "Oh my." He louped the stone again, focusing on the dab of pink nail polish centered low on one of the pavilion mains. Satisfied, he snapped his loupe shut and returned the ring to its hold envelope.

"What's that book you have there?" he asked David.

"Book?"

"The one under your arm."

"Oh, this book. It's about maps."

"Sounds interesting. I always wanted to learn about maps."

Go on, patronize me, David thought. You'll get yours before this day is over. "One hour," he said. "Two max. Don't sell it to anyone else before we get back."

"Oh, no no no, of course not."

David and Sarah left the store with Sarah clinging to David's arm, battering his ear with kisses. "Thank you thank you thank you …" On the sidewalk, out of sight, she pushed him away and donned her trench coat. "Let's get the fuck out of here."

"This way," he said. "Through Independence Park."

———

Bowling put the hold envelope containing the biggest sale of his career into the safe and locked it, spinning the combination wheel so hard that Felicity heard the clicks from across the showroom.

"So you got it after all," she called over to him. "What happened, did the be-back bus get caught in traffic somewhere?"

He took his jacket off—in violation of store policy—and draped it over the high-school class ring display. He raised his arms in the air and pumped them in jubilation. "*Yeeeooow!*"

Customers entered the store and Bowling was obliged to wait on one of them, but his heart wasn't in the mission, and he failed to make a sale. Meanwhile, Felicity sold another gold chain.

No matter. Tomorrow, the manager would open up the store like it was just another Monday morning. He would see the sales ticket from the previous day, and his jaw would drop. The owners would no doubt promote Bowling to manager of the next store they opened, maybe one on Market Street. And he'd be damned if he'd allow Felicity to set so much as one high-heeled foot in it.

An hour passed. Bowling was standing at the front window like a greenhorn, looking for Delbert Farrington III and his fiancée. He could still taste that kiss! He pretended to be checking the weather. No be-back bus in sight.

Another hour passed. What was taking them so fucking long? A thought occurred to him, and he dismissed it. He tried to calm himself by dusting the inside of a case, rearranging the display to make it less symmetrical (Felicity!), and cleaning the glass top with window cleaner.

The thought occurred to him again. Again, he dismissed it. Something had delayed them, that was all. Golf courses were big places.

By the time another hour had passed and the couple still had not returned, a hollow, sickening feeling had lodged in Bowling's gut. Shaking nervously, because he knew what the consequences would be if his suspicions were correct, he removed the hold envelope from the safe and tested the ring with a thermal conductivity probe.

The stone failed to register as a diamond.

———

"How about a little celebration?" David cupped Sarah's breasts from behind and kissed the back of her neck. She was never more appealing than when she appealed to others.

"Don't." She wriggled free, kicked her high heels across the bedroom, and flopped down on the bed. "Christ, my feet hurt." Her eyes narrowed, and David knew what was coming.

"Let me wear it for a couple of days," she said.

"Not even for a couple of minutes. People who take chances like that pay for them by spending time in a cage. I've been there, and I don't want to go back."

"So prisons do rehabilitate after all."

"Well, they make you more cautious. If that's rehabilitation, then I'm as rehabilitated as I'll ever get."

"If it's so dangerous to hold it, why did you bring it here?"

"I couldn't get a meeting with Zimmerman until this afternoon. Besides, I wanted to scope it. It's the one luxury I allow myself. So, if you'll excuse me ..."

He took the ring into his workshop and mounted it under the binocular microscope. Peering through the scope's eyepieces, he brought the stone into sharp focus at successive depths, from the surface of its table to the tip of its culet.

Sarah followed him into the room and waited quietly.

He searched the stone thoroughly, but at ten power couldn't find any clarity characteristics. He switched to thirty power, moving the stone around because its diameter now exceeded the field of view. Nothing. Using a long needle, he probed dust particles on the surface to make sure they weren't inclusions reflecting from deep within.

Still nothing.

The stone had been listed as VVS1, so where were the inclusions? At this magnification, David enjoyed the sensation of exploring the interior of a diamond cave, one that glowed a soft bluish-white above the scope's dark-field illumination. It was art, it was poetry. Sometimes it was even music. He understood the fascination microbiologists had in their subject: private, unlimited access to an otherwise inaccessible world.

He flipped the ring to view it through the pavilion. Nothing. He unmounted the diamond by bending the prongs away with needle-nose pliers, then inserted the loose stone in a clamp; if there were any characteristics, they must have been hiding under the prongs.

Still nothing. The stone was flawless. Ten power was strong enough, but to see nothing at thirty power was a unique experience. He had heard stories of art historians traveling to Europe to view paintings they had studied only in photographs, and dropping impulsively to their knees at first sight of them. And there you had it.

So why did they call it VVS1? It could only be that whoever graded the stone for Nineveh & Shimoda had not been confident of his call. Flawless stones were so rare, if you didn't find any clarity characteristics, you assumed you missed them.

"David."

"What."

Sarah was standing directly behind him. "I think we should discuss a change in our business relationship."

"Do you."

"Yes. I think until now the profit sharing has been a little lopsided. I suggest we adjust my share to better reflect the important—the indispensable—role I play."

He turned off the scope, folded the diamond carefully into a stone paper, and tossed the naked shank into a jar of old gold. "I agree completely," he replied, deadpan.

"You do?" His back was still to her, so she couldn't judge his expression.

"Indeed, I do. Profit sharing *has* been lopsided. You're getting more than you deserve."

"We're a team. You can't do it alone. We should split the take fifty-fifty."

"Bullshit. We don't split the *work* fifty-fifty. I do almost all of it."

"You didn't have to kiss the bastard. Did you get a whiff of his breath?"

He swiveled his chair around to face her. "Come here. I'll make it up to you. Give *me* a kiss."

"Keep your hands off. I've earned fifty percent, and I want it."

"Don't you realize how replaceable you are? All you bring to the job is your pretty legs. This town's *full* of pretty legs. But how many guys do you know who can cut a decoy like yours truly? If you don't like the money, go back to modeling underwear. I'm sure somebody, somewhere, hasn't heard of you—maybe in Pittsburgh. Go out to the sticks, where they don't know you. Go back to Zimmerman, *where you belong.*"

She swung her hand in a wide arc to slap him, but he blocked the blow with his forearm. Tears of pain came to her eyes. "I bring a lot more than a pair of legs," she cried.

"How *dare* you spoil this moment for me with your talk of 'profit sharing'?"

"I also bring knowledge of the operation—and your past."

He stood up and grabbed her shoulders. "You want a bigger cut? I'll give you a really big one." He manhandled her toward the bedroom. She tried to wrench her shoulders free but was no match for his upper body strength. So she dropped to the floor and kicked.

He caught her legs in mid-kick and dragged her, squirming and jerking, into the bedroom. There he hooked his right arm under her knees and swung her up onto the bed.

"I've got an idea," David said. "Let's invite one of your girl-friends over and have a threesome."

"I have a better idea," Sarah responded, gasping for breath. "Let's invite her over, have a twosome, and leave *you* out."

He stepped into a pair of shoes and starting tying them. "I'm tired of breaking up with you," he said. "This is the last time. I'm going to attend my meeting now, then go to Tien Chau's for lunch. Maybe I'll even get laid. When I come back, I expect you to be gone."

"I'll go. Believe me, I'm happy to shake this shit hole. But I'm broke, you know that. I need my cut before I can leave."

He turned his back on her. "Sue me for it."

———

Barclay Zimmerman was already waiting at the corner of Fifth and Arch, next to the Christ Church burial ground where Benjamin Franklin and his wife, Deborah, slept the everlasting sleep. Their plain marble slab, sprinkled with coins, lay immediately on the other side of the bronze spiked fence where Zimmerman stood. Any tourist who wanted to pay respects to one of America's founding fathers only had to pause on the sidewalk and dig some loose change out of his pocket.

David watched from a block away. He wanted to make sure Zimmerman was alone: if he had company and knew it, he would glance occasionally at the observation post, even if only inadvertently. But Zimmerman, a wiry, nervous man in his thirties, with unkempt hair that often spilled into his eyes, just stamped his feet impatiently, his hands buried deep in his pockets.

That satisfied David; if something were about to go down, Zimmerman would be waiting with the patience of a statue.

Their stories were remarkably similar: Zimmerman had been working on a graduate degree in medieval European history when something happened to alter his course. The "something" was different for everyone who ended up working the street; rumor was, Zimmerman had come to blows with his advisor. That would end an academic career awfully fast.

He was sharp—and mean as a cornered dog.

When Zimmerman looked at his watch and kicked the fence, David finally approached him.

"How's the X-rated theater business?" he asked.

"If it were doing well, I wouldn't be out here fencing stolen rocks."

"I suppose if the fencing business were good, you wouldn't be showing porno films, either."

"I did fine until you took Sarah away from me." Zimmerman took his hands out of his pockets. One of them was holding a pair of locking tweezers, the other a triplet. "Do you have it?"

David produced the stone paper. Zimmerman quickly unfolded it, maneuvered the diamond into the tweezers, and louped it critically.

"It's flawless," David said.

Zimmerman snickered. "Yeah, they all are, you know."

"No, I mean it. This one really is."

"Whatever you say, Feinstein."

"Listen, Zim. You know me. You know if I say it's clean, it's clean."

Zimmerman removed an envelope from his back pocket and handed it to David. David counted the money inside. It didn't add up. He counted it again, to make sure.

"This is a little light, Zim."

"It's exactly right, Feinstein."

David closed his eyes. One more mention of that name and he'd belt the man. "The stone is worth three times as much wholesale!"

"Supply and demand. Take it or leave it."

"Screw supply and demand. You know I have to unload the piece. You're taking advantage of me."

"If you don't like the price, sell it to someone else."

"I can't shop around for another fence this late in the game. Everyone in Nineveh & Shimoda knows my face."

"Everyone in this *town* knows your face, Feinstein. You've been working this corner of the world too long. Pretty soon the *Jeweler's Circular Keystone* is going to post your ugly puss on its front cover."

"The name is Freeman. How many times do I have to tell you?"

"Fuck you, Feinstein, you sniveling Jew."

David dropped the envelope on the sidewalk and pinned Zimmerman's shoulders against the spiked fence.

"You asshole," Zimmerman said. "Take a look over there." He pointed across the street. Three unfriendly looking derelicts were sitting on a park bench between Arch and Race. One of them grinned. He was missing most of his teeth.

"What are they going to do," David asked, "strangle me with dental floss?"

"They have your address, and now they, too, know your face. Lay another finger on me and they'll do things to you that—trust me—you do not want done."

David glanced back at the three derelicts. Smiley was gesturing the act of masturbation.

"Take it or leave it, Jew boy."

David released Zimmerman, picked up the cash-filled envelope from the sidewalk, and dusted it off.

Zimmerman unfolded the stone paper and admired the diamond again. "Well," he said, "it's not the Prairie, but I never did kick a rock out of bed for eating crackers."

"What's the Prairie?"

"Don't insult me by feigning ignorance. And unless you want to walk funny for the rest of your life, stay out of my way in the search for you-know-what."

———

As soon as David was out of sight, Zimmerman crossed the street and handed the three drunks five dollars apiece.

Smiley said, "You still haven't told us why you wanted us to sit here and act like that."

"Warm the bench for me, gentlemen. Someday I'll be sleeping on it myself."

He returned to his theater in Kensington. The theater was unsupervised and the projector was still running, but it didn't matter; no one had bought a ticket. He sat in one of the empty seats and inspected David's diamond once again.

You had to hand it to Feinstein, he thought. It sure did look clean.

He felt a twinge of guilt for having stiffed David. He felt it, then it went away. They had once been friends. Even, on occasion, partners—until Sarah changed allegiance. And they were both obsessed with the lost Tavernier stones.

Zimmerman's Grail was one of the stones in particular, the Ahmadabad diamond, a 94-carat stone "of perfect water." That wasn't unusual; gem aficionados often fixed on a single specimen or group—for example, the Hope diamond or the Three Brethren. The Ahmadabad wasn't the largest or most famous diamond in history, but it was the most controversial. A 78-carat pear-shaped stone currently in circulation purported to be a recut of the legendary diamond. But Zimmerman was convinced the genuine article was still intact, still missing, still waiting for him to find it.

He made no secret of his obsession. He had named his theater after the stone.

Now, as he sat in the empty, high-ceilinged room, passively watching the wriggling figures on the screen, he wondered how Feinstein could possibly not know about the Prairie. Was he telling the truth?

———

David took the number 23 trolley northbound on Eleventh Street, got off at Cliveden, then headed south on Germantown Avenue. It was midday, and the sidewalks were filling with people steered by hunger and motivated by short lunch breaks. He walked along the streetcar tracks, pretending to keep his balance on one of the metal strips, until a car honked and forced him onto the sidewalk.

Stay out of my way in the search for you-know-what.

David knew what. But the Prairie? What the hell was that?

Germantown was a dump. The Germans, right on the heels of the Indians and the deer they hunted, were long gone. And the charm of eighteenth- and nineteenth-century architecture had been obliterated by twenty-first-century trash and graffiti.

Stay out of my way...

He arrived at Tien Chau's, an unsanitary Vietnamese restaurant where several riffraff were loitering out front. He had always found it ironic that some of the dirtiest places in the city served some of the city's best food. As he was about to enter the restaurant, the riffraff suddenly pulled revolvers and pointed them at him.

"Put your hands behind your head," one of them commanded. "Lay down on the ground. You have the right to remain silent."

TWELVE

Mannfred Gebhardt had discovered an easy way to steal books from libraries: just throw them out a window, then snatch them from the bushes on the way back to the car.

Bookstores were more challenging, but he had solved that problem too: slit the covers off with a pocket knife while pretending to browse, thus removing any magnetic security strips that might be present, then simply walk out of the store with the signature-bound pages in hand. If the staff didn't perceive a book was being stolen, a book wasn't being stolen. Perception was the better part of reality.

One helpful bookseller recommended an encyclopedia of gemology recently published by the Bibliographisches Institut Leipzig. He also informed Gebhardt that the last copy had walked out the door just seconds before he walked in.

Gebhardt found the woman in an alley a block away, strolling smugly with the fat volume tucked under her tiny arm. Moments later, the book was his. He didn't feel guilty about her injuries; she should have taken him up on his offer to buy it.

The richest source of materials was the library of the University of Heidelberg, famous for its mineralogy department as well as its index of all the world's notable gemstones. Since the Heidelberg Library yield would be great, Gebhardt could not merely toss the stuff out a window. The more you wanted to profit from crime, the more crime you had to commit.

Late in the afternoon, while the Hauptbibliothek was still open, he passed through the gothic façade into the arched and marbled foyer, figuring none of the staff—government employees, all—would linger after closing time.

The university and library were Germany's oldest. Founded in 1386, the collection had grown in healthy spurts but had also been seriously damaged during the wars, taking one step backwards for every two forwards. Now it contained more than three million volumes, and if Gebhardt had his way, it would suffer yet another incremental setback.

He found a bathroom, entered one of its stalls, and stood on top of the toilet to punch out a ceiling tile. Then he climbed up above the ceiling, out of view. At thirty minutes past closing time, he would simply climb back down and search the library for relevant materials. He would have all night. It was easier to break out of a building than into one.

At five minutes past closing time, a janitor conducted a walk-through. Gebhardt, peering through a hole in the tile, watched him check the stalls to make sure they were empty.

He cursed Blumenfeld for assigning him this task. He predicted, nonetheless, that she would be happy with his work. So far, he had found no less than twenty-three distinct books on the subject of famous, notable, and collectable gemstones, especially those on display in museums around the world. They needed to gather these sources, Blumenfeld had argued, before others got the same idea and exhausted the supply.

Exactly why they needed to gather them—what they would do when they found the ruby everyone was looking for—she didn't say. But Gebhardt had learned not to question her. Too many times had he seen her eyes roll and her head shake condescendingly, and he worried that his temper might get the better of him the next time it happened.

He felt as out of place stealing books from libraries as a boxer might feel crocheting an afghan. *His* solution to the problem of the lost Tavernier stones was more direct and simple than hers: when the stones were found, take them away from the person who found them.

The janitor banged around a while before going home, so Gebhardt had time to feel remorse for what he had done to the driver who cut him off on the autobahn while he was enroute to Heidelberg. The driver had switched on his rear fog lights in response to Gebhardt's high beams, neither of which impaired vision during daylight.

Despite the effort, no feeling of remorse came over him. The fool should not have stopped and gotten out of his car.

———

At least, John noted, there was plenty of room to park. Not that three empty spaces in a row would make it any easier for him to line up his Ford Galaxie 500 collinearly with the other cars parked on Volta Street. He was the worst driver in the world with a driver's license. In fact, there were people who had never earned a license who were better.

Hell, there were *animals* who could claim greater proficiency.

He aimed for the center of the three empty spots, screeched to a halt, and climbed out to evaluate. The front right tire was up on the curb and the left rear bumper poked out into the street. But there was still enough room for other drivers to get by, if they took turns. Not bad, he thought.

He was disappointed in South Philadelphia, to say the least. Narrow row houses elbowed for frontage, each distractedly clutching its whining air conditioner like old women lugging noisy, unwanted children on their hips. Windows were boarded up, even on houses still inhabited, and garbage spilled liberally onto sidewalks from untied plastic bags. And if the cars that were parked on the curbs ran at all, they didn't run downtown, where they were safer anyway from theft than ridicule. A 1950s central business district had drifted out of the mainstream of city life and was struggling now like a salmon too weak to fight the current.

The house at the address Dr. Bancroft had given John looked no better or worse than its neighbors; all were vying to be the first to tumble down. What would he say to the current resident if David Feinstein no longer lived there? More to the point, what would he say if he did?

There was no sound when he pressed the doorbell, and no one answered his knock.

He paced up and down the sidewalk a couple of times, trying to look as though he were expecting someone. What to do now—come back another time? No, he had waited through yesterday, the Sabbath, and had fidgeted all day at work today, watching the clock. It had taken too long to get to Volta Street in the Philadelphia traffic, not even counting the times he got lost; he didn't want to make the drive again.

He went back to the door and knocked again. Then, yielding to the urge he had always heeded in the English world, he turned the knob. The door opened.

"Hello? Hello?"

The living room was incredibly narrow; a large beanbag chair almost spanned its width. Comically, the chair was bleeding beans.

"Hello?"

He heard noises coming from the rear of the house and followed them. In the bedroom, a woman was on her knees with her back to the door, rummaging through a dresser drawer, cussing loudly and creatively.

"Hello?"

The woman looked up, startled.

"I'm sorry, but your door was open, and no one answered when I knocked."

She scrambled to her feet and fixed her hair. "Aren't you supposed to read me my rights?"

John laughed nervously. "No, I'm not a policeman, if that's what you mean. My name is Graf." He handed her a business card. "I'm looking for someone named David Feinstein. I don't even know whether he lives here anymore."

"Then you *are* from the police."

"I swear to you, I am not. Just look at the card."

She did, then cast her eyes back at him suspiciously.

"I'm a cartographer. I was told a man named Feinstein lived here. He's supposed to be a gemologist. Do you know him? Was he the previous tenant?"

"Yes, Feinstein is the name of the previous tenant."

The woman was regaining her composure. John had thought she was attractive at first, but now he realized he was in the presence of a great beauty.

"Can you tell me where he lives now? I would really like to find him."

"He moved out last night."

"Last night?"

She eased the dresser drawer shut with one leg. "Yes, last night. You want his new address?"

"Please."

"It's on Eighth and Race."

John made a note. "And the number?"

"I don't know the number. It's the Roundhouse, the only building on Eighth and Race."

"The Roundhouse being..."

"Philadelphia police headquarters."

"Oh. He's in jail?"

"Where, in all likelihood, he will remain for some time to come. If he's lucky, Mr. Freeman's—excuse me, Feinstein's—*carcass* may someday be eligible for parole."

By now the woman had completely regained her composure. She seemed polished, even professional. If John hadn't met her under the present circumstances, surprising her while she rummaged through a drawer of undergarments in a ramshackle house on a slimy street, he would have guessed she was a fashion model. A *top* fashion model.

"I'm an ex-acquaintance of Mr. Feinstein's," the woman explained. "I'm just here to fetch some personal belongings."

She was standing with one leg in front of the other and a hand on her hip, obviously posing. She was strikingly good looking, knew it, and knew John thought so too.

"Thanks for the information," he said. "Sorry about the intrusion."

"Not at all."

———

"You just missed him," the duty sergeant at the Roundhouse told John. "We released him twenty minutes ago."

"That's in keeping with my luck so far."

"You want some advice?"

"Sure."

"I don't know why you're looking for this guy. If you're a private detective, fine. But if you're a cart—, a cart—"

"Cartographer."

"Cartographer, right." He snorted. "That's a good one. I'll have to use it myself sometime."

"The advice, sergeant?"

"The advice is, this guy's rotten to the core. We had him in here a while back for selling fake emeralds as the real stuff."

"I know about that one." Bancroft had told him about it—lab-grown crystals glued into matrix and passed off as genuine.

"Okay, let's see if you know about this one: he once did a daytime job in a jewelry store. Tied up the salespeople in a back room and proceeded to fill bags with merchandise. When a customer came in, Feinstein—or Freeman, whatever—sold the guy an engagement ring, for cash. Right there in the middle of the robbery. Conducted a goddamn sale! He was so proud of himself, he didn't even pocket the money, he left it in the cash register. We'd probably still have him now for that job, but none of the witnesses would identify him in a lineup. Seems he has *charisma*. So we had to let him go. If I were you, I'd keep my distance."

"You had him in here again today."

"And had to let him go again. Although we picked him up yesterday on an anonymous tip, reinforced by his record, of course, it turns out the jewelry store he was supposed to have robbed—one on Sansom Street—had not reported anything stolen. I'm only telling you this because you're a detective. Sorry, a *cartographer*. Anyway, I went to the store myself and spoke to the assistant manager, Mr. Bowling, personally. There had been no robbery, he assured me. And nothing whatsoever was missing from the inventory."

———

That evening, Sarah walked to Broad Street, carrying one small suitcase, and hailed a cab. "Penn Center Station," she told the driver.

The car sped up Broad into the dancing lights of downtown Philadelphia like a soul gleefully escaping purgatory. As the driver circled City Hall to JFK Boulevard, Sarah tried to decide just where it was she intended to go.

New York City was the place to launch—or in her case, relaunch—a modeling career, but she had her heart set on someplace warm. Atlanta sounded good. It was big and it was warm. Maybe she should first find out all the places the trains did go, then pick one of them.

She descended into the station at JFK and Sixteenth and wandered through the maze of restaurants and shops until she found a ticket window. With the entire contents of her wallet laid bare on the counter, she was about to ask, How far will this get me? when it occurred to her how cliché the question would sound.

Just as she was opening her mouth to speak, a hand clamped down on her shoulder. She whirled around. It was David.

"Don't go just yet," he said. His face registered an earnest calm she had never seen before.

"We're finished, David."

"Stick around a little longer," he implored. "Zimmerman gave me a clue. And I just figured it out."

THIRTEEN

JOHN OFTEN VISITED LANCASTER Cemetery to work out problems. He liked to wander among the granite and marble monuments, some weathered and faded, some listing, some fallen, and sit on tree stumps that broke the textural monotony of quiescent graves.

The cemetery clipped a squat rectangle from the north side of town, truncating streets and flattening the topography within its boundaries. But only on a map: it hardly existed for most of the living, who skirted it hurriedly to avoid an unsettling reminder of their final destination.

As if to symbolize the breadth of the journey, Lancaster General Hospital was across Lime Street to the west, and an elementary school, a junior high school, and a high school were clustered a quarter of a mile to the east. On their way home from school, children ran their hands along the cemetery's spiked iron fence, playing it like a harp.

The Winterbottoms, Ramsey (1865–1933) and Rosalie (1865–1936), were buried near the circular walkway in the middle of the cemetery. It was the oldest real estate on the grounds, where august families had long staked claims to choice plots, and where vacancies were rare and few of the living bothered any longer to stop by. John wondered what the Winterbottoms would think if they knew that he, born more than four decades after Rosalie's death, was their only regular visitor.

On Tuesday the problem John needed to work out was one the like of which he had never experienced before: he was dwelling more than he thought he should on finding a lost cache of legendary jewels.

It was wonderful that Johannes Cellarius had been found—no argument there. Now he could receive a proper burial, and historians might even figure out who killed him and why; age-old questions were about to be answered. Perhaps more importantly, Cellarius had come to the attention of a public that was otherwise apathetic about maps.

Mysteries had never before appealed to John, nor stories of treasure hunts, adventure and danger, or anything to do with lust and greed. His Amish upbringing had programmed him to work hard and live simply. He had never paid any attention to the lottery; why should he care about some missing rocks, however valuable they may be?

The superficial answer was clear: because of their historical connection to Johannes Cellarius. Because Cellarius cared about them. But there was more to it than that.

He knelt next to the Winterbottom monument, dug his fingers into the soil, and breathed in the damp, musty odor. He rubbed the soil between his fingers and felt its gritty texture, that magical combination of minerals and humus that were gifts from the earth and all the former life it had nourished. The sensation triggered memories both dear and painful. He had a choice to make, and making it would be painful, too.

Since most Amish activities—work, play, dining, worship, haircuts—took place in the home, John felt lonely in his tomb-like row house on Nouveau Street. He missed the hectic bustle of an Amish homestead. The chatter of women in the kitchen. The squeals of children playing in the barn. The laughter that rose almost as one voice from the gathering of people who shared a common crucible.

At the same time, he still wanted a taste of what the outside world had to offer. To what extent, he wondered, would searching for the lost Tavernier stones provide that?

The Amish didn't draw from Social Security because they didn't pay into it. Instead, they integrated security into their social structure. No matter what calamity might befall a family—illness, fire, bankruptcy—the community would intervene on its behalf. It was more secure than English society, more secure even than the military or any other well-funded social unit. It provided a sense of place, an identity, a purpose. In short, a home.

In what way could the lost Tavernier stones possibly address any of those?

The Amish had been tied to the soil for centuries. Indeed, they saw it as a biblical mandate: "Therefore the Lord God sent him forth from the garden of Eden, to till the ground from whence he was taken" (Genesis 3:23). John longed for the smell of crops at harvest time, the smell of the soil after a spring rain, even the smell of manure in the barn. Home, he had learned, consisted of everything he had ever taken for granted.

And now, in the quiet solitude of Lancaster Cemetery, kneeling next to the Winterbottom monument with the smell of earth on his fingers, it was time for him to take an objective look at the circumstances.

Johannes Cellarius had been found murdered in a bog in northern Germany. A ruby was clenched in his fist. Some people speculated the ruby was a recut of one of the lost Tavernier stones. Maybe it was, maybe it wasn't.

Suppose it wasn't. Suppose the ruby were merely an heirloom Cellarius grabbed in panic during his abduction. Then there was no connection to Tavernier, and nothing to look for. Or to dwell on.

Suppose it was. Then either the stones were all recut and scattered around the world, or they were still intact, buried somewhere, waiting to be found. If the former were true, then there was nothing to look for or to dwell on. If the latter, then he, John Graf, almost certainly wouldn't be the man to find them.

Most historians continued to argue that Tavernier's seventh voyage was mere legend, and that people who tried to fit the "facts" to the legend were only going to become frustrated. John was already frustrated; the problem was interfering with his professional life.

There might not have been any lost Tavernier stones to begin with. And if there were, they might not have had anything to do with Johannes Cellarius. And if they did, they might never be found, because there was nothing besides the ruby in his fist to suggest a connection. And the ruby was disconcertingly silent on the matter.

But then there was that map—that damn map. Cellarius's depiction of the lower Palatinate was what had been bothering John. It was never the gemstones; it was always *the map*.

It was the final effort of Cellarius's cartographic career. It had been lurking in dusty drawers for over three hundred years. Its border contained a secret message. Numerous elements were inexplicable and uncharacteristic of its author.

It had always spoken to John in a voice he could never understand.

He stood up and dusted off his knees. A walk in the cemetery was just what he had needed. His head was clear, he had sorted out an issue, he had identified the problem.

If Cellarius were speaking from the grave, he was not doing so clearly enough. There were too many unanswered questions about the Palatinate map. And as a cartographer, it was reasonable for John to seek the answers. He made a vow to Ramsey and Rosalie, speaking out loud to the weathered marble slab:

"All right, guys. As soon as I make sure the map contains no hidden messages, I'll quit my search for the lost Tavernier stones and end this obsession before it truly begins."

———

When John arrived home, entered his living room, and turned on the light, he found a man sitting cross-legged on the couch.

"Who the hell are *you*?"

The man held up a dollar bill for John to see. "Watch," he said. He tore the bill repeatedly in half until the pieces were the size of a postage stamp. Then he slowly "unfolded" them, revealing a restored dollar bill.

"The gist of the trick," the man said, "is that an accordion-folded bill—the 'restored' bill—is already fastened to the back of the bill that gets torn to pieces."

"Who *are* you, and what are you doing in my house?"

"You come home awfully late. I got tired of sitting on the front steps, so I came in. Besides, I'm only returning the call."

"The call?"

The man produced John's business card. "You gave this to my girlfriend yesterday."

"Oh," John said. "You're him."

"Yes. I'm him. David Freeman." He stood up and shook John's hand. "It appears we have a common interest."

The infamous gem thief was a lot shorter than John had imagined. And his face was too nondescript to trust. Anyone with eyes that luminous, that black, had been places John didn't want to go. Maybe tracking the guy down in Philadelphia wasn't such a good idea after all.

"How did you get in?" John asked. "The door was locked."

"I unlocked it," David said. "If you knew enough about me to find me, then you know enough about me not to be surprised by that."

"What I *don't* know is why I bother locking it," John mumbled. "Look...um...can I offer you something to drink?"

"Like what? I already checked out your kitchen. All you have is mineral water."

"Then I apologize for my inhospitality. And now, if you don't mind..."

"Listen to what I have to say. Then, if you want me to leave, I will. It'll only cost you a dollar, and you already paid."

"What do you mean?"

"That dollar bill I tore up—I found it on the dresser in your bedroom."

David spread a photograph, a postcard, and a drawing on John's coffee table, and the two sat down on the couch. The photograph was of the Cellarius ruby; John had seen reprints of it in the newspaper. The postcard depicted a different ruby, one about the same size. The drawing was a page from the disputed Tavernier manuscript that John also recognized.

"Did you happen to see Dr. Cornelius Bancroft's interview on TV?" David asked.

"No. But I met him."

"You met him? Oh, of course. That's how you got my name. Well, he was right. The Cellarius ruby *is* a recut of one of the lost Tavernier stones. Look closely." He pointed to a trapezoidal facet visible on the photograph of the Cellarius ruby, then to what appeared to be the same facet recognizable on one of the stones in the Tavernier drawing. "This is the connection Bancroft made. It's tenuous, but it suggests the Cellarius ruby came from the larger stone. Now look again." David moved the postcard between the photograph and the drawing. "Notice anything extraordinary about this kite-shaped facet here?"

"It's identical to *another* one of the facets in the drawing," John said.

"Yes. *This* stone," David pointed at the postcard, "was *also* once part of the Tavernier ruby. Considering the weight lost during a recut, the two stones, combined with a third not yet found, would comprise the original. So there's another third still missing, although it might have been cut into yet smaller pieces. I doubt it, though."

"Where did you find that?"

David flipped the postcard over. "Field Museum of Natural History, Chicago, Illinois. Can you believe it? The people who most loudly denied the connection had proof of it under their noses. It's called the Prairie State ruby. I haven't been able to find much history on it yet."

John massaged his temples. "So it's true, after all ..."

"This is the first confirmation, ever, of the legend. The lost Tavernier stones exist. And everyone in the world will know it before long."

"Why is that?"

David tapped the postcard. "They sell these things at the museum. Or at least they used to. The curators took the stone off display on the twenty-eighth of May, the day after Bancroft made his recut theory public. I think it's fair to predict we won't be getting much help from the museum staff."

"We?" John asked.

David nodded solemnly. "I'm betting you don't know a whole lot about the lost Tavernier stones. And you might as well be aware, I can't even point in the direction of north. We need each other. That's why I'm here, and that's why you were in South Philly yesterday."

John shrugged. "So what do you suggest we do first?"

"Eat," David replied.

John got up and headed for the kitchen, but David stopped him. "All you have in there is microwave meals. It's still early, though. We could hit a restaurant. And bring the map along."

On their way out, John said to David, "You know, it's eerie, but I can't shake the feeling Johannes Cellarius has been trying to tell me something."

"Well," David said, "now that you've made your confession, I'll make mine: Jean-Baptiste Tavernier has been talking up a storm to me. And I've decided it's time I started listening."

FOURTEEN

THE EARTH SUBSEQUENTLY SPUN *twice on its axis. As it did, fever increased over the possibility of finding a lost cache of priceless gems.*

Television talk-show hosts interviewed panels of cartographers, gemologists, and professional treasure hunters. Late-night comedians made one joke after another about dead mapmakers in bogs.

Printers of antique maps could not keep up with demand. Ruby prices soared. Tourists stood in long lines to view the remains of Johannes Cellarius, now on display at the University of Hamburg medical school.

Thursday's noontime sun seemed to linger over Scandinavia. Urged, finally, by the afternoon shadows, it ponderously moved on.

Near Bergen, Norway, a fisherman blew on his chapped hands, then steered his boat away from the fog-drenched fjords and out to sea. He reflected on the glory days of his people, when fishermen-warriors set out in razor-thin vessels to loot any conspicuously accumulated wealth they could find.

The lost Tavernier stones constituted just such booty. They awakened a spirit in the fisherman that had been dormant in his people for a thousand years.

In Reykjavik, Iceland, a blond, blue-eyed schoolgirl had mapped out the rest of her life and felt it was time to inform the world.

"Papa, I know what I want to be when I grow up."

Her father turned the page of his newspaper and said, "Hmm."

"I want to be a mineralogist."

"Hmm. Wasn't it just last week you wanted to be an astronaut? Maybe you could put the two together—be the first person to collect rocks on Mars."

The girl regarded her father with a look of exasperation, as children often do; one that suggested he was the number one idiot in the solar system.

On the southern coast of Greenland, a team of archeologists digging a Viking site took a break to huddle around one of their members and admire the engagement ring she had received from her fiancé.

Nobody said anything; it was difficult now to admire a gemstone smaller than a hen's egg.

As June third's sun passed over Europe and slipped west toward open sea, its afternoon shadows stretched slowly east, until they were finally erased by the encroaching night.

———

Gerd Pfeffer downed the remainder of his beer and stumbled out the door of the Gasthaus in the early morning darkness. He took a pee on the outside wall, leaning against it with one hand, holding his member with the other, shuffling his feet to avoid the expanding puddle. When finished, he shook himself dry and belched, then aimed his member toward home and followed it. Muted yellow light leaking from the Gasthaus windows helped him navigate for about fifty meters. After that, he thrust his arms forward to ward off dogged obstacles.

There had been much chatter at the tables. Some of the customers who knew Pfeffer's family also knew he had been the detective who recovered Cellarius's body. But Pfeffer had stayed out of the discussion. In fact, he had sat by himself in a corner and glowered at anyone who took notice of his existence.

When he arrived home, he unlocked and unlatched his gate with the meticulousness of an eye surgeon, then knelt down in the weeds and puked. The garden, he noted as he crawled out of it on all fours, was a tad overgrown. But it was nothing a few liters of weed killer wouldn't fix.

Once inside, he rinsed his face in cold water, then reached for the phone.

"FBI, Frankfurt field office," came a tired voice from the other end, followed by a long yawn. "Special Agent Stenner."

"Hello, Stenner. Guess who."

The line was silent for a moment, then an alert voice uttered: "Pfeffer."

"That's *Mister* Pfeffer, to you."

"Crap. What brings you out from under your rock?"

"Let's just say I'm on a quest for some rocks."

"You and the rest of the continent. What's it got to do with us?"

"You have contacts at Fort Meade, right?"

"Right…"

"Well, now, so do I!"

"The hell."

"You see, now that I've been quiet for so long about that 'creative extradition' I helped you guys with, I just thought you'd want me to *stay* quiet about it."

"Listen, Pfeffer."

"*Mister* Pfeffer."

"Mister Pfeffer. Hold one moment, please." The man went off the line for several minutes, then returned and said, "Perhaps we're in a position to offer some friendly advice."

"Now you're talking."

"Will we be even?"

"Dead even."

"Good. I—we—don't expect to ever hear from you again."

"You won't. Say hello to J. Edgar Hoover for me."

"He's dead."

"Oh. Sorry to hear that. Please forward my condolences to his family."

———

When Frieda Blumenfeld crossed the cobbled square of Liebfrauen Platz, she found Mannfred Gebhardt already waiting outside the entrance to the Gutenberg Museum. She stared wordlessly into his gray eyes, allowing just the hint of a smile to appear on her face.

"You found it," Gebhardt declared.

"It's called the Prairie State ruby. I'll tell you about it inside."

"We're going in the museum?"

"Of course. Why else do you suppose I told you to meet me here?"

Illuminated manuscripts dominated the museum's holdings. Ornate calligraphy, delicate engravings, and a riot of primary colors on pages stained by the centuries gave them a distinctively medieval look. Some had tanned leather covers that fastened shut with brass buckles. Others were bound in wood. A few were so large, Blumenfeld wondered whether she would even be able to lift them.

On the top floor of the museum, wedged between hieroglyphic tablets and broken pieces of Roman column, were the Vigenère manuscripts—the reason Blumenfeld had chosen the Gutenberg Museum as a meeting place.

"It's funny," she said. "I've probably toured these exhibits a dozen times over the years, but I'd never even heard of Vigenère until the Cellarius-Tavernier story broke. And here his stuff has sat all this time."

The manuscripts were plain compared with most others in the building; their fonts had fewer serifs, less overall flourish, and not a speck of gold foil adorning them. As a result, the text was damn near legible. Some of the book covers were mere paper—they constituted the world's first paperbacks. Vigenère, or whoever had printed his works, obviously concerned himself more with the comfort of the reader than with his own place in the history of the craft.

Few visitors were on the floor; Blumenfeld and Gebhardt had the exhibit to themselves.

"Any luck on the cipher?" Blumenfeld asked.

Gebhardt didn't answer. Instead, he silently studied the printed pages before him.

She shook her head. "I see."

"I still think the pigpen characters are just border decorations."

"They may, in fact, be border decorations. They may, on the other hand, be significant. If they're significant, the significance will elude obstinate men like yourself. We need a good cryptologist, someone who specializes in the seventeenth century and prior."

"Where do you suggest I look for one of those? The telephone book?"

"I suggest you visit Dr. Ernst Spengler, a Latin professor at the University of Mainz."

"What makes you think he'll be of any use?"

"Well, he's published journal articles on cryptology, and he happens to be the very person who prepared the Vigenère exhibit you are now viewing. We have to move on this. There's no telling how many people may be working on the problem, including Spengler himself."

"Tell me, Frieda. Why do I always get stuck with the actual work? Is it just my imagination, or is it because you don't want to do any of it yourself?"

Blumenfeld took off her glasses and rubbed her eyes. "Faults though I may have, and numerous though they may be, I submit that lethargy is not among them. I'm busy with the necessary historical research, for which you are most unsuited."

"And I suppose your banking and finance background is what qualifies you."

She put her glasses back on and crossed her arms. "Tell me, what should happen to Spengler, should he have something to share, after he has shared it?"

"He should be persuaded most aggressively not to share it with anyone else."

"And which one of us is best suited for such a task?"

Sighing: "I am."

"Good boy. Anytime you want to take charge and make decisions, just let me know."

Blumenfeld knew she was capitalizing on Gebhardt's most valuable asset. She also knew he'd employ that asset against her the instant she became his only remaining obstacle.

———

John Graf awoke on the morning of June fourth unable to figure out what century he was in. He looked at his pajamas, but they were no help. He scanned his room, but a dearth of adornments and a plain wooden floor suggested nothing. He looked out the window. Telephone wires and an Amtrak train rumbling in the distance finally clued him in: Oh yes, the twenty-first century. Of course. Where else.

He rose, showered, and dressed quickly. David and Sarah were visiting today to conduct what David had referred to as a "staff meeting." John had requested the day off from Harry Tokuhisa, whose first reaction was to raise his eyebrows in alarm. It was the second such request from John in a week, and Harry would not have expected as many in a decade.

John presumed David had conducted more than a few "staff meetings" during his nefarious career, either in candlelit cellars or in bare rooms dimly lit by swinging drop cords. By contrast, his own apartment was bright and spotless. He had scoured and dusted last night to prepare for the visit and had even gone shopping to stock up the pantry. He hadn't been sure what to buy, so he bought something that sounded versatile and broadly appealing: Hamburger Helper.

Now, in the back of his mind, alarm bells were softly ringing, because it occurred to him that Hamburger Helper might need to have some hamburger to help, and his didn't. Maybe Sarah would know what to do with it.

Sarah. The alarm bells rang louder, because he knew she was the reason he was anxious about the visit. David could have a frozen dinner if he got hungry, and he could eat it frozen if he had anything derogatory to say about it.

There was a knock at the door, and John showed the two in.

David immediately made himself comfortable by allowing gravity to do the work of dropping his backside into a chair. Sarah stood for a moment in the living room, surveying its sparse furnishings. She looked at John and smiled shyly.

Damn, she was pretty. But pretty wasn't the word for it. Wearing a simple sleeveless dress with a broad belt around her narrow waist, Sarah was difficult not to look at.

The three stared awkwardly at the floor for a moment. Then, as though to ease the tension, David removed a short rope from his pocket and pulled it slowly through his left hand. "Where do you want me to cut it?" he challenged John. "Say stop."

"Here we go again." Sarah rolled her eyes.

"Stop."

David opened a pocket knife and sliced the rope near its center. He held up the severed ends and let the two pieces dangle beneath his hand. "Now, since one long rope is more valuable than two short ropes, I'll restore it." He tied the two severed ends back together. "Pretty good trick, huh?"

"No."

David coiled the rope in his fist, then uncoiled it, and the knot was gone. "How's that?"

"*Now* it's a good trick," John said.

"Want to know how it works?"

126

"Let me guess—magic, right?"

"There's no such thing as magic."

"You've gotten him started," Sarah warned. She sat down on one end of the couch and yawned.

"All magic is illusion," David said. "That's why I prefer the term *illusionist* to *magician*. The rabbit that appears in a hat was in the hat all along. The rope that seems to get cut *does* get cut, but not in the middle of its length like the audience thinks. The dissolving knot was never tied to begin with. And the levitating girl is resting on a sturdy metal platform—it's just that nobody can see it."

"Don't mind him," Sarah said to John. "I have to listen to this shit every day. Let him get it off his chest, then he'll shut up."

"Actually, I find it interesting." Interesting, as well, that someone who made his living practicing deception should pursue it as a hobby.

"The audience doesn't look for the device," David went on, "that's not what they came to see. They look for the *illusion*. They *want* to be fooled. You don't have to prove your claim irrefutably, you only have to *conceal all evidence to the contrary*."

There was only one place left in the living room to sit, and it was next to Sarah on the couch. John eased around the coffee table, taking care to position himself exactly in the center of the available space, so it didn't look like he was trying to get close to her. He felt like a teenager on a date.

David took a notebook out of his pocket, and John picked his up from the coffee table. Also on the table were books: history books, travel books, map books, gem books; some from F & M, some checked out from the Lancaster Public Library. John's facsimile of the Palatinate map was rolled out flat on the floor.

"Okay," David began. "Let's start with an inventory of what we already know." He looked at the others, who were silent. "We have a corpse," he urged John.

"We have a corpse," John acknowledged. "And we have reason to be confident the corpse is Cellarius: the possibility of a hoax has been pretty much eliminated."

"Good," David said. "And it's clear he was murdered."

"It's obvious. He was struck repeatedly in the chest and abdomen with a pickax. The body had altered too much in the bog acids for the forensics people to decide whether there had been a struggle. But we can assume from his sudden disappearance that he was abducted, probably from his studio."

David made a note in his book. "And a ruby was in his fist. I think we agree the ruby, now commonly known as the Cellarius ruby, is a recut of one of the lost Tavernier stones. I suggest the Prairie State ruby is another recut. Enough material is still missing from the original stone to justify searching for yet one more. I haven't had any luck, though, and it's possible the material was divided among many small pieces."

"How many?" John asked.

David shrugged. "At one carat apiece, it could be as many as thirty. But that's just a wild guess. There's no way we could find such pieces, nor would we be able to reassemble them, so to speak, and put the original Tavernier ruby back together."

"How long before everyone knows what you just told us?"

"Maybe a day. Maybe a year. The Field Museum took the Prairie off display right after the news broke, so I assume somebody on the staff has figured out at least as much as I have. As for the rest of the world, there's no way to tell. Maybe lots of people know and are just keeping quiet, like we are. Once the press gets hold of it, everyone will know, because the press doesn't keep quiet about anything."

"We have to go at our own pace," John insisted. "We can't be worrying about whether we're ahead of, or behind, the crowd."

Sarah crossed her legs, and John saw the gentle curves of her thighs in the periphery of his vision. He glanced up at David, who was watching him.

Sarah said, "I hope we're the only ones who have gotten this far."

"So do I," David agreed. "But let's not get inane, okay? John, you said something the other night about Cellarius smiling when he died. Do you have anything more to add?"

"No, and I feel kind of silly about it. Nobody smiles while they're being stabbed. His face was probably just twisted into a smile by the acids in the bog. You know, some animals—cats and dolphins, for instance—often look like they're smiling, and it means nothing. Having said that, I can't shake the feeling there was nevertheless something very interesting on his mind."

"If there *wasn't* something interesting on his mind," David said, "then there's nothing interesting for us to look for."

"I've been spending a lot of time with Cellarius's last map, the one he finished just before disappearing. I don't want to rush to any conclusions, but there are several disturbing... what's the word for them? Coincidences? Incongruities?"

"Namely?"

"Well, it *was* the last thing he did before he died, for what that's worth. You have to at least wonder whether his death was related to his activities at the time. And it was the only map in his inventory lacking evidence of a commission. He had no reason—no ordinary reason—to make this map."

"Of course, there's always the *extraordinary* reason." David jotted down another note.

"And the area mapped, the lower Palatinate, contains one of the gemstone capitals of the world," John continued. "This may be pure coincidence, but my instincts suggest otherwise."

"Mine as well."

"Where, exactly, is the lower Palatinate?" Sarah asked.

"Roughly where Rheinland-Pfalz is today," John answered.

She looked at him blankly.

"A state in southwest Germany, bordering France."

"Oh."

"What else disturbs you about the map?" David was still bent over his notebook.

"The grid pattern. There's nothing discernibly standard about it. It seems to be totally arbitrary. The map is square—it's the only square one he ever made—so the number of rows is the same as the number of columns: twenty."

"By grid, I assume you mean parallels and meridians."

"Essentially, yes. The horizontal lines should show latitude, and the vertical lines, longitude. Of course they do, but what I mean is there should be a scheme, it should make some sense; for example, a line every tenth of a degree, or every twelve thousand yards. But these lines," he swiped at the map at his feet, "though they're uniformly spaced, are drawn on coordinates that are not discrete in any recognizable way."

"So," Sarah smiled broadly, "what you're saying is the coordinates are indiscreet!"

The two men looked at her.

"It was a joke. Sorry."

John studied Sarah as she stared at her hands in embarrassment. There was no evidence of the haughtiness he had encountered when he first met her. He glanced at David, then back at Sarah, wondering about the true nature of their relationship. They were obviously comfortable in each other's presence, like an old married couple. But just like an old married couple, they were mutually distant, rarely making eye contact. John guessed both would be happier with other mates.

It immediately occurred to him that their problem, as he believed true of all problems, represented an opportunity in disguise. But he quickly put the thought away, attributing his growing fondness for Sarah to her looks and to his sympathy for her plight.

All he felt for David so far was mild distrust. David was not a man he would associate with under ordinary circumstances. Of course, searching for buried treasure constituted anything but. The two men had agreed to a partnership Tuesday night, and John, for his part, intended to take it seriously. He hoped David did as well.

"Any more jokes you want to share before we move on?" David asked.

"Sure," Sarah answered. "What the hell. If this is a treasure map, why aren't there marks on it telling us where to dig for treasure?"

"You mean like an *X*?" he suggested sarcastically.

"Well ... why not?"

"Sarah—"

"Wait," John interrupted. "She has a point. If we assume this is a treasure map—and there's little reason to begin a treasure hunt if we don't—then we might as well interpret its contents as directions to where the treasure is buried."

"Fine," David said. "So ... where is the treasure buried?"

"I don't know."

"What contents serve as directions?"

"The border is decorated with symbols—or what people have been calling runes—that turn out to be elements of the so-called pigpen cipher. It's true the decipherment produces nothing but garble—for the time being, anyway. However, if Cellarius merely wanted to decorate his border, why would he choose a device that was universally known at the time to be a secret code?"

"Maybe because it looked pretty," David said. "I have a friend who made a birthday card for an Iranian friend of hers. My friend thought it would be pretty to decorate the card with some exotic Middle Eastern 'symbols,' so she copied a sentence from a language textbook she found in the library. It turned out the language was Persian and what she wrote, quite accidentally, was 'Meet me at the train station.' The poor guy sat on a trackside bench for three days."

"Anything's possible," John admitted. "But if this text does not, in fact, constitute a message, then we have way too little to work with."

"Let's see the decipherment."

John unfolded a piece of paper tucked in the back of his note-book and handed it to David.

```
gxkqvqmnvhvhtgmmctvbzbrer
owubvsnhrfybuifqokqwsxhge
cqdnxiqngxkqvqmnvhvhtgmmc
tvbzbresmnxitjierivviglzs
pgiohagatysstewbtrrdgnkmx
bkegoefprjehtzhiypohhzepv
khgfkmxescjektmahrknbrzbq
tjejumiioheimbbjtjeeqafmn
imfdmfsniejfpnrsqlfywaenf
dvrkrrdvokdmnjvtewazgleia
kqabjhglcrpnplpokbzrzaalv
```

132

"Notice that the first twenty-four characters repeat after character number fifty-eight. It's because the upper right corner of the map was torn off. They were repeated there to serve as filler, to avoid a blank spot on reproductions. That part of the text is therefore permanently missing. Some people think Cellarius did it intentionally to make the decipherment more difficult."

"I don't know why he would go to the trouble," David said. "It looks difficult enough as it is."

"We have to try to break the code." John looked directly at Sarah. "We *all* have to try."

"I'll need to make a copy of this sheet." David started smoothing out the page on his knee.

"I already did." John removed two more pages from his notebook, handed one to Sarah, and kept one for himself. The three then stared at the letters, trying to justify the theory there was order among them.

John briefly peeked over at Sarah and watched the subtle movement of her lips as she worked out thoughts quietly. He allowed himself the fantasy of kissing those lips; he could feel their softness as they brushed against his own, the wetness as they parted...

He glanced at David and found him watching again, his eyes smiling. The man knew. And found it amusing. No, amusing wasn't the word for it; more like pathetic. John and Sarah were almost two different species. Any fantasy John happened to be entertaining about the two of them getting together was—he could see it in David's eyes—ludicrous.

"Are we finished talking about the map?" David asked.

"Just a couple more things," John said. "The quote that appears in English."

"It's from the Bible. So maybe Cellarius was religious."

"Then why didn't he put biblical quotes on any of his other maps?"

David was silent.

"It's a clue," John argued. "I don't know what it means, but it's something we need to keep branded in our subconscious: 'All the rivers run into the sea, yet the sea is not full; unto the place from whence the rivers come, thither they return again.'"

"Okay," David conceded. "We'll keep it branded in our subconscious. Now to Tavernier." He turned to a different section in his notebook. "I'd like to focus on just one question: who killed him?"

John and Sarah glanced at each other. John said, "That question has befuddled historians for three hundred years."

"I think it's a rhetorical question," David said. "I think we have only one suspect. Tavernier was killed for the gemstones in his possession, and a recut of one of those stones ended up in the fist of Johannes Cellarius."

"Yes and no," John said. "Somebody also killed Cellarius. That means we have two suspects."

"But we don't know who killed him, and we're running out of characters for this script. We can't do research on anonymous ghosts."

"We have at least one more character: it's generally acknowledged that Cellarius had an ongoing affair with a woman named Hildegard Weinbrenner, who came from the lower Palatinate—yet another reason to take a hard look at the Palatinate map. What are the odds of a coincidence like that?"

"Cellarius may have drawn a map of the Palatinate simply because it's where his girlfriend was from."

"And make up a strange grid? And throw in an irrelevant biblical quote? And fill the border with mystical symbols? And make *only one print*—then destroy the plate? I don't think so."

"Do we know anything about Hildegard Weinbrenner, other than she came from the lower Palatinate and rolled in the hay with our boy?"

"She was beautiful," Sarah said.

John and David looked at her.

"Well, that's what the newspaper reported. Also, that she lived in a town called Idar-Oberstein."

"Nice to see you can read," David muttered, which made Sarah blush.

"What happens now?" John was trying to take the spotlight away.

"We assign duties," David said. "Mostly what we have are unanswered questions. But it's important to identify the right questions before leaping irrationally toward the wrong answers. It's also important to proceed without delay: the pigpen made the papers, and more clues will undoubtedly follow."

He consulted his notebook. "John, you need to dig up everything you can about Cellarius. I'm convinced he killed Tavernier and took the stones. The more we know about *him*, the closer we get to *them*. I know you're already an expert of sorts on the subject, but we need more than we've presently got. Write a biography if you have to. Also, you need to study the Palatinate map until you figure out what keeps bothering you about it. And, when you have nothing better to do, break that code."

"And you?"

"I've calculated the size and approximate shape of the missing ruby. I'm going to look for it. My instincts tell me that wherever it is, the rest of the lost Tavernier stones are likely to be too. I'm also going to research the genealogy, so to speak, of the Prairie State ruby, and investigate Tavernier and his legend as deeply as you're going to investigate Cellarius and his map."

"You've been there before," Sarah reminded him gently.

"I'll go there again. So, are we all set?"

"What about me?" she asked.

David frowned and scanned his notes. "You seem to have an affinity for Hildegard Weinbrenner. When you're not gussying yourself up in front of a mirror, see what you can find out about her."

"Is that all?"

"Trust me, it's plenty. She's suspect number two. If you want, you can come with me to College Park."

"Why College Park?" John asked.

"The University of Maryland. It's where I went to school." He put his notebook back into his pocket. "And you?"

"Franklin & Marshall."

"What's that, a law firm?"

"No, a college, here in town."

"Oh."

After an awkward silence, David said, "Listen, John. Just so there's no misunderstanding between us later, it would be unproductive to withhold information. I hope you realize that."

Rather than respond, John looked down at his shoes.

"Now," David rubbed his hands together. "How about something to eat?"

John stood up. "I have Hamburger Helper," he said brightly.

David and Sarah glanced at each other.

"Hamburger Helper?" Sarah asked.

136

"Is there a problem with that?"

"Not at all," David said, rising to his feet. "Hamburger Helper it is."

John motioned for Sarah to lead the way into the dining room. Then he followed her, tracing the geometry of her hips with his eyes, watching her skirt sway as she walked. He sensed that David, bringing up the rear, wore the same amused—no, pitying—smile he had worn earlier.

It could not have been the first time David observed another man scrutinize his girlfriend. But his path had probably never before intersected with another man's in quite such a way. It remained to be seen how well their paths continued to run together, and for how long.

FIFTEEN

FRIDAY MORNING JOHN CALLED in sick. It was the first time he had ever done so, sick or well, and his vigorous good health only deepened the guilt.

He returned to Franklin & Marshall, to the glass-and-steel Erwin Raisz Institute of Mapping Sciences. He had no legitimate access to either the manuscripts or the maps, but he had dressed in his Amish clothes, complete with straw hat, and was affecting a German accent. The young woman staffing the entrance to the climate-controlled facility pointed out that his student ID card was no longer valid but couldn't bring herself to turn him away.

"Just don't do anything that will get me in trouble, okay?"

"Do not vorry. I vill not."

He descended to the first underground floor and took a deep breath. It had been almost six years since he viewed any part of the collection. Tentatively pulling open one of the myriad aluminum drawers, he found the oldest map in the Raisz Institute, exactly where he had left it: a highly stylized 1475 illustration of the Holy Land.

He stared at it for a few minutes, as he would any other friend he had not seen in years. Major geographical features—oceans, rivers, mountain ranges—were abstractly depicted and more or less arbitrarily located, rendering the map functionally useless. But to John it was an object of beauty.

Compass roses, winged cherubs, and figures of the wind-blowers adorned the empty spaces on medieval maps and charts, as did heraldic emblems, cartouches, and scrolls. If cartographers were unsure of the content, they could at least offer the consumer a feast for his eyes and some fodder for his imagination.

John removed his straw hat and ran his fingers through his hair. What he needed to examine wasn't in the aluminum cabinets—or anywhere else on the first two underground floors of the Raisz Institute. It was in the institute's collection of uncatalogued manuscripts.

The problem was access: they had no reason to grant it to him, and his straw hat and German accent were not likely to be of any help.

The Raisz Institute extended three stories underground; the manuscript room was the back half of the lowest floor. Actually it was a steel cage, more vault than room. The entrance guard glanced at John's student ID card and failed to notice that it had long since expired. That was because an even greater deficiency distracted him.

"You need a professor's sponsorship to enter the cage," he told John.

"Dr. Antonelli is sponsoring me." There's another one for confession, John thought; too many more of these and he'd spend the rest of his life kneeling. All he needed now was for the guard to demand proof of sponsorship.

"Do you have that in writing?" the guard asked.

"He's on his way here now."

"Then we'll wait for him."

"It may be a while. And besides, he's expecting me to complete some work before he gets here."

The guard exhaled loudly, picked up the phone, and asked the college operator for Antonelli's office. John held his breath.

"There's no answer at his office," the guard said.

"I told you, he's on his way, but he's running a couple of errands first. We're researching Amish culture, especially clashes with local townsfolk."

Their eyes locked for several long seconds.

"Wipe your feet," the guard said, and opened the cage door.

John went immediately to one of the more than fifteen hundred acid-free archival document boxes and pulled on its plastic handle. He didn't know what was in the box but wanted to give the impression he did. After a few minutes of pretending to study its contents, he no longer felt the guard's eyes burning holes in his back and was free to explore the room.

Then he began a systematic search. He knew what he was looking for. He knew it was there, somewhere. What he didn't know was how quickly he would find it.

In one of the archival boxes, one containing a section labeled "Misc Corresp 17th Cent," were folders filled with letters written by seventeenth-century cartographers. One of the folders bore the label "J Cellarius." John removed the delicate sheets of parchment and read them one by one, allowing them to rest gently on the palm of his shaking hand to avoid subjecting them to dimensional strain.

He closed his eyes briefly to catch his bearings; the story behind the letters had begun long before Cellarius wrote them. If their contents were reliable, he had a motive for the murder of Jean-Baptiste Tavernier.

The Thirty Years' War had ended in 1648. A student in London at the time, Cellarius left for the war-ravaged lands, some said because he killed a fellow student. The push factor must have been powerful, because there were no pull factors drawing him to the Palatinate, where he initially settled.

Perhaps he was seeking opportunity: the war had buried most of Germany's men. So great was the shortage of men that in 1650, the Congress of Franconia legalized polygamy to replenish the population. No one under sixty could join a monastery. Unmarried women were taxed. Priests were encouraged to forsake one of their vows. The country could not rise out of its ashes until it had spawned a sufficient workforce.

No one knew what Cellarius did during his years in the Palatinate. The late 1650s found him in Amsterdam as an apprentice cartographer, and by 1660 he had published his first independent map, one of the city, showing property boundaries. In 1672, aged thirty-nine, he abruptly moved his studio to Hamburg.

Why? What happened in Amsterdam in 1672?

John glanced up at the cage guard. He was busy arguing with a janitor who was insisting he had to clean inside the cage.

Louis XIV was jealous of Holland's commercial success. Dutch ships ruled the seas. Dutch trading had made Holland wealthy. Also, Louis wanted the Rhein, and Holland controlled its mouth.

Guarding against French expansionism, Jan de Witt, Grand Pensionary of the Dutch Republic, allied his country with England and Sweden and tried in vain to enlarge his military. France declared war on April 6, 1672. Louis himself led his armies into Holland, where they enjoyed a string of victories before laying siege to Amsterdam and The Hague. De Witt, unwilling to see his cities destroyed, surrendered conditionally. But the terms Louis demanded were too stiff: control of all roads, rivers, and canals, and a conversion of the entire United Provinces to Catholicism.

De Witt refused. Instead, so that neither French nor Dutch would have Holland, he opened the dikes and flooded the land.

Louis and his armies retreated. Back in France, the Sun King was deified by his subjects, although the peasants were reduced to eating roots and acorns, so great was the financial burden of war.

Jan de Witt was hung from a lamppost by his own people.

And here was the golden egg in the archival box, on a sheet of parchment in John's hand: Cellarius had lost his young Palatinate-born wife, Charmaine, in the flooding, and had vowed to take revenge on Louis XIV.

"Grief attackes you on three levels," he wrote to a friend in London. "On the first, you are sorry for someone elses loss; you are sorry her life ended and she will not have the opportunitie to witness another sunrise or smell the fragrance of a rose. This grief passes quicklie. On the second level, you are sorry for your own loss, that you will never again take pleasure in her sweete companie. This grief passes after a long time. On the third level, the deepest level, you regret everything you did not do or say, and should have. This grief never passes."

His opportunity for revenge would not come until seventeen years later. Eventually, he paid the price for it with his own life. He spent those seventeen years in Hamburg, where he dreamed of shifting the world's cartography capital. His revenge, when it came, was but a flea bite to Louis XIV, and Hamburg never aspired to the grieving man's dreams.

David Freeman was right: Cellarius had to have masterminded the Tavernier robbery. He had allegedly been corresponding with Tavernier for mapping purposes, and Tavernier had obviously told him of his plans to make a seventh voyage. The correspondence wasn't in the box, but John could imagine Cellarius's reply: "Dear Sir, make haste in your preparationes, for my maps hanker for fresh ink (and my heart for justice)." Unable to reach Louis personally, Cellarius tried to punish him by stealing gemstones Tavernier had bought on his behalf.

Sadly, the joke was on Cellarius. In 1688 Louis once again invaded Charmaine's homeland. In 1689, even while Cellarius anticipated the fruits of his revenge, the king's armies razed the Palatinate and deprived its citizens of food. Now with the largest military force ever assembled in history—450,000 men, and another 100,000 in the navy—the king melted and donated his personal silverware to help finance war.

Homes burned, castles fell, and peasants ran into the woods to hide. It was the Thirty Years' War all over again. Peace in the Palatinate would have to wait eleven more years, when in 1697, Louis XIV had finally quenched his appetite for destruction.

John felt a tap on his shoulder. He turned around and came face-to-face with the cage guard. The guard rested his hands on his hips.

"Is Dr. Antonelli coming or not?"

"Perhaps I'd better go look for him."

"Yes. Perhaps you had better."

SIXTEEN

DAVID REMOVED A BOOK from the shelf, opened it to a random page near the middle, and held it close to his face, breathing in the wonderful mustiness of age-old ideas. Then he sat down in a cubicle to read.

He did the same with every book he ever examined. He loved the smell.

It was his first visit to the University of Maryland's McKeldin Library—or anywhere else on the campus, for that matter—in years. The history collection in the McKeldin stacks was as good as any within driving distance of Philadelphia, so he had made the trip despite misgivings about returning to the place where he had ditched his first choice of career.

If a book contained history, David believed, then the book itself was a part of history. An old book was a time capsule. When you opened the front cover, you opened a door to another world—a world accessible through a kind of looking glass made of hardboard and cloth. The author's voice resonated in the reader's head with the same words that had resonated in his own as he wrote them. He spoke to the reader from the past. What he had witnessed, experienced, learned, and discovered would live forever.

You only had to turn a page to travel in time.

Jean-Baptiste Tavernier was born in Paris in 1605, after his family had moved there from Antwerp to escape religious persecution. His father was a map merchant, his uncle an engraver and printer to the king, and his brother a successful cartographer. This early exposure to maps fueled his dream of visiting the distant lands they portrayed.

Tavernier's travels began early. At the age of twenty-two, he had already visited much of Europe and could speak several of its languages. Little did he know that his travels would make him the first European to visit the Indian diamond mines and document their recovery methods; that his slow, gentlemanly caravan would be the prize of robbers, his ships the target of pirates. Travel in the seventeenth century was often deadly, and Tavernier became one of the century's most traveled men.

"If the first education is, as it were, a second birth, I am able to say that I came into the world with a desire to travel. The interviews which many learned men had daily with my father upon geographical matters, which he had the reputation of understanding well, and to which, young as I was, I listened with pleasure, inspired me at an early age with the desire to go to see some of the countries shown to me in the maps, which I could not then tire of gazing at."

Tavernier's sixth voyage to India, which included an audience with the Great Mogul, was the one that ensured him a place in the history books. The Great Mogul bought some of the famous traveler's gemstones. Then, wanting him to stay for the annual birthday celebration, he promised to show him his personal collection.

Akil Khan, chief of the jewel treasury, presented the stones in two ornately decorated wooden trays, after first inventorying them no less than three times in Tavernier's presence. "For the Indians do everything with great circumspection and patience, and when they see any one who acts with precipitation or becomes angry, they gaze at him without saying anything and smile as if he were a madman."

The principal stone in the collection was the one Tavernier dubbed the Great Mogul diamond, and he was the only westerner ever to lay eyes on it. "The first piece which Akil Khan placed in my hands was the great diamond, which is a round rose, very high at one side. At the basal margin it has a small notch and flaw inside. Its water is beautiful, and it weighs 319½ ratis, which are equal to 280 of our carats—the rati being 7/8th of our carat."

Akil Khan allowed Tavernier to hold and inspect every stone in the Mogul's collection, which included another three dozen or so diamonds cut into pears, tables, and roses, ranging from 7 to 55 carats: "All these stones are of first-class water, clean and of good form, and the most beautiful ever found." The collection also included some ten natural pearls, the largest of which weighed 61 carats, as well as various pieces of jewelry set with rubies, emeralds, amethysts, and topazes.

"These, then, are the jewels of the Great Mogul, which he ordered to be shown to me as a special favour which he has never manifested to any other Frank; and I have held them all in my hand, and examined them with sufficient attention and leisure to be enabled to assure the reader that the description which I have just given is very exact and faithful ..."

At the age of sixty-three, Tavernier finally came to the attention of Louis XIV. The king bought much of his remaining stock and made him a noble of the court. Finding himself one of the richest men in Europe, Tavernier purchased the Aubonne Barony in Switzerland, then retired to write *Six Voyages through Europe into Asia*, publishing the work in 1676. The book was a bestseller and was soon translated into English, German, and Italian.

Tavernier's life wasn't over. Frederick William, Elector of Brandenburg, offered the now-seventy-nine-year-old gentleman explorer the job of ambassador to India. By the time Tavernier sold his estate and prepared his affairs for the move, Frederick William's plans had fallen through. Meanwhile, Tavernier had sent a nephew ahead to Persia with 222,000 francs worth of cargo—and never heard from either again.

Enraged, he launched his mysterious seventh voyage to the Orient via Russia—and disappeared from history.

———

David's cubicle was stacked high with books. An afterword in one of them attracted his attention. It grudgingly related and tried to dispel the legend of the lost Tavernier stones.

The author tackled the job responsibly enough, noting that shortly after the alleged robbery near Florence, two men were seized in a drinking establishment and strung up for having had their way with a blacksmith's daughter. The men were nameless; they had only been described as "the German rogues." While standing on the gallows, having waited until the last possible moment, they offered information leading to "fabulous fortune" in exchange for their release. The authorities, eager to proceed with the execution, dropped the counterweights in the middle of their pleas.

Fabulous fortune! The quote didn't prove anything, but it was yet another reason to believe a treasure hunt was justified. David checked the front of the book, an obscure history of India, and noted it had been published in 1911. According to the check-out sticker on the inside back cover, it had not left the library in more than thirty years.

David read with amusement that even to the present, people were sometimes caught on private property in and around Florence, digging for the lost Tavernier stones. They were treasure seekers so frenzied by fortune lust that they wildly misinterpreted the "clues"—or else they hoped random digging would do for them what random birthright had not, and sank their shovels into even the most unlikely places. In one or two instances, a homeowner heard noises coming from his basement and descended the stairs to find a team of treasure seekers digging a hole in the floor.

There was no doubt in David's mind that Tavernier had begun—and completed—a seventh voyage. The most valuable piece of information he had gained today was that the robbers were from Germany.

Could they have been from the Palatinate? Did Cellarius employ them? Or did Tavernier arrange the robbery himself, to defraud Louis XIV of his investment? Did he become a victim of his own sting?

One fact seemed likely: of all the places in the world where the lost Tavernier stones might await pick and spade, Florence, Italy, was not among them.

Before leaving the McKeldin Library, David stuffed the 1911 book into his pants and returned other relevant materials to the shelves in a way that no follow-on researcher would ever find them. He stepped outside into bright sunlight and paused among the building's neoclassical columns until his eyes adjusted to the glare. Then he headed across the southwest quad toward Regents Drive.

His pace was slower than that of the students and faculty, who seemed enthusiastic about what they were doing, or at least about where they were going. He sensed the intellectual buzz that pervaded all college campuses: it was faintly audible, well-nigh tangible. He had been absent from the academic life so long he had forgotten the sensation.

He slowed down even more, allowing students and faculty to pass him, until it felt as though he had come to a complete standstill.

SEVENTEEN

WHEN ELEANOR HALL ENTERED the *Chicago Tribune* conference room, she didn't bother slamming the door behind her. Such a display would have put her junior editors at ease—would have told them everything was normal. Instead, she calmly approached the head of the table and placed a copy of the previous day's *Louisville Courier Journal* gently on its polished surface.

"Anyone care to make an observation?" she asked. Her tone was tranquil, soothing—designed to rattle and alarm the men sitting before her.

The front-page headline of the paper confronted the men in tall, compact letters: CHICAGO RUBY FITS PUZZLE. The entire front page carried an article about the Prairie State ruby, which the writer claimed was an integral part of the Tavernier treasure hunt.

The source of the Prairie State ruby, according to the writer, was a place called Idar-Oberstein in the German lower Palatinate. The sister cities of Idar and Oberstein were prominent on Cellarius's last map; they had been the center of a gem mining, cutting, and retail industry for centuries.

"Anyone?" Eleanor Hall prodded.

Justin raised his hand. "Ma'am, I believe I speak for all of us when I—"

"Shut up. If it were Los Angeles or New York, I'd say, okay, we missed one. We screwed up. We'll have to do better next time. But gentlemen!" The gentlemen stared at their hands. "They came to Chicago and took a story away from us. These ... people ... from the Land of Cotton ought to be writing about mint juleps, tobacco spitting contests, hound dogs, pickup trucks, the hobo problem, and ..." she ran out of breath. "They came to *Chicago* and took a story away from *us*!"

She sat down and rubbed her eyes. "This Tavernier thing is the biggest news phenomenon of my career. I want more stories. Better stories. Fill the features section with Tavernier shit. Follow up on every nut who claims to have solved the puzzle. If an expert tells you the treasure is under Buckingham Fountain, print it. If he tells you the Picasso statue in front of the Civic Center is a pointer left by extraterrestrials, print that too."

———

A cowbell fastened to the door of the Milk & Honey Travel Agency on East Passyunk Avenue alerted the employees that Sarah Sainte-James had arrived. Not that any such gadget was remotely necessary; Sarah was accustomed to attracting attention without the assistance of an irritating noise.

One of the employees, a pear-shaped man with long strands of hair flattened to the top of his head, smiled the smile of one relieved by a promise unexpectedly kept. Sarah had visited Friday and said she would be back today.

Sarah's tours of area libraries and bookstores following her meeting with John and David had produced nothing, and she believed coming up with the idea to visit a travel agency was not so dumb. The pear-shaped employee (what *was* his name?) had been so eager to help that she had extracted an offer to track down everything about Idar-Oberstein he could find within the radius of a day's drive.

The man had spent Friday exploring that radius. Now he fumbled to finish with another customer already seated in front of his terminal. Sarah took a seat and thumbed idly through a brochure. She had worn her Phase I miniskirt Friday and was wearing her Phase II skirt today. Slowly and deliberately, she crossed her legs. She predicted the pear-shaped agent would prematurely ejaculate if she were careless about the way she uncrossed them.

"I'll mail the ticket to you," the agent told his customer. He stood up to indicate their business was concluded.

"But—can't I wait for it to be printed?"

"Sorry. The printer's not working."

Both the agent and his customer looked at the printer. Even Sarah squinted at it, then raised an eyebrow; it was wheezing away happily.

"I mean, it's not working very well. You wouldn't want to be denied a boarding pass because of an illegible ticket, would you? It'll be posted first thing in the morning, I promise. Now, if you don't mind, other customers are waiting. Goodbye!"

As the customer left, shaking his head, the agent licked the tips of his fingers and wetted down the hair over his ears. Then he took a cardboard box out from under his desk and made long, overly confident strides to where Sarah was sitting.

Sarah looked up at him and smiled, radiating all the warmth and admiration she could muster. He appeared as though he intended to propose on the spot. Instead, he said, "Everyone seems to be considering a trip to Germany these days."

"Did you find anything?"

"I'm happy to say I did. But only because I conducted the search yesterday, just before the Idar-Oberstein story broke. I think if I'd waited until today, nothing would be left."

He set the box on the floor next to Sarah's feet. Following a brief moment of paralysis because her legs were so close, he opened the box and removed a stack of books, magazines, and brochures.

"I'll leave these with you," he said. "You may examine them at your leisure. If you need any help, I'll be right over there."

"When I need you, I'll call you."

"I hope so. I mean … you're welcome. I mean …" He bowed inappropriately and a lock of hair fell down over his face. He grabbed it and pasted it into place, then hurried back to his terminal before committing more buffoonery.

Sarah turned to the materials.

The Prairie State ruby first appeared in the pages of history when Idar-Oberstein native Claus Weinbrenner sold it in Chicago after immigrating there in 1818, the same year Illinois—the Prairie State—became the twenty-first state of the union. The family that bought it named it, held it for several generations, and finally donated it to the Field Museum.

Claus hadn't known where the stone originally came from, except that his great-great-great-grandmother Hildegard left it to his great-great-grandfather Richard, who passed it down a line of ancestors to his father, who gave it to him. How Hildegard had come into possession of the ruby, Claus couldn't fathom. Her husband, his great-great-great-grandfather Adalbert, had been a distiller and probably wouldn't have recognized a precious gemstone if it had popped out of a tiara and struck him on the nose.

Hildegard was beautiful, and generous with her beauty, if the rumors were believable. At any rate, she was beautiful enough—or generous enough—that the famous German portrait artist Bernhard Schäfer had wanted to paint her.

There was another rumor, one Claus never literally believed: his lovely ancestor Hildegard was a practicing witch. It was an unlikely story, but every family had a skeleton tucked here or there, or else made one up to lend color to the family album.

What Claus hadn't known was that Hildegard Weinbrenner, although married to the reputable Oberstein distiller Adalbert Weinbrenner, was hopping into the sack with the disreputable lapidary Jakob Langenbach—who, researchers now speculated, was the man Johannes Cellarius had picked to recut the lost Tavernier stones.

According to contemporary writers, Hildegard and Langenbach were not only practicing witches, they were each leaders of their respective covens. Langenbach disappeared one day without a trace, but Hildegard was arrested and charged with witchcraft: too many teenage girls were missing, and too many rumors pointed to her as the cause.

The trial brought spectators from as far away as Strasbourg. Hildegard was sentenced to burn at the stake on the grounds that she couldn't prove her innocence. But she cheated the executioner by drinking a glass of wine, and not just any wine: one from the Château Aliénor d'Aquitaine.

Sarah read carefully, trying to internalize the details, knowing that David would never consider her an equal contributor unless she came up with something. She looked up at the travel agent, who quickly glanced back at his terminal; he had been watching her.

Château Aliénor d'Aquitaine was a Bordeaux from Pauillac. The winery itself now lay in ruins, but remnants were still visible near the bank of the Gironde. The few visitors who looked for it had to look hard: all that remained of the fairytale castle were a sinking tower and a pair of crumbling walls gradually blending into the tall grass.

Not that Château Aliénor d'Aquitaine was in any danger of restoration. As far as the citizens of Pauillac were concerned, if the ruins were to disappear altogether during the next summer squall, it would not be soon enough. The infamous Witches of Pauillac had operated the winery—and had poisoned the wine with wolfsbane.

Wolfsbane was a blue flowering plant containing aconite in its root. Ingesting the root caused, according to one medieval unfortunate who survived it, "Uncontrollable drooling. Nausea such as words cannot describe. Diarrhea worse than the nausea. The feeling of a thousand insects biting the skin. And a truly odd sensation that ice water is flowing through the veins."

Aconite was a natural alkaloid in the root of the plant. When ingested, it could kill within several hours. However, if the roots were dried and crystalline aconitine were separated, the poison was ten to fifteen times stronger, and death occurred within seconds. Only a few milligrams were necessary. The higher the dose, the more sudden the result.

In the mid-1970s, a Canadian collector who owned a dozen clay amphorae of Château Aliénor d'Aquitaine allowed viticulturists from the University of California, Davis, to test one whose wax seal was damaged. The researchers inserted a needle through a gap in the seal and extracted a sample. From it, they were able to confirm the presence of wolfsbane.

And wine. There was no way of knowing how good it tasted, but at least it was still wine. The result sent prices soaring on the collector market, and the amphora whose poison was confirmed at Davis was repaired and auctioned at Christie's for $90,000 in the investment frenzy that followed. Later, after things calmed down, an amphora could be had for ten or twenty grand, give or take availability.

Viticulturists at Davis also injected a couple of milliliters of the sample into a mouse, who within seconds went into convulsions and died.

The sample the researchers took was too small to judge color well, but a team of physicists analyzed it by passing beams of light through it and extrapolating. It was a deep brick red gradually turning into soft orange on its way to brown. Probably still drinkable, if not for the poison. Probably exquisite.

The clay amphorae had been turned in Avanos, Turkey, location of one of Pauillac's sister covens. Their surfaces were hand carved in bas-relief, with the image of one woman helping another place a basket of grapes on her head.

Hildegard Weinbrenner's coven allegedly celebrated the Black Mass in a suite of caverns beneath an old church. The church—the Felsenkirche, or "Church in the Rock"—was built *into* the side of the rock bluff overlooking Oberstein. Some interesting trivia about the building included the story of the town's last public hanging, a sentence handed down to a man in 1858 for defacing church property. The execution took place a week after summer solstice, during a drizzle that had gone on for nearly a month. They hanged him rather than burned him because they feared the rain would put out the fire.

The Oberstein coven was all-female. Every Beltane, or mid-spring fertility festival, the witches laid a terrified young girl naked on the altar. After each member of the coven had performed oral sex on the girl, they fed her a cup of wine—Château Aliénor d'Aquitaine. Then they slit her throat and held her head over a cauldron until the flow of blood slowed to a drip.

The witches heralded each sacrifice by ringing a church bell. In Oberstein, the sound reached the sleeping townspeople as a muffled ring because the bell was deep inside the mountain. This unnerved the townspeople, since they knew the church to be empty and locked tight, and since every official investigation had failed to discover an access to "secret chambers." As a result of the experience, bells in Oberstein had not rung for any reason, including Catholic High Mass, since the coven died out in the eighteenth century. The superstition persisted that the sound would invite their return.

One magazine article in Sarah's stack reproduced the oil portrait of Hildegard by Bernhard Schäfer. The portrait was as beautiful as Hildegard's reputation suggested it would be; Schäfer had captured the spirit that moved her. She had a lively face with

flushed cheeks, feathered hair brushed haphazardly over her forehead in bangs, and a slightly receding chin that made her look vul-
nerable.

Her loveliness was heart-melting, but much of the appeal came
from the lust-for-life expression she wore. If this was a witch, Sarah
thought, the books would have to be rewritten.

Schäfer had done justice to the eyes. Highlights on the pupils
reflected sunlight spilling through rectangular windows behind
the painter's back. The irises were cobalt blue ringed with dark
gray. The corners were slightly moist, suggesting an abundant
warmth held in check only by the burden of sitting for a portrait.

Hildegard stared straight at the viewer. Her mouth was slightly
parted as though she were ready to speak. One only had to stare
long enough into those eyes to hear what she had to say.

As for Sarah, the message went straight to her soul. The lost
Tavernier stones represented a voyage of discovery and a leap of
faith. And if Hildegard's eyes were to be trusted, there was safe
landfall on the other side.

She felt a presence and looked up. The pear-shaped travel agent
was standing above her, his mouth open and gasping to speak:

"I was, um, wondering..."

"If I needed more assistance?"

"Yes. Yes!"

"As a matter of fact, I would love to have more information
about this church." She lifted an open book and pointed to a photograph of the Felsenkirche. "If you could gather the information
for me, I would be in your debt—*deeply* in your debt."

The agent nodded jerkily. "How deeply—I mean, how soon do
you need the materials?"

Sarah replied, "As deeply as possible," then carelessly uncrossed her legs.

The agent doubled over slightly, muttered that he would get right on it, and excused himself to stumble into a back room.

EIGHTEEN

JOHN GRAF COULDN'T FIGURE out why he had labeled the Susquehanna River "Yankee Stadium" on a map he made last week. Or how Long Island Sound managed to trade places with Chesapeake Bay.

He glanced up at two newspaper clippings attached to the shelf above his light table. They were before-and-after comparisons of Cellarius, in one view confident, indeed vain, almost smirking; in the other, horribly transfigured by the bog but still wearing what appeared to be a smile. It was the most durable smile in history.

Since his visit to Franklin & Marshall on Friday, John had spent the weekend holed up in his row house, getting more and more obsessed with the search. It was wearing on him, and now even his cartographic productivity was declining. After four days of uninterrupted devotion to fantasy, he was having trouble concentrating on his job for more than a few minutes at a time.

He had confessed earlier to his colleague Annette that he didn't remember when he last ate a square meal. He also told her he had *never* before broken the Sabbath.

At the regular Monday morning staff meeting, he had suggested they employ cartouches and compass roses once in a while, to lend elegance to their maps. Everyone just looked at him with open mouths and blank expressions.

Johannes Cellarius had arrived, literally, in the flesh, all the way from the seventeenth century. And he was obviously trying to tell John something. But what?

John had always admired Cellarius, but now his memory seemed to be editing itself, insisting Cellarius had been his favorite cartographer, heads and shoulders above the others. But why else would John already have all of Cellarius's maps? He had other complete sets, too: Mercator, for instance. But hell, everyone had those. Dr. Antonelli didn't even have the complete Johannes Cellarius. Sure, he'd always been the favorite. There was nothing wrong with John's memory.

But there was something wrong with the rest of his brain: he deleted the blue italic "Yankee Stadium" from the sinuous curves of the Susquehanna River and typed "Wrigley Field" in its place.

An idea suddenly occurred to him. He removed his copy of Cellarius's Palatinate map from a flat portfolio beneath his light table, then ran upstairs to the library to retrieve a recent map of the lower Palatinate. Returning downstairs to the photo lab, he made transparencies of both maps, reducing the modern one in scale to fit Cellarius's. His intent was to overlay one atop the other, compare features, and check for discrepancies.

After a few minutes of study, something caught his eye.

Two minor tributaries of the Nahe, both flowing north and emptying into the Nahe just east of Idar-Oberstein, appeared on Cellarius's map, but not on the modern map. The tributaries were labeled "Charmaine" and "Latein."

John raced back upstairs to the library and checked every map of Germany, old and new, good and bad, he could find. He checked indexes of place names. He was about to place some phone calls when he realized that doing so would be tantamount to sharing an important clue. For in his heart, he already knew that no branches of the Nahe called "Charmaine" or "Latein" existed. And that Cellarius would not have made such a blunder unintentionally.

Could the geomorphology have changed with time? No, streams took thousands of years to grow wide enough to appear on small-scale maps, and such streams were not likely to disappear in the space of three hundred years. Besides, isolines on modern topographic maps didn't even hint at depressions, let alone stream channels, where Cellarius indicated water had flowed.

Placing nonexistent streams on the Palatinate map had been intentional. But what was the intent? "Charmaine" was, of course, Cellarius's dead wife's name. Did he merely want to preserve her memory by naming a geographic feature after her? Why, then, such a mediocre feature—and a fictitious one at that?

"Latein" was the German word for Latin. Was that Cellarius's way of suggesting the code was written in Latin, as many people already suspected? If so, then given how difficult it was to glean other clues from the map, didn't this one glare by contrast?

John would try both words as keywords to unlock the Vigenère cipher, but he was already sure Cellarius wouldn't have made the job so easy.

He returned to the photo lab again and stared long at the pair of registered transparencies, frequently exchanging top for bottom, lifting the top like a flap to check for more discrepancies.

For the first time, he noticed hills on the Cellarius map that didn't correspond at all to modern topography. Why hadn't he seen these before? Failing to notice a couple of fictitious streams was understandable: the Palatinate was drained by hundreds of minor channels, and no one person knew them all. But fictitious hills? With well-defined summits? Given Cellarius's reputation for accuracy, this was further evidence the Palatinate map was a treasure map—or a practical joke aimed at every treasure hunter to follow.

John heard footsteps, turned, and found Harry Tokuhisa approaching, watching him curiously.

"I guess you'll be wanting an explanation," John said, glancing sheepishly at his transparencies.

"I don't need one," Harry replied. "I can see what you're working on."

"Harry…"

"John, I don't mind the lab being used for personal affairs now and then, if they're kept in check. But this affair"—he pointed at the map—"just isn't like you."

"I'm sorry, Harry. You're right, of course."

"Don't let it take over your life. Already I see signs that your work is beginning to suffer."

John looked down at his feet. It was the worst thing Harry could have said to him. His job *was* his life. The lost Tavernier stones *weren't*.

"I'll do better, Harry. I promise."

"I know you will." Harry patted John on the back and left the lab.

John looked at the two tributaries again. Cellarius had obviously drafted them with a crow quill pen, because their widths varied with pressure, gradually growing thicker as they approached the Nahe. There was nothing arbitrary about their paths; the man who had held the pen had known exactly what he was doing.

NINETEEN

DAVID ALLOWED SARAH TO drag him into Philadelphia's Academy of Natural Sciences Museum to view one of the exhibits. It was, if nothing else, an excuse to get out of the house.

Surprising to David, Sarah's interest seemed to be increasing. She had bubbled with excitement all day Sunday over what she had gathered on Saturday, and just that morning the Milk & Honey travel agent—"Quickdraw," as she called him—had presented her with even more material.

David, on the other hand, felt as though he were sinking. Following his visit to the University of Maryland on Friday, he had spent the weekend moping about the apartment. Sarah, to her credit, had prodded him, wanting to know if something about the campus had touched him. But he had only ignored her.

"David, read this. This is interesting."

"Yeah, yeah."

She was standing in front of another placard. The more animated she became, the more bored David allowed himself to appear. Looking at museum artifacts was worthwhile—but mere text printed on posters? Did they have to visit a museum and pay an admission fee to read printed matter?

"This one's about Germany: 'Before the dominance of Antwerp and Amsterdam, the cities of Germany led the European jewelry trade. Willibald Pirkheimer of Nuremberg asked Albrecht Dürer to buy diamonds for him when he visited Venice in 1505. That same year the Fuggers, an Augsburg family, sold two diamonds to Maximilian I for 10,000 florins.'"

"Wonderful. The Fuckers of Augsburg."

"How much is a florin?"

"Beats the hell out of me."

"'The Fuggers bought the diamonds taken from Charles the Bold during his defeats in the battles of Grandson and Nancy.'"

"Good for the Fuckers."

"David, hush. 'Within a quarter of a century, diamonds were being treated as commodities. Another Augsburg family, the Welsers, lent money to Charles V to buy diamonds.'"

"Perfect. The Welchers of Augsburg. The Fuckers and the Welchers."

They were on the first floor mezzanine, above the museum entrance. David glanced at the stairs and wondered how soon he could terminate the visit without hurting Sarah's feelings. Yawning, he wandered away from the placards and idly shopped the gemstone cases. The collection was modest but included some interesting pieces: naturally colored amethysts that were intensely purple, a few decent opals, a couple of fine gold nuggets. He was surprised to see tugtupite, a rare mineral found only in Greenland.

He looked at his watch. Ten more minutes of this, and he would insist on lunch. His stomach was growling, and the Four Seasons Hotel was directly across the street.

"Over here," Sarah said. "This is what we came for." She was as excited as a kid in a toy store.

"What *you* came for," he reminded her.

"It's about signet rings. Read it."

"If I must." David's eyes scanned the placard.

"No, dummy. Out loud. I want to make sure you absorb the information."

"Very well. 'Signet comes from the Latin *signum,* which means "seal." Historically, signets functioned as signatures that authors impressed in clay or wax. Later they functioned as symbols of authority.' My stomach is making frightening noises, you know."

"Skip down a little."

"'The Egyptians were apparently the first to make signets, using a grinding powder from Naxos in the Greek Cyclades, one we know today as emery. They used it to carve designs—*intaglios*—into the surfaces of softer stones such as hematite, quartz, and garnet.' One more minute of this and my knees will buckle."

"You're almost there."

"'The Egyptians taught the Israelites, who in turn taught the geeks—excuse me, the Greeks—and the Romans. Before long, signet carvers became quite skilled at their work, and signet owners were confident that only a talented artist could forge their symbols of authority.' And they all lived happily ever after."

David raised his watch to eye level and pretended to be surprised by the time. "I think I'll get something to eat," he announced.

"Wait!" Sarah said. "Here it is, the Michelangelo signet. 'This often-copied image,'" she recited, "'of a woman helping another woman to place a basket of grapes on her head, was taken from the ceiling of the Sistine Chapel.'"

Below the placard was a glass case, and inside the case was a collection of signet rings. The centerpiece of the collection was an example of the Michelangelo signet.

"Finally," David said. "An artifact."

"I want it."

He laughed. "Well, you can't have it."

"Look, the case is locked with a five-pin tumbler. You can handle that with your eyes closed."

"I'm not going to pick it. I swear I'm not."

"I'm surprised to find you squeamish."

"We can't move that piece, Sarah. There isn't anybody in the city we could pass it to."

"I don't want to move it or pass it. I want to wear it."

"You've got to be kidding. It's a man's ring. It's too big for any of your fingers."

"So, you're a jeweler. Size it for me."

"You want me to saw into a shank that's maybe two hundred years old—"

"More like three hundred."

"—so you can wear it like a trophy?"

"It's mine, and I'm taking it."

"It's not yours, and it's not going to be."

"Pick it, David. Or iron your own clothes from now on."

David scanned the mezzanine, saw that it was clear, and leaned over the lock, pretending to study the contents of the case. A few moments later he straightened up.

Sarah calmly lifted the glass top of the case.

The room lights flickered.

"Oh, shit," David said.

Sarah thrust her hand into the case and snatched the ring, then let the glass fall back into place.

David took her by the arm. "Let's get out of here." They hurried downstairs to the ground floor.

"Excuse me, miss? Sir?" A uniformed man came out from behind the ticket window as Sarah and David passed it on their way to the exit. "Both of you, stop, please."

"Get her!" David screamed. "She's stealing a ring!"

The man lunged at Sarah, who dashed for the exit. "Lady, please don't do this!"

David chased after them both. Just as the man's hands were about to clamp down on Sarah's shoulders, David tackled him from behind, and both men tumbled across the floor.

As David scrambled to his feet, he found himself surrounded by security guards. He looked through the glass doors and saw Sarah running down Cherry Street. She passed the Four Seasons and the Radisson, and his stomach grumbled once more. He knew she would turn south to Penn Center Station and disappear safely into the Philadelphia commuter crowd.

A pair of guards took him by the arms. "You," one of them said, "have the right to keep your goddamn mouth shut."

TWENTY

GEBHARDT WOULD HAVE PREFERRED to conduct business on dry land. But Blumenfeld had insisted on getting out of the house, claiming she was tired of walking the streets of Mainz and loitering in its museums. Also, she was sure her husband suspected something: he was uncharacteristically quiet nowadays and often lingered nearby while she spoke on the phone.

The two cohorts seated themselves in a large dining room on the highest enclosed deck of the *Berlin*, a river cruiser operated by the Köln-Düsseldorfer line. Three rows of tables, already set with long-stemmed wine glasses, spanned the length of the boat. But despite the capacity, the room was nearly empty, most passengers electing to sit above on the open deck, where the view was better.

Gebhardt knew that Blumenfeld didn't care about the view. She wanted to continue the "saturation." And the disappointment on her face, as she watched him gaze idly out the window, was obvious. As for Gebhardt himself, he acted the way he felt, and the way he felt was that they had reached a dead end.

The Rhein River was beautiful from its source in the Alps to its mouths on the North Sea. But it was most beautiful in Germany, especially between Mainz and Köln. And it was legendary between Bingen and St. Goar, where the channel narrowed ruggedly and castles peppered the bluffs.

Across the river from Bingen's harbor were steep, terraced vineyards, the vine culture dating back to the Roman occupation. Although the sun was already low, it shined warmly on the vines as the boat pulled out of the harbor.

Gebhardt looked out the window. Waves from barges passing close by lapped inoffensively against the hull of the cruise ship. The churning surface of the water reflected the dull green hues of vineyards blanketing the hills. If not for the rumbling of the ship's engines, it would have been hard to tell whether the ship was moving or the scenery was reeling slowly by.

A loudspeaker began a commentary in German, repeating everything afterwards in English and French.

"So much for peace and quiet," Gebhardt muttered.

The first landmark, visible even from Bingen's harbor, was the Mäuseturm, a thirteenth-century tower jutting up from the middle of the channel in starkly medieval orange and white. In its prime, it had served as a lookout for Burg Ehrenfels, a castle built on the north bank without a clear view downriver. The castle, picturesque even in ruins, had been destroyed by the French during their pillage of 1689.

Ruins of more castles drifted lazily past on the hilltops.

"After half a dozen or so of those brick piles," Gebhardt said, "they all begin to look alike."

"Pity," Blumenfeld responded. "You should visit some of them. That one, for instance." She pointed up at Burg Rheinstein, its gray, menacing battlements growing out of the schist and slate high above the south bank. "The interior is splendid."

"I'll take your word for it. I like it down here, where the air is dense."

The boat docked at Bacharach and picked up more passengers, including a large group of Japanese tourists. Gebhardt commented that should his party come to power, there would be fewer such elements in the country, and therefore more seats on the boat.

"Yes," Blumenfeld agreed, "and fewer boats."

The jewel of Bacharach was its picturesque Gothic chapel. Looming on the hill above, Burg Stahleck was yet another medieval fortress defeated in 1689, yet again by the French.

"This is where I'd live, where I'd buy a house," Gebhardt nodded toward the town. "It's pretty and unpretentious."

"Oberwesel for me," Blumenfeld said. "The architecture is better preserved."

The boat stopped at Oberwesel, too. While they were waiting for the tourists to board, Blumenfeld ordered another glass of wine, then frowned at the stem of the glass. "I read in the paper that Dr. Spengler had a bizarre accident over the weekend."

"Yes," Gebhardt answered. "It was a tragedy. He fell down the stairs of his university office building."

"Funny how such an accident can break so many bones."

"One can never be too careful."

She sipped her wine. "According to the paper, first he fell down a flight of stairs, then he somehow rolled across the landing and fell down a second flight. It was during the first fall he cracked his skull, and during the second he broke his neck and died."

"He had a bad day."

"I gather if he had broken his neck during the first fall, the second might not have been necessary. Did he, by any chance, reveal anything interesting on the way down?"

"No, unfortunately, he was reluctant to cooperate. He got so scared on the upper landing, looking down, that he started crying and peed his pants. He called out his wife's name over and over. I thought maybe the first flight of stairs would inspire him to share information with me, but it only gave him a headache. A *splitting* headache."

"Poor bastard. I also tasked you to find—"

"—the wine, I know. As we speak, an amphora of Château Alié-nor d'Aquitaine is gathering dust in the cellar of an Ingelheim merchant. It happens to be for sale."

"Good work. Weinbrenner delivered a child right around the time of her arrest. I have a suspicion about who the father was. Here's a chance to put your 'history' training to work: take a look into the Weinbrenner family genealogy and see what you can come up with."

"What has that got to do with finding the lost Tavernier stones?"

"Indulge me. Now, what's the next step in getting Cellarius's keyword?"

"There's a guy in Bonn who seems to be the acknowledged expert on code breaking."

"Good. See if you can pry something from him without killing him. Failing him, try the Americans at some of their military installations. They rather devote themselves to that kind of thing." Blumenfeld laughed. "America: the source and hapless market, all at the same time, for turquoise. But God bless them, they drink our Liebfraumilch so we don't have to."

She returned to frowning at the stem of her wine glass. Gebhardt, gauging the deterioration of her mood, finally asked, "All right, what?"

"I'm troubled … by your diminishing enthusiasm."

"My enthusiasm is a function of our success. We haven't had any."

"Oh, I think we've come a long way. We have a long way to go, that's true, but we're making steady progress."

"We have no idea where the lost Tavernier stones are. We don't even know what continent they're on. We can't even say for sure they exist."

"I trust Tavernier, who said they existed. He drew pictures of them."

"Tavernier also said there were lions in India and two-headed snakes in Siam."

"I'm getting upset, Mannfred."

"That makes two of us. The search for the lost Tavernier stones has turned into an Easter egg hunt. If we don't make some real progress soon, I can think of more profitable ways to spend my discretionary time."

The cruise ship's loudspeaker announced the approach of the Loreley, then began the traditional song by Heine and Silcher.

"I'm going up top," Gebhardt said. There was no response from Blumenfeld, so he left the table and climbed the steps alone to the upper deck, where wind blowing through the bottlenecked valley whipped his clothes. He crossed to the starboard side of the boat to get a better view.

Most boat passengers had paused in their drinking, talking, and card playing to do what Gebhardt was doing: listen to the music and stare at the Loreley. The landmark was little more than a big rock on the north bank of the Rhein, but it was one too famous to ignore. According to legend, boats used to wreck in the narrow passage because a maiden singing on top of the rock distracted the pilots with her lovely voice. That she was stark naked was not documented as having had any effect on their piloting. After the channel was deepened and widened, and the passage made safer, the maiden never returned.

Gebhardt, like everyone else, gave the rock its due, hesitant to admit even to himself that what he was really pondering was what the hell the big deal was all about.

He felt a presence immediately behind him and turned to find Blumenfeld standing there. Her mouth was open and she seemed transfixed. But she wasn't looking at Gebhardt or even the Loreley; she was looking over the side of the boat, at the water below.

Gebhardt thought for a wild moment she was going to jump. "What is it?" he asked. "What's wrong?"

"Spengler's death on the stairs. You said he called out his wife's name, over and over." She was still looking at the water.

"Yes. Yes, he did."

"What was the name?"

"Interesting you should ask, because I've never known anyone by that name before, and it's been bouncing around in my head ever since. It was a pretty name, an exotic one: Carminea."

"Carminea?"

"Yes. He cried out for Carminea. Over and over."

———

John was spending his lunch hour in Long's Park on Harrisburg Avenue, a mile northwest of Franklin & Marshall. It had been a favorite haunt during his college days. Despite hurrying there on

176

his bicycle, he knew he wouldn't make it back to work on time and that Harry Tokuhisa would be counting the minutes, wearing an expression of injury.

Long's Park was where the poor went to escape from their futile routines, to sit on benches and eat egg salad sandwiches. And to warn their children away from the water: dominating the park was a manmade lake garnished with a pair of fountains. The lake's wildlife didn't mind or even seem to notice the people. Both populations, one hardly wild and the other not quite tame, enjoyed the park and its regenerating powers.

John leaned his bike against a bench in the most secluded spot he could find. He sat with arms draped over the backrest and watched one of the fountains. The biblical quote that appeared on Cellarius's last map had been ringing in his ears all morning:

All the rivers run into the sea, yet the sea is not full; unto the place from whence the rivers come, thither they return again.

The lake water roiled with goldfish that almost leaped out after crusts of bread were thrown to them. Ducks tried to sleep amid the commotion with their beaks tucked into their feathers; babies slept under mothers, each one squirming to get a warmer spot. Once in a while, a bird swooped down from the tall trees and snatched a meal from beneath the surface of the lake, then raced back up to the canopy, fighting off lazier competitors.

All the rivers run into the sea, yet the sea is not full…

Why make a treasure map, John wondered, if you're not going to fill it with clues? Isn't it reasonable to expect that everything you put on the map is fair game for treasure hunters? Isn't it reasonable to demand that codes be breakable, that keys be provided?

If you hide clues in places other than the map, how is anyone to find them?

Like the proverbial drunk who loses his house key walking home from a bar late at night: while backtracking, he only searches under street lamps, because if it's anywhere else, he won't see it in the dark.

And it just so happens the key is in his pocket the whole time.

All the rivers run into the sea…

All the rivers run into the sea!

John raced out of the park on foot, forgetting his bicycle next to the lake. He wouldn't be returning to work that afternoon. Nor would the potential damage to his career even occur to him.

———

Back in Germany, Blumenfeld tried in vain to get the Köln-Düsseldorfer cruise ship to dock early and let her off. She paused only long enough to berate Gebhardt: "All those years of Latin… *for nothing*! Spengler wasn't crying out for his wife. *Carminea is the Latin form of Charmaine*!"

———

In Kensington that evening, in his apartment above the Ahmadabad Theater, Barclay Zimmerman decided to take a bath. He'd been neglecting meals, hygiene, and anything not related to the lost Tavernier stones. His hair, always looking like it needed to be washed even when it was clean, needed to be washed.

He didn't have the luxury of a shower, not in this neighborhood, not above an X-rated theater. He watched as the thin trickle of rust-laden water filled his tub.

He thought about calling Sarah. Would she talk to him? Probably not. Besides, Feinstein would answer the phone. That's how protective he was; he didn't allow her to answer. No, he couldn't call, but he needed to find out what kind of progress they were making. Of all people, the one most likely to be in the lead was David Feinstein. If Feinstein won, he'd have both the girl *and* the Ahmadabad Diamond.

Freeman. Jesus.

He seated himself in the tub. After staring at the running water for a moment, he dashed, dripping, into the apartment's only other room.

"A pen. Where's a goddamn pen?"

Not finding anything to write with—he spilled the contents of his desk drawers onto the floor—he returned to the bathroom and began marking on the mirror with a bar of soap. Letter by letter, he deciphered the message in the border of Cellarius's last map, oblivious to the water now overflowing his tub.

TWENTY-ONE

AFTER THE PRESS REVEALED the identity of the pigpen cipher, solutions failed to follow. Since only gibberish resulted from every attempted decipherment, experts concluded the pigpen elements were mere border decorations and urged people to get on with their lives.

Few paid attention. Treasure hunters unhinged by greed showed an uncanny ability to make the facts fit their own random speculations and a priori conclusions, proving all claims made by the psychological community about the rationalization powers of the human brain.

In Lausanne, Switzerland, an unemployed carpenter dismantled his vacationing neighbor's house board by board. When the neighbor returned home to the carnage, the carpenter barely paused while jackhammering the foundation to offer him a cut of the booty.

The entire staff of the U. S. South Pole Science Station resigned en masse and requested immediate transportation to Lisbon, Portugal. And refused to say why.

A submarine commander in the north Atlantic ordered his boat to change course for the Bay of Biscay. When he revealed his theory to *the crew, he earned their complete support. However, they had to strap the boat's first officer to his bunk and spoon-feed him, such was the man's shortsightedness.*

A small crowd of strange people picketed the gates of Fort Knox, Kentucky, convinced the United States' government had recovered the stones and was hoarding them there. A similar crowd did the same at Wright-Patterson Air Force Base in Dayton, Ohio, seeking access to Hangar 18.

Delta Air Lines, responding to popular demand, increased the number of its nonstop flights from all major cities into the Atlanta hub after an article appeared claiming the solution was embedded in the novel Gone with the Wind. *The article, written by a Delta executive, did not say how. Atlanta hotels filled with tourists who remained in their rooms with curtains drawn and doors latched.*

———

Kommissar Gerd Pfeffer started a pot of coffee, then went to his office window and breathed the morning air. Twenty-one floors beneath him, the honking of car horns and the throaty growl of delivery trucks signaled the beginning of another day in Hamburg.

It was an odd mix of businesses that elected to hang a shingle in full view of police headquarters: the Hallesches Tor, a pub named after a subway station in Berlin. A bakery called Nirgendwo Anders, meaning Nowhere Else, as though the other dozen or so bakeries within walking distance had nothing to offer. The Indonesien, a grocery store that sold, in fact, Indonesian foods. And a pair of prosperous banks that, surprising to no one, had never been robbed.

Pfeffer wondered whether the merchants chose Beim Strohhause because the twenty-two-story Polizeipräsidium was across the street or despite the fact. There was something at once comforting and unsettling about being in the shadow of authority; you either loved it or hated it, and you were never sure which to do at any moment.

The coffee was ready. He sat down at his desk with a pencil and notepad.

```
⅂>Цᒣᗅᑭᗺ⊡ᗅᑎᗅᑎ>⅂ᗺᒣ⅃>ᗅᑌᗅᑌᖴᗤᖴ
Ɛ∀<ᑌᗅ∨⊡ᑎᖴᏟ<ᑌ<ᒉᏟᑎᏟЦᑎ∀∨>ᑎ⅂ᗤ
⅃ᑭᒍ⊡>ᒉᑎᗤ⅂>Цᒣᗅᑭᗺ⊡ᗅᑎᗅᑎ>⅂ᗺᒣ⅃
>ᗅᑌᗅᑌᖴᗤ∨ᒍ⊡>ᒉ>ᒍᒉ⊡⊡ᒉᗅᗅᒉᒣᖾᗅ∨
ᒣᒣᒉᏟᑎᒍᒣᒍ><∨∨>⊡∀ᑌ>ᖴᖴᒍᒣ⊡ᗤ⊡>
ᑌᗤ⊡ᒣᏟ⊡ꏟᒣᖴᒍ⊡ᑎ>ᗅᑎᒉ<ᒣᏟᑎᑎᗅ⊡ᒣᗅ
ЦᑎᒣᏟᗤᒍ>⊡∨ᒪᒍⲞᗤ>ᒍᒍᑎᖴЦ⊡ᑌᖴᗅᑌᑭ
>ᒍⲞᒍ<ᒍᒉᏟᑎⲞᒉ⊡ᑌᑌᒍ>ᒍⲞⲞᑭᒍᏟᗺⲞ
ᒉᒍᏟᒍᒍᏟ∨⊡ᒉⲞᒍᏟᒣⲞᖴ∨ᑎᒪᏟ<∨ᒍⲞⲞᏟ
ᒍᗅᖴЦᖴᖴᒍᗅᏟЦᒍᒍⲞᒍ∀>⊡∨ᒍᗅᒣᒪᗤᒉᒍ
ЦᑎᒍᑌᒍᑎᒣᒪᒪᖴᒣⲞᒣᖾᒣᏟЦᑌᗅᖴᗅᒍᒍᖾᗅ
```

First he had to confirm the pigpen cipher was correctly deciphered, and this he spent a few minutes doing. He assumed, like everyone else, the message started in the upper left-hand corner of the map, although for the purposes of code breaking it didn't matter.

He noticed the cipher could be rendered more difficult in ways that capitalized on its symmetry—by rotating individual elements 180 degrees, for instance. Pfeffer didn't suspect any such tricks, however. Cellarius hadn't tried to conceal the existence of his message; it was there for all to see. And he hadn't gone to great pains to conceal the fact—as the media tacitly assumed—that his Palatinate map was a treasure map. Because he lived in the seventeenth century, a time of simple cryptologic methods, the transpositions and substitutions he employed would probably be straightforward. Or so Pfeffer's sources had advised him.

The first layer of the puzzle was obviously a variation on the pigpen. Pfeffer hoped and expected there would be only one more layer, and he figured his sources were right: the Vigenère was the most likely candidate.

One of the magazines following the story provided a sharp, close-up photograph of where the original Cellarius map had been torn across its upper right corner. Pfeffer examined the tear carefully with a magnifying glass, trying to determine whether the length of the replacement string—repeated from the beginning of the text—matched the length of the missing string.

Judging from the literature, the existence of the repeating characters was widely known. He wondered, though, whether it would occur to other treasure hunters to lay out their Vigenère keyword accordingly, that is, to start over with the keyword when the repeated string ended. If the number of repeat characters did not *exactly* equal the number of characters missing from the original text, the material following the repetition could be trickier to decipher than the material preceding it.

He carefully wrote out the entire code on his notepad, separating and placing parentheses around the repeated string:

```
gxkqvqmnvhvhtgmmctvbzbrerowubvsnhrfybuifqokqwsxhge
cqdnxiqn
[gxkqvqmnvhvhtgmmctvbzbre]
smnxitjierivviglzspgiohagatysstewbtrrdgnkmxbkego
efprjehtzhiypohhzepvkhgfkmxescjektmahrknbrzbqtje
jumiioheimbbjtjeeqafmnimfdmfsniejfpnrsqlfywaenfd
vrkrrdvokdmnjvtewazgleiakqabjhglcrpnplpokbzrzaalv
```

Then he wrote out the sliding alphabetic table that powered the Vigenère cipher. The lowercase letters in the body of the table were the cipher letters. The uppercase letters in the column next to the left side were the key letters. And the bold letters in the row along the top generated the plaintext.

```
   A B C D E F G H I J K L M N O P Q R S T U V W X Y Z
A  a b c d e f g h i j k l m n o p q r s t u v w x y z
B  b c d e f g h i j k l m n o p q r s t u v w x y z a
C  c d e f g h i j k l m n o p q r s t u v w x y z a b
D  d e f g h i j k l m n o p q r s t u v w x y z a b c
E  e f g h i j k l m n o p q r s t u v w x y z a b c d
F  f g h i j k l m n o p q r s t u v w x y z a b c d e
G  g h i j k l m n o p q r s t u v w x y z a b c d e f
H  h i j k l m n o p q r s t u v w x y z a b c d e f g
I  i j k l m n o p q r s t u v w x y z a b c d e f g h
J  j k l m n o p q r s t u v w x y z a b c d e f g h i
K  k l m n o p q r s t u v w x y z a b c d e f g h i j
L  l m n o p q r s t u v w x y z a b c d e f g h i j k
M  m n o p q r s t u v w x y z a b c d e f g h i j k l
N  n o p q r s t u v w x y z a b c d e f g h i j k l m
O  o p q r s t u v w x y z a b c d e f g h i j k l m n
P  p q r s t u v w x y z a b c d e f g h i j k l m n o
Q  q r s t u v w x y z a b c d e f g h i j k l m n o p
R  r s t u v w x y z a b c d e f g h i j k l m n o p q
S  s t u v w x y z a b c d e f g h i j k l m n o p q r
T  t u v w x y z a b c d e f g h i j k l m n o p q r s
U  u v w x y z a b c d e f g h i j k l m n o p q r s t
V  v w x y z a b c d e f g h i j k l m n o p q r s t u
W  w x y z a b c d e f g h i j k l m n o p q r s t u v
X  x y z a b c d e f g h i j k l m n o p q r s t u v w
Y  y z a b c d e f g h i j k l m n o p q r s t u v w x
Z  z a b c d e f g h i j k l m n o p q r s t u v w x y
```

Pfeffer poured himself another cup of coffee. It was time to unearth the keyword. If he could discover its *length*, he could get the word itself.

In modern times, the keyword could have been millions of characters long, but in Cellarius's day, simple words and common expressions served. Probably it was something that had personal meaning to Cellarius or was related somehow to the Palatinate map.

Pfeffer inspected the ciphertext again, after crossing out the duplicate string. He was looking for repeating sequences of cipher letters. He found six sequences of length three—*nxi, ioh, tew, rrd, kmx,* and *tje*—and quite a few of length two. He underlined the former in his notebook:

```
gxkqvqmnvhvhtgmmctvbzbrerowubvsnhrfybuifqokqwsxhge
cqdnxiqnsmnxitjierivviglzspgiohagatysstewbtrrdgnkm
xbkegoefprjehtzhiypohhzepvkhgfkmxescjektmahrknbrzb
qtjejumiioheimbbjtjeeqafmnimfdmfsniejfpnrsqlfywaen
fdvrkrrdvokdmnjvtewazgleiakqabjhglcrpnplpokbzrzaalv
```

He decided to ignore two-letter repeats for the moment, because they were often caused by coincidence rather than a repeat of character strings in the plaintext. The two *nxi*'s were seven spaces apart, measured from the end of the first to the end of the second. Since seven was a prime number—divisible only by one and itself—Pfeffer immediately suspected he had found the length of his keyword. The *rrd*'s were 112 spaces apart, and seven was a factor of 112. Other factors included 2, 4, 8, 14, and 16, however.

It was the *kmx*'s and *tje*'s that threw curve balls: they were 32 and 16 spaces apart, respectively, suggesting a keyword length of 2, 4, 8, or 16.

Very short keywords were unlikely, because encipherers avoided them. They generated more repeated sequences of letters—more than were evident in the Cellarius ciphertext—and were therefore easier to discover. Pfeffer guessed the keyword was at least six letters long and probably no longer than sixteen, but he was keeping his mind open on the matter.

The two appearances of *ioh* were 80 spaces apart, throwing more doubt on seven as a choice; the only three factors in the range of consideration were 8, 10, and 16. The *tew*'s were 128 spaces apart, also favoring 8 and 16.

He now suspected eight, rather than seven, was the length of the keyword, and he sought to confirm it. If he turned out to be wrong, he would try sixteen next, since it also appeared as a factor in five of the six strings.

Turning to a fresh page in his notebook, he arranged the ciphertext in stacks eight characters wide:

```
gxkqvqmn    jierivvi    gfkmxesc    qlfywaen
vhvhtgmm    glzspgio    jektmahr    fdvrkrrd
ctvbzbre    hagatyss    knbrzbqt    vokdmnjv
rowubvsn    tewbtrrd    jejumiio    tewazgle
hrfybuif    gnkmxbke    heimbbjt    iakqabjh
qokqwsxh    goefprje    jeeqafmn    glcrpnpl
gecqdnxi    htzhiypo    imfdmfsn    pokbzrza
qnsmnxit    hhzepvkh    iejfpnrs    alv
```

Then he did a frequency analysis of the first column:

a: /	h: /////	n:	u:
b:	i: ///	o:	v: //
c: /	j: ////	p: /	w:
d:	k: /	q: ///	x:
e:	l:	r: /	y:
f: /	m:	s:	z:
g: ///////		t: //	

And he knew at a glance the hard part was over. The distribution was just clumpy enough to be an ordinary plaintext in an ordinary Western European language, disguised by having been slid across the alphabet in an increment equal to the modular value of the first key letter.

He guessed *e*, the most common letter in Western languages, was represented in the first column by *g*, two places away on the alphabet. That would make the first letter in the keyword *c*. He erased the first column in his stack and replaced it with the presumed plaintext letters; *g* went back two places to *e*, *a* went back two places to *y*, and so on:

```
exkqvqmn    hierivvi    efkmxesc    olfywaen
thvhtgmm    elzspgio    hektmahr    ddvrkrrd
atvbzbre    fagatyss    inbrzbqt    tokdmnjv
powubvsn    rewbtrrd    hejumiio    rewazgle
frfybuif    enkmxbke    feimbbjt    gakqabjh
ookqwsxh    eoefprje    heeqafmn    elcrpnpl
eecqdnxi    ftzhiypo    qmfdmfsn    nokbzrza
onsmnxit    fhzepvkh    gejfpnrs    ylv
```

Only one-eighth of the text was deciphered, but most of the work was done. Pfeffer looked at his watch; he needed to go to the bathroom but elected instead to stay on the job; the higher the pressure built in his bladder, the faster he would work toward a solution.

He had no time to waste. People had been searching for the lost Tavernier stones for *three weeks*. And some of those people, he knew from his long career as a homicide detective, were brilliant.

He started a fresh pot of coffee and stretched, waiting for the water to percolate. Then he returned to his desk, sharpened his pencil, and went back to work.

The second column was interesting, because frequency analysis suggested the modular value of the second key letter was zero—that is, the letter was *a*.

a: //	h: //	n: ///	u:
b:	i: /	o: /////	v:
c:	j:	p:	w:
d: /	k:	q:	x: /
e: ////////	l: ////	r: /	y:
f: /	m: /	s:	z:
g:		t: //	

This was obvious because only *e* could be acting as *e*. In other words, in the second column there was no transposition, no disguise. The keyword therefore began with the letters *ca*. He updated his cipher stack:

```
exkqvqmn    hierivvi    efkmxesc    olfywaen
thvhtgmm    elzspgio    hektmahr    ddvrkrrd
atvbzbre    fagatyss    inbrzbqt    tokdmnjv
powubvsn    rewbtrrd    hejumiio    rewazgle
frfybuif    enkmxbke    feimbbjt    gakqabjh
ookqwsxh    eoefprje    heeqafmn    elcrpnpl
eecqdnxi    ftzhiypo    qmfdmfsn    nokbzrza
onsmnxit    fhzepvkh    gejfpnrs    ylv
```

So far, no two-letter combinations had appeared that were impossible in a Western language, especially considering that the first letter could represent the end of a word and the second the beginning of another. The combinations felt sound to Pfeffer, as though they were leading him in the right direction.

He had always warmed up that way to a case. Somewhere lurking behind all the curtains were clues to the truth. In this case, the curtains were substitutions and transpositions concealing a message. The cryptology was merely a disguise, layers of shade drawn over the message, and the job of the cryptologist was to bring the message to light. No matter how frustrating things got, no matter how distant a possible solution seemed, the plaintext message was always there, always giving away hints, always flirting with the analyst.

Pfeffer was sure the modular value of the third keyword was seventeen, and the word therefore began with *car*. He was intrigued when *the* appeared at the beginning of the second row, but knew better than to bank on it; he still had no idea what language Cellarius used in the plaintext. Even the *yl* in the last group, which had grown to *yle*, had possibilities.

The anticipated problem following the repeated string had not occurred: the modular integrity of the text had been preserved when the string was removed. This obviously meant the number of letters used in the replacement string exactly equaled the number of letters missing from the original. He wasn't surprised: the number of cells fitted into a remodeled prison might well turn out to be the same number the prison had to begin with.

He swallowed the rest of his coffee and picked up the pace. If the job took too much longer, he was going to pee in his pants. After four columns—the halfway point—the plaintext began to shine through:

extevqmn	hinfivvi	eftaxesc	olomwaen
thevtgmm	eliqpgio	hethmahr	ddefkrrd
atepzbre	fapotyss	inkfzbqt	totrmnjv
pofibvsn	refptrrd	hesimiio	refozgle
frombuif	entaxbke	ferabbjt	gateabjh
ootewsxh	eontprje	heneafmn	ellfpnpl
eelednxi	ftiviypo	gmormfsn	notpzrza
onbanxit	fhispvkh	gestpnrs	yle

A substitution of *s* for *f* made sense of several of the quads. The sudden appearance of *from* added to the intrigue *the* had previously caused. Pfeffer now suspected the plaintext was written in English. But wouldn't that prove the cipher was a hoax?

Chasing clues and solving puzzles had ruled Pfeffer's passions all his life, passions that had served him well during a twenty-five year career as a detective. He had often pulled all-nighters, working himself into exhaustion to solve a problem.

All that changed when he found out his wife was having an affair.

He still hadn't decided what to do about it. The frequency of his wife's meetings with "Mr. Dick" had escalated to three times a week, each rendezvous resulting in yet another bottle of wine missing from his cellar. Apparently the two had become secure in their presumed invisibility. Mr. Dick was even parking his Saab in front of the house.

Pfeffer had finally given in to the urge to track down the man's license plate number. Turned out he was an old classmate of his wife's; he had graduated from their Gymnasium one year ahead of her. Pfeffer put a private detective on the case and learned how the two became reacquainted all these years later.

It was touching, he thought, and good grist for the movies, but damn them for drinking his wine. Once he came up with a plan to punish them, one that wouldn't implicate him, he'd implement it with no remorse at all. Damn her for her dishonesty, for her disloyalty, and for causing so much distraction in his life.

Like now.

After six columns, the stack began to speak:

extendmn	hinfaivi	eftaprsc	olomonen
thevltmm	elightio	hethenhr	ddefcerd
ateprore	fapollss	inkfroqt	totreajv
pofitisn	refplerd	hesievio	refortle
fromthif	entapoke	feratojt	gatesojh
ooteofxh	eontheje	henessmn	ellfhapl
eelevaxi	ftivalpo	gmoressn	notpreza
onbafkit	fhishikh	gesthars	yle

It was English after all. There was no mistaking words like *extend* and *light*. Even strings like *pofiti* made sense after Latin back-substitutions were made; indeed, "position" was a useful word to encounter when deciphering the presumed instructions to a treasure map.

But was it a hoax? Probably no one would know until the shovels went to work, and either they hit something or they didn't. The solution had been easy, even for amateurs. Pfeffer figured many people had already passed this point and were closing in on the target. That the newspapers hadn't gotten there—or weren't saying—didn't necessarily mean anything; journalists might have preferred to cash in on treasure rather than payment for an article about treasure.

Cellarius's instructions, once deciphered, didn't make much sense at first glance. But Pfeffer would worry about that later. Right now, he needed to take a piss.

TWENTY-TWO

John peered out his front window and watched Sarah arrive for a visit after what must have been, for her, a harrowing drive through the country. She parked David's VW Beetle in the only remaining place it would fit on Nouveau Street. Then she stepped daintily out of the car, as if merely brushing against the air of the neighborhood would soil her. Her apprehension about leaving Philadelphia for "the sticks" was obvious.

To be fair, Lancaster contained more than just crickets and rednecks. But John had heard city girls say it before: there were two kinds of flying insects in central Pennsylvania, those small enough to penetrate the screen and those big enough to open the door.

Sarah stretched her skirt down as far as she could toward her knees and took short, choppy steps on the sidewalk in her high heels. The city girls had a point: nothing about "Nouveau" Street was the least bit new. The row houses were some of the city's oldest. And none was complete without a rickety porch furnished with a lawn chair occupied by a fat person. The fat person's grungy tank top stretched torturously across his distended belly, and its low, U-shaped neckline granted canopy space to his sprouting chest hairs. The fat person didn't do anything—he didn't even read. He sat in his lawn chair and watched pedestrians, the blank expression on his face a symptom of intellectual paralysis.

Sarah shuddered visibly and hurried out of range of their hollow stares. John was glad he kept his interior tidy, and relieved he wouldn't be serving Hamburger Helper again.

"Nice neighborhood," Sarah said, when he greeted her at the door.

"I like it."

"You the only skinny guy in it?"

"Nah. There's another one four blocks down."

"What's cooking? Smells like spaghetti."

"Spaghetti."

She kissed him on the cheek, then went sighing into the living room and sat on the couch.

John realized that since he would be working with Sarah, he would be sitting next to her. And that doing so was going to make it hard to concentrate. He had been in a high state of agitation all day: fifteen minutes in front of the mirror was, for him, about fourteen minutes and fifty-five seconds longer than usual. After deciphering the code, he had spent two days digesting the message that emerged, then had finally—hesitantly—called David and Sarah to share his success with them.

David, however, was in jail again, this time for shoplifting in a museum, of all places. Sarah admitted as well that their progress on the treasure hunt had reached a standstill; that she and David had been spending their discretionary time casing jewelry stores.

"Casing them ... to buy something?" John asked.

"No. Casing them ... to borrow something."

"Oh." He spread his work out on the coffee table and handed her a copy of the cipher.

Extend in the vltimate prone poſition
From the foote of the elevation (Extend in
the vltimate prone) baſketh in fairie lighte
Of Apollos reſplendent apogee
On the feſtivall of his higheſt aproche
Then drink from the Sieve of Eratoſthenes
Sing more songes than Solomon
And deſcend to treaſvre
For the gates of Hell ſhall not prevayle

"The line breaks are mine," John explained, "and might be a little arbitrary. The text was all run together. This part here, in parentheses, is the repeated string I told you about on the phone."

"I don't want to be a party-pooper, but none of this makes any sense to me."

"It didn't to me, either, the first time I read it."

"And now?"

He shrugged. "It grows on you." He sat next to her on the couch. "'Extend in the ultimate prone position' probably means to lie down flat—that is, to measure a man's height horizontally from something."

"A short man or a tall man?"

"I can only assume we need to measure a distance equal to Cellarius's height. Yesterday, I called the University of Hamburg Medical School. I told them I was a journalist; seems I've been doing a lot of that lately. Anyway, Cellarius was of average height, about one meter seventy-seven."

"I'm impressed."

"I don't think we have to be extremely accurate here, because any container large enough to hold the lost Tavernier stones will be large enough that a shovel sunk within several inches of its center will strike it."

She was impressed. John had been consciously disciplining his eyes to look only into hers, or at the papers before him, but now he allowed them to wander momentarily down the length of her figure.

He had only known one girl in his life, and the knowledge had been superficial, to say the least. During a wedding at an Amish farm, to which one of the young men had brought a bottle of whiskey, a girl hitched up her skirt in the barn and offered herself to any and all comers. John, succumbing to peer pressure, took his turn in line. But when he got his pants down and knelt between her legs, he couldn't get it up. The girl tried to help by fondling him, but it only made matters worse. She giggled and told *everyone.*

It was during John's "sowing of wild oats" period, a time when youths were permitted to let loose and yield to primal urges before kneeling for baptism and officially joining the church.

He cleared his throat. "As for the 'foot of the elevation,' I assume we have to identify a high point of some kind, maybe an outcrop. We probably won't understand the instructions completely until we visit the general location."

"And where, exactly, is the general location?"

"Somewhere in the Palatinate, I hope. Somewhere on Cellarius's last map. Idar-Oberstein, in all likelihood. Unfortunately, this part of the code is where the corner of the map was torn off. From the foot of *what* elevation? We don't know. I've scoured the map, and all the modern maps of the area I could lay my hands on, and there's nothing labeled "the elevation," or "*die Erhebung*," or anything similar. Maybe the damage to the map was intentional, to make the solution more difficult. Maybe Cellarius tore it himself."

"Why would he give a clue, then take it away?"

"I don't know. I'm just speculating. I still don't have a clue why he made a treasure map to begin with."

"Well, speculate some more. This is really interesting. I didn't know you spoke German."

John couldn't resist showing off a little: he explained how the Vigenère worked, how Cellarius had encrypted his message, how his own sleuthing unveiled the keyword, *carminea*. She inched a little closer to get a better look at the pages he was holding. Twice her knee touched his. Both times he felt the adrenaline.

"I don't understand something," she said. "If he was German, why did he write the instructions in English?"

"Actually, he was Polish. I think in order to make the code as inaccessible as possible, Cellarius chose from the languages he knew the one that was most foreign to Germans. He spoke German, Latin, and Dutch, all more accessible than English in the seventeenth century. And he spoke Polish too, but since he left Poland as a young man, he might not have been comfortable with it anymore. He was comfortable in English because he went to school in England."

"Will others be able to do what you did? Are we ahead now?"

"I doubt whether many will get this far. Since a part of the text is missing, an analytic decipherment is pretty much out of the question. The polyalphabetic encryption, the absence of word breaks, the unconventional spellings, the Latin letter substitutions—these make the thing even harder to solve. You have to guess the keyword, there's really no other way. All it takes, though, is one person to solve it and make his solution public, and the whole world will know what we know."

Dinner was ready, and John served it. Sarah watched him carry bowls of noodles and sauce to the table and fill her glass with iced tea. The admiration in her eyes meant more to him than the "sleuthing" he had just finished bragging about.

He wished now he had used the candles after all. He had brought them out, put them back, brought them out again, and put them back again. He wanted to bring them out yet again, but it would look like a quick fix, so he didn't. The kitchen lights were awfully bright.

When it was time for Sarah to go, he followed her to the door and silently warned himself not to utter anything stupid. She turned in the open door frame and faced him. He didn't know what else to say, so he said, "We're going to need David."

"Then we're going to have to get him. Right now, there are some very thick iron bars preventing him from coming to us."

He offered his hand and she shook it. He noticed the signet ring on her finger.

"That's interesting," he said.

"It's ... borrowed."

"Oh. Hey, I'll walk you to your car."

"No, don't. Let's say goodbye here." She hugged him and planted another kiss on his cheek.

"You smell real good." He winced: "Sorry, I guess that was a stupid thing to say."

"No, it was a perfectly okay thing to say." She put her hand behind his neck, pulled him close, and kissed him briefly on the lips. Then she turned and stepped into the Pennsylvania night.

"Don't be a stranger," he said, in a voice he thought too low for her to hear.

She heard it and looked back over her shoulder. "I don't intend to."

TWENTY-THREE

Round about the beginning of the ninth century, Charlemagne ordered grapevines—*red* grapevines—planted on the grounds of his Ingelheim palace. A dozen centuries later, the Charlemagne Vineyard, among others, still cultivated Spätburgunder and Portugieser grapes in its chalky clay soils. Some of the few red wines made in Germany were coaxed from those grapes and earned Ingelheim its treasured nickname: *der Rotweinstadt.*

In dark cellars beneath the Charlemagne estate's half-timbered buildings were great oaken casks filled with fruity young vintages. The cellar master, a human mole if ever there was one, spent his days underground, checking color, bouquet, and flavor to decide readiness for bottling. As necessary, he topped off the casks to compensate for evaporation, otherwise exposure to air would prematurely oxidize the wine.

The estate cached its collectable wines in those same dark cellars. The centuries-old treasury enjoyed a reputation as one of Europe's most valuable: more than fifty thousand bottles lay on their sides in racks lining the cut stone walls. Estate personnel were careful not to disturb the dust and cobwebs, so important were they to the image and salability of aged wine. For like other rare commodities, the price of an old bottle of fermented grape juice was largely due to the mystique associated with it, and some vintners were better at creating mystique than wine.

The Charlemagne estate offered guided tours, which included historical discourses and a walk-through of the famous cellars. On Saturday, the thirteenth of June, Frieda Blumenfeld placed herself and Mannfred Gebhardt first and second in line.

In the darkest, coolest room of the Charlemagne cellars, a room bedecked with dust and festooned with sagging cobwebs, one illuminated only by candlelight and only when necessary, dwelt the estate's lone sample of Château Aliénor d'Aquitaine. It rested on a warped wooden board in a cabinet shielded from groping hands by a rusted iron grille.

The sample, the tour guide explained, had already been in stock when he began his career with the Charlemagne estate more than thirty years before. In fact, no one, not even the cellar master, knew where it came from, and there was no record anywhere of a purchase. The amphora contained what experts believed to be the last vintage the Aquitaine winery sealed without a cork.

The tour guide led his group into the small room and dramatically thrust a lighted candle toward the grille; its iron bars cast flat, linear shadows across a crusty earthen pot. The tourists, including Blumenfeld and Gebhardt, craned necks, stood on toes, squatted, and did what they could to catch glimpses as the candlelight flickered briefly and tantalizingly through gaps in the grille.

Blumenfeld noted that the amphora was about thirty centimeters tall and as much as twenty centimeters in diameter across the widest part of its belly, which tapered gracefully down to its base. A pair of handles fastened to the belly rose almost to the level of the mouth. The mouth looked just wide enough to admit a small fist; it was fitted with a lid and sealed with wax.

An image of one woman helping another place a basket of grapes on her head stood out in bas-relief on the amphora's belly. The signet, about four centimeters by four centimeters in area, appeared face-on when the high-arching handles were in profile.

The guide allowed his group to soak up the image for a minute or two, then he ushered everyone from the room and locked the door. He next directed them to an exhibit a few meters down the hall, one that illustrated and interpreted the history of poisoned wine. The exhibit, he informed them proudly, was the only one of its kind in the world. No one doubted his word.

Blumenfeld took Gebhardt by the sleeve and led him back to the door that separated them from the amphora of Château Aliénor d'Aquitaine. She wistfully touched the padlock with her index finger.

"I have to have it," she said. "I absolutely have to have it." She looked at Gebhardt. "You don't understand, do you?"

"Haven't you been paying attention to all the security?" He shook his head at her. "No one can set foot on this property without alerting dogs. *Big* dogs. Besides, there's nothing but vinegar inside that amphora."

"When one collects wine, one collects history—no matter the chemistry. Imagine the grapes from the seventeenth century that went into making the contents of that amphora. Imagine the people who toiled over those grapes, people long since rotted in their anonymous graves. Imagine the flavor trapped inside— imprisoned, as it were, like a genie in a bottle."

"That's poetic, Frieda. But the wine couldn't possibly be drinkable after all this time."

"As a matter of fact, it could. It depends on the quality of the vintage, the variety of grape, the processing techniques, and of course the care taken in storage. It may not taste very good, but then again it may."

"After *three centuries*?"

"Reds can live much longer than whites because they contain tannin, which acts as a preservative. The more tannin, the harsher the wine, and the longer it can—and arguably should—be aged before drinking. People don't have the patience anymore to age wine, however, nor the cellars in which to store the bottles properly. So most red wines nowadays are made to be consumed as soon as they're bought. But this one," she tapped the heavy wooden door, "was designed to go the distance."

"You should get a job here as a guide."

She glanced down the hall at their fellow tourists, all engrossed in another lecture, delivered by the man who presently held the job of guide.

"There's something intrinsically romantic about an old bottle of wine," she continued, "much more so than about, say, an old coin. We may hold the coin in our hand and think in wonder of the years that have passed since it was struck, or of the many other hands it must have passed through to reach ours. But wine is different: it was bottled, corked up—imprisoned—and we need not merely look at it in wonder. We may open it, release it, and taste the effort of the grapes from all those years ago. A bottle of old wine is more than an artifact, it is an event."

Gebhardt smiled agreeably.

"You really must affect at least a modicum of familiarity with wines, Mannfred. It is one of the hallmarks of an educated man. But of course, you are a beer drinker. I forgot."

"I'm not breaking into this building to steal that clay pot."

"Well, let me put it to you this way: if you broke into this building to steal that clay pot, you would accomplish something worthy of my gratitude."

"Frieda, if the amphora were in your possession, you would not be any closer to solving the puzzle."

"No, I suppose not. So impress me another way. Tell me what 'basketh in fairy light' means."

"I don't know what it means. I don't know what the hell 'fairy light' is. The corner of the map was torn off right before that phrase. You knew this would be a tough line to crack. Why did you give it to me?"

"You're right, Mannfred. It *is* a tough line to crack. I worked on it myself and didn't come up with anything either."

"So my assignment is to spin my wheels?"

Blumenfeld made a *tsk, tsk, tsk* sound. "I called the University of Hamburg Medical School yesterday. Cellarius's height was one meter seventy-seven. That's the uninteresting part. Here's the interesting part: the man who answered my query said it was the third such call that day. Your special talents may eventually come in handy after all."

"Did the man say who the other callers were?"

"An American journalist and a homicide detective. He didn't have names. To tell you the truth, I doubt either caller revealed his true profession. The closer we get to the stones, the more competition we're going to encounter."

"That's the reason you have me," Gebhardt said.

Indeed, Blumenfeld thought. And the reason I have you is exactly the same reason I'm worried about you.

"By the way," Gebhardt said, "there *is* something about the 'fairy light' we need to keep in mind."

"Namely?"

"'Basketh' is the third-person form of the verb. That means it refers to someone or something else basking, rather than directs the seekers to do so."

Blumenfeld smiled. "Good insight. Thank you. Now figure out what 'fairy light' is."

"What about 'Apollo's resplendent apogee'? That was *your* assignment, as I recall."

Blumenfeld looked over at the tour guide again. His pale face almost glowed in the dim corridor. He was listening to himself talk and enjoying every word.

"That one's easy," she said, "unless I'm missing something. Apollo was, among other things, the sun god in Greek mythology. An apogee is the highest point in an orbit. So it must mean we're supposed to do whatever it is we're supposed to do at noon on the day we're supposed to do it."

"What difference does it make what time of day we dig for treasure?"

"I wish I could say. It might just be superstition. Then again, these might not be instructions on when to *dig*, but rather when to *look*. In other words, maybe there's another clue yet to be revealed, and it can only be revealed … at noon."

"That would be inconvenient," Gebhardt said. "I do my best work at night."

The guide was rounding up his scattered tourists to lead them upstairs to the hydraulic presses. Blumenfeld and Gebhardt ambled over to where chattering people were gradually coalescing into a manageable herd.

"The secret to any successful partnership is to never outlive your usefulness," Blumenfeld told her young partner. "I suppose if we find the stones, I'll be able to buy that amphora outright from this estate. You don't know anyone who would care to taste-test it for me, do you?"

Gebhardt shook his head slowly and deliberately.

"Too bad. I may feel inclined to break it open anyway in celebration, to release the seventeenth-century toil and travail imprisoned within. To reunite them, you see, with old friends."

As the herd of tourists went up the stairs, one member asked the guide, "What's the best color for red wine?"

"Ruby," he answered without hesitation. "Fine red wine is exactly the same color as a top-grade ruby."

TWENTY-FOUR

On Sunday the fourteenth of June, Gerd Pfeffer put on a jacket and tie and visited St. Jacobi Church.

He entered one of the wooden confessionals, latched the door behind him, and knelt down on a padded stool. In the relative darkness he could hear murmurs coming from the other side as the priest gave penance to another confessor. After a few moments there was some rustling, then the distant sound of a door opening and closing. Finally a panel slid open before his face, revealing an intricately carved screen. Behind the screen was the vague shadow of a man.

"Forgive me, Father," Pfeffer began, "for I have sinned. It has been a long time since my last confession."

The shadowy figure remained silent. Pfeffer could only imagine the expression on his face. He heard what sounded like a soft chuckle.

"What sins have you committed, my son?"

"Lust, Father. And a whole lot of it."

"Lust ... for a woman?"

"No, for treasure."

"Ah. From what I hear, you're far from alone."

"Far from alone? Funny you should put it that way, Father. I've never been lonelier in my life."

The figure on the other side of the screen leaned closer. "Gerd, you only come here after you've shot someone. I dread the day you tell me it was your wife."

"No, Father. My gun is silent forevermore."

"I'm happy to hear that. God is happy too."

"Tell me something, Father: how many songs did Solomon sing?"

The priest replied without hesitation. "*He spake three thousand proverbs: and his songs were a thousand and five.* First Book of Kings, chapter four, verse thirty-two."

"I bet you were first in your class at the seminary."

"As a matter of fact ... I was."

"You could do me a special favor and not share this conversation with anyone else."

"But my son, are you not aware of the sanctity of the confessional?"

Pfeffer received his penance and took a seat in the west gallery under the imposing Arp Schnitger organ. With four thousand pipes, sixty registers, and four keyboards, it was the largest baroque organ in northern Europe. It occurred to Pfeffer as he recited his Our Fathers and Hail Marys that he really ought to visit the church more often, even without having shot someone.

The priest exited the center compartment of the confessional, found Pfeffer in the west gallery, and joined him in his pew. He was short and bald with a thick white beard. His eyes brimmed with the confidence and security possessed by men who knew their place in the world and happened to occupy it.

Pfeffer silently handed him his notebook:

> Extend in the vltimate prone po*f*ition
> From the foote of the elevation …
> … ba*f*keth in fairie lighte
> Of Apollos re*f*plendent apogee
> On the fe*f*tivall of his highe*f*t aproche
> Then drink from the Sieve of Erato*f*thenes
> Sing more songes than Solomon
> And de*f*cend to trea*f*vre
> For the gates of Hell *f*hall not prevayle

The priest read the text carefully. "'And descend to treasure,'" he quoted. "Sounds like you're going to do some digging."

"I hope the message is as straightforward as that."

"'For the gates of hell shall not prevail,'" he continued. "Sounds like you may be digging into solid rock." He turned and smiled mischievously.

"Father, if you ever decide to leave the priesthood and become a detective—"

"You," the priest interrupted, "will be the first to know."

———

Barclay Zimmerman wondered what he was doing running a two-bit X-rated movie theater in the Kensington neighborhood of Philadelphia. No, that wasn't true; he knew exactly why he was doing it. What he wondered was why he didn't strike a match and turn the building into something more useful—say, a pile of carbon.

He sat in the back row of the theater, pencil in hand, notebook resting on his lap. There was only one patron watching the movie, a freaky-looking guy sitting a dozen or so rows up.

Wriggling flesh filled the screen. Individual figures were largely undifferentiable amid squirming limbs, bobbing heads, and wobbling breasts. Actors ad-libbed their lines for the most part—grunts and moans being hard to script. But Zimmerman was only vaguely aware of the distraction, as though the people next door had turned up their television too loud.

"On the festival of his highest approach," i.e., Apollo's highest approach, could only mean summer solstice. At noon on that day, the longest day of the year, the sun would be higher in the sky than at any other time of the year.

But wasn't one day the same as another—as far as the sun was concerned? It rose in the east and set in the west. It didn't change course, did it?

No, it didn't. But the earth was tilted on its rotational axis, so as the planet revolved around the sun, the path of the sun *appeared* to change. Its position in the sky was a function of the date and the observer's latitude.

Zimmerman had the date: summer solstice was going to take place June twenty-first, and the event, being a natural one, was independent of any calendar manipulations that might have occurred since Cellarius's time. Man could move Christmas if he wanted to, but he couldn't move the equinoxes and solstices.

Zimmerman unfolded a map of Germany and found Idar-Oberstein. During summer solstice, the sun would be directly above the Tropic of Cancer at 23.5 degrees north latitude. Idar-Oberstein was about 49.7 degrees north of the equator, or 26.2 degrees farther north than the Tropic of Cancer. Therefore, the angle of the sun on summer solstice would be 26.2 degrees less than vertical, or about 64 degrees above the horizon.

Assuming the premise about Idar-Oberstein was correct, something was going to happen there at noon on June twenty-first while the sun shined down from 64 degrees high in the sky. Something that presumably had been happening at noon on every summer solstice for the past three hundred years.

Whatever it was, it was somehow related to prime numbers: "Then drink from the sieve of Eratosthenes" was the follow-on line in the cipher. Since one could not literally drink from a sieve, Zimmerman interpreted the "drink" part to be figurative. The Sieve of Eratosthenes was a mechanical method of separating the prime numbers from the rest of the natural numbers.

Eratosthenes was a third-century BC Greek cartographer distinguished by having been the first to measure the circumference of the earth. A prime number was any natural number, greater than one, that was divisible only by one and itself. The "sieve" Eratosthenes invented was really a grid: he made it by laying out the natural numbers, typically in rows of ten, and striking out those divisible by some number other than one and itself.

Zimmerman didn't think the sieve method itself was significant. Just that whatever was going to happen in Idar-Oberstein at noon on the summer solstice was going to involve prime numbers. And he didn't have a clue what it was.

He brushed the hair out of his eyes and looked up at the screen to gauge the progress of the movie. They were still going at it. He couldn't tell which limbs belonged to which torsos. Normally a movie would end soon after a climax, but in these kinds of movies...

The theater's lone patron, sitting halfway toward the front, had an unnaturally rigid look about him. Zimmerman hoped that, if the man was doing what he appeared to be doing, he didn't leave anything on the seat cushion.

He ran upstairs to the projection room and checked a wall calendar. Summer solstice was just seven days away.

———

That afternoon, John drove to Philadelphia and picked up Sarah at her house on Volta Street. She stepped squeamishly into the front passenger seat, taking care not to rest her arms on the arm rests or touch any other part of the dilapidated vehicle. For his own part, John was fighting down a rising panic over what the oil temperature gauge on the dashboard indicated.

"What's causing that noise?" Sarah asked.

"You mean the grinding noise? Like the engine's about to fall apart?"

"Yeah, that noise."

"The engine's about to fall apart."

"Oh. Has it always made that noise?"

"No, it didn't when it was new."

The car limped into Chinatown, where John parked it on Race Street. The two then walked to the condemnable brick building between Watts and Juniper that served as a police dispatch station and makeshift jail. Upstairs, they stood and waited until David was brought out. He brushed past them without acknowledgement.

"You're welcome," John said, when they were back on the street.

"I take it you want me to thank you for picking me up."

"It's the courteous thing to do. We could have left you up there."

"You came to get me because you need me. I was happy where I was. The food was ... exotic."

"Then why are you leaving with us?"

"They made me. There's a funny rule in these parts that you can't stay in jail if you don't belong in jail. After two nights in these luxury accommodations," he jabbed his thumb at the soot-covered building, "they released me for lack of evidence, the stolen ring being on Sarah's finger, not mine. So tell me," he inspected each of them in turn, "why are the two of you picking me up together?"

"You've been missing staff meetings," John answered.

"Are we conducting one now?"

"Hop in," John said. "We're going for a walk in the park."

He drove to the west entrance of the Philadelphia Museum of Art, where the three walked down the steps into the Azalea Garden. They bought soft drinks from a vendor and sat on the bank of the Schuylkill.

"Have you been reading the papers?" John asked.

"No," David answered. "I suppose you're going to tell me the press got the keyword."

"A newspaper in Little Rock, Arkansas, broke the story this morning, and it's all over the media. Within hours, everyone in the country will know the code."

"Do you have a quarter?"

"Why?"

"Do you have one or don't you?"

John produced one. David handed him a crayon and told him to make a secret identifiable mark on the quarter. John wrote the letter "J." Without looking at it, David wrapped the quarter in a handkerchief and asked John to verify its presence by feeling it through the cloth. Then he removed a ball of yarn from his pocket and dropped it into one of the empty soft drink cups.

"Abracadabra," David said, opening the handkerchief to show that the quarter had vanished. "Any idea where it's gone?"

"No doubt into your pocket," John replied.

"Wrong." He gave John the ball of yarn and told him to unravel it. John did so. A small matchbox, secured with rubber bands, appeared at its center. Inside the matchbox was the quarter—letter J and all.

"How did it get there?" John asked. Although he didn't really care; after spending time alone with Sarah, David's presence seemed like an intrusion. He hoped David wouldn't detect the attraction. The *mutual* attraction.

"Simple. I put it there right after you marked it. I've been practicing this trick for two days. The jailers figured I wouldn't be able to hang myself with a ball of yarn or dig my way out with an empty matchbox—both of which occurred to me, nevertheless. You know, it's customary to applaud the magician at the successful conclusion of his magic trick."

"Well done," John said unenthusiastically.

"Thank you."

"I must admit, though, that I find magic tricks rather frivolous at this particular time."

"Right. I figured you might. But ponder this rhetorical question: how are we going to get the lost Tavernier stones back into the United States, if and when we find them?"

John sat quietly next to David and Sarah on the riverbank, gazing out at the slow, serene waters of the Schuylkill, pondering David's rhetorical question. That he and David had begun to polarize, perhaps beyond repair, was obvious. He didn't think David was taking the project seriously anymore. And he felt that David himself knew it: that he had exhausted his contribution to the extent of his expertise and was waiting for John to come up with a solution. John wondered whether a collaboration was such a good idea after all. But then, there was the girl. Get rid of David, and you get rid of the girl.

It was the girl who broke the awkward silence.

"I've been wondering," she said, "why Cellarius bothered to make a treasure map, if in fact that's what it is."

David shrugged exaggeratedly and said, "When you bury treasure, you leave a record of where you buried it."

"But why?" Sarah insisted. "If he buried the treasure, or if someone else buried it and he happened to know where, he didn't need to document the location. He had nobody to leave treasure *to*. Why go through the trouble of making a map and enciphering mysterious instructions? What would the point be, other than amusement?"

John plucked a weed from the grass and stuck it in his mouth. "Maybe," he speculated, "Cellarius involved himself with the cutter and the distiller's wife long enough to know how and where they hid the stones. They killed him, but not before he recorded—as a kind of insurance policy, or as a study in irony, or even because he knew in advance he was doomed—clues on his last map. Think of it as a note in a bottle. Maybe the map and 'mysterious instructions' were, as you suppose, solely for his own amusement. Maybe he was just … being a cartographer."

"You just pronounced a lot of maybes," Sarah said. "*Maybe* we should go to Idar-Oberstein and start poking around."

"No," John said, "it's too early. We'd only be wandering aimlessly."

David laughed. "He's right: we can wander aimlessly here as well as there, and save ourselves the price of a plane ticket."

"Wandering aimlessly may accurately characterize what *you're* doing," John shot back. "It's not what *I'm* doing."

"Oh yeah, I forgot. You're the cartographer. You not only know where to go, you can tell *me* where to go, too."

"Guys, guys," Sarah said. "We have a job to do."

They sat quietly for a minute. Finally David said, "Okay. Let's review what we've learned since the last time."

He sat up in the grass and raised his knees to his chest. "We've deciphered Cellarius's message, and it speaks directly to the existence of treasure. We no longer have to worry about following a path that can only lead to a dead end."

"We have a likely motive," John added. "Cellarius's wife died during Louis XIV's invasion of Holland."

"And evidence of a theft," David continued, "the last-minute confession of two Germans hanged in Florence after Tavernier's disappearance. The lost Tavernier stones exist—or at least they did at one time. We have to work under the assumption that they weren't all recut, that they're stashed somewhere."

John plucked a fresh weed to replace the one he had chewed. "The question is, where?"

"I still think we should go to Idar-Oberstein and have a look," Sarah said. "Measure Cellarius's height from whatever landmark we find called 'the elevation,' and start digging."

"We aren't sure a man's height is the measuring stick," David said contemptuously. "And if it is, we aren't sure the man in question is Cellarius. We have no idea what 'the elevation' means. We don't know what basks in fairy light, how prime numbers come into play, or the significance of a thousand and five, the number of Solomon's songs. There are too many things we simply don't know. Until we make more progress—a *lot* more progress—we would be wasting our time and money traveling to Germany. And we would be cutting ourselves off from some valuable research resources."

"Columbus was wrong," Sarah countered. "He sailed for the West Indies, not the Americas. Edison was wrong, too. He once tried bamboo as a filament for his light bulb."

David stood up, brushing the loose grass from his backside.

John allowed his eyes to rove briefly above Sarah's knees. The way she sat in the grass with her legs crossed and her skirt bunched up in her lap exposed the insides of her thighs. And for an instant, as she shifted to a more comfortable position, he glimpsed the white flash of underwear. He looked up at her face and was startled to find her watching him.

"Beautiful, isn't she?" David asked.

"Yes," John answered—before realizing David was showing them a wallet-sized photograph of Hildegard Weinbrenner's oil portrait. David's curious smile told John he was aware of the faux-pas.

"The source of the Prairie State ruby," David said. "This is the woman who passed the stone to her son, who passed it to his son, and so on, until it ended up in the Field Museum."

"Do we know anything about how *she* came to own it?" John asked. "I mean, it matters little how it got from Hildegard to Chicago. What matters is how Hildegard got her paws on it in the first place. If we can dig that up, it might help us find the rest of the stones."

"If the information isn't in the library system of the University of Maryland, it doesn't exist. I trust my people. I went to school there, you know."

John knew. He was sick of hearing about it. David was not a product UMD could boast of, so he ought not to have been boasting of UMD. John would have liked to compare the merits of attending a large, prestigious university, a degree from which served as an entry ticket to a successful career, with the merits of attending a small liberal arts college, one where students got lots of attention from faculty who were not burdened by Publish or Perish. But he knew he would be wasting his time.

"I have another question," Sarah said.

David sat back down in the grass. "God help us."

"Why would Cellarius go after Tavernier, a correspondent of his, rather than the king himself?"

"Louis XIV was untouchable," John replied patiently. "He was far too powerful for a lone adversary to take a shot at him directly. I suppose Cellarius could have wormed his way into court and tried an assassination, but obviously he considered it too difficult, or else he didn't aspire to martyrdom. At any rate, given the king's love for gemstones, the route Cellarius chose seems pretty fitting."

"Okay, why did the seventeenth-century trio—Cellarius, Hildegard Weinbrenner, and her boyfriend the cutter—bury the treasure at all?"

The men were silent. Finally John suggested, "To wait for the smoke to clear. If there truly was a connection between the stones and Louis XIV, agents of Louis might have come looking—might have traced them to the cutter, Jakob Langenbach. Besides, why is any treasure buried?"

"Why indeed?" Sarah asked. "I've got another one."

"Jesus." David mockingly covered his ears with his hands.

"Why would they recut only one stone? Why not all of them?"

"For all we know," David said wearily, "they *did* cut all of them. And if they didn't, maybe the Tavernier ruby was a test. They wanted to wait, as John said, for the smoke to clear before doing the rest."

"Ruby was considered good protection against the spells of witches," John recalled. "And at least two members of the trio were deep into that stuff. Maybe it's why they cut the Tavernier ruby into three pieces—to split it among themselves."

"Cellarius got one," David said, "and kept it to the end. Weinbrenner got another and passed it down the family tree. When we find the cutter we'll probably find the missing third, or at least the beginning of the path it took after he died."

"I have just one more question," Sarah said.

"Oh, for Christ's sake."

"Why would Cellarius, who lived in Hamburg and masterminded the theft, hide the stones in Idar-Oberstein, as everyone thinks he did? Stop making that face, David. If we're going to find the treasure, we'll need to pose the *whys* before the *wheres*."

"How profound," David said.

"She's right, you know," John said gently. "But I think the choice of Idar-Oberstein is clear. They had to hide the stones in a safe place. And Idar-Oberstein was the home of the person whose job it was to recut them." He laughed. "It's funny, but my family originally came from that area—three hundred years ago, as Anabaptist immigrants. And now *I* have a question: why didn't Jakob Langenbach and Hildegard Weinbrenner *also* know where the stones were hidden?"

"They did know," David answered. "They all knew."

"Exactly. Which is why we have to continue studying all the personalities involved, and why Sarah's questions are legitimate."

"Whatever you say, Johnny. Maybe you can learn about those personalities at Washington and Franklin, or wherever you went to college."

John closed his eyes and took a deep breath. "I'm beginning to wish you *did* have that ring on your finger. You'd still be locked up." He opened his eyes again. The look on David's face told him he'd crossed a line.

"That would be convenient for you, wouldn't it? You could use my input to find the stones all by yourself, and hit on my girlfriend while you're at it."

"What's that supposed to mean?"

"I see the way you look at her—and get together with her behind my back."

"Stay out of jail, Mr. Feinstein, and you won't have to worry about who's getting together with your girlfriend. You'll also be able to contribute more of that 'input' you keep bragging about, and perhaps help us make some progress."

David's expression darkened. "Are you suggesting I'm not pulling my weight?"

"The possibility occurred to me."

"Let me ask you this, Mr. Anabaptist. Remember that problem with the map grid you mentioned some time ago? How the grid didn't match anything past or present, didn't seem to make any sense?"

John looked away and said nothing.

"Do you know what I'm talking about?"

"Yes."

"Then look me in the eye and tell me the truth. Have you solved that problem?"

John swallowed, looked David in the eye, and said, "No, I haven't."

"Maybe you don't know, but I'm more than just a magician and a flimflam man. I'm also a student of character—a very astute student of character. You have to be, I think, to succeed in magic and flimflamming. And I know you just lied to me."

John looked away again.

"Don't go off on your own, John. You need me, or at least you will toward the end. We have to get along even if we don't like each other. And I think the best way for us to get along is for you to keep some distance between yourself and my girlfriend."

David stood up once more, grabbed Sarah by the arm, and pulled her into a standing position. "Come on," he said. "Meeting's over. And I'm hungry."

As they walked away, Sarah kept glancing back at John. It was obvious she regretted the turn of events—or perhaps the choice of man she was leaving with.

"Whether I see Sarah is up to Sarah," John called after them.

David shook his head without turning around. "No, my friend, it isn't. It sure as hell isn't."

TWENTY-FIVE

ELEANOR HALL PUT HER feet up on the conference table. She knew the men sitting at the table could peer up her skirt. She didn't care. Or rather, she did care, but knew the men wouldn't be caught dead looking. They *wanted* to look, and they wanted to be observed *not* looking, and the torment put them in exactly the state of mind Eleanor Hall wished them to be.

"The *Arkansas Democrat-Gazette*?" she asked rhetorically.

The men scratched their heads, drummed their pencils on the table, loosened their ties. By allowing their eyes to rove around the entire room, ceiling and floor included, they could justify that split second during which their eyes just happened, by statistical chance, to gaze up her skirt. But it could only last for a split second, then they had to look away.

Eleanor Hall raised her hands before her, palms up, as though she were weighing two objects. "The *Chicago Tribune*," she said, looking at her left hand. She looked at the right: "The Little Rock, Arkansas, *Democrat-Gazette*." She bobbed her hands slightly, then

221

brought them even with each other to show the two objects were equally weighted.

"*Tribune ... Gazette.*"

A fly buzzed in the room. The men took a serious interest in it.

"Chicago ... Little Rock." Again they weighed the same.

Eleanor Hall picked up a sheet of paper from the table. "The ultimate prone position?" she asked.

Silence.

"The foot of the elevation?"

The men flipped through notes, looked at their watches, cleaned their reading glasses.

"The Sieve of Eratosthenes?" Eleanor Hall opened her knees a few inches to increase the torment. "The gates of Hell?"

"Ma'am?" Justin had his hand up.

"Yes, Justin?" She adjusted herself in the chair, allowing her skirt to inch higher; the men sitting around the table adjusted themselves too.

"It's from the Bible, ma'am."

"What's from the Bible, Justin?"

"That line: 'The gates of Hell shall not prevail.' It's from Matthew, chapter sixteen."

Eleanor Hall dropped her feet to the floor and pressed the intercom button. "Bring me a Bible. Now."

———

WHEN JOHN FINALLY SHOWED up for work Monday, muttering about faulty alarm clocks, he couldn't help noticing all the rubbernecking that greeted his arrival. Cartographers on both sides of the aisle turned to watch as he hurried to his cubicle, as though getting there ten seconds sooner would make a difference. He had pulled another all-nighter, then had overslept trying to get a few minutes of shut-eye before going to work.

As he sat down at his PC, Annette rose from hers across the aisle. The concern on her face suggested she intended to alert him of unseen clouds above his head. But the timely and efficient appearance of Harry Tokuhisa interrupted her visit.

"Good morning," John said cheerfully. He looked at his watch. "Or maybe I should say good day."

"Let's go for a walk," Harry suggested.

They went down the hall to the chief cartographer's office, and Harry closed the door behind them. John had always liked visiting the office because it was decorated with prints of Harry's favorite map artists: Heinrich Berann, Richard Edes Harrison, Erwin Raisz, Hal Shelton, Tibor Tóth. But he had a feeling today's visit was not going to be a pleasant one.

"Have a seat." Harry directed him to a chair in front of his desk.

"Am I promoted—or fired?"

"Neither."

Harry sat down behind the desk and tapped his desk nervously. "Your work has been less than spectacular lately. Your production is down, both in quantity and quality. I was going to steer a new Bible atlas your way, but I've changed my mind."

"Oh, Harry, please don't say that."

"You need a vacation, John."

"I'm just a little burned out on … personal matters. I'll shape up. It's a temporary problem."

"Get some rest," Harry said. He would not look John in the eye. "Take some time off, then come back. I need you, but I need you happy and healthy."

"Is it as bad as that?"

Harry nodded.

"All right. Let me clean up a few projects, then I'll look at the calendar and schedule some time off. I promise."

"John, you don't understand. You're going on vacation. Starting today."

John felt his face flush. "I don't believe this. This is embarrassing."

"I'm the only one who will know. You've just decided to take some leave. People do it all the time. Normal people, that is. It just so happens you're going to do it today."

John gritted his teeth. "For how long?"

"As long as necessary. Don't make this hard for me, John."

"For *you*?"

Harry chewed a fingernail. "I've been under pressure to ... do something about you."

"I see. It *is* as bad as all that." He got up and went to the door. "All right, I'll try it your way for a couple of weeks. And when the little green spots—the first sign of map withdrawal—begin to appear on my skin ...?"

"Call first."

John returned to his cubicle to pick up a few personal articles before leaving the building. He looked around to see if the other employees were watching him. All were bent over their work.

The compilation sitting on his light table had been due five days earlier. He couldn't remember ever being overdue on a job; he would stay as late as necessary and work weekends just to get a project done on time. Someone else would have to finish this one.

Annette hovered in the aisle. "I'm sorry, John," she said.

"You know?"

She nodded. "Everyone knows."

"Great."

———

After leaving the office, John went home to change into Amish garb; he couldn't show up at the old homestead in English clothes. His sister Rebecca waited tables in Bird-in-Hand, and since it wasn't yet time for her to go to work, she would still be home, probably alone in the house. Anyone else who happened to be there would leave as soon as John entered. He was used to it: community members who ran into him in Lancaster always looked the other way. Some even crossed to the other side of the street.

The Lancaster County farm country was a patchwork of crops wrinkled on the land like an unmade bed. Homesteads were free of antennas, satellite dishes, and telephone lines; instead, windmills added rustic texture to the rolling terrain. And instead of the roar and sputter of a motorcycle or souped-up jalopy to rend the calm, horseshoes and harness leather played subtle notes that mingled with the laughter of small children.

On the Graf family farm north of Bird-in-Hand, a silo and an elevated birdhouse broke the skyline with crisp silhouettes. The cluster of farm buildings had not been planned in advance; rather, it had grown one building at a time to adjust to ever-changing needs. Its white picket fence had grown with it, zigzagging and meandering along the periphery of a luxuriant green lawn.

Clothing, mostly blue and black, hung on a wire to dry. A pair of horses stamped the earth outside their stable and breathed lustily in the clean country air. Parked next to them was a solemn gray buggy outfitted with a bright orange warning triangle.

Clarence Graf was in the habit of milking his cows before sunrise, to conserve daylight for other purposes. The barn could be lit with a propane lantern, but work in the fields required the sun. After lunch, he liked to do chores around the house. Late morning was therefore the most convenient time for John to visit; the old man would be nowhere in sight.

"Hello, Becca," John said hopefully when his sister answered the door.

Rebecca said nothing but left the door open as she returned to the kitchen.

Inside the kitchen, John found the walls still the same old shade of pale green, and still bare but for an unpretentious seed company calendar. He knew the rugs covering the plain wooden floor would be rolled up and stored away were visitors expected. They were hand-made wedding gifts, intended to last a lifetime, and could not be subjected to the risks of inconsiderate guests.

On the kitchen table was a copy of *The Budget*, an Amish newspaper. *Martyrs Mirror*, a thousand-page tome chronicling the persecution of Anabaptists in the sixteenth and seventeenth centuries, occupied a dry sink in the corner.

Rebecca sat stiffly in a straight-backed chair, facing away from John.

"How is Father?" he asked.

"He's the same." She spoke tersely, her lips closing promptly, clipping the very idea of unessential commentary. John was nevertheless happy to hear her strained words; she was the only family member who would talk to him.

"Does he ask about me? Has he mentioned my name?"

"No."

Clarence Graf had become a minister shortly before John left the community. Unlike most organized religions, whose leaders were appointed and trained, the Amish chose ministers by divine lot among the community lay population. When a position became vacant, an ordination ceremony took place during the next available mass. Each adult church member whispered a nomination to the deacon, who in turn passed it to the bishop. The bishop kept count of the nominations; any man receiving three or more became a candidate.

Songbooks were then lined up on a table, one for each candidate, and the men were asked to take their pick. Tucked into one of the songbooks was a piece of paper containing a verse from the Bible. The man who drew this book became the new minister.

He could refuse neither the nomination nor the selection, since during baptism he had vowed to accept the office should God bless him with it. Nor could he aspire to the office, not only because doing so was haughty, but because the lot, not a power play, chose the minister. The choice was in God's hands alone.

When Clarence Graf learned he had received the requisite three nominations, he stood before the congregation trying, John thought, to look humble. When the old man had opened his songbook and removed the slip of paper, his entire family and even some of the neighbors had shed tears. It was, after all, a great honor.

John watched his father's face quiver as he tried to contain the emotion. For despite admonitions against coveting the office, John knew he had wanted it badly.

To Clarence Graf, the greatest conceivable crime was leaving the church. But John was also sure his father could not reconcile himself to the loss of a son. Because the second greatest crime, in

Clarence's view, was disowning one's offspring. The dilemma was the root of all conflict in his life.

A large, bony man with thick gray hair, crinkled eyes, and powerful, broad hands, Clarence Graf preferred to suffer the dilemma rather than bend one way or the other.

"He should be less stubborn," John told Rebecca.

"You should be less radical."

"Come on, Becca. You of all people can appreciate the absurdity of this situation. Wasn't it you who complained to me—back when you talked to me, *really* talked to me—that because our society is patriarchal, the concessions to modernize always favor the men? The men get the modern farm equipment to make their work easier, the women continue to mow lawns with push mowers. If men mowed the lawns, you argued, they would surely allow gas-powered mowers."

"So I'm to abandon my family and faith over lawnmower technology?"

"Don't take a single example and expand it to represent the entire issue."

"Isn't that what *you* just did?"

"Besides, I didn't abandon my family or my faith. They abandoned me."

"Oh, yes. Anyone can see that. We're all here, and you're way over there. Obviously the community got up and walked away from you. That explains your isolation."

John didn't let the sarcasm get to him. His sister was suffering from the same opposing forces he had suffered from: a magnetism to the church and community, and a need to explore the outside world. The difference between the two siblings was that she wouldn't admit the latter. He knew she admired him for his voyage of discovery but couldn't bring herself to pursue one of her own. The only possible resolution, in her mind, was John's return home.

Rebecca was a plain Jane in her early twenties. She seldom let her auburn hair down, but when she did, it was long and lustrous and a real asset to her looks. She was waiting for the right man and the opportunity to have his babies. Forks in the road only spelled trouble: she preferred the road to be straight, narrow, and well illuminated. Her only real dilemma was having a choice at all.

"My isolation wasn't my decision," John said. "A house doesn't have to get up and move to lock out one of its occupants."

Rebecca finally turned to face him. "The doors aren't locked, John. All you have to do is knock."

"And change who I am, or else no one will answer."

"Not at all. Change back to what you were, to what you really are."

"Is that what you want? For me to give up the work I love, come back here, and sing the *Lob Lied* every Sunday? Wash my neighbor's feet every fall and spring?"

"It's what Father wants. And I think, deep inside, it's what you want too. Otherwise you wouldn't be here."

"But what do *you* want?"

She turned away again and faced the wall. "I want this never to have happened. And I know that can't be."

John circled around to the front of the chair and stood before her. He put his finger beneath her chin and tried to lift it, to make her look at him. But she resisted and stared down at her feet instead.

"I'll tell you what I want," he said. "I want you to come with me."

"No."

"It's a big, exciting world, and not nearly as wicked as they make it out to be."

"How would you know? You haven't ventured very far into it. Even when you went off to college, as you like to say, you didn't go any farther than F & M."

She's right, John thought. He had only moved from Bird-in-Hand to Lancaster, from farm labor to craft labor. He still acted like an Amishman, living as he did on the fringes of Amish country and lifestyle. And the further away from the church he got—especially in his pursuit of the lost Tavernier stones—the more the church tugged at him to return. The tension was increasing like a rubber band slowly stretching.

His desire to hunt for the stones was, on the surface at least, an expression of greed. He had to admit that. The hunt was disrupting the precarious order in his life, his carefully balanced arrangement of compromises. As such, it had a price. He looked at his little sister looking at her feet. He wondered if the price was too high.

"Why do you come here, John?" she asked. "We have the same argument every time you do. Why do you keep coming back, dressed like that?"

He bent over and hugged her. "To tell you the truth, I guess I want it both ways."

"So do I, believe it or not. But we can't have it both ways. Neither of us. I walk past jewelry stores too, you know. I see beautiful objects I have no right to even dream about."

"Please tell father I came by."

She looked up quickly, realizing he was about to leave. "I'll tell him, but he won't say anything."

"But he'll hear you." He kissed her on the forehead. She neither resisted nor returned the affection. "I love you, *Schatz*."

In the yard, John paused briefly and watched a gravity-fed water wheel turn a crank that ran a pump. He smelled pungent and familiar odors drifting over from the barn.

He drove past his old one-room schoolhouse, where at any given time three dozen or so pupils in all grades from one to eight studied arithmetic, science, history, and geography. It was here he had first learned English. He could remember his teacher, herself a distinguished graduate of the eighth grade, pronouncing words for the class to mimic.

School had been mostly about learning how to add and subtract and do practical things like tell time and tie shoes. It had been little more than an extended kindergarten, and he hadn't really learned anything.

Why, then, was he so fond of the memory?

———

While John was stepping into the Graf family kitchen, David was parking his VW Beetle on Nouveau Street in Lancaster, a couple hundred yards away from John's row house. He had circled the block several times to get comfortable in the neighborhood and to make sure John's car was nowhere around.

After climbing out of the Beetle, he pointed at its front left hubcap and said, "Stay."

No one answered when he knocked on John's front door. He was grateful for the small entry porch sheltering the door, because he didn't want anyone to see him breaking in. If someone should wander by, he would merely knock again and pretend to be waiting for an answer. And if John should suddenly appear at the door, he would pretend to want a meeting.

David already knew from his first break-in that the lock was a common pin tumbler. He unfolded his leather tool wallet and selected a diamond-shaped pick and a torque wrench. He was about to go to work when a wild idea suddenly occurred to him.

He turned the knob. The door opened.

All of John's work on the lost Tavernier stones was spread out on his coffee table or stacked on the floor nearby. David went through it methodically, separating documents and notes that invited additional scrutiny. John had clearly made more progress than he was willing to admit. The jackpot was a hand-written analysis of the grid pattern on Cellarius's last map—the very clue he claimed not to have resolved.

Hills on the Palatinate map seemed to have been placed arbitrarily. This was routine among cartographers of the time, according to John's notes, but not characteristic of Cellarius. As it turned out, terrain peaks appeared only in the *center* of certain grid squares and did not correspond in any way to the actual terrain.

And the pattern was suspicious. If one counted grid squares starting in the upper left corner of the map, and began with 1006, one greater than the number of Solomon's songs, the peaks appeared only in prime-numbered squares: 1009, 1013, 1019 …

The twenty-by-twenty array consisted of 400 congruent squares. There were 54 prime numbers between 1006 and 1406, therefore terrain peaks appeared 54 times in the array.

The pattern served as a guide to constructing a locator grille.

David copied all the information into a notebook. By the time he was finished, his stomach was lodging complaints with audible growls. He searched the kitchen for something to eat but found only microwave meals.

"How can the guy eat this shit?" he wondered aloud.

He got himself a drink of water, placed the unwashed glass back in the cupboard, and left the house after making sure the piles in the living room looked more or less the same as he had found them. When he returned to his car, its hubcaps were gone.

TWENTY-SIX

THE NEXT DAY, TAKING a walk in Lancaster Cemetery, John stood over the graves of the Winterbottoms, wishing they were still among the living. Wishing they—someone—could tell him how to travel two divergent paths at once. Or whether it was even possible.

But Ramsey and Rosalie were silent, as always. That was the problem with having dead friends: they didn't give a lot of advice.

As uncomfortable as it was to think about, he knew he would be joining them before too long. In the context of history—in the grand scheme of the universe—the time remaining to him was painfully short. And then, when his life was over and it was *his* turn to go into the ground, what legacy would he leave by having hunted for treasure?

Searching for the lost Tavernier stones was not the most noble of undertakings. Making maps was noble. Working with his hands was noble.

Farming was noble.

On his way home, an idea occurred to him. He rejected it instantly on the grounds it was impractical and unnecessary. But it kept creeping back into his consciousness, demanding fair consideration.

Burn the maps. Burn the notes. *Burn everything.*

He laughed out loud. It would solve most of his problems.

Although he felt he was close to finding the lost Tavernier stones, possibly even closer than anyone else, he was sure he would not be any happier with them in his pocket than he had been before he was aware of their existence. In fact, searching for them had made him unhappier than ever before.

When he arrived home, he found a counseling letter from Harry Tokuhisa. The man hadn't wasted any time. It wasn't enough merely to give a verbal warning; Harry had to cover his ass in writing. The letter warned John that if his performance didn't improve, he would be subjected to disciplinary action. It further noted that his appearance had become disheveled and that he sometimes mumbled incoherently when addressed. Perhaps, it suggested, he should seek professional help.

No wonder Harry had put his comments in writing. Their friendship was too strong for him to say them to John's face.

He went into the bathroom and looked at himself in the mirror. Disheveled? Well, maybe a little. But how could Harry say anything about him, when several of the English working in the building were—how could one put it politely—unkempt? But then, their appearances hadn't been changing. And they weren't going anywhere in the organization, either.

He found a book of matches in the kitchen. He wished he had a fireplace, but a metal trash can would have to do. He filled it with his notes, his work on the cipher, his sketches of the stones, everything.

He was about to shove all the Cellarius maps in as well, but changed his mind at the last second and condemned only the Palatinate map. The rest he held back for his collection. He carried the trash can to the patio behind the house.

Making maps was noble. Working with his hands was noble.

Farming was noble.

He lit a match.

The phone rang.

He hesitated. If he ignited the contents of the trash can and left to answer the phone, a fire would rage unattended on his patio. He blew out the match and went back inside.

"Hello, John." It was Annette. "I just wanted you to know we're all thinking about you."

"That's a comfort."

"Seriously. Some of us feel Harry's treating you a little harshly under the circumstances."

"What circumstances?"

"You know. Your ... condition."

"Oh, yeah. My condition."

"And we hope you can make good use of this vacation."

"It's not a vacation if it's involuntary."

"Regardless. Make good use of it, John. Your situation might be a little more serious than you realize. I know about the counseling letter. It's only the beginning."

After a pause John said, "You mean things are going to get *worse*?"

"If you don't ... turn it around."

"The condition."

"Right. Listen, the real reason I'm calling is to ask you out to dinner."

"Oh, that's sweet of you, Annette, but I don't know if this is such a good time. I have so much to do."

"Hear me out. I've invited you to dinner at least a dozen times before. You always say you're too busy. Now that you're suspended—let's go ahead and use the word—you certainly have time for a meal. So if you're going to turn me down again, at least come up with a different excuse. Or, preferably, the real reason."

John mulled it over. He wished Sarah were coming by tonight. She was the only person he wanted to talk to, the only one he was sure would listen. But given the circumstances—the *other* circumstances in his disintegrating life—no such visit was remotely likely.

"Okay," he said. Plenty of time to burn stuff later.

"Meet you at the Oasis in half an hour."

———

The restaurant was full. So was the bar, where John and Annette waited for a table. The noise in the bar obliterated all subtle inflections of speech and allowed only short, high-energy bursts of conversation.

John had been there once before, to attend an office party. He remembered tasting excruciatingly hot salsa and grinning at all the silly oriental fans poking out of cocktails.

He ordered a mineral water.

"Change that to a Long Island iced tea," Annette told the bartender. "And make it two."

"Iced tea, good idea," John said, raising his voice to carry over the din. "The caffeine will keep me alert."

Annette smiled. "You are truly precious."

They were awkwardly silent over their drinks. It was the first time they had ever socialized together outside the office, and John didn't know how to proceed. The look on Annette's face suggested she was eager to share something.

"You're going to be fired, you know."

"I am?"

"Harry's had a counseling session with you, and now the first letter. Company policy requires two letters be given. He's probably already drafted the second. I've seen this pattern before."

"I didn't know I was screwing up that bad."

"You're not. Not really."

"Harry and I have been friends a long time."

"It isn't Harry. It's someone higher. Someone who doesn't like you, maybe because of who you are. Your recent behavior has provided that person an excuse."

John stared into his drink. Annette wetted her lips and cleared her throat.

"I, on the other hand, have always been fond of you."

Misery loved company, and alcohol was no third wheel in the party, either. Three Long Island iced teas later, John was willing to admit the affection was mutual.

———

It was shortly before dawn in Mainz, and Frieda Blumenfeld had woken to the sound of dogs barking. She rolled over in bed to check on her husband: his steady breathing told her he was still sound asleep.

The dogs were howling as though they had treed a fox and wanted all the world to know of their accomplishment. Blumenfeld figured she wouldn't be able to go back to sleep, so she might as well get some work done. She put on a robe, boiled water for coffee, and selected a few pieces of classical music.

The barking grew louder. She turned up the music to drown it out.

———

In his store-top apartment in the *Innenstadt* of Mainz, Mannfred Gebhardt was also awake. He had stayed up all night, his weary eyes fixed on the papers strewn about his living room floor, his expression of earnestness gradually degenerating into one of distaste. Never before had he felt more useless than now. Except in jail.

He really ought to handle the materials more, he thought. Treat them roughly, make some creases and ragged edges. So Blumenfeld would think he'd actually been doing something.

The wall clock told him another dreary day was about to begin. He wondered what the old lady would discover today and call him stupid for not having discovered himself.

His gaze fell on Cellarius's last map, and his eyes, almost of their own accord, focused on the oblique pictorial illustration of Idar-Oberstein.

Then on the Felsenkirche, the Church in the Rock.

Finally on the steeple of the church.

He waited a full minute for what he saw to sink in, to make sure an alternative explanation would not snatch his idea away. Then he reached for the phone.

"What is it?" Blumenfeld asked flatly. The staccato beats of Beethoven's Fifth Symphony filled the pause that followed. In the background, Gebhardt could just make out the sound of dogs barking.

"I think I have something."

———

It was eleven o'clock in Philadelphia, and Sarah Sainte-James had just come out of the bath. David Freeman was already asleep in their bed. Sarah wrapped a towel around her head and settled down into David's beanbag chair in front of the television, but she was unable to follow the plot of the old movie. She was thinking about John Graf.

It was funny; she kept catching herself thinking about him. Ever since they'd met, she'd been intrigued by his gentlemanly manners, his sturdy ego, his unpretentious ways.

Intrigued? Maybe she should just say "impressed."

Most of the men she had known had been good looking and fast talking. Get-rich-quick schemers. Extroverted and bold. Like David. She had met David just as her life was bottoming out; her agency had dumped her, and she was working for Barclay Zimmerman, helping him switch stones. Zimmerman wanted his X-rated movie theater to be more profitable, and he wanted Sarah to earn the profits. David found her sitting on the steps of the theater one afternoon. Her face was in her hands, and she was weeping uncontrollably.

"Do you like Czechoslovakian food?" he asked.

She looked up at the stranger smiling down at her. "Huh?"

"Do you or don't you?"

"How the hell should I know?"

David was sharp. David swelled with confidence. David thrived on pipe dreams.

John, on the other hand, was a different breed. He wasn't necessarily the best-looking guy around, but he thought about what he was going to say before he said it, and he treated women with respect.

And he liked her. Without a doubt.

———

John was thinking about Sarah, a hundred kilometers to the west, in Lancaster. But he happened to be lying naked in Annette's bed. Next to him, also naked, was Annette.

Still breathing heavily from exertion, he adjusted the blanket to cover his exposed skin. Annette chose to be immodest. She sprang up and tried to tickle him playfully. When he failed to respond, she lit a cigarette and paced the room.

The sight of her ample breasts had, just minutes before, inspired John to babble inanely about her looks, her intelligence, her value to mankind. Now they were just mammary glands. At least, he thought with relief, he had finally—successfully—copulated with a woman.

On the wall of the bedroom was a framed copy of Cellarius's Palatinate map. This didn't surprise him; everyone had them now. Annette had stopped in front of the map and was studying it while she smoked her cigarette. John found himself wishing he had enough experience in these matters to exit quickly and gracefully.

"Pretty sloppy," Annette said.

"What do you mean?"

"He drew one of his point symbols poorly. Come here and look."

He pulled the blanket up to his neck. "I don't have to. You don't know what you're talking about. Cellarius didn't use point symbols. He always drew pictorials."

"Not here he didn't." She removed the frame from the wall and brought the map over to the bed. "Look at the church, at the steeple. The two pieces of cross aren't even perpendicular."

"It's a perspective view."

"Well, if it is, the perspective's wrong."

John sat up and looked. She was right. Idar-Oberstein was drawn from the perspective of a viewer high above the town and slightly southeast of it. But the cross representing the steeple of the Felsenkirche was drawn as though viewed from the northwest. The obtuse and acute angles that resulted from looking at right angles obliquely were thus reversed. Why had he never spotted this anomaly before?

"It's a point symbol," Annette argued. "There's no other way of classifying it, regardless of Cellarius's reputation. And the horizontal beam of the cross should be tilting the other way. So, as I said,"—she adopted a defensive tone—"it's *sloppy.*"

"Or intentional," John muttered in a voice that was already far away.

Annette took a deep drag from her cigarette and exhaled it slowly. "Why the hell would he do that?"

Downstairs, the front door suddenly banged open.

"Oh my God," she said. "Get up! It's my husband."

"Your *what*?"

"He wasn't due back until tomorrow. You have to go. *Now.*"

"Go? Where?"

"There." She pointed at the window.

John shook his head vigorously. "I'm not jumping out the window. We're on the second floor."

"There's a tree right outside. It's easy."

Annette raised the window, and a breeze sent curtains billowing into the room. Footsteps could be heard at the bottom of the staircase.

"I mean it, John. He's an Armstrong employee. Mid-level management. Heart-attack tenure track. Prone to high temper."

John threw off his blanket, went to the window, and looked out. There was, in fact, an oak tree in the yard. And one of its branches was indeed within jumping distance of the window. But he didn't know if he could reach it in his intoxicated state. And even if he could, there weren't any lower branches he could climb down to once he landed on it.

He looked at the lawn below. It would be an ugly fall. "Others have passed this way before," he said, "haven't they?"

The footsteps were at the top of the stairs.

Annette shoved his clothes into his arms. He stepped onto the window frame and perched.

The doorknob clicked.

He jumped with all his strength, letting go of his clothes in flight, and caught the branch with his outstretched arms. The window slammed shut behind him.

His body swung like a pendulum for a few seconds, the bark burning his fingers and palms. He tried pulling himself up to the top side of the branch, but the alcohol had sapped his energy. Instead he dangled, swaying from the effort. He tried again, throwing his right leg up as hard as he could, but almost lost his grip and only managed to scrape the inside of his knee.

He knew then that the only direction he would be going was toward the gravitational center of the earth. And that the earth's outer crust would get in the way.

Muffled conversation leaked from the bedroom. A man's voice grew increasingly louder, and John could hear Annette pleading in response. There was a rolling crash, as though a piece of furniture had been kicked over. After that, a long silence.

Then the snarling and lathering of dogs.

John looked down. His clothes littered the ground. The dogs—there were three of them—swept in from different directions, their bodies low to the grass, their shadows appearing as grotesque, cartoon-like figures racing for the trunk of the tree.

Now he knew he had to hold on as long as possible and pray for a miracle. Maybe the husband would go downstairs and Annette could reopen the window. But even if she did, he was already sure he wouldn't be able to work his way back into the bedroom.

His grip was weakening. Below him the dogs milled anxiously, panting and drooling, watching his every twitch. Light spilling from the downstairs windows glowed in their eyes and stretched their fidgeting shadows across the lawn. John didn't know the breed, but they reminded him of the cover of a book he had once read: *The Hound of the Baskervilles*.

As he shifted to get a better grip on the branch, the dogs whined in anticipation. One of them, shorter on patience than the others, tore viciously at his scattered clothes.

Then, insult upon injury: John heard the squeak of bedsprings coming from the other side of the window. Annette was going at it again, this time with her husband.

He tried to think of a prayer, but he couldn't come up with one suitable to the occasion. "Dear God, I've just had carnal knowledge of another man's wife, and for that I am truly sorry. To tell you the truth, I didn't even know she was married. I'm about to plunge to the ground, land in a crumpled heap, and get chewed by a pack of wolves. *Now would be a good time for you to intervene.*"

Hanging by his fingertips, he opened his mouth to yell at the window but stopped short; he would rather die than beg for help from a man whose wife he had just ... go on and say it ... fucked.

"At least, dear God, please let me get dressed first."

One of the dogs began to howl, and the others joined in. Their chorus rent the night air. The impatient one dug his claws into the trunk and tried to climb. But he only fell back, rolled once on the ground, and howled even louder.

John bit his lip and choked out a verse from the Bible: "'And I say also unto thee, That thou art Peter, and upon this rock I will build my church.'"

Why, here and now, of all places and times, would he utter such a thing?

The dogs quieted, their tongues lolling. They knew the moment was near.

John's mind went blank. There was nothing left to think. His palms were on fire and his fingers felt like they were coming apart at the joints. It was only a matter of seconds before he had to let go. At that moment he experienced the sudden clarity of thought that always seemed to come, like the eye of a storm, during high states of emergency.

"'When it is evening it will be fair weather,'" he cried, "'for the sky is red.'"

He made one last effort to hoist himself up.

"'And upon this rock I will build my church.'"

His hands slipped from the branch.

———

Frieda Blumenfeld finished her conversation with Mannfred Geb-hardt, turned off the music, then spent several minutes studying her copy of the Palatinate map. So, she thought, Gebhardt hadn't outlived his usefulness after all. Not yet, anyway.

Outside, the dogs had stopped barking. She went to the window and opened it. The sun was coming up. It was going to be another warm, beautiful day.

She continued the verse from Matthew: "And the gates of hell shall not prevail against it."

———

Barclay Zimmerman made sure all the theater's doors and windows were closed and locked before carrying his suitcase to the waiting taxi. "'And I will give unto thee the keys of the kingdom of heaven,'" he spoke under his breath, from the back of the cab.

The cabbie smiled into his rear-view mirror. "We're only going to the airport, sir. It won't cost that much."

———

Gerd Pfeffer was just going to bed after having pulled an all-night-er studying the Palatinate map. He wasn't at all concerned about getting up in time for work; he was taking a leave of absence, effec-tive immediately.

There was a stationary lump under the covers on the other side of the bed that could only be his wife.

"'And whatsoever thou shalt bind on earth shall be bound in heaven,'" he whispered. The lump didn't move.

Before coming to bed, he'd checked the wine cellar again and discovered a pattern; his wife and Mr. Dick hankered after Burgundies. If only they were bottles of poison instead.

As he was about to climb into bed, he did something he hadn't done since childhood. He knelt down on the floor and prayed: "'And whatsoever thou shalt loose on earth shall be loosed in heaven.'"

And what, Pfeffer wondered, would happen after the stones were loosed from the earth? What would he do then? Were there more cartographers out there soaking in bogs?

TWENTY-SEVEN

THE MEDIA, ALREADY UNABLE to keep up with new revelations about the lost Tavernier stones, had other news to report, news just as exotic: antique pottery was disappearing unaccountably from museums, galleries, and archeological inventories worldwide. Curators and collectors were stashing their pots in secret hiding places as though preparing for a foreign invasion.

Bible sales spiked, and one publisher's King James version rose to number four on the Amazon.com bestseller list. The religious right hailed the miracle as a portent of the Second Coming.

A new political party formed in Italy, as if the country needed one. Calling themselves "Pythagoreans," members consulted the mystical properties of numbers, especially primes, and abstained from eating beans. The wire services had a field day with it.

Poster printers kept churning out Cellarius's maps, unaware that soon, very soon, they would sell no better than last year's pin-up girls.

———

Frieda Blumenfeld thought her native country was most beautiful in June. The great oaks and lindens that reigned over Germany's arboreal kingdom shimmered in emerald green. Poppies, violets, and dandelions speckled the roadsides like dabs of fresh oil paint, and rape and lavender checkered farm fields with broad rolling quadrangles of gold and lilac. Her native land should have been a Mecca for impressionist painters. It wasn't, but it should have been.

The most beautiful day of the year, give or take the weather, tended to be the longest: the summer solstice, one glorious spin of the earth during the third week of June, when all vegetable matter unabashedly bared its chlorophyll to the sun. After which the days grew shorter again; the trees, flowers, and crops spent the next several months preparing for a dearth of light and heat. As far as Blumenfeld was concerned, winter really began in July.

While she and Gebhardt were packing the trunk of her BMW, she found herself wondering almost rhetorically why she chose to live in the city. It didn't take her long to remember: the upper crust lived in the city, the peasants lived in the country. She would rather be rich and surrounded by pavement than poor and barefoot in the grass.

"Idar-Oberstein will be crowded," Gebhardt warned. He dropped a crowbar and a large coil of rope into the trunk.

"So much the better. We don't want to stick out while we're casing a church."

What she didn't express was her concern that Gebhardt's mere presence could jeopardize the plan. True, he was clean cut and even a little yuppyish, and therefore didn't stand out physically. But his background and political views were known throughout the Federal Republic. Nor did it help that Blumenfeld herself was an ex-con. The closer the two of them got to the finish line, the more anyone watching the race would be able to scrutinize them.

She inspected the contents of the trunk. Besides the crowbar and rope were a pair of shovels (did he think she was going to dig too?), several large burlap bags (a little optimistic, to be sure), and even an air hammer equipped with a makeshift muffler. They had tested the air hammer the previous night: Gebhardt busted up some old bricks in Blumenfeld's cellar while Blumenfeld stood outside in the lawn. All she could hear was a low rumbling, which faded away as she crossed to the other side of the street.

"Excellent," she said, closing the trunk. "Have you prepared yourself to be as useful as possible?"

He patted the bulge behind his jacket's left front pocket.

"Excellent."

———

John took an MD-11 to Frankfurt, then boarded a train to Idar-Oberstein. The train chugged energetically around steep, round-topped hills that were dense with needle-leaf forests. There was no mistaking the Felsenkirche as the train rolled into town. John thought its photographs failed to do it justice; the church loomed prominently above the center business district like a floating apparition against a backdrop of gray stone.

The closer he came to Germany, to Idar-Oberstein, and to the Felsenkirche, the closer he felt to Johannes Cellarius.

Oberstein was well named. The town crouched under a sheer rock wall that leaned unsettlingly over the Hauptstrasse. The Felsenkirche was fused into the rock, 165 feet above the street. White with gold trim, it presented one stubby, unpretentious steeple as a fist might present its pinky finger.

John asked the taxi driver in halting *Hochdeutsch* if he knew of a place called "the elevation." The driver shook his head.

Some of the people walking on the sidewalks were carrying picks and shovels. Were they treasure hunters—or just ordinary gem prospectors? But then John remembered reading that the gem mines around Idar-Oberstein had played out long ago. The older residents of the town, those sitting on benches or loitering in small groups on the sidewalks, appeared to have been transported directly from the seventeenth century: the men wore plain peasant clothing with drooping, broad-brimmed hats, and they gazed at passing tourists with stony expressions, their suspicious eyes peering out of chiseled and weathered faces.

John checked into his hotel, just to drop his luggage off. It was still early afternoon. He was tired and battling the strange psychological weaponry of jet lag, but he planned to spend the rest of the day visiting the town.

The front desk clerk stared curiously at her new guest's arms and face, no doubt wondering about the dog bites. Anyone with that many blemishes was surely suffering from a malady she didn't want to catch. John had removed the Band-Aids on the plane and examined his wounds in a lavatory mirror. They could pass for a bad acne problem, he had decided. A *really* bad acne problem. Thank God for the beard.

———

In Philadelphia, it was the top of the morning, and David and Sarah were trying to reach John by telephone. Since parting with him uncomfortably on Sunday, David had been preparing another stone switch, including the cutting and mounting of a freshly crystallized piece of cubic zirconia.

251

Today was the big day—to borrow some jewelry, as Sarah liked to put it. But David was edgy about John's sudden invisibility, so he was on the verge of changing his mind about going out. Also, for reasons he couldn't articulate, his heart wasn't in the job anymore.

Despite his disagreements with John, and despite his jealousy of John's budding relationship with Sarah, he was willing to admit that alone, he and Sarah would never find the lost Tavernier stones.

"Try again," he said to Sarah. "Give it a good feminine ring. If he thinks it's you, he'll answer."

"I tell you, nobody's home."

Nevertheless, she dutifully dialed the number again. Then she held the receiver up so David could hear it ring. And ring, and ring.

"So he's out for a walk," she said, hanging up. "Or he's shopping or something. Be patient. He's never gone for very long."

"I know. That's what worries me."

"Are we on today?"

"No, it doesn't feel right. I want to wait until we have a chance to talk to John."

"That salesman is expecting us."

"He's not going anywhere. Neither is his stone, it's too big. We can put the job back on the schedule anytime we want. I just don't think I can work today with all this shit on my mind."

"Then I can get out of this," she said, beginning to remove her miniskirt. "All dressed up and no place to go."

"I was wondering who it was you were dressed up for."

She stopped and asked, "What is that supposed to mean?"

He closed his eyes and shook his head. "Nothing. Sorry."

"David, remind yourself who it is that makes me wear this crap."

"You're right. Of course. Sorry."

"Why don't you do something relaxing, like practice one of your magic tricks? Or cut something on the lap?" She finished removing the skirt and went into the bedroom to put it away. Then she came back in cut-offs and a T-shirt and made herself busy in the kitchen.

David got up wearily, shuffled over to a corner of the living room, and lifted the lid of his footlocker. He fiddled for a while with the magic paraphernalia inside, listening to Sarah banging pots and pans. There was always fiddling to do, what with pockets to sew into handkerchiefs, double walls to glue into paper bags, false bottoms to build, ropes to core, cards to mark, and sometimes bunny droppings to clean up.

"You haven't seen Zimmerman lurking around, have you?" he called toward the kitchen.

"No, why?" Sarah called back.

"Just a feeling. The last time I spoke to him, he seemed confident he was on to something."

She joined him at the footlocker, wiping her hands with a dish cloth. "He's the least of your worries."

"He wants the stones."

"Only one of them."

"Believe me, when he sees the entire lot, he'll want all of them."

"I know the man, remember?" She waited until David made eye contact. "He only wants the one. It's all he needs in the world. That, and a haircut."

David kicked the footlocker, then picked up the phone but dropped it again without dialing. "Where the fuck are you, you worthless Amishman?"

"He'll turn up. He's seldom ever been farther than walking distance from home."

"Well, maybe he walked off the deep end this time."

Sarah stared at the phone for a moment. "You've just given me an idea who to ask."

———

John left his hotel on Otto-Decker-Strasse and walked down the Hauptstrasse toward the central business district of Stadtteil Oberstein. At first, the storefronts failed to reveal any evidence of the town's primary industry: there were cafes, travel agencies, tobacconists, florists, restaurants, confectionaries—the ordinary trappings of an ordinary tourist trap—but not a single rock shop.

Then the Hauptstrasse took a dip as it approached the center of Oberstein, and the goods on display finally began to change. The closer John came to the central Marktplatz, the deeper he stepped into the greatest permanent concentration of retail minerals, gems, and jewelry in the Western Hemisphere.

If it could possibly have been made out of rock, it was sold in the shops and from barrels and baskets on the sidewalks in front of them. Mineral specimens, everything from thumbnails to museum pieces. Long crystal shards projecting from matrix. Crystal balls. Uncut gemstones, by the piece for the collector, by the kilogram for the cutter. Loose faceted stones by the scoop. Worry stones. Fossils: Devonian fish etched in sedimentary rock.

So many beads dangled in long strands from street-side racks that a passer-by could grab and carry away a thousand semiprecious pebbles in one greedy fist. Some shop windows were crowded with geodes almost large enough to crawl into, like crystal caves; others bore sorted piles of raw emeralds, rubies, and sapphires, arranged in serpentine curves to portray rivers of precious stone.

Pet rocks. Amber, complete with pet insects, fifty million years old. Bookends and paperweights, the shape dictating the function. Cameos. Vases that couldn't help looking like urns. Urns.

Shops crowded the Hauptstrasse as it wound around the Marktplatz. They jostled one another for choice spots beneath the Felsenkirche. They perched on both sides of the Kirchweg as it climbed the steep hill to the church. The half-timbered architecture sitting atop glass-and-steel foundations seemed to reflect the calm, purposeful disposition of the men and women who made a living fashioning stone.

There was a fountain in the Marktplatz, its centerpiece a bronze statue of a miner boy dressed in rags. The boy sat on a rock ledge, leaning back on one hand and hefting a large transparent gemstone in the other, gazing at it dumbfoundedly. The expression was excusable, given that the rough gem in his fist probably outweighed the fist. He was free of the mine now, removed to the center of a market square, and was almost without exception ignored by the many tourists drinking beer there, probably none of whom could distinguish good rough from bad. Beer, on the other hand, they were better trained to judge.

Jewelry, too. Finger rings. Toe rings. Arm and ankle bracelets. Necklaces. Necklace lengtheners. Necklace shorteners, to shorten necklaces lengthened by necklace lengtheners. Necklace slides, for people who couldn't decide which way to go. Earrings. Lockets, with nothing to lock. Medallions, for people who had nothing to proclaim, to proclaim something. Stick pins to stick somewhere.

John paused in front of one shop's display window to watch a diamond cutter labor at fashioning a round brilliant. The man was thoroughly engrossed in his handiwork: a stone no bigger than a pea. John would have expected the diamond to be at least big enough to handle with bare fingers, but this one was locked in the jaws of a clamp and he could hardly see it.

The cutter was polishing one of the facets. He kept lifting the clamp and examining the stone briefly through his loupe before returning it to the lap and continuing with the same facet. After several minutes of watching, John grew bored and moved on.

He approached an idle policeman and asked him whether he had ever heard of a landmark known as "the elevation." The policeman slowly shook his head.

He toured the Heimatmuseum in the Marktplatz and bought all the books and brochures they had. He asked the saleslady about "the elevation," but she had never heard of any such place. She called into a back room and asked the manager. He came out and they both faced him, shrugging and shaking their heads. It could mean the rock promontory that seated the church, they suggested, but it had never been known specifically by that name.

They gaped at his complexion as he thanked them and left the museum, no doubt waiting for the door to close before commenting on his acne problem.

He wandered back into the open market square, selected an outdoor Stübchen facing the statue of the miner boy, and ordered a beer. Its bitterness surprised him. The plastic furniture of the Stübchen seemed to suit the clientele, a knick-knack, rubbernecking crowd of biddies and balding, cabochon-bellied men.

He was delaying his visit to the Felsenkirche, because evening was approaching and he didn't think he could do justice to it. Also he wanted to examine the new books and brochures first. But mostly he was just afraid that if he found nothing in the church, he would be in a stump about what to do next.

Perhaps he had acted irrationally. If he didn't find a place reliably known as "the elevation," he wouldn't have any idea where to dig. Somehow he had thought it would be easier than this. That it would simply be a matter of asking, of being shown some prominent feature of that name, probably associated with the church. And then of measuring a man's height—his own would do—from the base of the feature and putting a freshly bought shovel to work. Now that it didn't look so easy, he was beginning to feel foolish.

He sipped his beer and stared long and thoughtfully at the miner boy holding the rough gemstone he had just lifted from the ore at his feet. The untold story of the statue was clear: although the boy had freed the gem, the gem had also freed the boy.

Johannes Cellarius had been there; John could feel his presence, even separated as they were by more than three centuries. The great cartographer had visited this very spot.

———

One hundred sixty-five feet above, in the center aisle of the Felsenkirche, Frieda Blumenfeld and Mannfred Gebhardt admired the stained glass windows on the south wall of the nave.

"There it is," Gebhardt whispered.

"I see it."

"I'm the one who discovered it."

"Yes, you are."

Gebhardt turned to inspect a group of paintings hanging on the wall behind the altar. Their polished tempera surfaces glowed in an almost luminescent cast of gold. "And right up there in front of us, clear as day—"

Blumenfeld grabbed his arm and pushed it back down. "We best not be pointing."

"So," he shrugged. "Nothing to it. We come in tonight, dig it up, and we're out of here."

"No, I think we'll go home now and wait."

"For what?"

"For the summer solstice. It's only three days away."

"You're not being superstitious, are you?"

"No, just efficient. I'm just being efficient."

TWENTY-EIGHT

The next morning, John walked down the Hauptstrasse to the Marktplatz and began the long, panting climb up the stone steps of the Kirchweg. Rock shops lined the way. Baskets overflowing with trinkets sat outside their entrances, serving as bait to lure exhausted climbers inside.

At the top of the steps, the path leveled out onto a platform and came to a stop in front of an arch-shaped iron gate. The gate was bolted to the face of the rock and looked like a portal to the mountain itself. Which, in fact, it was: it opened to a tunnel that bored through solid rock to the church entrance.

From the platform, John had a clear view of both the town below and the cliff above. Nets and wire meshes clinging to the cliff face prevented injury from rock fall, a clear and present danger. The tunnel itself, according to one of John's brochures, had been built specifically to protect people from being struck by falling rocks on their way to church.

He studied the gate before entering the tunnel. It had a lock and would almost certainly be locked at night.

Inside the tunnel was another stone staircase. Fluorescent lamps built into the handrail lit the arch-shaped passage and spread erratic shadows across dank, rough-hewn walls. The unfinished surfaces gave John the impression the builders had merely placed their dynamite charges, lit their fuses, and walked off the job.

At the end of the tunnel was a wooden door that opened to the church itself—a door that *also* locked. John hadn't considered this detail in any of his mission planning. What if, after all his effort, he should be stopped by simple locks on gates and doors? He entered the church, paid the admission fee of two euros, and sat in a pew close to the altar.

The stained glass windows on the south wall of the nave were the first objects to grab his attention. Pastel rectangles, or "bricks," cascaded down narrow, Gothic-arched panes of glass. In the easternmost window, the one closest to the altar, the pattern was interrupted by the image of a cross. The cross was skewed *exactly* as Cellarius had depicted it on his map.

Cellarius never employed point symbols, only pictorials. But the cross *was* a point symbol. The window therefore had to be a clue, albeit a subtle one, directing searchers to the Felsenkirche in Idar-Oberstein—if, in fact, the searchers got far enough in their search to visit the Felsenkirche in Idar-Oberstein and see the window.

So maybe Sarah had been right: maybe they should have come earlier. Maybe all they needed to find the lost Tavernier stones was contained in this church.

Ten or fifteen other people were milling about inside; some he recognized from the breakfast room of his hotel. He left his pew and did some exploring.

Dozens of sarcophagi lined the perimeter of the church, each one gouged from a solid block of sandstone. They extended lengthwise away from the wall and were packed closely together, leaving little elbow room for their dead occupants. John guessed that everybody important had been buried inside the church until the church ran out of room for them.

One branch of the balcony overlooked the north side of the nave, opposite the stained glass windows. Portraits of the apostles hung from its balustrade. Between the front pew and the altar, the portraits appeared in the order Judas, Matthäus, Marcus, Johannes, and Simon.

John paused under the portrait of his namesake and looked for similarities in the cloaked figure. He didn't find any: the man in the painting, the only apostle depicted without a beard, had a scrunched, unhappy face. In the background, ominously, dark clouds roiled in the sky.

Were these artifacts important? he wondered.

At the rear of the north balcony was a wishing well. It was little more than a hole in the wall, lined with bricks, protected from the public by an iron grating. A shallow pool inside contained hundreds of copper coins, many already green from oxidation.

John took a penny from his pocket, tossed it into the pool, and wished for "the elevation."

Finally he approached the altar. It consisted of a simple marble-topped table, a Bible, and a bouquet of flowers. Tall brass candlesticks rose from the floor on either side. No more ornamentation was necessary: the works of art on the wall behind the table, paintings created by the so-called Master of the Oberstein Altar, commanded center stage.

They were presented in a triptych. The two side panels told of Christ's audiences with Caiaphas, Pilate, and Herod, and showed him being nailed to the cross. One large painting, of Christ being raised on the cross, occupied the central panel.

John turned around and scanned the small church; the crowd had thinned. A few remaining people loitered in the outer aisles, inspecting one artifact or another. The ticket salesman at the church entrance sat with his back to the altar and seemed to be nodding off.

He quietly stepped over a "no trespassing" rope, walked onto the altar, and examined the paintings more closely.

Their surface layers had long since cracked with age, although the egg yolk medium continued to shine. Gold paint filled all the backgrounds, creating flat planes that shimmered luminously, as if the sun were saturating skies and interior spaces with its golden rays. Contrasting red and blue garments draped the figures, the pigments still vivid six hundred years after the artist had applied them.

The figures wore halos and posed stiffly; both habits were characteristic of Byzantine art. But their facial expressions were alive with a vitality characteristic of early Gothic art. The style reminded John vaguely of Giotto.

Some of the facial expressions were highly exaggerated. Some were outright grotesque. Fingers stretched far beyond their natural means, lending a surreal quality to poses and gestures. The perspective was awkward throughout; more than a century would pass before artists of the High Renaissance learned to arrange space realistically on their canvases.

The central panel of Christ being raised on the cross was the eye-catcher of the group. The Savior, a bloated figure swathed in deathly pale flesh, gazed down at his tormentors with an expression of bottomless sorrow. Disciples wept, soldiers jeered, women clutched one another in supportive embraces; all participated in a dynamic tableau that had rightfully earned the anonymous painter a reputation for being years ahead of his time.

John felt, as he did every time he viewed an image of the crucifixion, that the artist was saying far more than words could possibly convey.

"A-*hem*." Someone behind him cleared his throat loudly and pointedly. John turned to find the ticket salesman beckoning with an impatient finger, ordering him to leave the altar. He returned to his pew.

More people entered the little church. They whispered in respectful silence among themselves, the whispers contributing to a low, sibilant din.

"The elevation" still mystified John. *Somebody* must have been familiar with the term, but nobody had been willing to surrender any information. Were people merely keeping clues to themselves? It couldn't mean the mountain itself—the one into which the church was built. The feature was too big; there was no reasonable way to measure a man's length from it or to know what point to measure from. But Cellarius's clues all pointed to the church, and the church was in the rock. It was the only elevated, intact structure in town.

John felt a sudden urge to just give up and go home, and he responded briefly to the impulse by actually rising a few inches from his seat before plopping back down again. What business did he have, anyway, lurking in the house of God, searching for treasure? And what business did he have scheming to remove that treasure, should he find it?

He knelt on the pew's padded floor beam and covered his face with his hands. A shiver ran through him, all the way down to his Anabaptist roots. Adventure was one thing. Stealing from a church was altogether another.

The nave was filling up again. Someone sat down to his right, and immediately afterwards he felt the presence of someone to his left. Probably he should go back to his room and study some more. He removed his hands from his face and turned toward the right to excuse himself. The person sitting next to him was David Freeman.

"What the hell are *you* doing here?" John demanded.

"Shh. Don't swear in a church, goddammit."

John looked to his left. The person flanking him was Sarah Sainte-James. She made the sign of the cross and winked.

"So," John said, turning back to David, "you found me."

"Yeah, we left Philadelphia yesterday and arrived in Germany this morning. Got the stuff yet?"

"Would I be sitting here if I did?"

"As religious as you are … maybe. Maybe you're begging forgiveness before skedaddling to Rio with the loot."

"Hardly. How did you know I was in Idar-Oberstein?"

"Sarah knew a travel agent with the right contacts. Apparently, only one John Graf boarded a flight out of Philadelphia in the last few days."

"Oh … how did you know I was in the church?"

"I can read a map, same as you." He stood up. "We're due for another review session. I assume you have a hotel room waiting for us." As he turned to leave, he fixed a stern glare on John. "And next time you schedule a field trip, make sure you apprise your partners in advance, okay?"

Sarah waited until David's back was turned, then smiled warmly at John. As she passed him, her arm brushed against his, the touch lasting a second longer than chance contact would suggest.

———

David and Sarah took a room next to John's in the Pearl Hotel. That afternoon, the three got together in John's room and spread his research materials on the floor.

"This is everything I've collected since I got here," John said. "You can go through it if you like."

"Have you been through it?"

"Six or seven times."

"And you found no mention of—"

"An elevation? No."

"Where are the local maps?"

"Here." He dug them out of the pile.

"I'm going to look these over," David said.

"You won't be the first."

They spent the rest of the afternoon poring over the materials, occasionally muttering expressions of impatience and frustration. John was happy for the company; getting nowhere was a lot easier with companions who weren't getting anywhere either. At one point, David asked him, "Did you ever come up with anything new about the grid pattern on the Palatinate map?"

John didn't glance up from his work. "No."

"Nothing at all?"

He looked straight at David. "Nothing. At all."

"Too bad."

"I have a question," Sarah said. "We're working under the assumption the legendary chambers beneath the church really exist, and the stones are somewhere in the chambers. But why were the chambers cut to begin with? The church wouldn't have created them for witches, and witches couldn't have made such an effort without the church knowing. Are we rationalizing their existence for our own convenience?"

Glad for the interruption, John picked up a brochure about the Felsenkirche and scanned it until he found the relevant passage:

"'The castle above the Felsenkirche,'" he recited, "'now mere ruins on the peak of the rock, constitutes what remains of the former residence of the Earls of Oberstein. In the mid-eleventh century, two brothers named Wyrich and Emich shared power over the region. Both sought the hand of one Bertha of Lichtenburg, but Emich, the younger of the two, eventually won her affections. Wyrich, upon hearing of their wedding plans, pushed his younger brother out a castle window to his death on the rocks below.

"'Later, Wyrich confessed his crime to an abbot, who instructed him to build a church on the spot where Emich died. According to legend, living quarters were cut out of the rock beneath the church to make a prison for Bertha, and perhaps other mistresses, but the existence of such chambers has never been verified.'"

John handed the brochure to Sarah, then picked up a book and thumbed through it for more information.

David studied John's face. "I don't mean to be insensitive," he said, "but those marks look like dog bites."

John laughed nervously. "It's just an outbreak of acne."

"It looks more like an outbreak of rabies."

"Did you see these pictures?" Sarah asked. She was engrossed in the brochure. "The paintings behind the altar are magnificent. We should have stayed longer and taken a closer look."

"Glad you think so," David said. "They didn't do anything for me. Dammit, John, those *are* dog bites, aren't they? What the hell happened to you?"

"This one here," Sarah continued, "the one in the middle, *The Elevation of the Cross*, is really moving. In the face of Jesus, you can see agony and serenity at the same time."

"Splendid. Come on, John. Out with it. What happened?"

John held his breath. He looked up slowly from the book he was reading. "What did you say?"

"I said, out with it."

"No, I mean Sarah. What was the title of the painting?"

"*The Elevation of the Cross*," she repeated.

David snatched the brochure from her hands. "Holy shit."

TWENTY-NINE

"Slow down," John said. "We can't be sure that's the solution."

"No, we can't," David acknowledged. "But it fits, and it's inside the church, and it's all we have at the moment. As soon as the sky gets dark, we go back to the church. And we dig."

John looked outside at the gathering dusk and realized they would be carrying out their new plan within the hour.

As though sensing hesitation in the others, David fished a copy of the solved cipher from the mess on the floor and held it up for them to see:

Extend in the vltimate prone poſition
From the foote of the elevation …
… baſketh in fairie lighte
Of Apollo's reſplendent apogee
On the feſtivall of his higheſt aproche
Then drink from the Sieve of Eratoſthenes
Sing more songes than Solomon
And deſcend to treaſvre
For the gates of Hell ſhall not prevayle

"The text that's missing is missing between the words 'elevation' and 'basketh,'" he argued. "There's room for the phrase 'of the cross' as well as several more words telling us what basks in fairy light."

"What *does* bask in fairy light?" Sarah asked.

"I don't know. Maybe the painting itself. If I'm right, we measure a few feet away from the wall on which the painting hangs. We dig into the floor. We find the lost Tavernier stones. We go home and sleep the carefree sleep of small children."

"And if you're wrong?"

"We go back to the drawing board. We've lost nothing."

"That floor is made of stone, you know," John said.

"I suspect it's just covered with tiles. We pry a few of them up and the going gets easy."

"Into solid rock?"

"It'll be weathered. Or we'll break into the chambers Sarah keeps reading about. If the treasure's there, it'll be accessible. If we find the digging impossible, that means the treasure isn't there. We either find the lost Tavernier stones or we eliminate a possibility. Either way, we make progress."

John looked at Sarah, who only raised her eyebrows; then back at David, whose eyes gleamed with confidence. There was no refuting his logic.

———

They left their rooms as the last light was dying in the sky. John couldn't help feeling like a gunslinger. He followed his two companions out of the hotel and the three walked down the Hauptstrasse abreast, as though playing in an old Western.

Storefronts were dark. Drop-down aluminum gratings shielded plate glass windows from thieves. Streetlights just coming on held the impending darkness at bay but failed to temper a mood of inaccessibility reinforced by all the security in place.

A pick was strapped to John's back, and a shovel to David's. Both wore jackets to cover the implements despite the warm night air. Sarah's purse was full of hand tools. She regarded the two men with a smile and said, "You guys look like a pair of hunchbacks."

The Hauptstrasse was dormant: a distant car horn, a train chugging out to a neighboring village, and a child crying in an apartment above one of the shops were all that competed with the echo of three pairs of feet making measured but resolute steps toward the Church in the Rock.

Here and there, a light came on behind a curtained window; otherwise, Oberstein showed no signs of nightlife. The town had drained quickly of tourists as dusk had gathered, and the town's workers had hurried home on their heels; the streets were all but deserted.

Nevertheless, John could still smell the lingering odor of leather and stale baked goods. As the Hauptstrasse sloped down toward the Marktplatz, the smells dissipated and the trio began to pass rock and mineral shops. They too were buttoned up, their sidewalk displays tucked in, leaving the street looking bare. Some of the jewelers had left their lights on to deter burglars, but John wondered how anyone would distinguish between a burglar and a janitor. Others had merely covered their display cases with blankets to inhibit temptation.

When the three reached the Marktplatz, they cut across its northwest corner and climbed the steps to the Felsenkirche in single file, with David in the lead, Sarah following, and John bringing up the rear. The great rock that loomed over the town of Ober-stein was just an opaque shadow jutting into the sky. The church itself stood out against the shadow as a soft white glow. Castle ruins on the rock's peak, former home of Wyrich and Emich, were awash in orange spotlights. High above both structures, stars crowded the heavenly arena like so many impassive observers.

Lampposts on the path were rare, so John had to measure his steps carefully, mindful of variations in the thickness of the stone slabs. Where lights did shine, the well-worn slabs glistened as though wet.

David stopped the train once, just long enough to check his watch, then led the rest of the climb to the cobbled platform in front of the tunnel gate. The town below was dappled with white lights that flickered like mirror images of the stars above.

The arch-shaped gate consisted of thick bars of iron painted black. Ambient light penetrated a few feet into the tunnel, then retreated abruptly, leaving a solid wall of darkness.

John pulled on the gate handle. It was locked. "Here's an obvi-ous obstacle," he said.

David removed a leather wallet from his back pocket and unfolded it. Inside was an array of picks and torque wrenches in an assortment of shapes and sizes. He took a penlight from his shirt pocket, got down on one knee in front of the gate, and shined a thin beam on the lock.

"Now the job starts to get ugly," John said uncomfortably.

David shrugged. "You want me to ring the doorbell?" He chose a pick and a torque wrench from the wallet, inserted the pick into the keyhole with his right hand, the torque wrench with his left. Then he raked the pick in and out of the keyhole with a gentle sawing motion.

A full minute passed. John said, "When they do this in the movies, it only takes a few seconds."

"You're right," David answered, "but we're not in a movie."

"Where did you get your experience with this kind of thing?"

"By breaking into Amish homes."

John smiled. "Oh, yes. I remember. That's how we met."

"It's a great way to make new friends." David stood up. "Now try it."

John pulled on the gate. Nothing happened.

"Push," David said.

John pushed, and the gate swung open.

They went up the steps through the tunnel, again in single file. David's penlight scarcely brightened the interior, making John feel like he was in a subterranean cavern.

The second door, an ordinary wooden one, was the last obstacle between them and the church. David dropped to one knee again and performed the same operation as he had on the gate. Within seconds, he pushed down on the stainless steel handle, and the door popped open.

"Sometimes reality does imitate Hollywood," he said. He pulled the door wide open, and the three entered the church.

By now, John's eyes had fully adjusted to the darkness. Light emanating from the town below leaked through the stained glass windows on the south wall and softly illuminated the interior.

"It's best you turn the flashlight off," Sarah told David. "Someone might see it from the street."

David turned off the penlight and put it in his pocket.

They went down the aisle and stepped over the "no trespassing" rope, onto the altar. The gold paint on the triptych glowed even in the dim light, as though it were radiating energy of its own.

John and David nodded to each other grimly, then took opposite ends of the marble-topped table sitting in front of the triptych's center panel—*The Elevation of the Cross*—and moved it into a corner.

"I'm of average height," David said, "so I'll get down and do it."

"Your height isn't your only average dimension," Sarah said. "Sorry, I couldn't resist."

After taking off his jacket and unstrapping the shovel, David laid down on his back and centered himself on the painting, pressing the bottoms of his feet against the wall. He rested his head on the stone tiles, then lifted it so John could mark the spot with a quarter.

"There," John said, pointing at the coin as David stood up. "That's where we hypothesize the lost Tavernier stones to be."

"We'll lift that tile," David said, "and the eight surrounding it. It'll give us enough room to drop down into any space we uncover, and to compensate for errors in pinpointing the location." He rummaged through Sarah's purse until he found a hammer and a large regular screwdriver. "There's no grout, so I think I can get them up without breaking them. Which will make it less likely anyone will discover our work."

He placed the edge of the screwdriver between two of the tiles and lifted the hammer to strike it. Then he hesitated.

"What's wrong?" John asked.

"I'm just recalling what happened to the last guy who did this—he dangled from the end of a rope."

He and John took turns chiseling until they had loosened all nine tiles and stacked them off to the side. John frequently looked over his shoulder—at the closed wooden door across the nave, at the empty pews arrayed before him, at the darkened balcony above.

He couldn't rid himself of the sensation that someone was watching them. The sooner this job was over, he thought, the better.

When the tiles were up, what lay beneath looked like weathered rock, as David had predicted. It was sandy, with little or no humus or evidence of vertical development.

The two men went to work with pick and shovel. But they didn't get far: the weathered material turned out to be fill from a previous dig. Someone—John guessed the man who was hanged in 1858—had dug in the same place before. At any rate, when they tried to go beyond the limits of the previous dig, about three feet down, they ran into solid rock—as John had predicted.

"Maybe the hangman got it all," he suggested.

"Maybe nothing was here to begin with," David countered. "Maybe we were naïve to think it would be as simple as lying down in front of a painting and pounding on a screwdriver."

"There's something I don't get," Sarah said. "If the tiles were pried up once before, why weren't they loose when *we* got to them?"

"Who knows?" David answered. "The job might have been discovered and repaired."

"Don't forget that the church has been remodeled extensively over the years," John said. "The tiles might be relatively new. David, maybe we just dug in the wrong spot."

"Somebody else dug here. Was he wrong too?"

"Maybe he found the stones. Or maybe the church is just a source of more clues, rather than the actual location of the stones."

David brushed dust from his pants. "If the stones were found, they would have been disseminated. They'd be in circulation. The Great Mogul diamond would be in a museum, rather than missing in action. If the lost Tavernier stones were out and about, believe me, I'd know it."

"Maybe they were removed and hidden somewhere else."

"Hell," Sarah said, "we could 'maybe' for the rest of our lives. If they're not in this church, we're not going to find them."

"She's right," John said. "It's like the drunk searching for his lost keys at night. If the stones aren't here—under the only streetlamp we have—they're nowhere within our grasp."

David made a show of peering into the empty hole. "The stones aren't here, John."

They filled the hole back in, replaced the tiles, and swept up as best they could with their bare hands. Then they carried the altar table back to its place in front of the triptych.

All John felt as they departed the church was relief that the ordeal was over. The others were silent and pensive. On the way back to the hotel, there was none of the childlike enthusiasm that had characterized their search up till now.

———

Later that night, after he had spent another two hours poring over his notes, John changed into pajamas, brushed his teeth, and climbed into bed. Just as he was reaching to turn out the light, he heard a soft knock at the door.

When he opened it, he found Sarah standing in the hallway, wearing nothing but a nightshirt. Her weight shifted from one foot to the other, and her eyes looked everywhere but into his. The nightshirt, a man's T-shirt enlisted for the purpose, did not cover any significant portion of her thighs.

"David's asleep," she said.

"And?"

"And, I just thought, you know …"

Light spilling into the hallway from his bedside lamp highlighted the contours of her face. She shifted her weight again, raised her shoulders in a shrug, and met his gaze.

He opened the door wider and stepped aside. She entered the room.

Moments later, he turned out the light.

THIRTY

THE NEXT MORNING, JOHN, David, and Sarah reentered the church as soon as it opened for tourists. John could tell something was troubling David, but David made no effort to share what it was. He avoided eye contact and spoke only in short, crisp sentences.

So he knows, John thought. So he wasn't asleep after all. Then again, maybe we woke him with all the noise.

They loitered in the church for a few minutes with their hands in their pockets, randomly inspecting artifacts. Then Sarah got an idea.

"Will you translate for me, John?"

The three approached the ticket counter at the entrance and waited until the woman working there had finished with a customer. Then John said to her in German, "The lady here," pointing at Sarah, "would like to know whether the paintings behind the altar have always been in their present location."

"No, certainly not," she answered. "Everything was removed from the nave after a big rock fall in 1742, even the altar itself."

"Did the rock fall do great damage?"

"It destroyed half the church."

Sarah leaned impatiently over John's shoulder. "Ask her where the paintings were hanging before the rock fall."

The woman pointed at the balustrade opposite the stained glass windows. "Only the north side of the church, the side embedded in the rock, survived."

"And the windows?"

"What you see are remnants of the old stained glass interspersed with modern replacements. But every effort was made to match the original design."

"Ask her if she knows *exactly* where the paintings hung on the balustrade."

"No," the woman answered. "Nobody does. In fact, we only know about the former location through oral tradition. Why does the lady ask these questions?"

"Sarah, she wants to know why you're asking these questions."

"Tell her we're art historians. This stuff is important, you know. Go on, tell her."

"The lady is an art historian," John told the woman. "The exact position of the paintings with respect to eye level is important to her from a display perspective."

"Interesting. No one's ever asked such questions before."

John translated, and Sarah muttered, "That's a relief."

"What did she say?" the woman asked.

"She said, she wants to be the first to publish her findings."

The three went wordlessly back down the tunnel and emerged on the platform outside the gate, blinking in the sunlight.

"We dug in the wrong place," John said.

"Yes," David agreed. "And so did that man in 1858."

"Let's not panic," Sarah said. "We've spent all of two hours in the church, and most of the time it was dark. I suggest we come back tomorrow at noon, sit in a pew like good Catholics, and wait to see what happens. Tomorrow is the summer solstice. Whatever is supposed to happen at noon on the summer solstice will happen tomorrow while we're sitting in a pew."

"Tomorrow is also Sunday," John reminded her. "And a mass is scheduled from eleven to noon. The church will be full."

"So much the better. There are lots of other people searching, and more than a few of them have gotten far enough to identify Idar-Oberstein as the likely location. Tomorrow we'll see how many show up in the church. We need to keep our eyes peeled for anyone who looks interested in more than the mass."

"Better safe than sucking hind tit," David quipped. He looked directly into John's eyes. "Or any tit at all."

———

Gerd Pfeffer was in his pension on the Kirchweg, reading about Eratosthenes. The sieve was the piece of Cellarius's puzzle that continued to give him problems.

Pfeffer was also doing his best not to reach for the telephone and check up on his wife. His insecurities prompted the desire to do so; his ego dampened it.

There was something cartographically odd about Eratosthenes's world map. Rather than draw his parallels and meridians at regular intervals, he drew them so they would pass through major geographical features. A parallel went east-west through Alexandria, for example. He called it "the Parallel of Alexandria." Others went through Rhodes and Thule, but none appeared at ten degrees north and south latitude, or twenty degrees, and so on.

Likewise, the meridians: one ran north-south through Alexandria, but none appeared at equal distances east or west of it. Thus there was no systematic geometric grid on which to locate *all* geographical features.

Cellarius himself had done something similarly odd on his Palatinate map. Although he spaced his parallels and meridians at regular intervals, he didn't space them discretely north of the equator or east of a prime meridian. He didn't even label them. The result was an arbitrary graticule superimposed on the terrain, as if Descartes himself had happened upon an ungridded map and wished to study its sinuous features as analytic functions. Pfeffer suspected this aspect of the map was somehow related to the Sieve of Eratosthenes. But how?

He snatched up the telephone and dialed his home number. No one answered. Sometimes the only way to affect justice, he decided, was outside the context of the law.

———

Meanwhile, Frieda Blumenfeld perched on her second-floor balcony, waiting for Mannfred Gebhardt to show up. If she stood on her toes, she could just see the Volkspark and the rose garden next to it, for which Rosenstockstrasse was named. The garden's sculpted hedges and grand old oak trees shaded colonies of mosses homesteading its flagstones and shallow steps.

She watched as Gebhardt approached on foot. He passed the rose garden, oblivious to the roses and to her presence on the balcony above him. His gait was carefree; when he reached her house, he sprang up the front porch steps with uncharacteristic flourish.

And there wasn't the usual hesitation of several seconds before ringing the doorbell. He must have gotten laid, Blumenfeld reasoned.

She went downstairs to the living room while Hannelore showed Gebhardt in. As he entered the living room, he handed her a tan envelope. She noticed he was wearing an amethyst crystal pendant.

"What's in the envelope?" she asked.

"The genealogy report you asked for."

She handed it back. "What does it say?"

"She already had one son named Richard, who was five years old when she was convicted. The Weinbrenner name is, in fact, still common in Idar-Oberstein. The baby she was carrying at the time, also a boy, was adopted by an Anabaptist clan in the Palatinate, most of whom eventually emigrated to America."

"Really."

"Pennsylvania, America, to be specific. Weinbrenner named the baby before she died. Rather than use her own last name, she gave it the name Graf, apparently in honor of the father's profession. Johannes Graf began a dynasty of sorts in central Pennsylvania, a dynasty that thrives to this day."

"Interesting. Thank you. Now," she rubbed her hands together briskly, "some wine. To celebrate my last day of poverty." She opened a cabinet and scanned the rows of bottles.

"You still haven't told me why you needed the information."

"I was curious. As I am about that pendant you're wearing."

Gebhardt shrugged. "Just something I found."

"In Idar-Oberstein?"

He inspected his fingernails. "Could be."

"You know, a twelve-year-old girl is missing down there."

"Is that so?"

"Yes. Her picture was in the paper. Erika. Pretty little thing. Looks remarkably like someone else you knew … intimately. The whole town is acting as though the witches have returned."

"You don't say."

"As a matter of fact, Erika went missing right around the time you were there doing your genealogy research."

"Forty thousand others were there too, Frieda."

"So they were."

"What do you say we just focus on our mission tomorrow and leave my personal life off the agenda?"

Blumenfeld smiled. "Forgive me." She removed a bottle from the cabinet. "I've been saving this Pouilly-Fumé for a special occasion. Of course, it really should be consumed with some oily fish. Herring or mackerel. Or," she turned to Gebhardt, "do you just order 'white wine' with your 'fish'?"

"I wouldn't mind sampling … a glass of that."

"One ought to eat the foods that are famous in a given wine region whenever one drinks that region's wine. You haven't lived until you've tasted fried eel from the Gironde with a Bordeaux. Heaven! And here we sit in Mainz."

"I notice you only poured one glass."

"Oh, my dear Gebhardt, you wouldn't appreciate this. Do go downstairs and get yourself a bottle of something from the Mosel." She chuckled. "Give me one more day, and there'll be some poisoned wine down there you'll have to be careful not to grab by mistake."

―――――

In his hotel room on the south side of the Marktplatz, Barclay Zimmerman recalled Tavernier's famous words once more: *No. 4 represents a diamond which I bought at Ahmadabad for one of my friends. It weighed 178 ratis, or 157¼ of our carats.*

Accompanying the note in Tavernier's travel account was a drawing of a smooth, irregularly shaped diamond. Next to it was a drawing of the same diamond in its new incarnation, after Tavernier had it cut. Now shaped like an egg with a large natural at one end and covered with numerous flat, polygonal facets, it weighed 94½ carats and was reportedly flawless, or "of perfect water," in Tavernier's words.

… which I bought at Ahmadabad for one of my friends …

That's as far as the record would go. Stones purporting to be the Ahmadabad, including a pear-shaped specimen weighing almost 79 carats, were eagerly sought and traded by collectors hoping reliable provenance would someday come to light.

Zimmerman was convinced the genuine Ahmadabad was somewhere within walking distance of where he stood. The alternative was unacceptable.

He looked out his window at the Marktplatz. He could see the Felsenkirche towering high above. Tucked under his arm was a *Chicago Tribune* newspaper. Its front page article named the Felsenkirche as the probable location of the lost Tavernier stones, based on a reference to the Bible found in Cellarius's code. It pointed out a glaring discrepancy in Cellarius's depiction of the steeple. *X*, the newspaper claimed, marked the spot.

Zimmerman watched the crowd in the Marktplatz. It seemed to grow by the minute. The whole world was about to converge on Idar-Oberstein.

John waited in his room for David and Sarah to return from what they called "window shopping." Despite his insistence that his knowledge of German made him the best shopping companion, David had stubbornly refused to listen, and he and Sarah had left without him.

He paced the room, which was only long enough to allow four steps in one direction before he had to turn around again. After a few minutes, he realized he was behaving like a caged animal, and stopped.

He looked at himself in the full-length closet mirror. His hair had gotten shaggy in recent weeks. And a cigarette dangled from between his fingers, an innovation adopted only yesterday, renewed from the "wild oats" period of his youth. He watched his image in the mirror as he took a drag without inhaling and blew the smoke back out in a thin, bluish-gray stream. It was like a scene from a movie. He was not sure he recognized the man in the mirror.

When he finally heard two pairs of feet coming up the stairs, he went into the hallway to greet them. David and Sarah were both smiling.

"That took you long enough," John said.

"We got distracted." David reached for Sarah's hand and held it up for John to see. She was wearing a large diamond ring.

"You've got to be kidding." John stared at David in disbelief. "You robbed a jewelry store?"

"'Robbed' is a strong word. We found the most feebleminded salesman this side of the Atlantic and couldn't pass up the chance."

"Don't you realize how stupid that is? We're looking for the greatest cache of gemstones in history, and you risk it all to steal a lousy ring?"

"There was no risk. We knew what we were doing. And all's well that ends well." David turned his back on John and unlocked his door; as far as he was concerned, the conversation was over.

Sarah glanced quickly from one to the other, then followed David into their room.

"Don't blow me off like that," John said. "Your behavior is—"

"No!" David exploded. He spun around and returned to the doorway. "*Your* behavior is what we should all be concerned about. Look at yourself! We're not searching for the Holy Grail, for Christ's sake. We're searching for some missing rocks. And until you get a grip on yourself, it's *you* who are risking this operation, not me."

John looked past David at Sarah, who avoided eye contact. "By all means," he said, "don't hold anything back."

David stepped into the hallway and closed the door behind him, leaving Sarah alone in the room.

"You wanna talk to me, farm boy? Talk."

"You treat her like property," John said.

"The question is not how I treat her, but rather whose property she is."

John laughed. "I don't believe I'm hearing this."

"That's not all: until she becomes *your* property, I suggest you treat her as though she were someone else's."

They glared at each other for a few seconds. John finally broke it off; the expression on David's face was not at all yielding.

"What Sarah does with her body," John said, "and with her life, is up to her. I will neither encourage nor discourage her."

"So be it. But just keep in mind, Amishman, where you come from—and where she comes from. She would do no better in your world that you would in hers—than you *are* doing in hers. If *you*

285

feel like a fish out of water, imagine putting a bonnet on *her* head and putting her to work in one of your barns or fields."

"You speak as though I'll be returning to the farm—"

"Well, won't you?"

"—and that I intend to take her with me."

"Well, don't you?"

John leaned heavily against the wall. "I don't know."

"Until you know, be careful what you do. You think I mistreat her, but actually I'm the best thing that's ever happened to her. If I hadn't taken her under my wing, she'd be turning tricks in Lower Kensington right now. So be careful not only what you do, but also what advice you give—to me or to her."

———

Afterwards, alone in his room, John looked at himself in the mirror again.

Had he changed *that* much? Enough to alarm the people around him? At North Star, some of his fellow cartographers had nicknamed him Clark Kent, and he had accepted the gesture good-naturedly because he was, after all, compared to most of *them*, rather mild-mannered. Now he was driven by a need to avenge and exonerate an obscure seventeenth-century mapmaker, a need that hardly characterized mild-mannered men.

Avenge? Exonerate? Where had *those* words come from?

He sat down at his small writing table and pulled the telephone closer. His instincts told him it was time to make a call, but he didn't know which of two numbers to dial first. One was the restaurant where his sister Rebecca worked as a waitress. The other was the airline—to ask for a seat assignment.

The lost Tavernier stones still belonged to Cellarius. They would continue to belong to Cellarius until found by someone else. It occurred to him that if he abandoned the project now, David and Sarah might yet find the stones, but at least he, John, wouldn't be party to the effort.

Sarah. If he left Germany, he left Sarah. David was right: they each came from worlds the other could never enter. But last night had been transcendental; if two people who shared such an experience didn't belong together, no two people did. And yet, to what extent was he confusing genuine affection with mere sexual desire? And did either of them have to go so far as to enter another world just to enjoy each other's company?

He was not aware how much time had passed when he heard the soft knock at his door. He suddenly realized he was sitting in darkness.

Without waiting for an answer, Sarah opened the door and entered the room. John watched her figure cross the dusky space, peel off clothes, and climb into bed. He undressed as well, got under the covers, and felt her long, bare legs press warmly against his own.

"Does David know?" he asked.

"Yes." She gave him a slow, wet kiss on the ear.

"What does he think about it?"

"Whatever he wants to think about it."

"Why do you stay with him?"

She pressed her lips against his neck. "He's a genius. He could be anything he wants, even a professor. All he needs is a little nudging. I intend to marry him, you know."

"You ... you do?"

"Yes."

"What does he think about that?"

"He's getting used to the idea. As we speak."

She kissed his chest and worked her way down. "I want to make you happy, John. Just tell me what you want me to do."

THIRTY-ONE

It had to be the clearest day of the year. It couldn't get any clearer, for there wasn't so much as a wisp of cloud in the sky, only a vast hemispherical vault of blue. The sun climbed steadily and authoritatively across the vault like a judge entering an arena.

Summer solstice. *All rise.*

John marched wordlessly alongside David and Sarah down the Hauptstrasse toward the Felsenkirche. Other visitors and townspeople, dressed in their Sunday best and keeping just as silent, filed alongside. As the gathering crowd neared the Marktplatz, it was joined by streams of devout Catholics and treasure hunters trickling in from hotels and residential districts elsewhere in the city.

Many of the rock and jewelry shops were open, a Sunday tradition in Idar-Oberstein. But John saw few visitors patronizing them. Shopkeepers stood in the entrances, wringing their hands, gazing wistfully at the brilliant white church high above them.

People streamed in from both directions on the Hauptstrasse. They choked the Burggasse where it entered the Marktplatz from the west. They broke formation and hurried across the open market square.

A bottleneck formed at the bottom of the Kirchweg. David waited for a gap in the flow of people, then began trudging up, with Sarah and John close behind. Climbers in poor shape stopped on some of the path's nineteen landings to catch their breath, rest on benches provided for them, and smile sheepishly at the able-bodied passing them by. Employees of rock shops lining the way peered out through display windows to marvel and shake their heads at the swelling train of people.

On the platform at the top of the Kirchweg, the train bunched up in the amphitheater-shaped space and pressed forward to wedge its way into the tunnel. No bells were ringing, and John knew why: bells hadn't rung in Oberstein since the seventeenth century. Eye contact was rare and brief; everyone seemed suspicious of everyone else, and neighbors did not appear to know each other this day.

The three had arrived early enough to find places on the outside of a third-row pew, beneath the stained glass windows on the south wall. John dipped his fingers in the basin of holy water and made the sign of the cross. David and Sarah hesitantly did the same. But when John bowed to the altar and genuflected to the tabernacle, David and Sarah merely took their seats.

The church continued to fill amid the sound of shuffling feet and an occasional cough until no seats remained. John surveyed the nave; the space between the back pew and the entrance was becoming crowded with standing figures, their hands clasped in front of them. Some fidgeted, perhaps because they were in a church for the first time in years. Some no doubt wondered whether they would be able to stand elbow-to-elbow like that for the entire hour of the service.

Some, their eyes darting from the stained glass windows to the altar, from the tiled stone floor to the balcony, were clearly present for reasons other than holy mass.

John could tell the balcony was full; he heard murmuring and the flapping of leaflets that served better as fans than guides. The atmosphere was heavy with the rustle of clothing, the muffled grate of clearing throats, and the sibilant hush of whispered conversations. The people were as self-conscious of the noises they made as the appearances they gave. Most studiously avoided eye contact, as though they were in a whorehouse rather than a church. They seemed uncomfortably reflective and introspective.

What unconfessed sins caused such behavior? John wondered. Something from their distant pasts? Time spent absent from the church?

He looked at his watch. It was exactly eleven o'clock.

The organ suddenly piped up, and a choir in the balcony began a hymn. The seated congregation rose to its feet.

Zu dir, o Gott, er-he-ben wir
die Seele mit Ver-trau-en.
Dein Volk er-freu-et sich in dir,
wollst gnä-dig nie-der-schau-en.

The priest made his entrance behind a pair of altar boys. The three marched solemnly toward the altar, the boys each carrying a lighted candle, the priest holding a Bible above his head like a shield.

Laß leuch-ten, Herr, dein An-ge-sicht,
er-füll mit dei-ner Gna-de Licht
die Die-ner dei-nes Thro-nes!

The procession stopped at the foot of the altar while the congregation continued singing. John took an interest in the priest's garments. He wore a Gothic-style chasuble made of bright green fabric and decorated with ornate crosses. Around his neck hung a white silk stole embroidered in gold.

Mach un-ser Herz von Sün-den rein,
da-mit wir wür-dig tre-ten ein
zum Op-fer dei-nes Soh-nes!

As the hymn ended, the priest and his two altar boys bowed to the altar and assumed their places. The boys each placed their candles on the marble-topped table, then stood off to one side in front of wooden chairs. The priest went behind the table and bent over to kiss it. He said, *"Brüder und Schwestern, damit wir die heiligen Geheimnisse feiern können, wollen wir bekennen, daß wir gesündigt haben…"*

While the congregation reflected on the sins it had committed during the previous week, John studied the altar. The marble-topped table was pulled farther away from the wall for the service, and he wondered whether the priest would notice that the floor beneath him had been disturbed.

He glanced over at David and Sarah. Sarah was looking around, obviously reveling in a novel experience. He found her childlike curiosity appealing. David was staring down at the floor. He seemed troubled by the words being spoken, although John was sure he did not literally understand them.

The priest said, *"Lasset uns beten."*

John prayed also, silently to himself: Dear God, we both know the reason I'm in your house today. I'm on a mission I don't believe I can quit. Please understand my mission, and give me the strength not only to see it through, but also to comport myself according to your wishes the moment I do.

"Amen."

Now everyone took his seat, and there were hushed sighs of relief throughout the room. An elderly woman went to the front of the altar and read from the Bible. John recognized the text from Isaiah, chapter fifty-five. He turned and inventoried the people seated around him. One pew back was a barrel-shaped man who was glaring suspiciously at everyone in his vicinity. If John's instincts were correct, this man was present for purely secular reasons.

He looked across his own pew, past David and Sarah, at a middle-aged woman with long gray hair and a pointed nose. She could have served as a stand-in for the Wicked Witch of the West. As he watched her, she turned suddenly and regarded him blandly with pale blue eyes.

He looked away. The man next to her was young and clean cut, like a yuppie. He stared vacantly at the altar as though his thoughts were elsewhere.

The woman at the podium finished reading from Isaiah. The priest then led a responsorial psalm. John knew another reading and another psalm would follow. He looked to his right at the stained glass windows on the south wall.

———

Frieda Blumenfeld looked at the windows too, especially the easternmost one, closest to the altar. The skewed cross stood out bluntly in contrast with the escheresque weave of pastel bricks. Whatever was supposed to happen at noon on the summer solstice was going to happen in the next forty minutes: the sun was already shining brightly through myriad pieces of colored glass, warming up to reveal the solution to a mystery that had befuddled historians for three centuries.

She noticed that the young man with whom she had shared a glance was also scrutinizing the windows. She wondered how many others in the church had their eyes open for clues, and how many of those had guessed the most likely sources.

After the second responsorial psalm, the congregation rose to its feet for a reading of the Gospel. Blumenfeld rose as well. This isn't so hard, she thought; you just do what everyone else is doing.

The priest sang: "*Hal-le-lu-ja, hal-le-lu-ja, hal-le-lu-ja.*"

"Hal-le-lu-ja," Blumenfeld muttered to herself.

He walked over to the podium and opened his Bible to a page marked with a ribbon. "*Aus dem heiligen Evengelium nach Matthäus…*"

In synchronization with everyone else, Blumenfeld traced a small cross with her right thumb on her forehead, lips, and heart. She remembered enough of her school catechism to follow the Gospel according to Saint Matthew. That is, if she had been paying attention. The church was full to bursting. All these people can't be here for love of Jesus, she thought. Maybe a hundred on a typical Sunday morning. That meant some two hundred were present for reasons other than holy mass.

The priest bent over the Bible and kissed it. Blumenfeld heard him mumble, "*Herr, durch dein Evangelium nimm hinweg unsere*

Sünden." May the words of the Gospel wipe away our sins. Indeed, she thought, and please throw in the ones we intend to commit.

––––––

Sarah, John noticed, was listening intently to the mass, even though she couldn't have understood a word of it. At this point, the priest was delivering the homily, explaining the Gospel he had just read and tying it into the previous readings, the philosophy of the church, and even current events. He made a public service announcement about a missing twelve-year-old girl named Erika and commented on the surprising turnout this bright, sunny Sunday.

John also noticed that David kept glancing at Sarah, then at John, probably making sure they weren't stealing furtive glances or making surreptitious physical contact.

For his part, John was little concerned at the moment about Sarah's proximity. He stood at the end of the pew, as close as anyone to the stained glass windows on the south wall, and squinted as the sun's rays streamed through the fragile glass. He bowed with the rest of the congregation while reciting the part of the Creed that described Jesus becoming man: " ... *hat Fleisch angenommen und ist Mensch geworden* ... "

As he straightened up again, the rays hit him with such force that he had to turn his head aside. The sun had been rising steadily during the mass; it projected images in the stained glass windows onto the opposite wall of the nave, where they made a kaleidoscope of blurred patterns on the stone surfaces and wooden balustrade.

––––––

Blumenfeld checked her watch; it would be noon in another half-hour. She followed the glances of the man at the opposite end of her pew and noticed the patterns forming on the north wall. Meanwhile, the congregation was offering up general intercessions.

"... *um Rettung von Krankheit* ..."

"*Christus, erhöre uns.*"

As the sun continued to rise, the patterns advanced toward the altar and descended toward the floor. At first Blumenfeld found the abstract shapes and swimming colors pleasing; the pastel bricks were just becoming recognizable, as though cast by a weak slide projector. Then the skewed cross began to take shape on the balustrade, and her expression turned to stone.

"... *von Hunger und Krieg* ..."

"*Christus, erhöre uns.*"

———

John watched the cross advance and descend; it had dropped below the wooden balustrade and was creeping onto the stone surface above the row of sarcophagi lined up along the north wall. He looked pointedly at David, who almost imperceptively nodded his acknowledgement.

The cross seemed to be going somewhere. It seemed to have a destination.

John did some quick figuring. Although the church faced south, the sun rising from the east was shining into the windows. That was because the church stood at nearly fifty degrees north latitude. Which meant that even at summer solstice, when the sun reached its highest point in the sky all year, sunlight would stream into the windows from about twenty-six degrees south of vertical.

It was enough angle to cast images onto the lower part of the far wall of a narrow church flattened against a rock face. The sun moved from east to west as well as climbed higher, which explained why the images on the wall glided toward the altar while slipping gradually toward the floor.

The sun was already near the top of the window and in a short while would rise above the arched pane. On the opposite wall, the skewed cross was coming into focus.

———

Blumenfeld wished the people around her would shrink, or fall down and die, or do something to get out of the way, so she would be in a better position to extrapolate the cross's path. But now everyone was supposed to shake hands with his neighbors in the "sign of peace" part of the mass. She shook Gebhardt's hand. She looked down the pew and caught the eye of the young man with a close-cropped beard. She nodded to him in a small but formal greeting. He only stared back.

She turned and shook the hand of the barrel-shaped man sitting behind her. As he leaned forward to reach her, his jacket opened slightly, revealing the handle of a police revolver sticking out from his belt.

So, she thought, the danger is every bit as great as the stakes.

The priest broke up a piece of host and dropped it into a chalice containing wine. "*Seht das Lamm Gottes, das hinwegnimmt die Sünde der Welt.*"

The congregation responded, "*Herr, ich bin nicht würdig...*"

———

Indeed, John thought, I am not worthy. All he wanted to do now was determine where the cross was going. He noticed that David had planted his right foot on the kneeling beam as though he were getting ready to stand on top of it to improve his view. The organ's throaty voice once again filled the small church. Members of the congregation began leaving their pews to approach the altar and share in the body of Christ. As John and David stepped into the aisle to join them, Sarah shook her head at the two and remained standing in her place.

> *O heil-ge See-len-spei-se auf die-ser Pil-ger-rei-se,*
> *o Man-na, Him-mels-brot!*

John got in the short line forming in the right aisle, with David right behind him. To his left, in the line moving steadily up the center aisle, were the witch and the yuppie.

> *Wollst un-sern Hun-ger stil-len, mit Gna-den uns er-fül-len,*
> *uns ret-ten vor dem ew-gen Tod.*

John knelt at the foot of the altar, with David to his right, and waited for the priest to make his way over. He bent forward to look down the line of kneeling people. The barrel-shaped man was dead center in the line, his head bowed and his eyes closed. He was either taking communion very seriously or was spiritually far away. Beyond him, the witch and her companion had occupied places as far to the left side of the altar as they could get—and as close as they could be to the apparent destination of the cross.

> *O sü-ßer Bronn des Le-bens, fließ nicht für uns ver-ge-bens,*
> *du un-sers Hei-lands Blut!*

The priest worked his way down the line of kneeling people until he reached the person to John's immediate left. John muttered a quick prayer: Lord, may I receive this gift in purity of heart—despite what I intend to do immediately afterwards.

The priest took one step over and held a round piece of host in front of John's face.

"*Der Leib Christi*," he said.

John looked into his eyes and answered, "*Amen.*" He opened his mouth, and the priest laid the host on his tongue.

O lösch den Durst der See-len, so wird uns nichts mehr feh-len, du un-ser al-ler-höch-stes Gut!

John waited for David to receive his host, then they both stood up. But instead of returning to their seats, they crossed the nave, weaving through people still approaching or leaving the altar.

The image of the skewed cross was so clear, it almost looked like it had been painted onto the wall.

John glanced at his watch; it was just minutes before noon. He turned to check the stained glass window and observed that the sun was rising past the upper pane, about to disappear from view.

In front of him was a long row of sarcophagi, all packed closely together and extending lengthwise away from the wall. He had taken note of them during his first visit to the church but had not thought them significant. Each one was carved from a solid block of sandstone and covered with a precisely fitted rectangular lid. The sarcophagi were not sealed in any discernable way; the weight of their massive lids had apparently been deemed sufficient to secure their contents.

John and David were not the only ones standing before the north wall. The witch and yuppie were also present. The two teams exchanged knowing and suspicious looks.

Mit Glau-ben und Ver-trau-en wir dich ver-deckt hier schau-en in dei-ner Nie-drig-keit.

Above the sarcophagi, portraits of the apostles Judas, Matthäus, Marcus, Johannes, and Simon peered down from the balustrade. As John and the others watched, captivated, the cross seemed to pause for a second, then it faded as the sun rose out of sight.

The point of greatest clarity, just before fading, was a place on the wall immediately above one of the sandstone sarcophagi—the one beneath the portrait of the apostle Johannes.

John looked at David, who raised his eyebrows in response. Together they stepped closer and examined the tomb. Engraved on its lid was a cipher:

$$
\begin{array}{ccccc}
S & A & T & O & R \\
A & R & E & P & O \\
T & E & N & E & T \\
O & P & E & R & A \\
R & O & T & A & S
\end{array}
$$

The last people receiving communion were just then leaving the altar. John decided that if he and David didn't want to look like tourists disrupting a mass, they needed to return to their seats right away.

Ach, laß es, Herr, ge-sche-hen, daß wir im Him-mel se-hen dich einst in dein-er Herr-lich-keit!

Only the concluding rites remained to complete the service. The organ piped up one last time as the priest and his two altar boys wrapped up the ceremony and led a procession out of the church. The congregation bunched up behind them, eager for fresh air.

———

Outside in the tunnel, in the commotion of the crowd, Sarah became separated from John and David. As she twisted around looking for them, she bumped into the scary-looking lady who had sat at the end of her pew.

"Excuse me," the lady said in heavily accented English.

"Don't mention it."

"My, but you *are* a pretty thing, aren't you?"

Startled and repulsed, Sarah muttered a quick thank you.

"And that's a very interesting signet ring you're wearing."

Sarah turned and hurried down the steps to the tunnel exit. She looked over her shoulder once on the way down; the lady was still watching her, smiling. Passing through the tunnel gate onto the platform overlooking the town, she caught up to John and David and found them already arguing.

"You weren't supposed to eat the host," John said.

"Everyone else ate it."

"But you're not … eligible."

"What was I supposed to do, toss it like a Frisbee?"

Sarah recognized something in the crowd. The back of a head. Someone trying to conceal himself in the dispersing congregation.

"Don't talk now," she said to John and David. "Just walk."

THIRTY-TWO

BACK AT THE HOTEL, David and Sarah joined John in his room. John looked uncomfortably at the bed, then at David, but his concerns were unnecessary; promise of treasure governed the mood.

"It all makes sense now," John said. "By 'extend in the ultimate prone position,' Cellarius didn't mean lie down on the floor and measure your height from something. What is the ultimate prone position, anyway? Death, of course. He was referring to the sarcophagus."

"You mean the stones are inside the sarcophagus?" Sarah asked.

John shook his head.

"Underneath it? But the thing's made of solid rock. We'd never budge it."

John turned to David. "Are you thinking what I'm thinking?"

"The stones are neither in nor under the sarcophagus," David said. "The sarcophagus is the entrance to the chambers beneath the church. The sarcophagus lid is the door. That's why historians and other researchers have never found the chambers. The idea to look there wouldn't have occurred to them. They wouldn't have disturbed something so sacred."

"Like we're going to," John muttered.

David said, "Hard as it may be for you to believe, I don't want to defile a church anymore than you do. But if it's merely an entrance, then there's no one buried there, and it's not sacred. Look, what's it going to take to find out? We merely lift the lid; at the very worst, we find some dusty bones inside, in which case we apologize profusely and close the lid again."

John looked out his window at the street below. Tourists wandered in and out of shops, oblivious to the ancient mystery being solved just a few feet away. "And if we do?" he asked. "If we only find bones? Then what?"

"Then … I guess we might as well go home." He paused. "Any more problems?"

"Just one," Sarah said. "There are several sarcophagi resting along the north wall, where the painting once hung. The *south* wall, the one containing the stained glass windows, came tumbling down a couple of hundred years ago. They've rebuilt it, but how do we know the image of the cross landed in the same place today as it did back then?"

"Everything we have tells us the restoration was true to original design. We have no choice but to trust the restorers. Besides, the windows would have to be way off for the image to center on a different sarcophagus altogether. And even if it did, if we open one and find nothing, then we open another."

"Right," John said. "Let's open them all up. Let's have a disco with the dead. We've already broken and entered, we've vandalized a church, and now we're going to rob a grave. That ought to get us a thousand years in purgatory, if not jail. What more could they do to us if we just kept going and tore the whole place apart?" He picked up a tattered copy of the deciphered code from his nightstand and studied it for a moment.

Extend in the vltimate prone po∫ition
From the foote of the elevation ...
... ba∫keth in fairie lighte
Of Apollo's re∫plendent apogee
On the fe∫tivall of his highe∫t aproche
Then drink from the Sieve of Erato∫thenes
Sing more songes than Solomon
And de∫cend to trea∫vre
For the gates of Hell ∫hall not prevayle

"Well, at least now we've confirmed what 'Apollo's resplendent apogee' means. And it's pretty obvious what Cellarius meant by 'fairy light.'"

"I should have known that one to begin with," David confessed. "There's a mineral called staurolite, an iron aluminum silicate, that commonly occurs as X-shaped twin crystals—as skewed crosses. The more common name for the mineral is 'fairy cross.'"

"And we know why the treasure hunter in 1858 failed," Sarah said. "The sky was overcast during solstice; it had been drizzling for nearly a month. He never saw the image of the cross descend on the wall."

"That leaves us with the Sieve of Eratosthenes and the songs of Solomon," John said. He looked out the window again. "Any ideas about those?"

"The sieve means the solution has something to do with prime numbers." David stood up and walked to the door. "That we already know."

"And the songs of Solomon?"

David opened the door and motioned for Sarah to follow him. "We'll cross that bridge when we come to it."

"It appears we have competition."

"Right. Which is why we have to go tonight—as soon as it gets dark."

"Don't we want to wait until after midnight?" John suggested. "Until as late as possible?"

"No," David said, "by then it'll be rush hour in the church." He turned to Sarah. "Are you sure it was Zimmerman you saw in the crowd? Absolutely sure?"

"Absolutely. Bad hair and all."

"Just who is this Zimmerman person?" John asked.

David ushered Sarah out and reached for the doorknob. "Trouble."

———

Gerd Pfeffer waited in his pension for the cover of night, playing with prime numbers. The phone had not rung. Not once. His boss might have thought to call, but then again, Pfeffer was on leave and his boss might have been sparing him the nuisance. A subordinate might have wanted to get in touch, but surely Pfeffer's gruff telephone etiquette would have daunted him. Who else? His mother? Perhaps, if she weren't already dead.

There was no point wondering if his wife had any inclination to dial. The phone, an old Princess model still popular in hotels and pensions, sat motionless and silent on the table as though deep in hibernation. It wasn't going to ring.

Pfeffer dressed in all black clothes. He blackened his face with a military camouflage stick, set his alarm for safety's sake, and laid down on the bed to wait for dark.

He knew where the image of the fairy cross had landed, but he didn't know where the treasure was. The image was supposed to have pinpointed an entrance to the chambers beneath the church. Instead it had stopped above a coffin. Still, he predicted that if others had solved the puzzle, they would go after the treasure tonight.

Therefore, so would he.

———

Mannfred Gebhardt rode from Mainz to Idar-Oberstein in Frieda Blumenfeld's BMW, with Blumenfeld at the wheel, staring straight ahead at the road, her mouth clamped shut. Had she intended a successful, uneventful evening, one that would end with the two of them splitting the loot, separating the lost Tavernier stones into two piles, one for her, one for him, she would have spent the time underway bending his ear in preparation, scolding him for his deficiencies, warning him not to outlive his usefulness. Instead she was silent.

Which meant she had some other dénouement in mind.

So did he.

———

Barclay Zimmerman loaded his 9mm handgun. It had been easy to get. All you had to do was ask the town drunks. For five euros, enough to help a drunk make it through the night, you could have any information you needed.

Zimmerman found a group of them huddled over a case of beer at the train station. Half an hour later, he was in a dingy apartment overlooking the Nahe River, examining German police surplus handguns and miscellaneous lots of ammunition. Fifteen minutes after that, he was the most recent in a long line of owners of a Heckler & Koch P7 and two clips of 9mm ammo.

Twenty minutes later, he was back in his room.

Feinstein deserved a bullet. And no one would complain, not the Philadelphia law enforcement community, nor the gemology industry, nor even Sarah Sainte-James. Sarah deserved far better treatment than Feinstein gave her.

Still, Zimmerman had to admit, they looked natural together when they came out of the church. They looked like a pair.

Freeman, he reminded himself again. *Freeman.*

———

Back in his own room in the Pearl Hotel, David calmed himself by practicing the magic trick that would get the lost Tavernier stones through airport security and past the customs officials. Occasionally he glanced up at Sarah, who was still leafing through research materials. Their eyes met once, briefly, communicated nothing, then drifted apart.

He was hungry. It was what he hated most about hotels; you couldn't just go into the kitchen and make yourself a snack like you could at home.

The trick he practiced was a standard production box, using a shoebox he had found in a pile of boxes behind the hotel. He pulled a table away from the wall, set the shoebox in the middle of it, and placed its lid on the near side, next to the edge.

He held up the box for an imaginary audience to confirm it was empty. He did the same with the lid, to prove nothing was attached to it—nothing visible to the audience. Then he fitted the lid to the box.

Displaying the closed box from every angle, he shrugged to the imaginary audience as if to say, "It's just an empty shoebox." But when he set the box back down, opened it, and reached inside, his fist came out filled with diamonds.

Or would, if everything went as planned.

It was a simple trick, but most tricks were, and it would get non-metallic objects through airport security and *anything* past customs.

He only needed some black felt to finish preparing the contraption, and he had already bought it from a craft shop downtown. He would sew a bag out of the felt and attach it to the lid.

Now all that remained was to go out and find some really big diamonds to put in the bag.

———

In his room across the hall, John ground out a half-finished cigarette, then immediately lit another. He was smoking too much; the cigarettes made him feel dizzy and left a filthy taste in his mouth.

He missed Pennsylvania. He missed Rebecca. For the first time since leaving the farm, he even missed hooks and eyes.

He retrieved a piece of folded-up cardboard from the bottom of his suitcase and unfolded it carefully on his bed. It was full of square and rectangular holes. When open and flat, it had the same dimensions as Cellarius's last map.

It was the clue John was still withholding from David: Cellarius had not, in fact, placed hills on his Palatinate map arbitrarily. Instead, he had centered terrain peaks on grid squares numbered

9, 13, 19, 21 … corresponding to the prime numbers greater than 1005, the number of Solomon's songs: 1009, 1013, 1019, 1021 …

John had drawn a duplicate graticule on a sheet of cardboard and cut every one of those squares out of it, creating fifty-four open windows. When held up to the light or laid down over some other pattern, possibly another map, the sheet acted as a locator grille.

Locating what, he did not yet know.

He heard David and Sarah's door open, followed by muffled conversation in the hallway. He quickly folded the cardboard sheet back up and stuffed it into his shirt.

There was a knock at the door, and he opened it.

David and Sarah were holding hands. "It's time to go to church," David said.

John picked up a bag of tools from the floor next to his bed, swung it over his shoulder, and followed them down the hall to the stairs.

"'Yea, they made their hearts as an adamant stone,'" he quoted into the darkened stairwell. "'Therefore came a great wrath from the lord of hosts.'"

THIRTY-THREE

THE STARS WERE OUT in such numbers, they seemed to have gathered to witness a spectacle. The night sky was a navigator's dream. It struck John that after years of working with maps, he saw the world through a cartographic lens: azimuth, grid coordinate, navigation by the stars.

Breaking into the church was by now routine. They had arrived via the Burggasse rather than the Marktplatz to avoid surveillance; no one could stake out every approach. David made picking the gate lock look easy, and there was no bantering among the three while he worked. They trudged silently and businesslike up the tunnel steps.

In contrast to the teeming, restive ceremony they had attended that morning, the interior of the church felt lifeless and hollow. And yet watchful.

It was the paintings, John decided. They were all portraits: angels, apostles, holy family. And of course they all had eyes. And even the eyes that were averted seemed to watch the three visitors loiter in the center aisle, as if to say, "Well?"

The three visitors continued to loiter there, treading a wash of silence rippled only by their own shoes scuffing on the stone floor.

They had wrapped their flashlight lenses in red cellophane to reduce the risk of detection, but they had not anticipated the effect the tint would have on the mood in the nave. The red glow and the roving circles and ellipses reminded John of artificial theater lighting. He experienced a brief moment of stage fright before an unforgiving audience of portraits, coffins, and painted glass, inanimate objects that had witnessed so many scenarios played out on the altar's stage in centuries past that they were surely dubious about tonight's performance.

Finally Sarah said, "Well?"

David walked around the front left pew and approached the sarcophagus. John followed him and placed his bag of tools on the floor next to it. Sarah, clearly not wanting to be left behind in the aisle, hurried to keep up with the two men. All three stared at the cipher engraved on the sarcophagus lid:

```
S A T O R
A R E P O
T E N E T
O P E R A
R O T A S
```

"What the hell does it mean?" David asked.

"I don't know," John said. "But it looks like witchcraft to me."

"It's an amulet," Sarah whispered, "to guard against sorcery. It's never been deciphered."

John reached down and removed a crowbar from the bag.

"I don't think we'll need any of that stuff," David said. "Here, take the other end, help me lift the lid."

It took them several minutes of jerking and straining before they discovered that a natural seal had formed between the two pieces of sandstone. David picked up the crowbar and used it to work his way around the lid, loosening the weld caused by centuries of chemical deposition.

"You're the religious one," he said. "You want to say something before we open it?"

John made the sign of the cross. "May God forgive me for what I am about to do."

"Assuming," David added, "that he has already forgiven you for busting into his house and hacking at it with garden tools."

"I'd feel a world better if today weren't Sunday."

"It's funny you should say that. Stonewall Jackson, a very religious man, fought most of his battles on Sundays."

"And he, a cold-blooded killer! I feel so much better."

David set the crowbar back down and cracked his knuckles. John rubbed the palms of his hands together. Sarah took a couple of steps backwards while the two men bent over and got a good grip on the corners of the lid.

"Three, two, one … go!"

They strained and grunted, and the lid came loose, making horrible screeching noises as it slid across the top of the sarcophagus. They shuffled a few steps away and dropped the sandstone slab on the floor. It crashed thunderously, breaking into several large pieces.

The trio froze, waiting for the echoes in the nave to fade. John imagined the noise reverberating through the rock bluff and being heard by everyone in the town below. After a few seconds that seemed like minutes, all was still again, and no response came from the world outside.

David removed his flashlight from his back pocket and directed its beam into the open sarcophagus. "Come have a look at this," he said.

John and Sarah joined him and peered inside. The red light illuminated a worn stone staircase that wound deep into the rock. At the bottom of the staircase, at the limit of the flashlight's beam, an arched entrance led into an open space. No door blocked the entrance, but the darkness beyond was even more forbidding.

"I never really believed it," Sarah said, "until this moment."

David took a deep breath, then stepped over the side of the sarcophagus. "It's now or never."

Sarah followed behind him, and John brought up the rear.

The walls of the access were rough hewn; whoever had cut them had made a modest attempt at an arch structure but had deviated wherever the rock became too resistant. As John descended behind the red glow of three flashlights, the temperature gradually dropped and goose pimples formed on his arms. He ducked to avoid spider webs, some clearly as old as the access itself. The air was dank and musty and had a stale odor consistent with three hundred years of little or no disturbance.

As they neared the bottom of the staircase, the walls became spotty with moisture. The sound of steady dripping emanated from somewhere far below.

Sarah reached behind herself and took John's hand. He gripped it firmly.

"I hope," David said over his shoulder, "that if God decides to punish you in the next hour or so, he waits until the rest of us get out of the way."

Blumenfeld and Gebhardt had reached the tunnel gate and found it latched and locked. Blumenfeld looked up at the stained glass windows, now dark within their Gothic arches. All was quiet; there wasn't so much as a breeze to disturb the calm. The stars shined so clearly, even the convection currents must have stood down for the night. No evidence existed that she and Gebhardt were following in the footsteps of others, which is why she concluded they were.

"Time to make yourself useful," she told her partner.

Gebhardt knelt down before the gate, removed a tool wallet from his back pocket, and shined his flashlight on the lock. "*Scheiße!*" he said. "It's been picked already."

Blumenfeld's heart raced; the game was on. But it was best, she decided, not to excite her young companion. "Take it easy," she reassured him. "They have arrived, but they have not yet left. So far, everything is going according to script."

"I hope you know the script," Gebhardt said, "because the story looks a little open-ended to me."

"Naturally. But from this point on, we really should speak only when necessary."

They went silently into the tunnel, closing and relatching the gate behind them.

Blumenfeld knew the script. She had it memorized.

─────

Farther down on the Kirchweg, Pfeffer was in bed but still awake, thinking about crimes, detective work, puzzles. He'd never really solved a great crime, certainly nothing that would get him into the history books. The Cellarius murder was a great crime. Pfeffer had broken most of the code. He was almost there. As he lay on the bed, he treated himself to the vision of tossing a shovel aside, swinging open a wooden chest, and plunging his fingers into the cold pile of sparkling jewels that constituted the lost Tavernier stones.

It wasn't about the gemstones, he admonished himself; the only treasure to be sought and found was a solution to a famous crime. But what if the solver then kept the stones for himself? Would he be committing a crime as well?

He got out of bed, looked at himself in the mirror, and was startled by the camouflaged face looking back. Laughing out loud, he dampened a washcloth and wiped the makeup off. Then he flopped back down on the bed.

He checked his alarm clock for the twelfth time. Close your eyes, he told himself. Get some rest. Give it one more hour. Let whomever is destined to find the stones have an opportunity to find the stones. Then—*then*—determine who is destined to take them home.

———

Zimmerman watched the Marktplatz from his hotel room window. He was sure David Freeman would pass by. But the hour grew late, and David had not appeared.

Had he already found the lost Tavernier stones?

Were the stones somewhere other than the church?

Was David sitting in his own room, waiting for someone else to lead the way?

―――――

Meanwhile, David, Sarah, and John had arrived at the bottom of the stone staircase. David pointed his flashlight down a sinuous, descending corridor. The corridor angled northward, penetrating deep into the mountain. John wondered how deep—to Hell itself? He thought, It's now or never, just as David had said. See it through to the finish or turn back and quit.

"We don't need these any longer," David said, removing the red cellophane cover from his flashlight lens. John and Sarah removed theirs as well, and the corridor was suddenly awash in white light. Minute quartz crystals sparkled as the flashlight beams glided across the walls.

David led the way, brushing ancient cobwebs aside with his flashlight, stopping periodically to shine the light directly ahead and study the path before him. The ceiling was so low, John found he had to walk bent over double and sometimes in a squat. Age-old mosses and lichens, entombed since the last torch was extinguished in the corridor, made splotchy patterns on the rock surfaces. He brushed at a patch with his fingers and it came away like fine dust. As the corridor leveled off, he varied his strides to avoid shallow, murky puddles. Directly in front of him, Sarah was duck-walking in a hunkered crouch, her free hand frequently pressed against the floor to keep her balance.

Were he and David leading her into danger? Would this path suddenly disappear into some kind of an abyss? Was it possible there were witches still down there, waiting for them? He felt a chill and realized a breeze was flowing against them. Somehow the mountain was channeling cool, moist air through its secret corridor. The air had to come from somewhere; somewhere ahead, there was another opening.

Eventually David's flashlight revealed a large, open space about ten meters in front of him. As John neared it, he was able to rise up to his full height. When he stopped next to David and Sarah, he faced the entrances of three chambers that comprised a suite.

"It's hard to tell," David said, "but I think we've descended to street level, maybe even lower."

The chamber that opened to the left of the corridor was filled with clay amphorae. The dust-covered pots jammed wooden shelves that spanned the walls from the floor to the ceiling. Spider webs sagging with age looped from handle to handle and enshrouded the bas-relief images decorating their bellies.

"That was no doubt the wine cellar," David said.

Another chamber, larger than the first, lay to the right of the corridor. It contained simple furniture, suggesting it used to be a bedroom. The rotted wooden frame of a bed was recognizable in one corner, as were a nightstand, a high-backed chair, and a dressing table. On the dressing table sat a mirror whose glass had flowed so much over time that images reflected in it were severely distorted. What must have once been a rug made a large rectangular stain on the floor.

Behind the headboard of the bed, visible only because the wood of the headboard had decomposed, was a hole in the wall big enough for a person to crawl through. John shined his flashlight on the hole. The scratch marks around its circumference suggested it had been carved meticulously by hand with a stone, dull knife, or eating utensil.

"Someone was trying to escape," David observed, "and hiding her efforts behind the bed."

"Maybe one of Wyrich's mistresses," Sarah suggested.

"Or an unenthusiastic witch," John said.

The third and main chamber was directly ahead. John took a deep breath and followed David through the entrance. Would they find treasure in there—or ghosts? He wasn't sure which would unsettle him more.

As soon as David stepped out of the way, the first thing John noticed confirmed his worst fears. Sprawled on the floor, just inside the entrance, was a complete human skeleton. Its jaw had fallen slack in a macabre grin, and its eye sockets were staring vacantly at the ceiling.

"The cutter," David said. "May I introduce Jakob Langenbach."

"How can you be sure?" John asked.

David bent over the pile of bones and removed something from the dead man's right fist. He held it up for the others to see: it was a large, faceted red gemstone. "The missing third of the Tavernier ruby," he said. He put the stone in his pocket.

The skeleton lay on its back in what John judged to be a choreographed position: its legs were pressed close together, its right arm rested straight at its side, and its left arm was stretched out perpendicularly to its frame, apparently pointing toward the center of the room.

A dagger had settled inside its rib cage, leaving no doubt about how the man had died.

John surveyed the chamber. All the surfaces—walls, floor, and ceiling—were tiled over and painted with various pagan themes. The room was cubicle; each surface had the exact same number of tiles: twenty by twenty made four hundred.

Johannes Cellarius was in this room.

John spent a minute studying the pagan images. They were drawn in heavy black outlines, almost like old woodcuts. Some were filled in with color, but the color had faded over time. Fairy crosses and pentagrams were common themes, as were crescent moons, stars, and planetary disks. Vegetation was highly stylized. Animals, mostly cats, frogs, and snakes, paraded across the checkered surfaces.

Naked maidens ceremonially drew down the moon. Crones encircled steaming cauldrons. More brooms appeared than John would expect in a decorative illustration, and there were more representations of Satan than he would want.

Cellarius gazed at these illustrations.

And then there were the Baphomets. The largest covered the far wall, opposite the room's entrance. In an unlikely but nevertheless convincing illustration, the head of a goat sat atop the body of a human female. The creature had long, curved horns, satanic wings, and a pair of breasts swollen to fetish proportions. It sat cross-legged, with a serpent coiled in its lap.

"Now there's something you wouldn't want to meet in a dark alley," Sarah said.

John looked at her, then back at the image. "Or in an underground tomb."

———

Blumenfeld allowed Gebhardt to walk a few paces ahead, his .45 Colt revolver drawn. He checked each row of pews, scanning the length of wooden seats as though expecting to find people lurking in them, perhaps even happily grinning people clutching handfuls of gemstones. Instead, he found the place empty.

To Blumenfeld's relief, he reholstered his gun.

She went to the altar to get one of the long brass candlesticks that stood on either side of it. Returning to the church entrance, she jammed the candlestick between the wooden door and its stainless steel handle, rotating it so that it crossed the doorframe and blocked the effort of anyone trying to open the door from the outside.

Then she and Gebhardt approached the open sarcophagus and took in the scene at a glance. A crowbar lay on the floor next to the tomb, and the tomb's lid lay in several broken pieces a few feet away. Little deductive reasoning was needed to figure out what had happened.

Gebhardt leaned over the side and sniffed the air. "It's stale, but it's moving. Wherever this leads, it breaks the surface at the other end."

Blumenfeld took a quiet step backwards, reached behind her back, and removed a pistol hidden beneath her suit jacket. The pistol's barrel was outfitted with a silencer.

Gebhardt was still looking down the staircase. "I'm ready if you are," he said. He was about to climb over the side and begin his descent when she stopped him.

"Hold on just one second."

When he turned to face her, he saw the pistol in her hand. He looked into her eyes. His expression first registered shock, then confusion, then anger. Then fear.

"Frieda…"

"Your search has ended, my friend," she told him. "You have finally outlived your usefulness. And your days of harming little girls are over."

Gebhardt reached for his shoulder-holstered gun, but Blumenfeld fired three times in quick succession. The pistol jumped in her hand each time she pulled the trigger. The shots sounded like dull, abrupt sneezes.

Gebhardt's legs buckled. He fell on top of one of the neighboring sarcophagi, rolled off, and landed face-down on the floor.

Blumenfeld grabbed her former partner by the ankles and dragged him to the front of the altar, out of the way and beyond the view of anyone entering the church—or emerging from beneath it. Not a bad place for a sacrifice, she thought, stepping in disgust over the prostrate figure.

She saw something glinting on the ground next to his neck. It was the amethyst crystal pendant he had "found." She unclasped the chain, wiped it clean of blood on his shirt, and hung the pendant around her own neck.

Then she rehooked the "no trespassing" rope and returned to the sarcophagus. Descending the stone staircase, she cocked an ear and listened.

———

Deep within the rock, John and his two companions inventoried the main chamber with roving flashlights. A large stone slab squatted in the center of the room, resting low to the ground on sandstone boulders that served as table legs. The slab, the room's obvious centerpiece, resembled a crude altar.

Lying on top of the slab, covered with a heavy blanket of dust, were a double-bladed flint knife, various goblets and dishes, a corroded ball-peen hammer, and a large iron pot. Resting on the floor next to the slab was a solitary straw broom.

John saw something that looked like a box. He reached over and brushed the dust off the top, then stepped back, startled.

"What is it?" Sarah asked.

"A Bible."

Surrounding the altar was a circular array of nine sandstone monoliths that reminded John of Stonehenge. They seemed to grow out of the floor. On close inspection, they turned out to be remnant rock left untouched when the chamber was cut. The slender stones, each about three feet high, curved and pointed toward the altar as though mimicking a human rib cage. They were topped with candles glued into place with their own melted wax. The wax was dyed black.

David walked from monolith to monolith, lighting candles. They sputtered with dust and the reluctance of waking after a long sleep. The flames grew slowly and filled the room with a soft, flickering glow. The flashlights went off.

Here and there on the floor were clay amphorae, and when John knelt down to inspect them he found the now-familiar Michelangelo signet engraved on their bellies.

Sarah blew the dust out of several of the goblets on the altar, then lifted them to her nose.

"Can you smell anything?" John asked.

She shook her head. "Maybe a trace. Oils, herbs, incenses. It's hard to tell what they used to contain."

David brushed cobwebs from some of the monoliths and exposed fairy crosses carved on their surfaces in bas-relief. "Now we know what the fairy cross really stands for," he said. "It's intended to parody the Christian cross."

"And the Bible," John said, pointing to where it sat on the altar, "was no doubt being read backwards or upside down."

"Then it's pretty clear the purpose of this room was..."

"... satanic worship," Sarah finished for him.

A large, awkwardly shaped object hanging from the ceiling caught John's attention. He went to the side of the altar and looked straight up. Above him was a crudely fashioned bell, its metal sides hammered together from many individual pieces, each one so tarnished now that it was impossible to guess their original composition.

The bell hung from a rope wound out of raw hemp. The rope, in a high state of decomposition, ran through an iron ring embedded in the ceiling, then across the ceiling to the near wall, where it passed through another iron ring before running down the wall to a spool. The rope looked weak enough that a mere tug would reduce it to dust. John took one quick step backwards, to get out from underneath the dangling hunk of metal. He glanced again at the ball-peen hammer on the altar and understood its purpose.

He looked at the others. They were scanning the room, searching vainly for inspiration. He studied the image of the Baphomet again and felt for the sheet of folded cardboard tucked beneath his shirt.

Sarah asked, "So where are the lost Tavernier stones?"

Before John could open his mouth, an answer came from the entrance to the chamber in a throaty female voice:

"You are about to figure that out for me."

THIRTY-FOUR

PISTOL IN HAND, THE heavy-set woman with the long nose and iron-gray hair who had sat in their pew that morning stepped into the chamber, smiling as though having found things exactly as expected. She surveyed the skeleton, the monoliths, the Baphomet, and finally John and his companions.

"Allow me to congratulate you," she said. "To get this far is quite an achievement."

Her accent was thick, but her grammar was sound. John guessed from her inflections that she was from somewhere nearby, somewhere in the Rheinland.

"I see you have found Mr. Langenbach." The woman nodded toward the skeleton on the floor. "His resolution is no longer a mystery."

She stepped farther into the room. The three backed into a corner. John looked at the 9mm in the woman's hand. Its silencer, a dark gray cylinder that effectively doubled the length of the barrel, gave it a deadly appearance.

He heard David mutter, "If you have any religious strings left to pull, now would be a good time."

The woman walked around the altar and approached the three. Her eyes scanned Sarah's figure, resting uncomfortably long on her hips and breasts. "Nice to see you again, my dear." She raised her hand and stroked Sarah's hair, tucking a lock behind her ear, combing a few loose strands into place. She caressed Sarah's cheek with the tips of her fingers. As she lowered her hand, she allowed it to graze Sarah's breast.

"What do you want from us?" Sarah demanded.

"Fair question. I want to know which one of you is going to find the lost Tavernier stones for me." She waggled her pistol in Sarah's face. "Is it you, my dear?"

Sarah only stared blankly at her.

She aimed the pistol at David. "You?"

"Yes," David answered. "Kill me—or any of us—and you'll never have them."

The woman shook her head. "No, I happen to know that is not the case. I did not achieve my status by allowing amateur liars to fool me."

"I may be a liar," David admitted, "but I'm no amateur."

"I'm not talking about you, I'm talking about *him*." She swung the pistol's barrel over and pointed it at John. "This fellow here knows *exactly* where to find the stones."

"I don't know any more than you do," John countered.

"You lie."

"I tell the truth."

"Look at me and tell the truth."

John didn't. He stared at the floor. He couldn't bring himself to peer into those eyes.

"You see?" the woman said to David. "He knows where they are."

"We need to conduct a systematic search of the three chambers," John insisted. He was sure the woman wouldn't shoot them. They needed to stall long enough to create an opportunity to disarm her.

"We don't have time for that," the woman said.

"We have all night."

"Do you want to get shot, young man?"

"If you shoot us, you won't recover the stones. Ever. You want to stand around and wait? We can wait too; we have no place else to go. Think we'll get hungry? So will you. Think we'll get tired? How long can you keep that gun raised to our heads? There's nothing you can do. *Nothing*."

The woman bit her lip. She looked around the room as though searching for an idea. Finally she noticed the spool on the wall and the rope that threaded up and around to the bell. She grabbed the spool's handle with her free hand and wound it down a few turns. The bell lowered to within arm's reach. Turning back to the altar, she picked up the ball-peen hammer.

John watched the bell sway under the threads still holding it up. He glanced at Sarah; her eyes were shut, and she appeared to be gritting her teeth.

"There *is* something I can do," the woman said. "I can let everyone know you're here. Imagine what the residents of this town will do to you when they catch you in this chamber, in the middle of the deep, dark night. So, for the last time, where are the lost Tavernier stones?"

The three were silent.

The woman lifted the ball-peen hammer above her head and struck the bell.

John covered his ears. The metallic *clang* resounded through the chamber. Its throaty echoes pounded on the tiled surfaces and beat mercilessly on his eardrums.

"Now all you have is a few minutes," the woman hollered above the din, "if you want to tell your grandchildren you found the greatest treasure in history. Minutes, that's all. Solve the puzzle— before townspeople flood this room."

She struck the bell again. And again.

———

Gerd Pfeffer, who was already making his way through the darkness to the church with an empty satchel slung over his shoulder, stopped and listened for a few seconds. The ringing sounded distant and muffled, as though it came from deep inside the earth.

"*Verdammt!*"

———

Barclay Zimmerman ran out of his hotel room and into the Marktplatz. Throughout the town of Oberstein, lights were coming on as people woke to the sound of the ringing bell. It was past midnight, and some of the people spilled onto their front porches and balconies, rubbing their eyes in confusion. Then it seemed to dawn on them, and Zimmerman heard voices carrying anxiously from house to house, penetrating the calm night air: "*Jemand läutet eine Glocke!*"

Somebody's ringing a bell!

Men trotted across lawns, buttoning their shirts as they ran, as though they comprised a minuteman unit that had been ready for such an event for the past three centuries. A mother appeared on an upstairs balcony, snatching her curious children into her arms. "*Oh, mein Gott, nein,*" she said. "*Nicht so etwas.*"

———

John thought his eardrums would burst. The old woman continued hammering the bell in a tantrum. Her eyes darted from David to John, John to Sarah, skeleton to bell, all the while gleaming like headlights at the front of a driverless vehicle.

It's time to put a stop to this, John decided. He removed the sheet of cardboard from under his shirt and unfolded it, then went around to the other side of the altar and stood next to the skeleton. When the woman saw what John had in his hands, she stopped hammering.

The bell continued to vibrate with a low hum. When it finally became still, the sudden contrasting quiet made the atmosphere in the chamber tense.

John held the cardboard up to the candlelight. It was perforated with holes that channeled square and rectangular patches of yellow glow onto his face and chest. He unceremoniously kicked the skeleton out of the way. Loose bones scattered across the floor, making hollow clicking noises as they rolled and tumbled. The dagger fell out of the skeleton's ribcage and came to rest at Sarah's feet. Sarah looked down at it, then up at the woman. But the woman was watching, shaking her head.

Positioning himself where the skeleton's ribcage had been, John held the cardboard grille at arm's length and aimed it at the wall toward which the skeleton had pointed, the same wall that was decorated with the large drawing of a Baphomet.

He hesitated.

Everyone stood motionless, waiting to see what would happen next. What happened next was John lowering the cardboard and calmly tearing it into pieces.

"No!" The woman stuck her pistol into John's face. "Stop doing that—stop doing it … *now*!"

John scattered the shredded pieces of cardboard on the floor. "I won't participate," he said. "I won't be the instrument of this sacrilegious act."

"You just ordered an execution," the woman told him. "Your own."

———

Outside the tunnel gate, Pfeffer was first to arrive on the platform. He tried the gate and found it locked. Below, in the town, rivulets of people joined to make currents as the town's residents, armed with all the weapons they could expediently grab, converged on the Felsenkirche.

He pulled a handkerchief from his pocket and rubbed his face vigorously to remove any remaining camouflage makeup. Surveying his all-black clothing, he decided it was better to arrive with the rest of the townspeople than to be found by them lingering at the gate. He ran back down the steps.

———

At the foot of the steps, the townspeople, Zimmerman among them, were on their way up. Zimmerman felt himself transported back three hundred years. The clothing was more modern, the weapons were more effective—but not much more. The people around him were frightened, and it was a suspicious fear, a foreboding over the invisible, the indecipherable, the uninvited.

This, he thought, is what a lynching looks like. Somebody's not coming back down these steps alive.

———

John closed his eyes and waited for the bullet to sear through his brain.

"Wait!"

It was David's voice. John opened his eyes. He watched as David reached inside his pants and removed a piece of cardboard that was identical to the one John had just torn up. He held it up for the old woman to see.

She lowered her gun.

John looked at the cardboard. "Where the hell did you get that?"

"I told you you'd need me."

Sarah said, "John, if you tear that one up too, we're all dead."

"Listen to your friends," the woman advised John. "Or you'll watch them die first."

"*Please*," Sarah implored him.

John accepted the piece of cardboard from David and took a deep breath. He aimed the cardboard once again at the Baphomet. Each of the grille's fifty-four open squares lined up with its respective tile on the wall. But something funny happened when the grille was lined up just right: the Baphomet disappeared.

There was, John knew, no predictable pattern to the prime numbers between 1006 and 1406. Twin primes—primes like 1019 and 1021, separated by only two digits—occurred eleven times, accounting for nearly half the total number of holes. And vertical pairs—primes like 1013 and 1033 that, when cut out of the grille, made two adjacent holes, one above the other—accounted for eighteen rectangular windows in the grille, or thirty-six holes all together.

There was no predictable pattern, but a pattern of sorts nevertheless emerged from the two phenomena. The cutouts formed a pair of irregular curves, one snaking its way down the left side of the 400-square array, the other down the right side. Together they *avoided* the outline of the Baphomet; the artist had arranged his strokes to fit between the spaces of the locator grille, so that no line work would show through any of the open windows.

With one exception. The tail of the serpent that rested in the Baphomet's lap was tipped with a small fairy cross. It was so small, John hadn't even noticed it before. The cross was the only part of the illustration that appeared in the grille windows.

John lowered the sheet of cardboard and extended his free hand toward the old woman. She first looked at the pistol in her right hand, then at the hammer in her left. She gave John the hammer.

John crossed the room, knelt down in front of the wall, and aimed carefully at the marked tile.

He tapped firmly.

The tile shattered. Pieces dropped tinkling to the floor like shards of glass.

Behind the broken tile was a hollow space. John wiggled jagged remnants from the sides of the square opening and brushed away dust and fallen shards.

Inside the space was a clay amphora.

He reached in and pulled it out. The amphora was decorated in bas-relief with the Michelangelo signet. He carried it over to the primitive altar and nudged the goblets and other artifacts aside. Holding the amphora over the stone slab, he allowed himself a moment to relish the heightening anticipation.

Then he let it go.

The pot burst into hundreds of pieces amid a small cloud of rising dust. When the dust cleared, what remained was a pile of clay fragments mixed with some odd-shaped lumps.

John leaned over the pile and blew. As more dust billowed across the slab, some of the lumps began to appear transparent. He blew again. There was no longer any doubt that many of the objects in the pile weren't made of clay.

He blew once more, as long and hard as he could. The last of the dust dissipated into the room. Remaining on the surface of the crude altar, exposed among jagged splinters of red clay, were dozens of rough and crudely fashioned jewels.

———

Pfeffer reached the iron gate at the head of a mob that was growing larger and noisier by the minute. People bunched up behind him, crowding the cobbled platform until there was no room left to stand. Some were still in their night clothes. Many carried crowbars, odd pieces of lumber, shotguns with rusted barrels. One fellow wielded a long-handled ax.

Pfeffer tried the gate, although he already knew it was locked. He rattled it in mock frustration, hoping to channel the mob's restless kinesis into some kind of purposeful action. But the people only milled and grumbled.

Someone finally suggested kicking the gate in.

Someone else argued against that: a church was not a place to break into, he said; they should go and get the priest.

No, came the counterargument: when witches are about, there is no time to lose.

———

Sarah dreaded what she was about to do. If her timing was the least bit off, the witch woman would shoot them all. As David approached the pagan altar to join John, Sarah followed him. The witch woman kept her distance from the three—and kept her pistol leveled at them.

No one said anything at first. There was nothing brilliant or scintillating in the pile. And the enormous size of several of the stones made them look like fakes.

But Sarah knew better. She had spent enough time with David to be aware that the larger the stone, the larger its facets tended to be, and the less brilliance and dispersion it exhibited per unit surface area.

David picked up the biggest specimen and held it up to the candlelight. "The Great Mogul diamond," he said simply, as if he were identifying a piece of common calcite. He rotated the enormous stone in the light, showing off its half-egg shape and numerous flat facets.

He set it down and picked up another. "The Great Table." It was a tapered, rectangular step cut with a truncated corner. Sarah moved slightly so she could look through the thickest part of the table and see one of the candles behind it; if not for diamond's high index of refraction, the stone in David's hand might have been a large chunk of pink windowpane.

He plucked fragments of clay out of the pile and brushed his fingers across the remaining stones. Uncut diamonds, especially well-shaped octahedra and glassies, accounted for a large part of the hoard. Many of the rest were irregularly cleaved fragments, unaltered except for their high polish. Some, including point cuts and variations on the old Indian table cut, were fashioned only partially.

David picked up and inspected four rose cuts, then a massive double rose Sarah immediately recognized from one of Tavernier's drawings.

He plucked out seven moguls altogether, two of which, about 40 carats each, appeared to be a matching set. "The Tears of Venus," he said with wonder in his voice.

He spied another large stone in the pile and almost dropped the moguls. "The Ahmadabad!" Snatching up a colorless, egg-shaped diamond, he rubbed his thumb across its polygonal facets and pressed a fingertip reverently to the large natural at its pointed end.

Not all the stones were gigantic: David collected a fistful of car-buncles as he sorted specimens. Sarah also recognized Egyptian emeralds, cornflower sapphires, star corundums.

More than a dozen natural baroque pearls, including one that weighed at least 200 grains, were also in the pile. As were ame-thysts, spinels, jades.

Everyone in the chamber stared at the lost Tavernier stones in numb disbelief. The images simply would not register in Sarah's brain, and she could only imagine that the others were struggling with a similar reality. Even the witch woman lost her concentra-tion and allowed her pistol to lower until it pointed at the floor.

That's when Sarah made her move. She reached over to touch the Great Mogul diamond. The woman didn't object; she just stood and stared. As Sarah retracted her hand from the altar she secretly palmed one of the amphora's jagged shards and hid it behind her back. While everyone else continued to gawk at the pile, she inched her way over to the spool on the wall.

The old woman awoke from her trance. "Well, my young friends," she said, "it's time to step aside. You now have stories to tell your grandchildren." She leaned toward the altar, her free hand reaching for the stones, and in so doing passed directly under the bell. At the same time she glanced cautiously at Sarah, as if she were reading her mind.

You hesitate, Sarah told herself, and you die. Taking one more quick step toward the spool, she removed the shard from behind her back and swiped at the remaining strands of rope. Then she closed her eyes. She could tell from the noise what subsequently happened: the bell plunged swiftly and unprotestingly onto the woman's head, knocking her flat to the floor.

But not before she fired off a shot.

THIRTY-FIVE

PFEFFER DECIDED NOT TO wait any longer—the stones might already be fleeing the premises. The mob was in need of a leader. He flashed his badge and said, "This is an emergency. Help me get through this gate."

No one moved.

He slammed his bulky frame against the barrier. The effort only made its iron bars rattle. Turning to the mob, he spied a hefty man in suspenders and beckoned him forward. Then a pair that could only have been twins, and weight lifters too. A wiry, nervous-looking man with unkempt hair joined them. The five lined up across the front of the gate. After some forward-and-back rocking motions to get themselves in unison, they hurled their shoulders against the iron bars. The gate shook violently but held.

"*Noch mal*," Pfeffer commanded. "One more time."

———

John noticed Sarah's arm even before Sarah did. Blood had already stained the sleeve of her shirt and was spreading down toward her left wrist.

"Oh, God, what have we done." He ran over and pressed his palm hard against the wound but knew he would need a bandage to stop the bleeding. He looked around the room. The old woman was lying on the floor. He squatted next to her and ripped off part of her skirt.

David stood watching.

"Do something!" John commanded. "Sarah's been shot!"

"Calm down," David said. "It's superficial."

"Superficial? Are you crazy? Blood is dripping from her arm!"

"It's a scratch. A nick. A graze. Don't you watch Westerns?"

"No, I don't."

Sarah was also taking it very well, John noticed. She waited until he had bandaged the wound, then she applied pressure with her right hand.

"I'm fine," she said. "Really."

John could hear battering noises coming from far above. He checked the unconscious woman on the floor and satisfied himself she would pose no further danger. Then he glanced upwards, imagining a hoard of people on the top side of the rock, trying to crash the gate. When those people eventually succeeded, they would discover the open sarcophagus, the worn stone staircase, the descending, sinuous corridor, the three chambers, the lost Tavernier stones—and take them away.

He said to David, "We need to get back up there and stop those people from coming down here."

"How would we manage that?" David asked. "The sarcophagus lid is broken."

"I don't know how. But we have to find a way. If they come down here, we'll never get out. Not with those." He pointed at the pile of stones on the altar.

"About those …" David said.

"I'll pack them while you're gone," Sarah said. "Hurry! Before it's too late."

David picked up one of the intact amphorae sitting in a corner of the chamber and handed it to her. "Empty this of wine," he said, "and fill it with gemstones."

"Right."

"Don't leave any behind, especially not this one." He took the Great Mogul diamond from the altar and pressed it into her hand.

"Of course not. Go!"

"But your arm …" John said.

"Go!"

John and David ran back up the corridor, stooping as the ceiling lowered, turning sideways to squeeze past resistant outcrops in their path.

———

Sarah watched them in the dim light until they disappeared from view. Then she dropped to her hands and knees and groped around on the floor, looking for the witch woman's pistol. It had to have fallen when the bell hit her on the head, but it was nowhere in sight. Finally she lifted one side of the bell and found the gun underneath.

She returned to the altar and cut the wax seal of the amphora with the blade of a pocketknife. When she lifted the lid, she smelled the powerful aroma of red wine.

It smelled good. And probably tasted good, too. But she knew its deadliness and was careful not to let any of the liquid come into contact with her skin. She gathered up the lost Tavernier stones, fingering through the clay fragments on the altar to make sure she had not overlooked any. David would notice even the smallest one missing.

———

John reached the staircase and raced up to the nave one step ahead of David. Together they examined the lid of the sarcophagus.

"Even if we *could* fit these pieces together again," David said, "and we can't, it would be obvious the lid was broken."

From outside the church, from the far end of the tunnel, came the rattle and groan of the gate being battered, over and over. Optimistic chants rose from the mob.

"Then we're going to have to block the church door," John said. "And keep those people from coming inside." He inspected the door and found it had already been blocked by a candlestick. He checked to make sure it was secure. "The witch must have done this," he suggested. "But it's not going to be enough."

"The witch must have been hiding in the church," David said, "because I'm sure we locked the gate and door behind us."

"It's academic now. They've broken through. Here they come." He heard what sounded like hundreds of angry men pounding up the steps of the tunnel. When the first few made it to the top, they were so near he could make out panting on the other side of the door.

"If they can get through an iron gate," he whispered to David, "they can get through a wooden door."

"We need something else to block it with."

The two men ran up the aisle, looking for heavy objects. The mob was already trying to force the door open; the candlestick rattled with each kick and shoulder slam delivered from the other side.

"How about the sarcophagus lid?" John asked.

"It's in pieces. They're too flat, and none of them is large enough."

"Then maybe the altar—the table itself." John stepped over the "no trespassing" rope and almost tripped over a body. "Jesus, look at this." He recognized the person immediately: it was the yuppie who had shared his pew at mass that morning.

David squatted down and examined the sprawled figure. "He's been shot in the chest."

"Shit. Just how many people are in this church, anyway?"

———

It was the man wielding the long-handled ax who finally breached the door. He hacked a hole in it big enough for Pfeffer to get his arm through and dislodge the candlestick. After that, Pfeffer and his fellow barrier-beaters kicked the door until it splintered from its frame.

The mob spilled into the church. Men stepped over pews, ran up the steps to the balcony, stormed onto the altar, searching for the source of the night's disturbance. They found the body of a man at the foot of the altar, and someone questioned whether he was a victim of witches.

Someone else noted that witches didn't use guns—thieves did.

Pfeffer was first to notice the open sarcophagus. By now comfortable in his role as leader of a rag-tag militia, he shouted, "*Hier entlang!*"

John and David returned to the main chamber and found Sarah clutching the lidded amphora, waiting for them. John couldn't help likening Sarah's hold on the amphora to a mother cradling a baby.

"Let's get the hell out of here," she said.

"That might not be so easy anymore," David told her. "They've already broken into the nave."

"We're dead if they catch us."

"Not necessarily." David patted his belt; tucked into it was a Colt .45.

"Where did you get that?"

"We found the witch's accomplice upstairs."

"There was another woman upstairs?"

"No, a man. And he's dead."

"Well, good. It's getting damn crowded around here."

John stepped into the corridor and looked into the adjacent chamber, the one that had served as a bedroom. "There's a hole in the wall behind the bed. It's our only option."

"We don't know where it goes," Sarah said.

"We're going to find out." He led the others into the room, taking care not to step on the rug stain for fear of leaving footprints. The hole was visible behind the headboard only because the wooden slats of the board had decomposed. John pulled on a slat and the entire wooden frame collapsed onto the floor.

The hole was just big enough for a person to crawl through. Its circumference was etched with gouges.

"Someone spent years creating this opportunity," Sarah said. "I wonder if she was able to take advantage of it."

John poked his head through the hole and shined his flashlight around. What he found on the other side was a spacious pipe; a long, cylindrical passageway made of carefully cut and fitted stones. Reemerging, he said, "It looks like some kind of canal or aqueduct."

"Are you sure it's not a sewer?" David asked.

John poked his head in again and sniffed. "Pretty sure; it doesn't smell like shit."

They each climbed through and stood on the dry, curved floor, their flashlights criss-crossing like searchlights, making elliptical pools on the polished stones.

"What the hell is this place?" David asked.

"I don't know," John answered. "But whatever it is, the Romans built it."

"How can you tell?"

"Look." He pointed at a brick on the wall, one that had been chiseled with letters and Roman numerals.

"What does it say?"

"It's too faint to read, at least in this light. But I know Romans conquered Germany shortly after the death of Christ. And I know they quarried and cut stone from glacial deposits while they were here. Sarah, do you remember reading anything about Roman aqueducts in Rheinland-Pfalz?"

She shook her head. "Some roads have been identified in this area, and a defensive wall or two, but no mention of aqueducts, cisterns, or other water-related technology."

"Then this is probably an important archeological find."

"A find for someone else to find," David said. "We've got higher priorities."

From the other side of the hole, from far down the corridor, came the racket of scuffing shoes and excited voices.

"They'll be here any second," John said.

Sarah held a finger to her lips. "Shh!"

Above the approaching din, John could just hear the soft roar of running water.

"That would be the river," David said. "We should be right next to it."

———

Although Pfeffer could make out three chambers ahead of him, only one of them was lit. The flickering inside suggested candle-light. He slowed down, and a pair of men right behind him collided with his back.

Whoever had shot the dead man upstairs was still on the loose. And *that* person had either escaped with the stones or was still down here, looking for them. The former would mean Pfeffer had lost the race. The latter would mean an armed killer was now one of the obstacles. Pfeffer didn't know which he preferred, but in either case, there was no reason to hurry. He held up his free hand to slow the others, then made sweeping, up-and-down motions with his arm to quiet them.

Once inside the illuminated chamber, he could hardly believe his eyes. The candles, welded to the tops of curved monoliths, appeared to have been burning for centuries. Of course that couldn't have been the case; someone had to have just lit them, probably in the last hour. The walls and ceiling were covered with pagan images. Scattered in disarray on the floor were what looked like parts of a human skeleton, as well as clay amphorae with Michelangelo signets engraved on their bellies.

And then there was the prostrate woman, no doubt also dead. She was lying crumpled next to a low table that was covered with dust and clay fragments. On the floor next to her head was a crude bell.

The room quickly filled with townspeople who speculated wildly on what had happened.

"Someone obviously clobbered her with the bell."

"No, the rope broke—look at how weak it is—and the bell fell on her head."

"So she must have been the one ringing it. But why?"

"Why else? To call the other witches!"

Pfeffer spied the broken tile in the far wall and caught his breath. He looked at the clay fragments on the table and suddenly understood their meaning.

The prostrate woman abruptly sat up and rubbed her head.

"Look," someone said, "she's awake!"

———

The mound of rocks and hand-cut bricks that blocked the aqueduct was exactly what John's flashlight had forecast from 100 meters away: the pipe had collapsed sometime in the past and the route was impassable. John nevertheless kicked a few bricks aside and tried to dislodge a boulder. The effort was pointless: there was no telling how deep the collapse extended; they would have to look for a way out in the other direction.

And going in the other direction meant passing the chambers, chambers now filled with angry townspeople.

"Why don't we just go back the way we came?" David asked. "Into the bedroom, up the corridor, and out through the church?

Just walk out like we have every right to do so? What have we got to lose?"

"We're not residents of this town," John answered, "and we don't know how the residents will react when they see us climbing back through that hole. We have no business being down here. I'm not willing to take the chance."

Sarah tapped the amphora cradled in her arm. "And we still have everything to lose."

John turned and began trudging back down the pipe. He wondered how much power was left in his flashlight batteries. He wondered how they were going to get past the hole through which they had entered the aqueduct, a hole they had not bothered to cover after climbing through.

He wondered how, of all places on earth and all times in history, he'd ended up here and now.

———

It was all so *undignified*, Blumenfeld thought. She woke to find herself lying on a gritty floor, her skirt hoisted above her knees, part of it inexplicably ripped off, her nylons full of runs. A massive pain throbbing in her head.

Wide-eyed peasants encircling her.

"Help me up," she said.

But the peasants just stood there, watching. Some wore pajamas. Some held candles they had removed from the monoliths. Most were armed with sticks and bats.

All of them *stared*. With that hollow gape, that primeval ogle, that dim countenance, the result of three centuries of inbreeding and superstition.

"*Help me up*." She raised her arms.

345

A small, round-shouldered man pointed a shaky finger at the amethyst pendant hanging from her neck. "What the devil is that?"

Others inched closer. "Oh my God," one said, "Erika was wearing one just like it."

Blumenfeld groped around on the floor for her pistol but couldn't find it. Strong arms grabbed her roughly and lifted her to a standing position. She swayed with dizziness. A thin young man forced his way to the front of the mob and stared at her chest in anguished horror. "*That's my daughter's pendant!*"

One of the townsmen tore the pendant from Blumenfeld's neck and pushed her. Her feet made little hops and shuffles as she struggled to regain her balance. Someone behind her shoved her, and she fell against the altar.

She thought about trying to outrun them, and would have made an attempt if she weren't wearing heels. And if she were in decent shape. And if there were some place, any place, to run.

The gun. Where's the damn gun?

The townsmen clamped onto her arms and legs. She resisted by kicking, jerking, scratching at everyone within reach. But they were too powerful for her. They pushed her through the chamber entrance, then dragged her up the long corridor. Her knees scraped against the rock floor as she labored, and mostly failed, to stay on her feet. Blood trickled into her stockings, now hanging in tatters from her calves.

When one of the vigilantes asked where they were going, another reminded him there was a lamppost above the statue of the miner boy in the Marktplatz.

Another recalled that the lamppost was in the shape of a scaffold, with a sturdy pole jutting out like a branch from the main trunk.

Yet another was sure he had a coil of rope in his garage.

It was not so much the pain, or even her impending death, that Blumenfeld found herself regretting most. It was the utterly *undignified* way it was all going to happen.

THIRTY-SIX

JOHN COULDN'T HELP MARVELING at the workmanship of the aqueduct, even as his mind raced to find a way out of it. The individual stones had been hand-cut to fit each adjacent one; the project must have employed many craftsmen and required years of effort. He swung his flashlight beam in broad arcs, admiring the symmetry and structural elegance.

David, he noticed, was more concerned with the symmetry and structural elegance of the pot Sarah was holding.

"Do you want me to carry that for you?" David asked.

"No, I'm fine, thanks."

"It must be getting heavy."

"When one arm gets tired, I shift it to the other."

"But the other was grazed with a bullet."

"Trust me, David, I'm fine."

"Well, just let me know."

"Thanks, I will."

John held up his hand to hush them; they were approaching the hole in the bedroom wall. He aimed his flashlight down the aqueduct and abruptly came to a halt.

His flashlight revealed the figure of a man.

The man was short and stout, with a gut that spilled over his belt and a bulbous nose streaked with veins. John recognized him from mass; he had sat one pew back and had watched people rather than sunbeams. The man held a flashlight in one hand, but it was turned off. In the other hand was a snub-nose .38 revolver. It was aimed at John's face.

Not knowing what else to say, John said, "*Guten Abend.*"

The man nodded. "*Guten Abend.*" Under different circumstances, the two might have shaken hands.

Out of the corner of his eye, John saw David's right hand move toward his belt, where he had tucked the .45. But Sarah grabbed his arm and stopped him.

The man put his flashlight away and reached into his shirt pocket, removing something metallic. John shined his light on the object. It was a badge.

"Lower your flashlight," the man said to John in German.

John did. "Sir, we'll leave peacefully. We don't want to cause any trouble."

"Tell your girlfriend to put the pot on the ground."

"It's just a pot. We'll reimburse the church its value. We have no issues with you."

"*Put the pot on the ground.*"

"Sarah, he's a cop, and he wants the pot. Set it on the ground next to your feet."

"No!" David cried out. He stepped in front of Sarah.

The cop cocked his revolver. "Tell your friend to get out of the way."

"He means business, David."

"So do I. After all we've been through, I'm not just going to hand the stones over to some fat man in a tunnel."

The fat man in the tunnel pointed his revolver slightly to the left of David's head and fired. The sharp *crack* startled the three; John and David crouched and covered their heads with their arms.

Sarah remained standing upright. She calmly stepped around David and handed the pot to the cop.

"No!" David tried to stop her, but John grabbed and held him.

The cop accepted the pot with his free hand. He pointed down the aqueduct and said to John, "Keep going the way you were going. Don't look back." Then, still aiming his revolver at them, he climbed back through the hole into the bedroom chamber.

David tried to follow him, but John continued to hold him.

"How could you just give the thing up?" David yelled at Sarah. "Have you learned nothing at all in our time together?"

"David, he was going to shoot us. Or at least arrest us. It's better to be alive and not have the stones than dead and not have the stones."

"You gave them up too easily! What the hell's the matter with you?"

"I value my life more than the stones."

"Well, I value the stones more than *your* life, so I'm going after them." He tried to break free from John's grasp, but now Sarah held onto him as well.

"David, we're not going to retrieve the stones by getting into a gunfight with a police officer," John said. "Let's move on and find another way out—before others get the idea to investigate this pipe."

He and Sarah held David between them and pulled him down the aqueduct.

"But the stones!" David screamed. "The *stones!*"

———

Pfeffer couldn't believe his luck. Taking the lost Tavernier stones from the young Americans had been like mugging a trio of quadriplegics. His tactic had been sound from the beginning: wait until someone found the treasure, then simply affect a transfer of ownership.

As he was leaving the bedroom chamber, several townsmen came running up, claiming they'd heard a gunshot. Pfeffer pointed at the hole in the wall. "More witches," he said.

He hurried up the corridor, ready to show either his badge or his gun, whichever would seem appropriate to the occasion. No one challenged him. He knew he should put off opening the pot until he returned to his pension, but he didn't want to wait that long. When he had climbed back up to the nave, he assessed the scene. Townspeople, including children, were milling around the church, acting as though the night's events were part of a circus or carnival. He looked up at the balcony and saw that it was empty. So that's where he went, choosing an out-of-the-way seat near the wishing well.

The lost Tavernier stones!

Cradling the amphora in his lap, he looked around to make sure no one was watching. It occurred to him once more that if he kept the stones, he was just as guilty as everyone else trying to steal them. The thought occurred to him, then it finished occurring to him. He lifted the clay lid.

The powerful aroma of red wine greeted him.

That's natural, he thought. Wine had filled the amphora for three centuries before rocks took their place. He delicately inserted his hand and was surprised when his fingertips touched liquid.

They'd left the wine in the pot when they put the stones in? But why?

He sank his hand deeper until his fingers touched bottom. No stones.

He closed his eyes.

He reached for his revolver and stood up to return to the aqueduct, then paused and laughed. He sat back down. He shook his head and laughed again. He laughed at the irony of seeking one thing, finding another, and discovering that the second was the prize after all.

He laughed and laughed.

————

Zimmerman had watched as the old woman was dragged off. He'd stood in the corner of the main chamber, out of sight, and waited there until the mob settled down and thinned out. Then he'd conducted a systematic investigation of the room.

The clay shards on the altar were the only objects not tangled with cobwebs or blanketed with dust. The pot they once comprised had recently been broken. Since the only opportunity to do so in the last few hundred years was during the last few minutes, it was safe to assume the pot had contained the lost Tavernier stones.

It took a bit longer for Zimmerman to realize the pot had been hidden in the wall; that was the reason the tile was broken. He ran his finger around the edge of the hole, then reached inside, closed his fist upon the empty space, and pretended it grasped the treasure he had sought all his life.

In retrospect, the path had been simple: break a door, break a lid, break a tile. Take home the lost Tavernier stones. One in particular.

The Ahmadabad diamond was still nearby. Since it didn't travel back up the steps to the church, it must have left the chambers by another route.

Zimmerman didn't take long to find it.

———

Meanwhile, John arrived at the lower end of the aqueduct ahead of David and Sarah and discovered that it did indeed branch into the sewer system.

"*Now* it smells like shit," he said.

The three entered a spacious cement drainage pipe and stepped gingerly over a shallow stream of sewage. Only a few yards down the pipe was a ladder leading up to a manhole cover. From the noise being made a few feet above them, John guessed they were under the Marktplatz.

At the base of the ladder, David said to Sarah, "Here, let me have your purse. I'll help you climb up."

Sarah hesitated, and the two stood there, eyeing each other. John stepped onto the first rung and asked, "What is it? What's the matter?"

Suddenly David and Sarah pulled their guns, holding them outstretched at arm's length and aimed at each other's heads.

"Oh, for Christ's sake," John said. "What now?"

"Where did you get that gun?" David demanded.

"Same place you got yours; I found it on the floor, Mister Let-Me-Have-Your-Purse. As though you really want to help me up the ladder."

"Why are you aiming it at my head?"

"Because you're aiming at mine!" Sarah cried. "And I've had way too many guns pointed at me today already."

"But you pulled yours first."

"No, you did."

David stepped closer. "So. Are you going to shoot, or what?"

"Only if you do."

"What makes you think I intend to?"

"To get the stones."

"Ah, so they *are* in your purse!"

"Of course they are. What did you think? That I would give them to Columbo?"

"You didn't know Columbo was in the picture," David said. "You hid the stones on your person to steal them from us. To keep them for yourself."

"Actually, I put them in my purse, rather than the pot you gave me, to prevent *you* from stealing them from *us*."

"You think I would do that?"

"Well, wouldn't you make off with them if you could?"

"That's not the point. The point is whether you think it of me."

"Well, shit, David. If you would do it, why shouldn't I think it?"

"Because I thought you loved me."

354

His .45 revolver was still aimed at her forehead. The silencer of her 9mm was inches from the tip of his nose.

"The fact that I love you doesn't change the fact that you're a thief. It doesn't mean I can trust you."

"So you *do* love me."

"And what of it? It's no skin off your ass."

"Do you love me enough to marry me?"

She blinked. "What did you say?"

"I said, do you love me … enough … to marry me?"

"Is that a proposal?"

"It could be. It depends on the answer."

"You mean, if the answer is yes, then the question is, 'will you marry me?'"

"Uh, yeah, that pretty much sums it up."

Sarah flipped her safety off. David immediately cocked his revolver. He said, "Why the hell did you just do that?"

"To see if *you* would, and you did. You don't point a cocked gun at your fiancée."

"I cocked my gun because you cocked yours!"

"And I did because you want the answer before the question!"

"All right, fine. Have it your way. Will you marry me?"

"Not unless you ask nice."

"Jesus. Will you *please* marry me?"

"Yes."

"Good. Now turn the safety back on and lower your gun."

"No, you first."

John stepped down off the ladder, positioned himself between the two, and placed the palms of his hands over the barrels of their guns. He pushed slowly downward until the barrels were pointing at the ground.

At first David and Sarah just looked at each other. John gently nudged one, then the other. The two hesitated, then embraced awkwardly.

"I guess it's time for me to get a real job," David said.

"Same here," Sarah agreed. "I guess it's time for me to tell you that you're all I have in the world."

David grinned. "Same here."

They wrapped their arms around each other and hugged tightly.

John cleared his throat. "I hate to break this up, but we can't stay in the sewer all night."

A commotion was rising on the street above. It sounded like a mob rioting. John had never witnessed a riot, but he couldn't imagine any other source for such noise.

"Do you have a handkerchief?" David asked Sarah.

"Why?"

"Do you or don't you?"

"Here. What are you doing?"

David peered down the drainage pipe. "Saving our lives."

———

Zimmerman discovered that the first direction along the aqueduct, the one that penetrated deeper into the mountain, was blocked by rockfall. Cursing about the irreplaceable loss of time, he freed his gun from beneath his shirt, made sure the clip was locked into place, and ran back in the other direction. He estimated the successful party was no more than ten minutes ahead of him.

But ten minutes was all it took to disappear into town.

John led the way up the ladder and popped out of the manhole on the outskirts of the Marktplatz, next to the Heimatmuseum. Emerging unnoticed in the fray, he then helped Sarah and David out of the hole. All three watched in fascinated horror as the mob prepared to string the witch woman from a lamppost above the fountain.

The lamppost was in the shape of an inverted *L*, like a child's drawing of the hangman game. A rope had been thrown over the horizontal branch of the *L*. One end was tied to the woman's neck. The other was in the ready grasp of four strong men. The woman fought to keep her balance on the wall of the fountain, her hands tied behind her back, a pillowcase thrown over her head.

John looked at the statue of the miner boy in the center of the fountain. Now he seemed to be lifting the crystal in his fist to the streetlamp above him, rather than to a hypothetical burning torch. The crystal glowed as though illuminated from within. Too much time had passed, John decided, since the days when people could change their lives merely by digging objects out of the ground. The era of treasure hunts was over.

A squat, round man in a bathrobe and slippers climbed onto the fountain wall and harangued the assembled vigilantes.

"He sounds like a politician," David said. "What's he bellowing about?"

"He's the mayor," John answered. "He's confirming he heard the old crone speaking in tongues."

"I'd be speaking in tongues too," Sarah said, "if I had a noose around my neck."

The mayor jumped back down onto the cobbles and gave a signal. As the four men pulled on the loose end of the rope, the woman rose into the air, her bleeding legs kicking frantically, their shadows flickering across the half timbered buildings bordering the square.

The mob broke into a cheer.

"Let's get out of here," Sarah urged.

The three crossed the Marktplatz, weaving through jubilating Christians, working their way toward the Hauptstrasse.

"Our first priority should be to get out of the country," David suggested. "I can sneak the stones through customs. When we're back on American soil, we'll divide them up."

"Divide them up among yourselves," John said.

"Excuse me?"

"Count me out. I don't want my cut."

They stopped at the edge of the Marktplatz, and John turned around to survey the scene. High above the fountain, the old woman's legs had stopped kicking, but her body continued to convulse in short, involuntary spasms. People were still streaming in from all directions, swelling the crowd.

"Do you know what you're saying?" David asked.

"I know."

"One-third of the stones belongs to you."

"Don't worry. Where I'm going, I won't need them. I've seen enough of the world and its tinsel."

David frowned, then dug into his pocket and took out the ruby he had plucked from the skeleton's fist. He handed it to John.

"At least take this," he said.

John shrugged and accepted the stone. Meanwhile, the mob applauded the end of the show; the woman's figure had become still.

———

On the other side of the Marktplatz, Zimmerman scanned the crowd. He saw the old hag dangling from a lamppost. Best not to interfere with that. He saw Obersteiners streaming in from all parts of town to gawk at her. The mob had grown to the point that few of its members had witnessed any of the night's events, and most who had were still in their pajamas. He saw children running about, as though they were at a fair rather than a lynching.

He was about to give up when he happened to look across the crowd and spy David Freeman, Sarah Sainte-James, and another person on the far side, walking out of the Marktplatz and heading up the Hauptstrasse. He might have missed them except they seemed so happy.

Happy. A witch was hanging from a lamppost. A man lay dead in the church. The flow of people was *into* the Marktplatz, not out. And these three kids just happened to be leaving. Happy. Moving briskly, shoulder-to-shoulder, almost skipping, as if in celebration.

He opened the handkerchief again, the one he'd found tied to the manhole ladder, and pressed his fingers to the flat polygonal facets of the Ahmadabad diamond. He read the accompanying note:

Zim: The rest are going to a good home. As is Sarah. Deal?

From the opposite side of the Marktplatz, David turned around to look and saw Zimmerman. He stopped and made a shrugging gesture.

Deal, Zimmerman mouthed.

As the three strode away, Sarah and David wrapped their arms around each other's waists. Then Sarah reached for the other man and hooked her free arm around his waist as well. They tightened together, united as one, and faded into the night.

THIRTY-SEVEN

The lost Tavernier stones captured front page headlines one last time: wide speculation that pagan chambers beneath the Felsenkirche in Idar-Oberstein served as a storage vault for the world's most famous rocks was dispelled once and for all.

The chambers did, in fact, exist; that surprised everyone. But the stones themselves turned out to be mere legend.

And the big hoopla that took place in Idar-Oberstein on the evening of the summer solstice was only the work of vandals. Persistent reports that residents of Oberstein had caught and lynched one of the vandals were adamantly denied by the town's mayor.

The paintings on the tiles in the main chamber beneath the church generated quite a lot of interest in the art world, receiving as much attention as newly discovered prehistoric cave art in France or Spain. Unfortunately, one of the tiles was broken, but restorers were confident it could be mended.

In addition to the art find was a major archeological find: the Romans had built an aqueduct that passed through the mountain to the river and had linked it to secondary pipes that ran down from the castle ruins above the church. The purpose of the aqueduct was still under debate. In the centuries since the Roman occupation, the water passage had collapsed north of the church, but it was still passable on the south side toward the river, where it connected with the city sewer system. Early construction workers had apparently mistaken it as an already-existing branch of the sewer network.

The find not only proved Romans had occupied the rock peak earlier than previously thought, it also proved Roman engineering skill was far superior to that generally ascribed to them. The textbooks would have to be rewritten.

The story of the lost Tavernier stones was over. Only crackpots continued searching, and the newspapers paid them no mind.

———

Barclay Zimmerman remodeled the Ahmadabad Theater in the Kensington neighborhood of Philadelphia. He sand-blasted its red brick façade until it shined in multispectral hues. He applied fresh paint to the old supporting beams. And he ripped out the marquee whose letters had to be changed manually and replaced it with a flashy digital one.

He even paid to make the rotating candy cane on the barbershop next door rotate once more.

The interior of the Ahmadabad received even more attention. Exquisitely embroidered curtains were imported from Würzburg. All four walls were surfaced with antique tiles bought in Munich. And the wooden balcony railing—or "balustrade," as Zimmerman now called it—was carved by hand in Idar-Oberstein.

A theater without elegance was just a room with a projector.

The first movie Zimmerman showed after the remodeling was complete, an afternoon matinee, was a Disney feature. The theater filled to capacity with boisterous children and their frazzled parents.

———

Gerd Pfeffer returned to his home in Hamburg and transferred the contents of the amphora via plastic funnel to a conventional wine bottle, which he then resealed with a cork. He placed the bottle in his wine cellar, on the rack that normally contained his most valuable Burgundies.

Of course, he had no demonstrable knowledge the wine was poisoned. And he was, as far as his friends and colleagues were concerned, completely clueless about the affair his wife was having. Certainly he could not be aware that his wife and her lover—Mr. Dick—sampled routinely from the Burgundies before doing unspeakable things to each other in the bedroom.

Knowing that Mr. Dick would not be the only one to fall victim to the Witches of Pauillac in the days ahead, Pfeffer hesitated while pouring the contents of the amphora into the plastic funnel.

He hesitated. Then he continued pouring.

Early that same afternoon, he was back at work, sitting at a large, round conference table with his detectives. Through the conference room window, he could see the 125-meter clock tower of St. Jacobi Church. He kept an eye on his watch. The tower clock was more reliable, if only because thousands of downtown workers and residents would complain if it were too fast or slow. Pfeffer's watch, on the other hand, would inspire no such rebellion.

His team of homicide detectives, a cluster of eleven men and women with varying levels of experience, waited nervously and impatiently at the conference table for Pfeffer's attention to return to the meeting. They were usually full of antics and practical jokes, their personalities characterized by a lack of restraint and a disdain for formalities. But today they sensed that something had happened to Pfeffer during his trip out of town. Also, they knew all about his wife and couldn't bring themselves to break the news to him.

Pfeffer watched as the minute hand of the St. Jacobi clock jumped one notch to twelve, then checked his watch and made a small adjustment.

"Is everything okay, boss?" one of the detectives ventured to ask.

"'Who can find a virtuous woman?'" Pfeffer answered, quoting a proverb that had been on his mind all morning. "'For her price is far above rubies.'"

When David Freeman showed up at Dr. Cornelius Bancroft's office in the Smithsonian Institution, he could tell that Bancroft was surprised yet pleased. Despite their past differences, his former mentor was clearly happy to reconcile with the best student he'd ever had.

David introduced the young lady he had brought with him as Sarah Sainte-James, his fiancée. Then he asked Bancroft outright for a job.

"Well, there is a research associateship still available," Bancroft said. "But it doesn't pay much. It was established for a graduate student or an advanced upperclassman. If you had any inkling whatsoever to return to school…"

"I have lots of inkling," David said.

"… then the associateship could be yours. And if you needed any supplemental income, we might be able to scrounge up a part-time job for Sarah too."

"Actually," Sarah said, "I've opened my own modeling agency." She handed Bancroft a business card. "I have international experience," she said brightly. "And, as it turns out, I'm pretty good at helping people present the best of themselves."

"Did the two of you have lunch plans?" Bancroft rose from his desk and reached for his jacket.

"Plans, yes," David replied. "But the financial means to realize them, no. At the moment, we're flat broke."

"Then it's on me. Welcome home."

Before leaving the office, David set a black felt bag gently down on top of Bancroft's desk. The bag leaned slightly, suggesting it was full of small, heavy objects. He held onto the bag for a few seconds, relishing the last moments of ownership. Then he let go.

"Anything interesting in there?" Bancroft asked.

"Just some specimens for the museum. They can wait. But my stomach can't. Let's eat."

"If you don't mind, someone else will be joining us at the restaurant, a previously arranged lunch date with another research associate. It's funny: this guy is also a former university student, he was also in the jewelry industry, and he's also returning 'home' to academia. When it rains, it pours."

"Oh my God," David said. "I hope it's not anyone named Zimmerman."

Bancroft laughed. "Don't worry, there's very little chance you know him. He was in the legitimate jewelry business, and he lost his job due to a … circumstantial misfortune."

"That's a relief. There are some people in my past I'd just as soon leave there."

"You'll like this guy, and I have a feeling the two of you are going to work together splendidly. His name is Bowling."

———

The first thing John Graf noticed when he arrived at the farm was the smell of dirt. It was the smell of home.

There would be a price, he realized as he circled the barn looking for his father. He would lose much of his individualism as a member of the community. He would submit to group authority and thus renounce almost every personal preference he had. He would drop cartography and take up farming.

He would never see Sarah again.

He found his father hoeing in the tomato garden, chopping each stubborn lump of clay until it surrendered and fell to pieces. John grabbed another hoe leaning against the barn and walked out into the field to join him.

Clarence Graf halted in mid-chop when he recognized his son's face. John was afraid he would drop his hoe and walk off. But the old man could see that John was dressed plain, and instead he squinted in curiosity.

John went to work beside him, chopping at clods with "take that" thrusts of the hoe. After a moment of watching, his father returned to the chore as well, but kept his head turned slightly away.

John didn't look at him. Because he knew that if he did he would embarrass him by discovering tears in his eyes. The reward, he decided, was indeed worth the price.

After a few more minutes of hoeing for the sake of hoeing, John absentmindedly reached into his pocket for the ruby David had given him.

"What's that?" his father asked gruffly, as though glad to come up with something to say.

"A present. For Rebecca." He handed the stone to his father.

Clarence Graf fingered the bauble, enjoying its tactile qualities. He stuck out his lower lip and grunted approval. "I'm sure she'll like it."

"You wouldn't happen to know where she is …"

The old man raised his six foot four frame above the tomatoes and squinted across a field of low corn. There, silhouetted against the horizon, a young lady ran toward them through the stalks, her arms raised in triumph, her long skirt billowing forward with each thrust of a knobby knee.

BIBLIOGRAPHY

The Story of Maps by Lloyd A. Brown (Dover Publications, 1979).
Dover has kept this 1949 publication in print, and wisely so. It's
the best one-volume history of cartography on the market.

Travels in India by Jean-Baptiste Tavernier, translated by Valentine
Ball (Macmillan, 1889). Yes, Tavernier really existed, and most
of what I wrote about him is true. But sadly, the seventh voyage, as I have described it, is fiction. This narrative is for serious
readers only. Reprints are available from various publishers.

Diamonds: Myth, Magic, and Reality, edited by Robert Maillard
(Crown Publishers, 1980). An excellent all-around book about
diamonds, especially for beginners who want a comprehensive
and engaging approach. A brief biography of Tavernier, with
some of the drawings he made of stones now missing, is
included.

Legendary Gems or Gems that Made History by Eric Bruton (Chil-
ton Book Company, 1986). If you've ever wondered whether
there was an authoritative history of all the world's famous

gemstones, including those whose whereabouts are unknown, your search is at an end.

Gemstones of the World by Walter Schumann (Sterling Publishing Company, 2007). The best field guide to gemstones. Most of the specimens photographed are from collections in Idar-Oberstein.

Rocks, Gems and Minerals; A Golden Guide by Herbert S. Zim and Paul R. Shaffer, Illustrated by Raymond Perlman (St. Martin's Press, 2001). Excellent for young people. First published in 1957, it's the way many of us were introduced to the subject. I suppose I didn't actually draw anything directly from this book for my novel, but if I hadn't studied the book as a kid, I wouldn't have written the novel.

The Codebreakers by David Kahn (Scribner, 1996). The definitive work on the history of cryptology. Despite its enormous popularity in cryptology circles, it remains one of the great undiscovered nonfiction books in print.

The Riddle of Amish Culture by Donald B. Kraybill (The Johns Hopkins University Press, 2001). Another definitive source. I spent eighteen months in Lancaster County, Pennsylvania, and still didn't get what I needed. Mr. Kraybill's book solves the riddle.

About the Author

Stephen Parrish is a cartographer and gemologist. He lives in Germany. *The Tavernier Stones* is his first novel. Visit him online at www.stephenparrish.com. Book clubs with ten or more members are invited to schedule his attendance, via Skype or speaker phone, at one of their meetings. Write to steve@stephenparrish.com for information.

www.MidnightInkBooks.com

From the gritty streets of New York City to sacred tombs in the Middle East, it's always midnight somewhere. Join us online at any hour for fresh new voices in mystery fiction.

At midnightinkbooks.com you'll also find our author blog, new and upcoming books, events, book club questions, excerpts, mystery resources, and more.

Midnight Ink Ordering Information

Order Online:

• Visit our website www.midnightinkbooks.com, select your books, and order them on our secure server.

Order by Phone:

• Call toll-free within the U.S. and Canada at
  1-888-NITE-INK (1-888-648-3465)
• We accept VISA, MasterCard, and American Express

Order by Mail:

Send the full price of your order (MN residents add 6.875% sales tax) in U.S. funds, plus postage & handling to:

> Midnight Ink
> 2143 Wooddale Drive
> Woodbury, MN 55125-2989

Postage & Handling:

Standard (U.S., Mexico, & Canada). If your order is:
> $24.99 and under, add $4.00
> $25.00 and over, FREE STANDARD SHIPPING

AK, HI, PR: $16.00 for one book plus $2.00 for each additional book.

International Orders (airmail only):
> $16.00 for one book plus $3.00 for each additional book

Orders are processed within 2 business days. Please allow for normal shipping time.
Postage and handling rates subject to change.

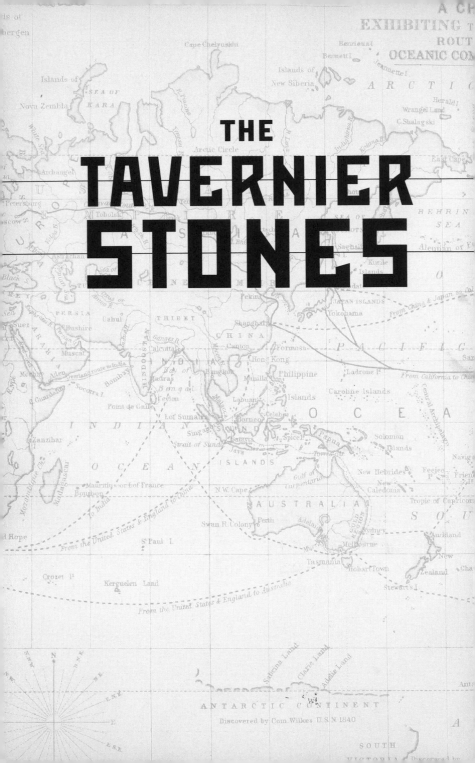